SHADOWS of ATLNTIS

Book One: Awakening

MARA POWERS

"An absolutely fantastic read that had me turning the pages obsessively from the very beginning. Once I started this book, I simply could not put it down, it was that good."
–Readers' Favorite 5-star review

"More than fantasy or mythical fiction. It offers a fascinating prospect to what might have once been very close to an otherworldly truth."
–Mission Date Night

"The stakes are of biblical proportions and characters unique and intriguing"
–What is that Book About

"The book is a work of art, one definitely worth reading! If you want a fresh take on the Atlantis myth, this is a solid choice."
–Blogger Andy Peloquin

"Mara does a beautiful job of tying fact and fiction in such a way as to convince the reader she has solved the mystery of Atlantis."
–Amazon Reviewer

"A masterwork!"
–Amazon Reviewer

"Fantasy, mythology, philosophy, romance, tragedy, humor, horror, adventure, thrill... this book lacks nothing."
–Goodreads Reviewer

"So incredibly engrossing that the reader will be captivated and impressed by the author's intuitive and solid understanding of ancient Atlantis."
–Amazon Reviewer

"A beautifully written, attention holding fantasy science fiction novel. Mara's keen knack for expressing a high level of imagery in just the right amount of detail transports you into her world."
–Amazon Reviewer

"The fall and rise of consciousness demonstrated in the book reflects a

lot of the dynamics existing in humanity today."
–Amazon Reviewer

"This story weaves a Tolkein-esque tale of love, monarchy, and sibling rivalry... An allegory of the current state of our world."
–Amazon Reviewer

"The stunning Atlantean universe is saturated with dazzling imagery which leaves you longing to go there."
–Amazon Reviewer

"Right from the start this world captures your imagination."
–Amazon Reviewer

"The beauty of this work lies in its relevance to those of us who are working to change the world."
–Ignite.me

"An original and deftly crafted novel from beginning to end, the Shadows of Atlantis series demonstrates exceptionally entertaining storytelling talents."
–Midwest Book Review

"Author Mara Powers has done a fabulous job in creating characters that her readers will truly care about and connect with. Her ability to create a fantastic but believable world is simply second to none"
–Reader's Favorite Book Review

"An absolutely fantastic read that had me turning the pages obsessively from the very beginning."
—Readers' Favorite 5-star review

"More than fantasy or mythical fiction. It offers a fascinating prospect to what might have once been very close to an otherworldly truth."
—*Mission Date Night*

"The stakes are of biblical proportions and characters unique and intriguing"
—What is that Book About

Published by *Shadows of Atlantis*, LLC
Fort Collins, Colorado
Santa Monica, California
USA

www.ShadowsofAtlantis.com

Editors:
Judithann Powers, D.F. Lyoness, Susan Peters

Cover Art:
David Lawell

Map:
Carrie Russell, Mara Powers

Illustrations:
Natasha Murray, Audrey McNamara, Ruslana Shybinska

Borders:
David Lawell, Stuart Smith

Publisher's Note
This is a work of fiction. Names, characters, places and incidents are a product of the
author's imagination. Locales and public names are sometimes used for atmospheric
purposes. Any resemblance to actual people, living or dead, or to businesses, companies,
events, institutions, or locales is completely coincidental.

Shadows of Atlantis— *awakening* / Mara Powers
PB ISBN— 978-0-9967652-0-6
EB ISBN— 978-0-9967652-2-0
HB ISBN— 978-0-9967652-1-3

Library of Congress Control Number
1-2443719021

This book is dedicated to the awakening of humanity;
the memory of a forgotten utopia
that will one day live again.

In the Back of this Book:

Starting on P. 261

you will find a letter from the author,

a Character Index

and a Glossary of Atlantean Terms.

These Atlantean terms are not invented by the author, rather, chronicled here as a parable intended to warn the reader of the detriments brought about by the willful ignorance of humanity's inherent connection to nature.

If you feel connected to this chronicle,

please consider spreading the word

and leaving a review on your favorite online retailer.

www.shadowsofatlantis.com

Book One
Awakening

*"On these infinite mountains of light,
now barr'd out by the Atlantic Sea,
a new born fire stood before the starry king…"*

—William Blake, *Marriage of Heaven and Hell*

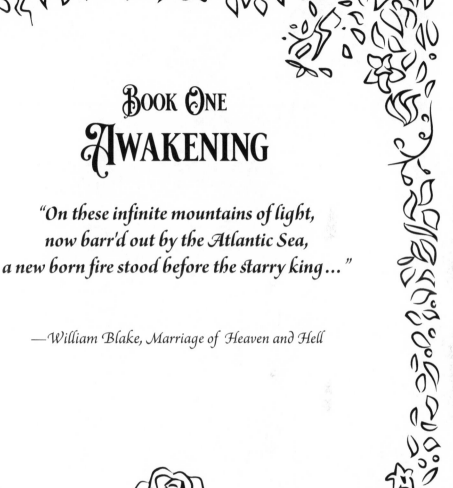

EXCERPT FROM THE
SACRED CANTOS
OF BELIAL

And it came to pass that the goddess Sophaiya fell from the heavens and took form as a celestial sphere, orbiting the great eye of Ra. She made her appendages into the minerals and plants, the animals and elementals of the Telluric Realm. And when she saw that she was complete, she sent her resonance into the celestial currents, and summoned the expressions of Source to beget their human project to dwell within her many realms.

Humans would have the ability to gather themselves into completion as they ascended through the cycles of incarnation among the realms of Sophaiya. And yet in their creation occurred a schism, born of the goddess's descent into matter. Their task would be to rise to the highest vibration in the face of adversity and break through the paradigm of duality.

And thus, the motherland of Lemuria grew into a state of grace and perfection, while the Bloodfire nations, born of envy, would be their natural enemy. War ignited between them, ravaging the purity of the mother Sophaiya. And when she had her fill, the elements rose up and decreed peace once more. The fire nations were frozen into ice, and Lemuria sank into the sea. The Watcher Belial absconded through the depths of Subterra, spiriting the Nexes of all knowledge to one of the eight remaining colonies of the motherland. The bountiful islands became home to the most shining achievement ever to be seen on any shore in any time.

Soon the schism would emerge again and cause its beauty to crumble upon itself. The fire nations would grow restless in their icy prison, and cast a shadow of vengeance over the shining shores of Atlantis ...

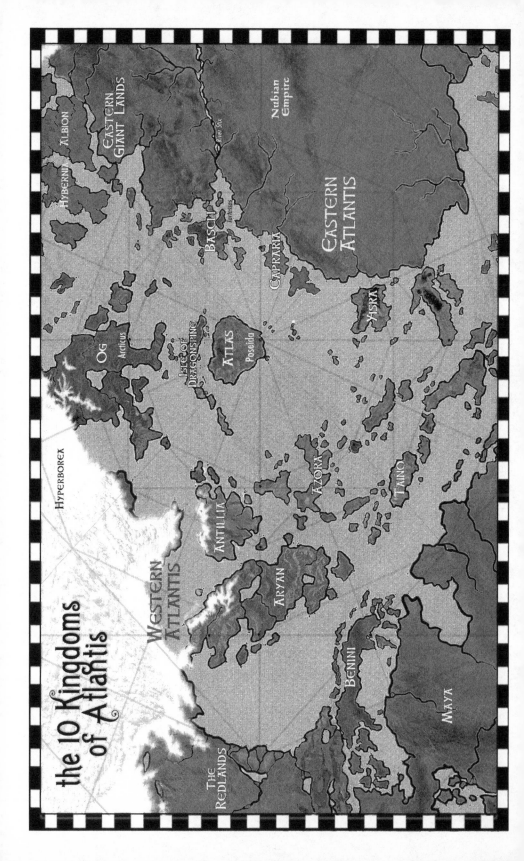

the 10 Kingdoms
of Atlantis

HYPERBOREA

WESTERN
ATLANTIS

The
REDLANDS

ANTILLIA

ARYAN

BENINI

MAYA

Og
Arcticus

Isle of
DRAGONSPINE

ATLAS
Poseida

AZORA

TAINO

EASTERN
ATLANTIS

XISRA

CAPRARIA

BASCU
Tartessus

River Stx

EASTERN
GIANT LANDS

HYBERNIA ALBION

Nubian
Empire

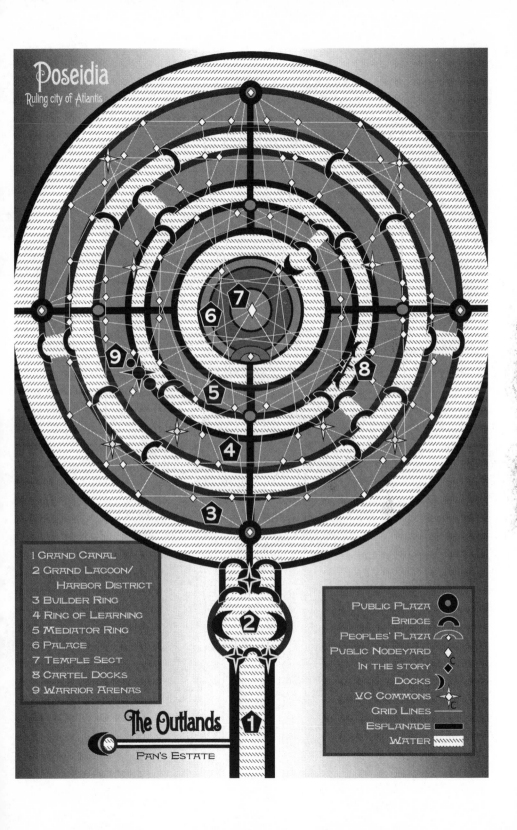

Poseidia
Ruling city of Atlantis

1 GRAND CANAL
2 GRAND LAGOON/
   HARBOR DISTRICT
3 BUILDER RING
4 RING OF LEARNING
5 MEDIATOR RING
6 PALACE
7 TEMPLE SECT
8 CARTEL DOCKS
9 WARRIOR ARENAS

The Outlands
PAN'S ESTATE

PUBLIC PLAZA
BRIDGE
PEOPLES' PLAZA
PUBLIC NODEYARD
IN THE STORY
DOCKS
V.C COMMONS
GRID LINES
ESPLANADE
WATER

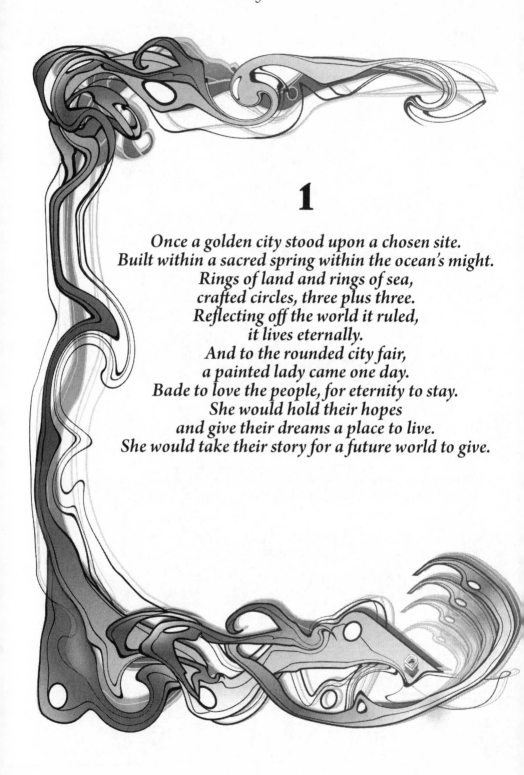

1

Once a golden city stood upon a chosen site.
Built within a sacred spring within the ocean's might.
Rings of land and rings of sea,
crafted circles, three plus three.
Reflecting off the world it ruled,
it lives eternally.
And to the rounded city fair,
a painted lady came one day.
Bade to love the people, for eternity to stay.
She would hold their hopes
and give their dreams a place to live.
She would take their story for a future world to give.

Leaving the Dreamvale would mean Brigitte would gradually forget growing up on the rocky shores of the mystical islands. She stood in her favorite place high above the dreamclan village watching the ocean dance with the cliffs. It would be her last chance to behold the glory of sunset before boarding the galleon bobbing in the cove below.

Evenings were always a masterpiece of color, the best time to behold the splendor of nature's art. Clouds of rainbow prisms had the look of creatures billowing in the sky. But in the distance, a wall of storm opened like the jaws of a predator, drifting ever closer to the peaceful, green island.

"Brigitte." A male voice echoed through her contemplation. She felt a pang of disappointment. Leaving would mean the beginning of a journey she had feared all her life. With one last lingering view of the panorama, she held her breath, reached out her arms and leapt from the cliff. As a mass of dancing particles, she bounced down the ragged rocks toward the village, one with the wind. Taking her time would be rude, so she kept moving until she filled the inside of her room.

Her brother Lukias was a dreamseer, finely tuned to the invisible. As usual, his hair was a shock of chaos that pointed in every direction. The amber of his eyes sparkled with gold flecks as he stood over her body with arms crossed. He looked right at her dream form. "The council has called us," he said with a hint of impatience.

Brigitte sank back into her body and opened her eyes.

"I warned you not to dreamwalk too much." He turned his back as she reached for her travel clothes. "You could separate from

1

your body and forget how to return. Especially here in the Dream-vale."

"It hardly matters anymore." She watched the sun's rays shoot dusty light through holes in the walls. She thought about the pattern it made every day at this time, the royal symbol of Atlantis. "In Atlantis we will be bound to our bodies."

Lukias reached out a caring hand and patted her shoulder. "There will be ways to dreamwalk in the realms of matter. It will just be more… challenging."

She smirked, knowing he always loved a challenge. He could always find humor even in the grimmest of circumstances. They exchanged a few moments of unfolding memories until, with the final boot in place, she stamped her feet and started for the door. "You coming?"

Together they walked to the center of the village where the council was gathered in a semi-circle facing a woman. She wore the leather of seafarers, her face shaded by a wide-brimmed hat. With one hip thrust to the side, her demeanor was unruffled with a twist of amusement.

Their father Denikon raised his booming voice for all to hear. "Captain Ofira Pazit of the Dreamship *Vex Voyager*, I give you my daughter Brigitte, emissary to Atlantis. She is the first true Moirae born into our dreamclan for seven generations."

The captain wrinkled her chin. "Impressive. Embodied Watchers are rare, even among dreamclans." Her chameleon eyes shifted in the fading light. "If you are ready, I think it wise that we set sail before that shadow storm arrives, don't you?" Her eyes slid toward the horizon. "This storm has struck more than one dreamclan. All of them were to send emissaries for the renewal of the Telluric Treaty. None of them have been heard from." She turned back to the council. "Are you certain you want to risk staying? It would be a tight fit, but we can evacuate the rest of you."

Brigitte glanced at the grim face of her tutor Indrius. The mysterious Atlantean woman had always been a curiosity to the clan. Though she had spent many years among them, she was never one of them. She was riddled with tragedy from a past she never spoke of, a past born in Atlantis.

Denikon answered, "Those who remain have chosen to face the shadows." His voice was steadfast though regret lingered in his eyes. He exchanged a nod with Indrius. "I am sending Lukias, my son and heir, to accompany his sister. If we fall, he will be the future of our clan. But trust me, we will not go down without a fight."

The council had argued for many moon cycles, trying to decide the fate of their people. It was important for Brigitte to escape. Her path was evident. The first ships had already departed, taking women and children to places of refuge. The rest stayed, devising a strategy. Though they were hopeful, they worked with the solemnity of people who faced their demise.

She squinted at Lukias as he and Indrius said their goodbyes. Theirs was always a close relationship. But everyone liked Lukias. Her time spent with Indrius was always strained at best. She offered him a gift. The sun flashed off a crystal dangling from a silver chain. Brigitte could feel the telluric consciousness radiating from the multi-faceted quartz. It pulsed with a longing that made her fidget.

After a whispered message to Lukias, the white-haired woman turned to look at Brigitte. Her green eyes were gray with emotion. She brushed Brigitte's cheek with her fingertips. "You know your task," she began. "Remember your Watcher powers. It has become exceedingly difficult to travel between realms on this planet. I fear this shadow storm will make it even more difficult. Atlantis is suffering from a disease. It will try and take you, too. Do not be attached to your human wishes and emotions. For humans, attachment can turn to weakness and suffering. This only serves to feed the shadows. Your path will not be easy."

"I will do what it takes to find a cause and a cure for Atlantis. I will be mindful of your warnings."

"Therein lies the trick. As you descend deeper into the Meridian Realm, you will forget my warnings. Take steps to hold them in your heart." She lingered in Brigitte's eyes for a few awkward moments. "I have prepared you as best I could, my child. I regret how I've treated you." She faced Brigitte and held her shoulders. "Know that I loved you like my own daughter. My treatment toward you was an attempt to prepare you for the task you face. Atlantis will not be kind to you."

"I understand, Indrius. You had no choice." Brigitte wanted to cry. But her tears had long since dried up.

Fire burned on the horizon. The storm stretched its tentacles to consume the peaceful cove. The *Vex Voyager* made a hasty departure. On deck Brigitte and Lukias watched their clan gather on the shore to take a stand against the approaching elemental threat. Her eyes fell on the white dress of Indrius. She held a dabrina in her hands. Together with the remaining magi of the clan, she played its chiming chords to mingle with their singing spells. A bubble of light appeared above them.

The dreamship let loose its sails to expedite their escape. At its curved bow stood their navigator. Her dark hair was bound into wild tendrils. It was her job to gain favor with elementals and direct the ship's course. This one was a rare arcane practitioner with supernatural talent, and the reason Captain Ofira had a functioning dreamship.

The navigator held up her arms with eyes closed. Three magi surrounded her. Their incantations joined with an ethereal chorus drifting from the ocean. Brigitte leaned over the railing. Surrounding the hull of the dreamship floated the colorful heads of oceanids, sea-people who were the denizens of the Oceanus Realm. They gazed at her with blinking silver eyes. Their hair rolled in the tide, a cascade of iridescent fins. Brigitte lifted her hand to salute them. Their answer came telepathically. They, too, were in the service of the Watchers, and would infiltrate Atlantis in their own way.

Brigitte shivered. Elementals responded immediately to their summons. Fog rolled in around the ship, lifting from the ocean like rolling steam. A celestial wind gathered the sails. Brigitte grabbed hold of the railing as the ship lurched and picked up speed.

The storm closed around the shores of the island. She buried her face into Lukias's shoulder. The crystal that now lay at his chest sent her a pulse of comfort. She stared at it in wonder, allowing it to become a focal point of distraction. Lukias looked back. But all he saw faded to a blur. Propelled by the songs of the oceanids, the ship seemed to fall off the edge of the world. The sails at its sides tilted, and the ship took flight into a starlit sky where they became wrapped in a muted silence.

Shrill screams and curses punctured the afternoon's sunny still-ness. Emerging from a flower-framed archway, a man ducked to escape missiles of pottery aimed at his head of messy curls. His childlike expression beamed with amusement as a woman's voice pursued him into the narrow street.

"You have no business showing your face here!"

D'Vinid rarely expended energy unnecessarily. Even in flight his movements had a feline elegance, which carried him lightly to the end of the lane where a set of twins waited purposefully, perched on a low wall. Their faces were painted with smug amusement as he exploded from the fragrant corridor, his long legs expediting his escape. They rose to their feet with light applause, thespian admiration written on their faces.

Adorned with bright noble attire, the twins stood out among the commoners, turning the heads of all who passed. Both had long sharp features and devilish eyes. Thin beards framed their wrinkled smiles.

D'Vinid stopped to straighten his clothes and adjust the floppy hat that flattened his wild curls. He reached back with momentary panic to make sure his musical instrument was still safely strapped to his back.

"What are you two doing here?" he asked, his eyes narrowed.

Kayden Aello had slightly wider features than his brother. It was the only means by which to tell them apart, though sometimes if they were not together, even that difference could fail to distin-guish one from the other. "Good job, D'Vinid!" he cried. "As usual, you never fail when it comes to getting the show started!"

Jensyn, the other twin, always prefaced his words with a dra-matic gesture of some sort to emphasize his "thoughtful" nature. "We've come to make sure you keep your appointment to per-form at our father's revelry tonight." Jensyn draped an arm over D'Vinid's shoulder with a genial smile.

"I was on my way there!" D'Vinid protested. "Your father does not have to monitor me." He trailed off, looking back at the seldom-used corridor. "How did you find me? A locator-crystal? I don't seem to recall imprinting one for you."

Their looks were too innocent for anything but guilt.

"You say you were on your way to Father's revelry?" Kayden interjected with an index finger thrust into the air. "What a coincidence! That's where we're heading. We can go together."

D'Vinid smirked and took one regretful look back at the florid home of his attacker. With a sigh, he waved his hands in surrender and stepped into the bustling market.

D'Vinid intensely disliked being held to his appointments. But he understood their father's caution. He had become notorious for getting swept away on other adventures, which often led him to spontaneously cancel his musical appearances.

In fact, just this very day while heading for the Aello estate, somehow his feet adopted a mind of their own and walked him to the outer ring of the citadel. Today he blamed it on thoughts muddled by a maddening dream that awakened him far too early. It pointed to aspects of his fractured past and propelled him on a mission. Thus far, however, it had proven more difficult than he could imagine. Apologizing to those he had slighted with his negligent nature seemed to generate the opposite of the desired effect.

The old dabrina strapped to his back made it more difficult to dodge through the crowded marketplace. Though it was as homely as dabrinas came, he believed its depth of tone to be the reason for his popularity. No other resonance could compare to that which came from the heirloom passed to him by his mother. Though he could not remember her face, sometimes when he played he imagined her laughter in its ethereal song. Throughout his life, the instrument had become his most steadfast and loyal friend.

D'Vinid inhaled the salty air. It had been a misty morning, characteristic of Atlantean days. As always, music danced in his head, and soon his brooding thoughts were swept into the silent melodies only he could hear.

A cold gust whipped through the corridor of buildings. D'Vinid shivered. He noticed the world slow. Feeling dizzy, he reached to steady himself on a nearby wall. A flood of emotion smacked him into a funnel of buzzing darkness. He wanted to run but had enough presence of mind to keep his wits about him.

He closed his eyes. In the darkness a vision was burnt into his mind like he had been staring into a light. Blood red eyes gazed at him with sinister menace. He cried out.

The world was suddenly back to normal. Just as he thought his mind was playing tricks on him, he froze at the sight of cloaked figures standing at the entrance to a side street along the twist of a

7

canal. Though he could not see their eyes from the shroud of their hoods, he knew they stared right at him. Their faces were covered in what seemed like painted runes, and their arms wrapped in the bandages of death rites. He stumbled backward.

Kayden reached out to steady him. "You ok? Too many elixirs?" He laughed.

D'Vinid looked again at the dark figures. They were gone.

Flanked by the twins, he slowly made his way, as if escorted toward a prison sentence. He looked over his shoulder, stumbling as he walked.

The twins reached into satchels at their hips and produced golden hover-discs, inlaid with gems and geometrical patterns. As if in rehearsed choreography, they tossed their discs with the same flippant flick of the wrist. The discs clicked open as they fell, and a magnetic force cushioned them a few inches above the ground. They leapt atop the gleaming contraptions, which bounced at their added weight.

"Where's your hover-disc?" Kayden, the twin with the wider features, called out while hovering in a fluid pattern. Jensyn joined in, and soon the twins circled like jeering hecklers.

D'Vinid shook his head, replying, "I don't have mine anymore, remember?"

The twins jumped to the ground and stomped on their discs to make them bounce back into their hands. The movement automatically retracted the footholds with a click.

Jensyn leaned in close. "You don't *have yours*?" he marveled after a contemplative pause.

"It was taken away in the renegade revelries," D'Vinid admitted. "But I thought you knew that."

"You were one of the great hover-tricksters! How could you not get a new one?" Kayden exclaimed, throwing his hands out.

"You forget what happened to me when King Koraxx, in all his wisdom, decided to ban hovering outside the road mounds." D'Vinid sank into a dark expression. "Being so close to his sons, I was too high-profile, and he made an example of me. I am not allowed to even possess one."

Jensyn crossed his arms in a puzzle. "I'm sure your banning period is over by now. Koraxx isn't even king anymore. Just go through the mediators and get it resolved. How do you even get around?"

"Please spare me the questions! You don't know how hard it is to break the bond with a hover-disc. I still haven't gotten over it," D'Vinid admitted, though he knew there was a real truth he always avoided. As much as he tried to hide from King Koraxx, his son and successor, King Kyliron, was far worse. D'Vinid would do anything to avoid his attention. "I'm in no rush to get anywhere, and if I am, I just take the vailix needle," he pointed up at the shining bullet-shaped public transport, silently gliding on its wire around the city ring.

D'Vinid started walking, throwing a tentative look over his shoulder. He wove in and out of people gathered along the busy streets. The twins tucked their discs into their hip bags and followed closely. As they approached the Grand Esplanade, which cut through the rings of the city, a gathering crowd blocked the bridge across the water ring.

Jensyn threw up his hands.

"See," teased Kayden, "if you would only just allow our father to get you a new hover-disc, we would be past this in a hurry."

D'Vinid stared at him as if he were a lunatic. "How would that help right now?"

Kayden shrugged indifferently.

Jensyn rose to his toes, trying to catch a glimpse over the many heads. A parade of noble mediators inched along the esplanade, displaying their fancy hover carriages and feathery regalia.

The market was bubbling with festival fever. Banners and streamers billowed in the gentle breeze, and a general cheer abounded. It was the week of Ka-Ma-Sharri, when Atlantis celebrated the beloved myth of the separated Watchers, Belial and Kama, soulmates who vowed to unite only when they needed to act as a bridge for humanity's evolution.

All Atlanteans celebrated by taking a lover at the height of the festival. It was the most exalted time to join a couple as life-mates, or take on a nameless lover, offering oneself up as a channel for the divine beings to possess. The passing parade was a display of debauchery, signaling the start of the night's festivities.

Ka-Ma-Sharri lasted three days and happened repeatedly through the seasons when the sun and moon met in the sky. Human separation was represented by the celestial bodies that brought day and night to Sophaiya, and great celebration ensued when the two divine lovers could again merge during an eclipse. It was one of D'Vinid's favorite festivals. He often pondered the deeper meaning of the Ka-Ma-Sharri and wondered why many citizens had begun to objectify the ritual to a point of greed and lust, rather than the celebration of divine union as it was meant to be.

With the passage of time, though, he had begun to tire of the ritual. The temptations and pleasures of beautiful women were all just a part of his daily routine, and the pattern had begun to repeat itself enough that he was losing interest in the excitement of the festival. There was only one explanation he could think of to justify his endless string of lovers: D'Vinid was in love, and he did not know with whom. Somewhere along the line he had been struck with apathy, and it had spread through his entire being like a disease.

Guilt had taken up residence in his heart. Dark times had fallen over Atlantis. Everything felt wrong. For a long time, D'Vinid thought his uneasiness came from his own gloomy depression, but the feeling was beginning to seem more widespread. Perhaps the whole city felt it. An image from his dream flashed again in his thoughts. *A woman, standing at the bow of a ship. She was surrounded by clouds and swirling colors.* It was her. Or at least he thought it was her.

Who she would appear as next was always a mystery, an enigmatic vision that captured his heart like no other. She would materialize periodically in the eyes of a lover, only to be replaced in the laughter of another. She was the ever-unreachable, unattainable object of his desire. And try as he might to keep a steadfast heart to those he met, he always followed the trail left by that abstract lover.

His eyes landed on a strange phenomenon along the horizon at sea. One of the clouds seemed to take the shape of a ghostly galleon rising out of a cloud bank. Magically, like an image in a dream, the enormous cloud drifted ever near the central city of Atlantis. He fell into a trance. Focusing on the horizon, his eyes flashed orange as he quietly began singing words that popped into his mind, as words always did for him.

"On a ship of clouds and air
came she unto Atlantis fair.
Traveler from o'er the sea,
come to us and set us free.
For we are full of sorrow true.
Listen!
Atlantis calls to you!

The maiden of the moon is she,
the lover of Belial.
Seer of the shadow storm,
revealer of denial.
We shall wait to hear from you.
Listen!
Atlantis calls to you!

Where one rose grew are truly three,
and only one shall stand alone.
Its path begets the fourth and final,
fallen back to home."

Waves of sun-drenched chestnut hair blew across the contours of Brigitte's face as she stood at the bow of the shifting galleon. "Listen, Atlantis calls to you," she whispered. The ruling city of Atlantis was called Poseidia. Situated on the island of Atlas, it rose like a gem against the sky as they approached. They marveled at its glimmering radiance and majestic elevations.

Standing by her side, Lukias melded with her thoughts. He heard a melody spinning in her head, one neither of them could remember having heard before. Perhaps it was one of the Atlantean songs Indrius used to sing to them. But the words weren't familiar.

Dressed in the loose travel clothing of their clan, Lukias was short of stature. His dreamseer eyes revealed the depth of his perceptions. In many ways the siblings looked alike, with the same high cheekbones and almond-shaped eyes the color of amber. Though Brigitte kept herself impeccably groomed, he often neglected his appearance. Both had a presence that cast a spell over

11

anyone they crossed. Even the most charismatic of souls would become tongue-tied in her presence.

They had stayed on deck from the moment they sighted Poseidia. The city was perfectly round, built into a mountain with alternating rings of land and water, forming a target pattern with each ring stacked higher toward the center. Magnificent terraces and impressive spires stretched into hazy heights, cradled by an expanse of rolling hills. As the galleon reached the ocean entrance, they marveled at the massive golden gates that marked the water channel leading up to the circular citadel.

Reconstructed in an age when wars with foreign lands were considered a thing of Atlantis's past, these gates remained rusted open as a sign indicating all were welcome in her mighty ruling city. The entry channel stretched for five miles across farm and trade communities known as the Outlands. Most sea commerce took place along those bustling banks until the channel opened into the citadel's golden rings.

Brigitte gnawed on a thumbnail. A crosswind billowed the sails, pitching the hull abruptly. She slipped her hand across the rail, gripping tightly while widening her stance. Along the journey she had discovered the secret of sea legs: allowing herself to stumble in whatever direction the deck would present itself, in an always-random sense of stable ground.

Brigitte savored the moments remaining before she would have to adopt city fashion and take her place at the side of the man bound as her betrothed by the Watchers. Their joining as mates would serve the Telluric Treaty, a marriage of necessity for the good of all. Her thoughts swarmed, wondering what his young face had grown to become. He remained in her dreams since their meeting as children. She wondered if there would be love.

Obscured by elemental magic, the shifting ship of clouds went unnoticed by port authorities. They anchored offshore away from other vessels. She closed her eyes, trying to block out the memory of their flight from the Dreamvale.

Lukias touched her hand, and she startled back to the present. "You will soon forget," he assured.

She stifled the swell of emotion. "We will never see them again." A tear slid down her cheek. "I still don't understand. Why did they attack our people?"

"I believe it is the alliance between Atlantis and the dreamclans they want to destroy. The only thing you can do in retaliation is stay alive and fulfill your destiny." His eyes fixed ahead. "Leave the revenge to me."

She glanced at him. "That's your plan? Revenge? Perhaps you should focus on bringing to light these shadows of Atlantis."

He chuckled. "I knew you would say that."

She scooped up the crystal into her fingers. "Indrius gave you this?"

He snatched it away. "She said it would lead me to someone she wants me to find."

"Who?"

"Someone important." He tucked it into his shirt.

"Oh, I see! I'm not good enough for her secrets."

Lukias messed up her hair with a sideways smile. His eyes clouded over with the dreamseer's haze. "You will know him before I do. And soon you will have your own secrets to keep."

A gust of wind gathered the sails, propelling the dreamship toward shore. The captain stood on the highest deck watching them with her shifting eyes. In a single acrobatic motion, she deftly moved from where she stood, down the stairs, and onto the main deck. "The magi are preparing to send you ashore." She looked at them searchingly as she spoke. "I am not sure I feel comfortable sending you two alone. I don't feel like my job is done until you get to the palace."

Lukias glanced at his sister before explaining. "Captain Ofira, you have been a generous deliverer. The Watchers have chosen you wisely. They also directed me on this path. We must have faith in their guidance."

Ofira gave up. "Then allow me to increase your list of allies." She snapped her fingers in a spiral, and a vial of blue liquid appeared in her hand. "This will allow you to see the signs of the conclaves."

Brigitte reached for the vial and examined it. "What's in here?"

"Various plant medicines with a base of sha'mana."

"The Treasure of the Watchers." Brigitte's eyes widened as she swirled the elixir. "Who are these conclaves?"

"Some call them the Children of One. They are the future of Atlantis emerged from the secrets of her past." Ofira's expression illustrated her care toward the matter. The captain had demonstrated unwavering integrity in their short time together. She nodded toward the elixir. "This will allow your eyes to see the blue-dream frequency where they alone can tread."

Brigitte nodded and swallowed the contents of the vial. Ofira produced one for Lukias, who followed his sister's lead in trusting the jaunty sea captain. Brigitte made a sign to Poseidon as the liquid slid down her throat and a tingling sensation spread through her body.

This was the moment for which she had prepared all her life, her arrival to Atlantis. She hardened herself to the fear. Dolphins and oceanids circled the ship's luminescent hull. Sea birds danced in and out of misty obscurity.

A circle of sulfur was cast on deck. The magi awaited them, held entranced by chanting. In the blink of an eye, they would be teleported to shore.

The crew of the dreamship gathered silently. Brigitte and Lukias exchanged telepathic respect and farewells with their brave deliverers. Brigitte nodded to the captain. She sucked in a deep breath as if preparing to leap into the ocean. Lukias took her by the hand, and they stepped together into the circle. The magi maintained their chanting cadence to will them to another place.

The chanting escalated to a loud drone. Sunbeams bent inward around them, casting radiant rays to brush their faces. Mist swirled in a vortex. The voices gradually disappeared. Molecules danced, effervescent across space. Fog poured around them, sweeping their vision into gray.

Moments later they found themselves inside a circle of standing stones where many road mounds intersected. Their bodies buzzed. In the center was a ten-foot tall obelisk made of solid quartz crystal. A ball of polished quartz balanced on its tip, held in place by a spiral of copper wiring. Sunbeams poured through patches of fog. Tiny particles of radiant light swarmed around their heads.

On the island of Atlas, the majority of the populace dwelled in the countryside. The heart of the ruling city was a citadel, with the outer ring serving the working classes. The central ring was reserved for learning and leisure, and the inner ring housed the opulent estates of mediators, those born to the ruling elite. The island apex of the target pattern was home to the royal palace and the Temple Sect.

Brigitte and Lukias had not appeared far from the entry channel connecting the ocean and the canals of the citadel. Esplanades with their numerous markets bordered both sides of the waterway. These were the main thoroughfares for land passage. Road mounds were carefully formed along natural telluric lines in the surface of the planet. Using magnetic propulsion, Atlanteans were able to activate their levitation devices, allowing them to hover along the mounds and transport themselves, or carry loads of goods from place to place.

The siblings stared at the obelisk, knowing it was one of the nodes of the Crystal Grid that powered Atlantis. These were resonant capacitors that stored the mindlight donations of the people, so the Grid could be supplied with psychic power. Brigitte placed her hand against the crystal surface, feeling its great age, and the life force it exuded. Lukias did the same, and for the first time, both of them connected with the mighty Crystal Grid of Atlantis.

Brigitte startled when Lukias batted her hand away from the obelisk. "It's in their Grid. The shadows came from here. This is what came to destroy us. Come," he encouraged, attempting a smile. "Let's get to the city as soon as possible. The Watchers will deliver us to where they wish us to go."

The road mound they followed snaked through rolling emerald hills slanting toward the ocean, whose shifting surface sparkled in the sun. The rugged country was shadowed with towering green crags and cliffs. Parcels of patchwork farmland and circular villas framed their destination. The citadel gleamed like a formation of crystals.

They passed villas overgrown with vines and fragrant hanging blossoms, making the structures seem as outcroppings of the land. The sound of an approaching vehicle could be heard coming from behind as they entered the valley. An older man appeared, floating on a hover-disc along the road mound. A wire connected his disc to a larger sled carrying a covered load. A group of boys sat on the back of the sled with their feet dangling over the edge. Their chatting and laughter rose above the gentle hum of the vehicle.

The mound joined with the market and led to the esplanade along the main waterway. Children ran in packs along the streets among colorfully clad pedestrians. Vendors barked their wares. It was hard to distinguish between the clattering of goods, the bustle of foot traffic, the din of voices, and the hum of levitating vehicles. To a person used to quiet, such racket could be maddening.

Traffic along the wide road parted at the passing of the travelers. Brigitte's cycles of silent studies and teachings left behind any need for peace. She allowed herself to enjoy the excitement and exchanged a glance with Lukias expressing her secret hunger for this adventure.

A flimsy purple scarf wrapped her hair. The scarf's edges fluttered in the warm salt breeze whipping through the corridor made by multi-storied buildings. She began to relish the elation of walking among crowds. The brush of their memories, hopes, and dreams rippled across the surface of her emotions. The feeling gravitated to the core of her soul, and she bathed in it as if swimming through a sea of consciousness.

They passed rows of shops and street carts nestled in sunken courtyards. Here, merchants displayed foods and exotic crafts for trade. Sinuous alleys and side streets wound off the esplanade. The crowd's energy was thick with activity. Brigitte could hear their thoughts, a noisy chorus of intent, focused on purposes and destinations.

It was alluring and overwhelming at that same time. She burrowed her face in the scarf to hide, even though not a soul took interest in their passing. She was amazed at the extent to which Atlantean telepathic presence seemed diminished. They did not have the awareness of the dreamclans. They were much more self-absorbed than Brigitte was accustomed to. The Crystal Grid kept them connected, though she sensed its very existence had made Atlanteans less aware of their once keen telepathic powers. The Grid had become a mental crutch.

She stopped to watch an older man shambling down the street. Equally perplexed, Lukias did the same. The man's dark-rimmed eyes swiveled in his head as if he had lost control of their movement. His face was dimpled with creases, his skin was blotched and faded. Everyone who passed pointedly ignored him. He begged for their attention in a nearly unusable voice.

As he drew near, Brigitte could not bring herself to look away, and the very act of looking drew his focus. His eyes pleaded for her to give him comfort. His stumbling steps propelled him toward her. Instinctively, Brigitte reached into his mind. Tears stung her eyes as she felt the utter loneliness and madness holding him prisoner inside his own head. She opened her eyes to dreamsight and recognized the shadowy creature that had attached itself to him. Trembling, she stepped closer to Lukias. "These people don't even know these shadows are taking over their minds!"

As the man reached out to grab at her cloak, Lukias stepped between them.

Brigitte could tell the shadow had become symbiotic with the man, feeding off his dark emotions, while at the same time stimulating them so it could constantly feed. It was a parasite.

Desperately, she tried to stifle her own fear, so she wouldn't accidentally react, as she had so often done growing up. She remained transfixed, as the hand of another gripped the invalid from behind and turned him the other way. "Here you are, sir," a man's voice said calmly.

Brigitte watched the stranger produce a piece of bread, which captured her assailant's attention.

"If you sit over there, you can eat this without being disturbed," he spoke as if to a child. Something about him seemed to soothe the helpless old man.

As Brigitte examined her savior's face, it lit up with a dashing grin, and she marveled at his stunning features. He was dressed in sloppy courtier fashion, with a loose-fitting tunic of dark green tied at the waist by a thick sash. A floppy hat rested on a head of dark curls falling to the middle of his neck. Strapped to his back was the hump of a dabrina. The depth of his brown eyes captured her heart. His smile reached into her soul. Lukias took note of a pair of twins nearby causing a scene with wild gestures and raised voices.

"I see you two are new to the city," he chimed in a cheerful voice, regarding their clan travel garb. "You should try and stay away from the madness. Some people say it's contagious if you touch them." He winked with a crooked smile. When he saw she didn't find his humor appropriate, he shook both hands at her. "I don't believe that myself, though." He noticed her lingering shock with compassion. "I see you haven't witnessed the madness yet."

Brigitte shook her head. "I don't understand why they are not taken from the streets and cared for. Why are they just ignored? Doesn't the Temple Sect have healing centers?" she demanded, glancing at her brother, who had gone into a dreamseer trance.

The handsome stranger fidgeted with his hip bag. "So many questions." His teasing smile made her stomach flutter. He pulled out an orange fruit. "You see, the healing centers are full. There's not much that can be done about it, and they're not much of a danger to the community, anyway, just to themselves. Although," he leaned in, looking around to make sure no one could hear, "sometimes the warriors come through and take them. But no one knows where to." He casually placed the fruit into the old man's needy grasp. "It has been said there is no cure. It's rather sad considering the advanced healing techniques of the Temple Sect. That man is probably someone's father or mate. He probably wandered away, and they can't even find him. Not that they would even recognize him if they did. The madness twists them into empty shells of who they were." He shivered visibly.

Brigitte felt drawn to the stranger's carefree manner. She could not take her eyes off his face.

Lukias focused inward. His lips moved as if he were muttering silently. He fidgeted with the crystal pendant.

The stranger's eyes flashed, entranced. "Is that a soul-crystal?" His demeanor shifted to seriousness.

"I don't know this term," answered Lukias.

"You should hide it." The stranger's voice wavered as he looked around. "The use of soul-crystals is banned in the city. Tool-crystals are used all the time, but they are not the same as soul-crystals. This will be taken from you if one of the king's guardians sees it." He turned to leave. "Well, I have a musical engagement to attend. My patron will be furious if I don't show up." He tipped his hat. "Be careful out here. You never know what trouble you can get into on Ka-Ma-Sharri. You and your mate should have a lovely time." He hesitated, looking at Lukias with a hint of envy.

"Brother," she said with forced reserve. Something about this stranger was alluring and terrifying at the same time.

"Excuse me?" The stranger leaned in closer. Her body buzzed at his proximity.

"He's my brother. Not my mate."

The stranger smiled. "Is that so?" He paused. "I would invite you to the revelry where I am playing … if you would like to attend."

"We are not here for revelry," interjected Lukias.

"Well, you came on the wrong night," he laughed in response.

Through the crowd, the twins came stalking toward them, waving and smiling. "Oh, D'Vinid! There you are!" one of them bellowed.

D'Vinid bowed and took her hand to his lips. A spark erupted at their touch, igniting a memory of some long-forgotten dream.

An unfolding rose glimmered in the sunlight. A twinkling tree swayed in a moonlit courtyard. A great hole into a starry sky opened in the base of its trunk.

Brigitte and D'Vinid jumped apart.

"Thank you for your assistance." She made a sign of farewell, pulled by her brother's mental summons. "Be well, stranger."

"Wait! I think this is for you." He opened the dabrina case where a red rose was tucked away inside one of the open cavities of the instrument. With a sigh, he handed the rose to Brigitte. She stared at it.

"It's yours. As a ... a welcome-to-Atlantis gift."

When she took it he seemed relieved. He muttered the traditional blessing of the festival, "Happy Ka-Ma-Sharri. May your soul find union," quickly closed the case, and continued on his way.

Everything about him turned her stomach in knots. She dared not look back as Lukias led her in another direction. She resolved to try and forget how electrically peculiar he made her feel. As she brought her purpose back into focus, she sniffed the fragrant aroma of the rose, and thought it was just as well she would never see him again.

2

In the arms of prophet's song
while singing words of destiny.
Free-will is a shadow
in the crying song of misery.
Once along a passing phase
in life and love and more.
Distant words of yesterdays
appear there on the door.

The sun sank toward the horizon. Brigitte and Lukias reached the last neighborhood before the circles of the citadel. Here the market faded into residential areas where the channel branched off into coves. Careful to blend in as they moved through pedestrians, they navigated by his dreamseer instincts.

The crowd parted ahead to avoid a woman of stately composure standing in the middle of the esplanade. She wore a hooded overcoat falling to her ankles with wide sleeves almost touching the ground. The hems were lined with light blue embroidery. Its swirling patterns stood out from the dark blue of the fabric. Her hair was uncommonly blond for an Atlantean, though she had it covered with the pointed hood of her coat.

She focused on Brigitte and Lukias with large blue eyes that absorbed the world like a dreamseer's.

Lukias headed straight for her. "Greetings," he spoke, bowing respectfully. It was the first exchange he had chosen to have since they entered the city. "I believe you are waiting for us."

She nodded slowly. Her glacial eyes studied the travelers. "I am Allondriss. I have seen you in my visions." Her eyes bounced to Brigitte.

"And you have been in mine," he responded steadily. "I am Lukias, High Seer of Poseidon's dreamclan. The Watchers have guided us to your care."

Brigitte flinched. It was the first time he had introduced himself as the high seer of their clan. With their father gone, the title had fallen to him.

Allondriss hesitated, taken aback by the implication of his dreamseer mastery. "My master is loyal to the Watchers and their

21

dreamclans."

"Your… Master? Are you not of the Temple Sect?" asked Brigitte.

"I am a servant to an influential mediator household, my lady." She bowed.

Brigitte found her station a curiosity. From what she understood, a fair-skinned maiden with fair hair would be seen among the high-born Temple Sect, not as a lowly servant. Her mannerisms were deliberate, as a servant's would be, yet graceful to suggest the delicate training of the temple priesthood. Neither did her clothing allude to a lesser status.

To avoid curious glances, she led them through a side alley to the gates of a private estate along one of the coves. Allondriss peered back over her shoulder before running a crystal bracelet over the locked gate. The motion set off a clicking mechanism, and the gate swung open.

"A stranger told us soul-crystals are banned for use here. How is your crystal different?" Brigitte asked.

Allondriss pulled it from her wrist and handed it over. "This is a tool. A crystal-accessor, to be exact. It is merely a hollow shell, because its telluric consciousness is harnessed into the Grid. Our entire Grid is run by crystals. Our hover technology is run by torsion-crystals and imprinters. These are all tools. We can connect with soul-crystals far deeper than we can with tools. Only the Temple Sect is allowed to use them, but only to program them."

Brigitte pursed her lips in thought, handing the bracelet back. "Is there a reason for this ban?"

Allondriss pressed her lips together. "One can take the official reason for truth. The technology was being abused by the few, and therefore forbidden to the whole. But then there is the unofficial reason." She motioned for them to enter, then led the way through a tunnel of creeping vines, which opened to a breathtaking view of palatial gardens and serpentine paths built around one of the coves. Their pace was no more than a promenade, which gave them the chance to absorb their surroundings.

"What is the unofficial reason?" Brigitte pried, as they curved around the water.

Allondriss took a moment to examine Brigitte, pondering the openness of her mind. "It is said the rulers of Atlantis do not want the people to have their personal power, that slowly the rules have been changed to take it all away from us. But most say this is the stuff of paranoia. It is said these are simply stories made up to try and undermine the wise powers that govern us." Her voice began to take a sarcastic tone. "The fact remains we have been denied the freedom to use the gifts that nature has given us." She lowered her voice to a whisper, "But nature always finds a way."

The main estate came into view along the edge of the water. Curving walkways extended from the house over the cove they had been following, bridging a series of stilted walkways and dome-shaped bungalows over the water.

"My master is celebrating the Ka-Ma-Sharri. There are guests at his court for the three days of the festival. He is very fond of revelries."

Lukias motioned for her to lead on. "If we may see him in private…"

"I will be happy to arrange that," the servant answered, her blue eyes surveying them carefully.

Having grown up with her brother and father, both dream-seers, Brigitte understood the subtle intricacies with which they conducted their affairs. They seemed to be aware of everything without even speaking. Allondriss had the same look to her. She guided them along the waterline toward the main house until they reached a round black door. Brigitte ran her fingers over the edges of golden glass embedded in its dark wood. It formed a symbol she recognized with profound awareness.

Allondriss watched, curiosity overcoming her aloofness. "You like the artistry?"

"This pattern…" Brigitte mumbled, her thoughts flying away.

Allondriss's expression darkened. "It is the symbol of the Order of Nexes."

Brigitte glanced toward Allondriss, speaking softly. "The Archives Nexes. Given to the people by Belial. The key to the Crystal Grid." She buzzed with a familiar tingle. "Is your master a member of the order?"

"It's always fashionable to discuss Atlantean origins among social circles. My master tries to be the most fashionable at all times. The order is an elite society of families who follow the ancient teachings. This symbol can be found throughout the city. It is built

23

into everything."

"The teachings of old Atlantis," Brigitte's voice flew away. "A fascinating subject." She traced the outline of the symbol, two serpents coiled up the center of a six-pointed compass within a twelve-pointed star. Twelve stars encircled the symbol. Allondriss's eyes remained on her.

"The serpentine mother of all knowledge and wisdom, as given to you, oh children of the sun, by the nations of light beyond the stars!" Brigitte delivered the passage from Belial's Cantos, breaking the spell with a cheerful lilt.

"Sometimes the Nexes Order is called the Order of the Serpent," Allondriss admitted. "The serpent humanoid was the original form taken by Belial and his brother. They were the Anunaki who designed the human project. One became the overlord. The other, the liberator."

A wordless eternity passed as Allondriss studied Brigitte. An unspoken bond formed between them. Lukias looked on in clouded dreamsight. Allondriss broke the moment, and cordially directed them into the house.

The large room beyond spanned nearly the entire structure of the main house. It featured a lush indoor garden with fountains of polished stone and hanging greenery growing in all directions from large baskets. The high ceiling displayed a checkerboard pattern, alternating amber glass with smooth, onyx tiles.

"If you'll excuse me for a moment, I will fetch my master." Allondriss walked to an alcove across from the entrance, braiding her hair quickly, her gaze on Brigitte. "Please make yourselves at home in the atrium until I return."

Mediator Pan Aello had a habit of talking incessantly. He was engrossed in his own story when Allondriss approached. He excused himself mid-sentence and turned an eager expression to his servant.

No words passed between them. She nodded, and he nodded back. Without a word to his guests he strode toward the house, hands clasped behind his back, a smile forming on his lips. "So, my special guests have arrived just as you said they would!" he exclaimed, clapping his hands and rubbing them briskly, a movement he often made in excitement. His long stride quickly brought them to the atrium.

Pan Aello was an older man with gray-streaked hair, which he usually kept swept back and tied behind his head. With a stroke of his goatee, another of his many idiosyncrasies, he greeted his guests with twinkling eyes. Many deep smile lines made his nature apparent.

Brigitte noticed Pan's aristocratic composure. She probed him closely, remaining quiet. Her brother stepped up in greeting.

"I am Lukias, High Seer of Poseidon's dreamclan." A silence opened at his words.

"High Seer?" Pan's thoughts flew away. His expression fell for a moment. High seers had the power to guide entire dreamclans. This was a man of great importance, despite his apparent youth and unkempt appearance. "My servant is a perceptive one," Pan continued, regaining his pace. "She knows the Lemurian dream-clans are forever welcome in Atlantis. In fact, she had a vision of your arrival earlier! I am most pleased the Watchers have brought you to us! I bid you welcome to my Outlands estate, and to Atlantis!" He bowed deeply. "I am Pan Aello of the royal line of Atlas, mediator of the fireball games. You are just in time for my grand revelry."

"I wish I could tell you our visit is for leisure and revelry," said Lukias tiredly. "We have been traveling for quite some time now, and, to be honest, the Watchers have guided us here because we require your assistance. My sister is an emissary of the Telluric Treaty. But our clan has been decimated by dark sorcery. Whatever sent that storm has enslaved the elements and used them against us."

Pan's smile faded. Standing straighter, he adopted a serious expression. Feeling needed was what he lived for.

"Your mediator line champions the Warrior Sect," Lukias continued.

"Only one aspect of the warriors," Pan corrected.

Lukias nodded. "I believe this is why our journey has brought us to you, Pan Aello. We need a warrior escort to reach the palace."

Pan seemed confused. "Our Crystal Grid keeps us linked telepathically so no one can bear to hurt one another. You could enter with a royal parade if you wish! I will arrange one if you would like. Parades and pageantry are what we Atlanteans love best. Dreamclans have immediate audience in the palace at all times." He paused from his rambling, reconsidering for a moment. "Why would you feel you need protection here? Inside the Grid you should feel safe."

Lukias lifted an eyebrow. "How do you know the storm didn't come from your Grid in the first place? You may not be aware of the dangers lurking in the shadows of your beautiful city, Mediator, but this doesn't mean they don't exist. When the dreamclans send emissaries to Atlantis, our coming often marks a change of history. You and I are both aware of this fact." He leaned in closer to Pan's fading smile, "and you must be aware that the Telluric Treaty is in jeopardy. Our coming is anticipated, and yet someone or something is trying to prevent it. We must reach the palace unknown and unhindered." His pitch raised into steady urgency. "You must believe me when I tell you we have great need for protection."

Pan made it his business to remain aware of the machinations of the Watchers. Their domain was Dreamtime, the subtle fabric surrounding reality, like water surrounding the ocean floor. It permeated everything, and Watchers existed in it comfortably as mere humans could not. People traveled there in their sleep, the only time they might release hold on a world shaped by eons of thought-created reality. Dreamseers had the ability to navigate Dreamtime consciously, and as such, they were the link between humans and Watchers.

"Of course, I will help you," Pan spoke clearly. "It is my duty." He studied the chestnut-haired beauty, the emissary. A ferocity burned in her eyes, which grabbed him enough to venture a second look. He admired her strong jawline, softly curved nose and the fullness of her lips. Both had a lighter skin color than the average brown Atlantean, though the sun had given them a golden hue. "I will summon a warrior escort for you immediately. But I would suggest, if you sense danger, that you wait until morning to travel. Night is the time when the shadows are thickest, after all. And there will be much chaos on the streets this night."

Lukias nodded in grim agreement.

"Please accept my hospitality!" Pan clapped his hands together and rubbed them briskly. "You may join the revelry, if you wish. I have some of the finest musicians in the land entertaining my

26

court this night. I have spared no expense for the Ka-Ma-Sharri."

"Pardon us, Mediator Pan, but we are not here to attract attention, or to celebrate," Lukias protested again.

"Well, that's okay, my young foreigner, this is why we have revelry disguise in Atlantis. I will see to it my servants supply you."

"I'm afraid it is not humans we are hiding from."

A movement at another entry to the atrium interrupted their debate. Brigitte's heart lurched. The stranger from the marketplace made an animated entrance followed by the same pompous twins. Their noise surged, then immediately ceased when they noticed who was standing in their path. The light in his eyes had seared her soul since they had parted. With a shiver, Brigitte silently cursed the Fates for joining their paths again.

"Ah! My sons! I see you've brought D'Vinid!" Pan exclaimed, throwing his arms open in delight. "Well done, boys! He is a difficult one to procure."

The twins waved off his praise, eager to find an elixir to soothe their tired muscles. "We had to walk the whole way because D'Vinid won't get a new hover disc," Kayden complained.

Pan waved off the comment. "My dear guests. This is D'Vinid, known as the Prophet Singer. He is the finest dabrina player in all of Poseidia, and in my employ for the revelry. He will be entertaining you this night."

Lukias observed his sister's reaction. His hand slid to the crystal pendant, which he had hidden beneath his clothing. It sent a jolt into his finger and he drew his hand back, surprised.

D'Vinid scowled at the rose Brigitte still held.

Pan clapped once again. "Allondriss here shall guide you to your chambers. And my sons will hand-deliver word to my associates in the Warrior Sect at once. Do not even think of wanting for anything. I shall ensure you are well cared for."

Jensyn's expression faded. "You want us to do another errand? We just spent the whole day getting D'Vinid!" His hands flew out to his sides in protest.

When Kayden realized what was being said, his eyes widened. "But the revelry!" he exclaimed.

Pan raised his palm at them with a feeble giggle. "All the more reason to leave with expedience. Look on the bright side, this time you can hover." He turned to Brigitte. "You must excuse their rudeness. They are fatigued and have forgotten their courtly manners. Alas, I find myself needing to remind them of their current punishment, and how this errand will perhaps erase it."

D'Vinid chuckled. The twins were always in some sort of trouble. But his attention shifted again to the strangers from the market. She was his muse come to life to once again haunt his heart. Whoever she was, her presence made him tremble. He quickly excused himself with a wink in her direction.

His dabrina needed to be tuned without delay. It was a plausible explanation for a hurried exit. Her amber eyes pursued his escape into the blinding sunlight, urging him to turn around. When he reached the doorway, he succumbed to her silent demand and immediately regretted the queasy feeling she aroused.

If he would choose anyone to be his Ka-Ma-Sharri lover, it would be her. But it seemed the Watchers had chosen her for him. He resolved to resist their temptation at all costs. With a wrinkle between his brows, he turned and walked away.

Sunset washed the city with gold. Business traffic faded on the Grand Esplanade. Shops closed. Every evening the gentle resonance of crystal-nodes engulfed the city rings. Their radiant song called the citizens of Atlantis into silent contemplation. Lights began illuminating the streets.

Pan's servants had spent the late afternoon setting up tables and cushioned lounge spaces throughout the gardens for the festivities. Exotic women, scantily clad and overflowing with charm and hospitality, led guests to tables and took orders for any number of intoxicating services, from oil massages to flower-essence oxygen treatments, tonics, perfumes, and mood-enhancing elixirs. Pan treated his guests like royalty.

D'Vinid and the other musicians set up their instruments on the deck of a larger bungalow over the cove. He sat tuning his dabrina strings while dolphins chattered in the water, doing tricks around the kitchen where servants tossed fish for their evening meal. He watched the city's starry lights come to life amid the song of the crystals.

The nodes were resonant capacitors that harnessed Atlantis's power through the focused thoughts of its citizenry. These mindlight donations fed power to the Great Crystal. For so long, D'Vinid had neglected his duties to meditate during illumination rituals. It was yet another source of his recent guilty conscience.

"This song reminds me of the oceanids," Brigitte's voice interrupted his brooding.

He caught his breath and turned to face the woman who had not left his thoughts since their meeting. "Sunset is always my favorite time of day," she admitted.

"Mine, too." His smile brought out the dimples in his cheeks. "Evenings have always held my heart. The song of the crystal-nodes, the color of the horizon, the lights of the city. Wait until you see it from the rings of the citadel. You will be amazed."

She gazed around with delight, sighed deeply, then smiled, unsure how to react to the feelings his presence aroused in her. The resonant chiming continued.

"That sound!" she gasped.

"It's the Temple Sect sending resonance through the nodes. We call it nodesong." It was a sound he loved to the core of his being. "It's supposed to call us to illumination rituals, though I'm afraid most of us just listen to it these days."

As they absorbed the sound, it seemed that every part of them reached toward one another, like water flowing downstream. Their tenuous silence was consumed with the desire to succumb to the pull. The longing bordered on pain. They knew it when their eyes met. He wanted desperately to resist the temptation. Had she stayed away, he would have eventually purged her from his thoughts. But the Watchers were clever. Women were his greatest weakness.

She cocked her head, wishing to ask him many questions. It seemed much easier to link telepathically, but this was not something Atlanteans did anymore as they had in their history. It was a burden for her to think about communicating with only words.

He returned her examination, feeling strangely at ease under the caress of her entrancing eyes, despite his initial urge to run away from her. He brushed aside a lock of hair that had fallen over her eye. Her dangerous beauty blossomed even more as he examined her face.

"You know," he said, "this is the height of Ka-Ma-Sharri, the night when Belial's mate, Kama, comes to him. I am always moved

by the thought of their union… The tragedy of lovers separated forever, and the glory they must feel to be united once more." He raised an eyebrow. "It is customary to take a lover during this festival." His eyes betrayed his admiration as he looked back at the twinkling lights. "There is a woman who haunts my dreams. She is a light within the dark, a queen on a hilltop whom I cannot touch. She holds my heart somehow. But she is ephemeral. She appears for moments in the eyes of a lover and then disappears again."

Brigitte began to tremble. She could feel the pull of his words. The story of Belial and Kama made her anxious. She longed for this man without reason. Though he was devastatingly beautiful, it made no sense how she could love him so immediately and entirely.

He gently cupped her fingers and lifted them to his lips, holding her gaze with a roguish spark in his eyes.

Her stomach turned to knots. "I go to the bed of my betrothed tomorrow," she blurted, breathless.

"Why are you not with him tonight? To perform the joining ceremony at the height of Ka-Ma-Sharri is the most exalted moment to take a mate. Obviously, the *Watchers* have other plans for you."

She puzzled over his question. Her hand buzzed in his light grasp. Her inner dialogue argued with his words. She shook her head and lightly pulled her hand away.

"Do you know him?" he asked softly.

She shook her head again and looked downward.

"I didn't think so," he jeered. "Our ways are civilized, yes? What sort of alliance do the Watchers have in store for you? Will it be pleasurable? Will there be love?" His hand slid to her hip. Panic gripped her throat. His lips brushed in a whisper across her ear. "Love and familiarity should be the basis of mating, not perpetuating bloodlines based on genetic alliances. We're dealing with peoples' lives here."

"Some of us are born to the task!" she protested, pulling away in muted anger. "In case you forgot, mating is the only known method for perpetuating bloodlines."

He laughed at her offense. "The Fates can be amended, my lady. Free-will is our highest law, after all. This is why our genetically controlled Mediator Sect takes on kallistas. Our *civilized ways* have made it so love can at least be tasted, even if these betrothals deliver a mate we despise. So, our dream kallista gets all the love, while the one bearing our bloodline is emotionally rejected. You can take on a kallisto lover if you wish," he suggested alluringly. "It is the Atlantean way."

"I must not venture down that path. It is my choice to meet my betrothed with a clear heart."

D'Vinid laughed. "A clear heart! Do you suppose the Watchers have that planned for you, as well?"

"I do as the Watchers bid."

"And what if it was they who brought us together? How else do you explain it? I ask you again, why are you not with him right now?"

She watched every move he made. Her desire grew stronger. Suddenly her voice seemed to escape her lips without permission. "If a kiss would not break my betrothal…"

Without letting her finish, D'Vinid took her into his arms. His eyes flashed an eerie orange as he lowered his lips to hers.

Everything went black.

They floated in a vision among a million shards of starlight falling to the planet. She stood by his side on a hill, overlooking pyramids in a lush jungle valley below. In the span of one kiss, their love transcended all time and space.

His eyes glowed a brighter orange. "Beloved Kama," a strangely familiar voice escaped his lips. "I have waited for you, my love. It is time for my return, and for us to unite once more."

Brigitte caught her breath and stepped back. It was as if a different person had suddenly appeared before her. She knew him, and she loved him beyond measure.

He shook his head. The light in his eyes faded. "What happened?" D'Vinid pressed his fingers to his temples.

"I don't know… You changed," she stammered.

He reached to steady himself on the railing.

She placed her hand on his back for support. A wave of apprehension rippled over her body. "I'm sorry, I… I couldn't help it."

"Neither could I." He collected himself, taking note of his surroundings once more, feeling pulled in impossible directions. Vertigo flooded his head as he stepped away. He touched her cheek, drinking deeply of her beauty. He could barely control his body. He had not meant to kiss her.

"This is Watcher trickery," he said. Something had overtaken him, and it only ignited his resentment for those meddling Fate weavers who stole away the free-will of the people. "You're right. We cannot continue."

He looked out over the cove with his jaw clenched. He had vowed to never be manipulated by them. "You should go," he grumbled, and tore his eyes away to avoid her reaction.

The streets of the city filled with revelers wrapped in their finest regalia. It was customary to wear dark jewel tones for the height of Ka-Ma-Sharri. As such, the crowd was a rainbow of dark colors. Elaborate lace masks covered their faces. It was a night to be anybody but themselves.

A group of foreigners skirted the edge of the revelry, winding through the back streets of the Outlands to avoid the amorous chaos. Their leader, Torbin, was shorter than the rest, stocky of build, his head covered with a brown hood. By his side was his daughter Loressai. She was a woman of exceptional beauty, dark and sleek. She scanned their surroundings, her eyes fixed in nervous caution. They were accompanied by four magi who cast an energetic net around them.

As they passed onto the esplanade running beside the Grand Canal, they tried to remain discreet. But they couldn't avoid noticing the needy attention of the madness. Something had stirred the zombified victims of the strange ailment. Revelers ignored them, focusing on the intentions of their own lustful desires. Citizens had become used to the mutterings of those who had fallen to the epidemic.

Loressai and her father, however, took note of the strange behavior and shook their heads at the disgusted ignorance the city dwellers cast on the misfortune of their own people.

In one of the plazas, a group of ragged people suffering from the ailment shuffled toward them, calling out in desperation. The foreigners pulled into a tight circle. Loressai glanced around and froze in terror. On the edges of the plaza stood strange hooded silhouettes. The beating of her heart pounded at her chest. She had seen them before. Their faces were covered in black runes, and their limbs wrapped in the bandages of those who were prepared for sacred death rites. They were shadows, incorporeal, phasing from sight as if they were but hallucinations. She blinked, hoping they would disappear. But they remained, staring at her, empty and ominous.

Their whispering thoughts consumed her mind in a chanting chorus. As if in a trance, she walked toward one of them, who reached out his bandaged hand to touch her forehead. "*Queen of the Blood Triad, we welcome you.*" His voice sliced into her mind. The rest of them bowed in reverence.

"Loressai!" Her father's voice interrupted the trance. She turned around, realizing she had wandered away from the safety of the magi. She pressed her fingers into her temples. The air felt like thick liquid. Obeying her father's summons, she hurried back to the magic circle. She knew then that she should have stayed in the safety of their home in Subterra. Every time she journeyed to the surface into the Grid of Atlantis, she suffered from memory lapses. Gripped by a chilling fright, she allowed her father to lead the way to the estate of Pan Aello. Looking back, she realized the black figures had vanished.

"Brigitte?" Lukias called across the walkway. "There you are!" He jogged toward them. A spark jolted from the soul-crystal. He stopped in his tracks and studied D'Vinid, squinting.

The musician glanced at her. There was at once banishment and regret in his eyes. An anxious burn heated her body until she was red in the face.

Lukias spoke. "You should get back to the bungalow, Brigitte."

"I was heading there, anyway," she answered.

D'Vinid's regret soured his expression. He nodded toward the shore. "It's for the best. Good night, my lady."

She stormed off. Dolphins leapt from the water, following her path, chattering persistently. A planter of flowers mysteriously withered at her passing.

D'Vinid watched her departure. His mouth hung open by the time she reached the shore.

Lukias studied the dolphins' peculiar behavior. His eyes blurred into Dreamtime, revealing the subtle currents of light swirling above the surface, the same currents dolphins could see naturally.

He took a step back to widen his perspective. A cord of light extended between Brigitte and D'Vinid. "Who *are* you?" he asked in amazement. The crystal pulsed on his chest.

D'Vinid returned to tuning his dabrina strings with more attention than was necessary. "I'm no one special," he muttered. "Just a musician. But your sister… No one makes dolphins act like this." He stopped tuning and looked toward the planter of withered flowers. "She is not entirely human, is she?"

"I know what my sister is." Lukias shook his head. "But you, I don't know. You are marked by the Watchers."

D'Vinid stood from his instrument, standing close enough to Lukias as to make the dreamseer shift his feet. "Free-will is my master and mistress. I choose to live a simple life. I choose to *not* be marked by any Watchers. And it is my right to choose this."

Lukias traced the lingering subtle currents with dreamsight. They trailed after Brigitte as she disappeared in the direction of her bungalow. He eyed D'Vinid carefully. "I don't think you've ever had free-will, my friend."

"Nonsense. All humans have free-will."

"My sister is the Moirae of our dreamclan. She was born for one task."

"I'm afraid I've never heard this word before." D'Vinid sat again and picked up the dabrina.

Lukias clutched the crystal at his chest. "Our people are the ancestors of Lemuria. We live on the border of Dreamtime. We carry the blood of the Watchers. When Watchers are born among us, they are called Moirae. They are the weavers of fate in human form, and she has been chosen by virtue of being born. She doesn't have free-will. She is ruled by her destiny, one that she chose before incarnation."

D'Vinid dropped his head, cursing his decision to get out of bed that morning. "I'm sure you're both noble people. And you will do as you must. I would very much prefer to be left out of it, if possible." D'Vinid struggled to speak the words. His interest in Brigitte scorched his soul. He tried to keep himself from shaking. This word *Moirae* seized his heart in panic.

Lukias eyed him. "My sister and I were raised by a woman from Atlantis named Indrius. Does this name mean anything to you?"

D'Vinid's head tingled at the sound of the name. But he had

never heard it before.

"Where did you learn to play dabrina?" Lukias added.

"I've always known." He tuned another string, listening carefully for the proper tone.

"Interesting," Lukias smiled slightly, and without another word strode off in pursuit of his sister.

Alone at last, D'Vinid lost himself in a chord progression. His head spun. Fragments of the dream that awoke him that day fractalized in his psyche. It had to be prophetic. He focused his thoughts on Belial. Being the patron of free-will, he was the only Watcher D'Vinid felt comfortable praying to. Somehow the thought of Belial always calmed his mind. He felt as though he sat in the eye of a storm, plucking out a melody at the end of the world, somehow knowing it was a pointless project.

Night transformed the estate into a glowing forest. Guests wandered around the bungalows as they flooded into the revelry. The dreamseer's words made him think of the last time he saw Prince Bavendrick. He thought of their exchange, remembering every detail as clearly as if it happened at this moment.

"What is it they call you these days? The Prophet Singer?"

D'Vinid recognized the voice. His heart leapt at the sound of it. He turned with a grin. "Another name given to me by your mother."

Prince Bavendrick lowered the scarf covering his face and clapped D'Vinid into a brotherly hug. "She always liked to give you names. She used to call you 'Prince of the Sea.'"

"She only liked me because I was her captain's son." D'Vinid looked around at the interior of the queen's flagship, Dafni's Enigma, which had been his home most of his life. When the queen died, the ship was decommissioned. And here she sat in permanent berth, transformed into a social hub, a monument to the beloved queen. D'Vinid played music on the stage since he retired from his days at sea, unsure how to proceed with his life. Despite increasing notoriety for his music, he felt lost.

"She loved you because you didn't have a mother. She was always a sucker for orphans." Bavendrick laughed, running his finger on the etchings in the carved wood of the stage. Even wrapped in sadness, his handsome face had a glow to it. In that sense, he was much like his mother.

"I must say, it's good to see you, brother. What are you doing out of

the palace?"

"I figured I would give your free-will credo a try for the day. It's been liberating, I must admit."

"For the day? Oh, come now, buddy. This is your chance! There's an entire world out here for you to explore."

There was sadness in the prince's eyes when he laughed. "Believe me, I've given that some thought."

D'Vinid longed to ask him for a recap of their time apart, but leaving the courts was a reminder of the stack of guilt that was beginning to weigh on his soul. Kyliron was king. It should have been Bavendrick. And as monarch, the young king was gradually ridding himself of all those who truly loved him. His actions promised to take their father's folly to an entirely new level of mishap.

"I brought you something, D'Vinid." Bavendrick produced a glimmering rose from his pack. "I found this growing in my mother's shrine. When I took it, I had a vision of you. I don't know why."

D'Vinid threw his hands up as if touching the rose would burn him. "I can't take this! It's Watcher magic!"

"Then give it to someone. A lover, perhaps." He offered it again. "Go on, take it."

D'Vinid absently reached for the rose. His eyes flashed orange.

Bavendrick took a step back. With silent reverence, he made a sign to the Watchers, but chose not to address it. "Kyliron hasn't been the same since you left."

"What are you talking about? Kyliron hates me."

"He's jealous of you, D'Vinid."

"Why? Because Loressai wanted me and not him? He couldn't have her. I did him a favor. He's got a betrothal obligation and she wasn't a kallista."

"You don't need to talk to me about betrothals." Bavendrick laughed. His eyes glazed over. Negotiations for his third were under way. "D'Vinid, if I go through with this joining, it would be going against the Telluric Treaty. My generation is supposed to join with the dreamclans. Kyliron wants to unite the ten kingdoms. The only way to do this is to join with Og." He cradled his head in his hands. "He should promise his firstborn to Og, not his brother. I have an obligation to Atlantis." He threw up his hands. "I don't want to bore you with politics."

D'Vinid patted him on the shoulder. "Why is Kyliron even king? What happened?"

Bavendrick closed his eyes. *"Our father named him successor. What else could I do except for strongarm my way in there? Ignore my father's last wish? I am not my brother."*

D'Vinid rolled his eyes. *"Koraxx had the madness, Bavendrick. How could his decisions be taken seriously in the end?"*

"Perhaps all of Atlantis suffers from the madness," Bavendrick sighed.

"Don't let your moral code be the downfall of us all. If Kyliron plays dirty for his politics like your father did, then you need to stand up to him. Don't let yourself wallow in self-pity like I do. You're supposed to be king, stupid." D'Vinid grabbed him by the shoulders and gave him a shake. *"You were born to be a leader. Kyliron pretends to be able to lead. That's the difference between you."*

D'Vinid sighed. What he said to Bavendrick on that day made him a hypocrite. He had confirmed the dreamseer's assertion that the Fates overruled free-will from the moment of birth.

He thought of the rose. He was finally rid of it, and yet it had come back in the hands of a Watcher in human form. He hardened his thoughts with indignation. He accepted that perhaps those with birthrights had fates. Someone like Bavendrick. Or perhaps Brigitte. But not someone like him.

3

Singer's song to silence meet,
amid the shadow's site to greet.
Rest his head to quell the fear,
the meeting of the muse is near.
Magi whispers words of fate,
flying to its primal mate.
Underneath the dying lights,
standing in the darkest night.
Calling in the violet flames,
they can find the shadows' names.

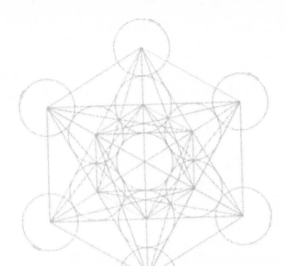

Gossamer drapes fluttered in the window of the guest bungalow. Smells of blossoming flowers wafted across the open-
air patio and into the single circular room. The air was cold.
Such a sudden change in temperature was unheard of in Atlantis.
The Crystal Grid did not allow the ten kingdoms to suffer the
same cold as the rest of the planet's icy reaches.

Tortured by her confinement, Brigitte chose to retreat into
meditation. Slipping into a lotus position, she stilled her mind.
Her eyes opened to dreamsight. She had not yet tried entering
dreambody in the Meridian Realm. How hard could it be? Her
soul stretched and squirmed in its heavy shell. She lacked the
intensive training of her brother. But as a Watcher, being in dreambody was her natural state. She tried again, breathing slowly. Soon
her agitation melted, and she was drifting above the bungalow.

She floated above the cove like a ghost. What she saw filled her
with terror. Despite their cheerful demeanor, the courtiers had
shadows swirling around their heads. The creatures reached invisible tentacles into their dreambodies, feeding off their essence
through gaping holes. The people seemed helpless, paralyzed as
if bitten by venomous creatures subduing their prey. Their only
escape seemed to be the pursuit of sensory pleasures.

She noticed the arrival of a small group at the entrance of the estate. They were dressed in simple travel clothes. One of them was
a woman. Examining her, Brigitte recoiled. The woman was consumed in shadow, but this was no ordinary shadow. It had the look
and feel of an original Nephilim, half Anunaki Watcher and half
human. These Nephilim were dangerous, and had been banished

from the Meridian Realm, doomed to wander as demon spirits, much like the shadows. Or perhaps the shadows were like them. Brigitte sank deeper into Dreamtime and watched with fascination. She never thought she would see one in her lifetime.

When the original Nephilim lived on the surface of the planet, many became drunk with power, and participated in the subjugation of humanity. It was Belial who had banished them from the Meridian Realm by activating the Fire Crystal of Atlantis to destroy their oppressive empire. But in so doing, he also set the elements off-balance and nearly destroyed the world. The icelands were what was left of the Nephilim empires.

Since then, the knowledge of the Fire Crystal was sealed among the highest initiates of the Temple Sect. Meridian settled into a denser vibration. Thus, in order to take physical form, all Watchers and, by proxy, their Nephilim offspring, needed a human shell. Brigitte knew this was impossible unless they entered through the birth process, thereby accepting the amnesia of birth.

She had taken incarnation the easiest way possible by entering through the dreamclans. They maintained the lineage of Lemuria, and the original bloodlines of humanity as created by the Anunaki. Until now, she had allowed herself the ignorance of surrendering to her human condition. As much as she wanted to wait, she knew it would soon be time to awaken.

This creature was trying to create a Neter. This would entail possessing its host while fully conscious of the process. The only way to do so would be to spend time altering the host to its vibration, then finding a way to eject the soul that had already taken up residence in the body. Unless the soul was willing, this was exceedingly difficult, and could take decades.

There was a third way for a Watcher to dance with physical incarnation, and perhaps the most common – the taking of an Avatar. It involved sharing a body with a human host. The control of the Watcher was limited at best. An Avatar could be the beginning of a Neter, but the process was undesirable.

The Neter woman had been blessed with profound beauty; eyes of coal, jet black hair and a golden complexion. But her auric field had been all but consumed by darkness. The creature had come a long way toward its goal.

She was accompanied by a group of magi. As they entered

the compound, the woman excused herself and headed into the revelry. If an original Nephilim had returned, Brigitte knew without a doubt its intentions had to be discovered. It was hard to tell who exactly was in charge, the woman or the demon creature. She drifted higher to avoid being detected and followed the woman into the revelry.

"And what, my friend, makes you think you can come here at the height of Ka-Ma-Sharri and interrupt my revelry? I realize you Subterrans don't celebrate our celestial events." Pan Aello flipped his hand toward Torbin. He was keymaster from the realm beneath the surface of the planet. "What do you have down there to mark your sacred revelries? Constellations of bioluminescent moss? Or do you forego sensory pleasures and study all the time?" He grinned widely, kicking up his heels on the desk of his private reception chamber.

A picture window allowed them a view of the gardens below. Pan surveyed the revelry, hoping to catch a glimpse of something delightfully scandalous. Torbin was a man of Pan's age, though younger in appearance, as all Subterrans lived to be thousands of years old. He was of stocky stature with hair grown out long and smooth. This was an antiquated style, but it suited his features, so Pan chose not to chide his old friend for not being able to move with the times.

"Subterra has a staying power you will never have on the surface, Pan Aello. One day, when Atlantis is merely a myth, we will live on and still be as we are today."

"Sounds positively boring. So, what brings you to ruin my revelry this evening, my dear, boring friend?"

"It isn't I who brings ruin to your revelry, Aello. But perhaps I can save it. I'm afraid this celestial event of yours has brought about a doorway between realms," Torbin admitted solemnly.

Pan leaned back in his chair and stroked his chin, letting himself sink into deep thought. He loved all things secret. The Order of Nexes always had a sense of exclusivity that enticed him on every level. Torbin was also a member of the order, but obviously for different reasons. He was of the Luminari, who acted as liaisons between Subterra and Atlantis. The man never made a visit without purpose. He only called on Pan in times of need on behalf of the order.

"The signs are all in place, Pan. Belial has returned to Atlantis. It is time to prepare for what is to come."

"Excellent!" Pan sat up, rubbing his hands together.

"Belial must enter through a human host," Torbin spoke as he paced, his arms folded in front of his chest. "He will not return through the birth process. He will hide behind the identity of whomever he infiltrates. A living avatar. Perhaps a Neter."

Pan contemplated, stroking his goatee with a smile.

"But he must enter at the height of Ka-Ma-Sharri when the celestial doorway is open. Unfortunately, there seem to be other Watchers trying to enter through the same doorway, ones who may not have the best intentions."

Pan stood up and strode to the window, wondering what excitement he'd missed at his grand revelry. He placed his fingers in a steeple. "Let's not get carried away with conspiracies. All will become clear in time."

"If we can find out the entry point of the Watchers with dark intent, we may be able to tip the scales in favor of Belial's arrival."

Pan smiled wickedly. "Don't be too sure the evil doesn't enter right under your nose, my dear friend. It is easy to be fooled by the darkness." He poured an elixir and swirled it around in a crystal goblet. "But rest assured, Belial is a master of the Cunning. Whatever scales you wish to tip may already be tipped. His arrival will be glorious. You can depend on that." He took a swig of the green liquid. "In Atlantis, our existence is about leisure and pleasure and love. To be afraid of this is to invite darkness into the soul. Fear makes itself stronger, especially with the state of the Crystal Grid these days! You need to get out of Subterra more often and into the light of Ra, my friend! Come now and enjoy my revelry. I have spared no cost to celebrate Ka-Ma-Sharri this cycle."

Torbin's seriousness melted.

Pan strode toward the door with a gracious smile and the intention to leave.

A knock sounded as he approached. He threw the door open with a flair. Allondriss waited on the other side, accompanied by a man behind her on the stairs. She seemed unfazed by the immediacy of his response, but she was used to his antics.

Allondriss was Pan's favorite little toy from the servant house. Engaging a fair-skinned temple outcast from the house of servants bordered on black market affairs, but to appease the balance of karma, he had vowed to one day set her on another path more suited to her talents.

"Master Pan." Her ocean blue eyes dug into his soul. "One of Master Torbin's companions wishes to speak with him."

Pan backed up with a sweeping bow to present them to Torbin, all the while keeping his eyes on Allondriss. The man who entered bore the emblem of a Subterran magi. His eyes were wide with anticipation. The magi bowed to Torbin and glanced hesitantly at Pan.

"You may speak for him to hear," Torbin permitted with a wave of his hand.

"My friend! I am flattered!" Pan laughed. "Let's hear what he has to say!"

Torbin knew Pan's manner. He was not inclined to trust the scoundrel. But Pan was initiated into the higher levels of the Nexes Order, and so was entitled to their findings.

"Master Torbin," the magi spoke gravely. "There is a Watcher here."

Torbin perked up. "Explain."

"We detected a powerful dreamwalker here on these grounds. It is a very advanced level of training. We would not have noticed it, but we were tuned to dreamsight to see what danger was here."

Pan prepared another elixir, listening intently.

Torbin turned to Pan. "May I have your permission for my magi to ignite the violet flame over your estate?"

Pan nodded in the midst of a stretch. "Yes, do as you will. I would not want my revelry spoiled."

Torbin looked to the magi. "Ignite the flame immediately. And find my daughter."

The magi nodded and left the room. Torbin turned again to Pan. "The Queen Impending is in the city somewhere. Our dreamseers have seen terrible visions of her demise. We have taken it on ourselves to find her."

"You mean Kyliron's betrothed, *from the dreamclans*?" he emphasized the phrase over-enthusiastically. "Why would she not go straight to the palace for Ka-Ma-Sharri?" Pan seemed to have an idea. He fumbled with his clothing, comically intoxicated. "Perhaps she also suspects she is in danger and has perhaps found refuge somewhere the Watchers deem safe." He answered his own question with an index finger pointing upward.

Torbin nodded, amazed at the conversation Pan was having with himself. "By your leave, then, I shall go collect my daughter, and when the magi are done, we shall be on our way. It is imperative we find the Queen Impending before the height of Ka-Ma-Sharri."

Pan bowed dramatically and ushered Torbin out the door. After the Subterra Keymaster descended the spiral stair, Pan whispered in Allondriss's ear. "Please see to the safety of our special guests at once."

Music began in the gardens. Atlantean classical music was designed to weave the delicate harmonies of nature and emulate frequencies from the universal spheres. It had evolved in modern times to a more primal reminder of human existence, with multi-layered rhythmic pulses as its basis. It had become popular at revelries to feature the dark, grooving textures of percussive instruments run through resonance amplifiers. The dance style to this tribal heartbeat music was an individualized expression of character and personal power.

D'Vinid, like all dabrina players, studied classical music. His unique contribution was to run his instrument through the same resonance amplifiers to modulate universal frequencies. The ensuing melodic textures were in juxtaposition with the fierce, pulsing rhythms. His legendary ingenuity had started a trend, and he was well known as the inventor of the fusion.

He was at war with his desire. All he wanted was to find Brigitte in time for the Ka-Ma-Sharri. The draw was so powerful he almost felt he would be sick if he didn't follow it.

The garden had been set up with swirling lights and long, draping streamers to disorient revelers and give the feeling of walking in Dreamtime. Revelries were a cultural mainstay all through Atlantean history. They believed it to be their birthright as humans to enjoy the pleasures of sensory perception, while reaching for the bliss of higher consciousness. They had found the best way to do this was through revelries.

D'Vinid wandered aimlessly, pacing through the gardens in unsettled thought. He lowered his head to avoid laughing courtiers as they chased through the garden pathways. He thought perhaps an elixir would soothe his torment. Just as he had the thought, the path emptied into a small patio where a mixologist had set up a portable case of tiny glass vials on a low, round table.

Courtiers relaxed on cushions around the woman's tiny costumed form. She had a painted face that glowed in the twinkling lights, and a feathered headdress with plumes rising into a collar. Her eyes landed directly on D'Vinid as he appeared on the patio. She gestured a delicate hand toward an empty cushion. The other courtiers gazed up at him with eager eyes and mimicked her gesture, urging him to join in their search for just the right form of intoxication.

"What is your pleasure?" she asked in a singsong voice. "Are you sad and lonely?" She waved her hand over the vials, pushing their tops gently to make a fragile chiming sound as their various glass shapes clinked together. "Do you need me to slip you a feeling of sexual arousal? Are you longing to see the other side? Or perhaps you need some excitement and adrenalin!"

D'Vinid carefully thought of his answer. Pan had the best elixir mixologists, and any feeling he wished to have, she would deliver. "I need to not care."

Her expression darkened. "This is a specific feeling you ask for. You have many things haunting your thoughts. Do you wish to forget? I can give you temporary amnesia."

One of the courtesans rubbed his thigh and leaned in to whisper in his ear. "Go for arousal. I will help you forget." She giggled and fell back, landing in the arms of the man behind her, who caught her up in a greedy kiss.

A commotion caught everyone's attention for a moment, but drunken agendas gradually distracted the group again. Refreshed and ornamented, the Aello twins swaggered into the lights.

"D'Vinid!" Kayden exclaimed with a wave.

D'Vinid returned the greeting with surrendered resolution. He tightened his jaw as he spoke and leaned in closer. "Do you have anything to counteract the feeling of guilt?"

She sat up straighter. "I see your struggle. You have been infected by a sweeping guilt that makes yours feel stronger. Everything you have done that you regret feeds this guilt. I have just the thing for you. Fendesia. It will numb your feelings and raise your spirits so you can join the revelry." She ran her fingers over the vials and plucked a multi-faceted jeweled bottle sealed with a cork.

The twins found their way into the midst of the quasi-orgy, amplifying the din around them. D'Vinid leaned in closer to the mixologist, narrowing his eyes to slits. "Will it make me do anything stupid?"

"Only you can do that." She moved closer and breathed his aroma, electrified by his natural sensuality. She pressed his fingers around the vial. "The side effects of fendesia may cause you to see with dreamsight. If anything else, a light euphoria will linger a few hours. Your mind will be numbed enough for you not to care about whatever brings you guilt."

He nodded and opened the cork, took one last look at her painted face, and swallowed the purple liquid. The debauchery continued around them. Music pulsed in the distance. Colorful lights flashed. Jensyn and Kayden tag-teamed a valiant story, capturing the attention of those who felt obligated to pay respect to their hosts. Before too long, they ventured into intoxicated politics.

Jensyn positioned himself closer to D'Vinid, dragging one of the women with him. She tumbled into his arms, giggling wildly. He swiveled his head to stare at each of the gathered courtiers with intense punctuation.

"It is Bavendrick who should be king." The creases of his face deepened as his smile spread, and he lifted an elixir to his lips.

"Long live King Bavendrick!" the others mimicked.

D'Vinid raised a glass of tonic. "For that you will get no argument from me. Long live King Bavendrick."

The fendesia began to kick in. At first, D'Vinid felt light-headed, and then his heart seemed to burst into a million shards of unspeakable ecstasy. He scanned the garden and coiled back in astonishment. His vision swirled into dreamsight. The air seemed as if it had transformed into liquid. Bright waves of colors outlined the people.

The mixologist began slithering toward him, her lips searching for a kiss. He reached out to embrace her, gently exploring her slender curves. He skimmed the surface of her skin with his lips, succumbing to the beast of passion he tried to keep locked away.

A movement at the entrance of the courtyard distracted him from the mistake he was about to make. A woman came into view. Her simple robe lacked the pageantry of the others. Beguiled by her raven beauty, his eyes summoned her to join him until he realized who she was. His heart stopped. She glared at him. He released the mixologist, who landed in a heap of pillows. He quickly rolled to his feet and followed Loressai into the garden.

It was the perfect test of the fendesia. If anyone would make him feel guilty, it was Loressai. They walked quietly, wrapped in memories of their past. Theirs was a tumultuous affair that ended with his leaving the palace and never speaking with Kyliron again. Her appearance was yet another thread in the trap he was being lured into by the Watchers. She was so out of place that he hoped she was a hallucination. But then she spoke, and the reality of her presence was made real.

"What are you doing here, Loressai?" he said.

Dark circles framed her once beautiful eyes which now devoured him, flashing between anger and pity. "I came with my father's contingent. They're here to consult with Pan Aello. I heard you were playing music. It makes sense to find you here in the arms of a woman instead." She frowned and waved off her annoyance. "There's something wrong with me, D'Vinid. I should not have left Subterra. Here it grows stronger. This city is cursed." She stopped and faced him. "But I had to come. I had to warn you."

"Me? Warn me? Why?"

"They want you, too. We are Kyliron's weakness. Both of us. To control us is to control him." She raised her hand to see that it was shaking. She quickly tucked it under her arm. "You can still stop it, D'Vinid." She lowered her voice to a breathing whisper.

He stepped away. Her body tensed. Her eyes shifted. A reptilian gleam sparked in her expression. She stepped closer to him. "Unite with me for Ka-Ma-Sharri." Her voice was different. She kissed his neck. He lit up at her touch, remembering all too well the intensity of their passion. There was no guilt to make him stop. He was helpless in the trap of their attraction. The elixir was working the wrong way.

The light of the moon dimmed as the shadow of the planet began its Ka-Ma-Sharri journey. The taste of her lips became irresistible. His mind shifted to Brigitte. His eyes flashed orange. With a sudden burst of strength, he pushed Loressai away.

As much as the wounds were festering, Brigitte could see a flicker of light at the core of the Neter woman's soul. She was fighting the possession. Her spirit was strong, and Brigitte knew she needed help. Shadow tendrils imprisoned her like she was the woven feast for a spider. When she spoke to D'Vinid, the shadows enclosed around her throat. The tentacles reached toward him as if they intended him for their next victim.

Brigitte had learned to create dreamlight with her thoughts. Gathering drops of luminescence from the fabric of Dreamtime, she wove them into a pattern. When she was satisfied with her creation, she sent it hurling to ignite the dull flame in the woman's heartlight. When it hit, the flame sparked into a blaze. The woman turned away from D'Vinid.

The black tendrils withdrew from him and closed in to strangle her newfound strength.

"Please don't feel rejected," he pleaded. "I didn't want to stop kissing you, Loressai. I just…"

"D'Vinid, shut up! I can't… be near you… It gets stronger. It wants us both." She began jogging away. He tried to follow. "Go away!" She warned. "Do not come near me again." She picked up speed and ran toward the entrance of the estate.

When she reached the gate, a swath of violet light appeared out of nowhere, sweeping through the grounds in a flaming burst. In Dreamtime, the shrieking of shadows could be heard as they were ripped from their hosts by the passing of the light. Brigitte recognized the chanting of magi as they cast their incantation to purify the revelry.

D'Vinid clutched his head as if he had been freed from a spell.

He stopped, staring after her, bewildered. Brigitte could feel his confusion. In dreamsight he was surrounded by an orange outline of light. She noticed a displaced dreambody around him. It beckoned and gazed at her with fiery eyes. An ancient passion sparked in her heart. She recognized the feeling it caused her. The orange displacement turned toward her and smiled with a pointed finger at its lips.

It was then that D'Vinid noticed she was floating beside him.

Loressai ran from the estate of Pan Aello, desperate to escape. Every cell in her body burned to stay with D'Vinid for Ka-Ma-Sharri. The voice in her head tormented her to stay. *"You can have D'Vinid,"* it screamed. *"He is your chosen mate."*

She covered her ears and squeezed her eyes shut. The streets blurred. Her feet carried her as far as she could go. A growing mound of anger, despair, jealousy, rage, and betrayal threatened to bury her once more. The pile of resentment grew past the point of no return, until she forgot where it was coming from in the first place. It was part of her now.

She finally came to a stop on an empty balcony overlooking the Grand Canal. Small watercraft gathered below in a cluster of floating revelry. Everywhere she looked, couples were kissing, celebrating the union of Belial and Kama. She wanted all of them to die. But her own death would do nicely.

As she placed her hands on the railing of the balcony to throw herself in the water, white heat consumed her trembling body.

A symphony of chanting rose up in dissonant refrain. Beings in black materialized from the shadows and enclosed her in a shrinking circle. She tried to scream as she felt her consciousness struggle against the sensation of falling. In one final cry for help, she felt herself disappear, and all turned to emptiness.

"Who are you?" D'Vinid stepped back in awe. "You really are a Watcher!" he breathed, recognizing Brigitte's ghostly figure. His skin melted into effervescence. His vision washed with a veil of orange. He grabbed his head. The light faded for a split second, and a profound chill of fear overloaded his soul.

The apparition of Brigitte began to fade. Her ethereal limbs wrapped around him, enticing him forward.

His legs moved against his will, directing him toward the eastern bungalows. His human mind was unsure where she was, but his body knew exactly where to go. The dome bungalows were framed by smooth waters reflecting the starry sky.

With her dreambody again merged with her physical form,

Brigitte moved to the deck overlooking the cove. A sudden gust of wind sent her hair blowing wildly as she leaned against the railing. Dolphins gathered below, smiling up at her. D'Vinid watched the curves of her outline as she emerged. She was a sight to behold against the starry night. His heart raced as he neared the bungalow. Sensing his approach, she moved to open the door.

Allondriss stood nearby in the darkness. She took a few steps toward the door of the bungalow, unsure what to do. A heavy hand fell on her shoulder, and Lukias regarded her with warning. His mess of hair caught the fading moonlight as the eclipse began to reach its height. He shook his head slowly. "*This is meant to happen. Can't you feel it, young dreamseer?*" His thoughts became one with hers.

"My master wanted me to check on you..."

"We are fine," he interrupted and then paused. "I have cloaked her so no one can find her in Dreamtime. We have no further needs for the night."

Allondriss nodded slowly, entranced. His face in the dim garden lighting seemed just as captivating as the sight of Brigitte and D'Vinid uniting in the entrance of the bungalow.

In dreamsight they were illuminated by a golden beam as they kissed under the eclipse of the moon. At the height of Ka-Ma-Sharri, the world pulsed with life. Allondriss blinked, perplexed as flowers and vines began to visibly bloom around them, just as the light of the moon became covered in shadow.

The crystal pendant flashed on Lukias's chest like the light of a star. She could not help but stare at it. Her blue eyes glowed in the crystal's light. Lukias raised her face to look at his and shook his head.

"A soul-crystal." She wondered at its brilliance.

"You should go now, little dreamseer."

Without argument, she turned and wandered into the garden, stopping only to look back at Lukias's outline in the eerie garden lighting under the eclipse of the Ka-Ma-Sharri. For the first time in her life, she wished she could participate in the ritual. But she lowered her head and stepped into the darkness of the night without a word.

As Brigitte closed the door, D'Vinid pinned her against it, placing a hand above her head. He looked her solidly in the eye. He was himself, and yet entirely unbridled. His hands shook. The same otherworldly force seemed to take over his movements again. Tears poured from his eyes, and he pulled her into his arms. All time seemed to stop. A wave of passion erupted from the depths of their souls, and they swept one another into a tender, ravenous kiss.

Golden light saturated the room. Brigitte pulled away, panting. His eyes burned with a fiery glow, holding her suddenly motionless. The presence within the room seized her in a state of euphoric tension. The air warped. She wanted desperately to move. Every limb ached to be in his embrace.

She recognized her situation and capitulated, allowing her mind to surrender to the hopeless web in which she had become entangled. An ethereal orange light illuminated the whites of his eyes as a smile crept onto his face, a smile Brigitte somehow recognized. *"My love…"* His words echoed through her mind, triggering distant, faded remnants of memories, leftover dreams lying dormant in her subconscious.

She felt Dreamtime close in around her, encasing her in an invisible chamber of serenity. "Belial," she breathed.

D'Vinid's voice laughed, its pitch shifted with possession. *"I am he who the Watchers fear and protect. I am he who brings knowledge from the stars and gives it to humanity. I am he who walks through Dreamtime. The traveler of worlds. The fallen star. Protector of that which all hold dear. I am darkness within the light… the lightness within the dark… Master of the Cunning."* His words trailed with an ethereal echo.

"I have watched, too, my love. And I await the end times with great anticipation, when we can be reunited at last. On this night, the eve when these fine people celebrate our reunion, let us be one again." He sank to his knees, clutched at her hand, and kissed it as if it were the source of nourishment to a hungry man. *"As above, so below. As within, so without."* His voice dripped like honey in her thoughts. *"You are the light in the darkest night, Kama, protector of humanity, mother of Atlantis. Let your seed maintain the Telluric Treaty."* He

pulled her closer, running his hand through her hair, and squeezing her scalp with his fingertips. She leaned her head into his touch.

His burning hand reached to touch the skin on her side. She erupted into blue ethereal flames. Passing a hand before her eyes, she inhaled with apprehensive fascination, watching the flames incredulously.

Their movement together was as natural as two streams of water uniting. Their limbs intertwined, and a connection was made like that between atoms. As two primordial beings, passionate for one another and parted for centuries, they combined into a burning pillar of rapturous bliss.

The Nephilim sank into its human vessel and used her lips to smile. The shadow of the planet reached to swallow the moon. Her eyes glowed red in the moonlight. The ancient creature had trouble maintaining its hold on the body of its host. The daughter of Subterra was strong-willed. Hollowing her out with the shadows of human suffering was a long process. But now that she was separated from the protection of her Subterran Luminari brethren, she had fallen into the creature's snare.

"Shadowmancers," she croaked in her new voice. "The convergence has begun. I have failed to retrieve the host of my mate this night. We will take him when we can. For now, we must prevent the arrival of the dreamclan emissary." They watched the shadow grow across the moon, chanting in preparation for the celestial portal to open all the way.

When the phenomenon was almost complete, the circle parted, and two cloaked figures stepped into the center. Each held captive a man and woman. She stepped toward them. With a surge of desire, she took the woman by the hair, extending her head to look into the eyes of her prey. Sniffing deeply of the surging blood, the fear made her stronger. She nodded to the captors and took a step back as they reached up knives to the throats of their prey.

"Receive this sacrifice, oh queen of the Blood Triad. May you gather strength from this sacré moré and seal your hold on this human vessel as shadows eclipse the light." The shadowmancers began chanting, a rolling serpentine cadence.

Then to the shock of all, their prisoners shifted weight, disarming their unsuspecting captors. In one confusing moment, they turned from prey to predator. A flurry of bursting light rippled through the plaza. Free from the grasp of those who would sacrifice them, the couple gathered light to the movement of their hands.

A new resonant chorus interrupted the evil blood ritual. Blue mist materialized out of Dreamtime, revealing translucent silhouettes on all sides. The flash of crystals raised to their ethereal lips revealed the source of the sonic attack. The black-cloaked figures shrank from the sound and realized they were outnumbered.

Loressai began to feel her body again. Her consciousness fought to escape the sticky black ooze that trapped her in a psychic prison. Her hand fought against her as she raised it, trembling to her face. Her body hunched into writhing pain. The creature fought to keep her contained. The eclipse grew darker.

With the finesse of a dancer, one of the shadowmancers tucked into a tumble. His movements drew shadows to his hands. The others resumed their chanting. The area was obscured by swarming, dark masses with yawning and treacherous faces.

Just as quickly, the translucent attackers changed their pitch, and beams shot from the crystals at their lips. A web of light threaded through the plaza. The couple, now free from their impending death, summoned light to the weaving movement of their hands. The light turned to a glowing sword in the hands of the man. The woman now wielded the shape of a round blade that she held up as a shield.

They flanked Loressai. She fought furiously to gain control. Doubled over with the pain of the fight, she ripped the hood from the shadowmancer closest to her. He had a shaved head, and black death runes covered his skin. She bent her arm to hit him in the temple with the pointed force of her elbow. He fell to the ground.

The ones who had come to her rescue saw that Loressai was on their side now. The man began speaking to the shadowmancers. "You were warned to stay out of Poseidia. You had to know we would track your blood magic." He held the light blade up, illuminating his face. He was dressed in wealthy attire. His dark eyes shone in the reflection of his sword.

"It would be in your best interest to understand our intentions," one of the shadowmancers hissed. "We have all been chosen to purify Atlantis. You are chosen, too, brother. The shadows can be your servants, not your enemies."

"From where I stand you just tried to kill me. I don't think your intentions will be in alignment with me or anyone else in the ten kingdoms of Atlantis."

"You survived, didn't you?" The shadowmancer sneered. "You are among the strong. One of the purifiers, the chosen ones. It is the life force of the weak that must be used to allow the Blood Triad to help us cleanse the Grid. We can harness the shadows and correct the mistakes of those who have become their sustenance. It is their lazy arrogance that has allowed the shadows to corrupt the Grid."

The eclipse reached its perigee.

"Step aside, Children of One. The rulership of Atlantis has failed us. Oh Blood Triad! Accept my blood to increase your strength!" With a smile of release, the shadowmancer lifted up his hands. The shadows swarming around him formed into a wavering blade. "Let the shadows be your tools, brother." He reached the swarming dagger to his throat and stabbed himself. Blood spurted from his neck.

As he crumbled to the ground, the tattooed runes on his face wriggled and turned to wavering movement. In the eerie light of the lunar eclipse, shadows twisted free from his skin and formed a spiral around his twitching body. Like a liquid whirlpool, it flowed toward Loressai. The creature's icy touch took hold of her heart once more.

"Stop them!" she cried.

But it was too late. The others copied their leader. Their tattooes came to life and wrapped around Loressai. The two Children of One withdrew, frowning at her with wrenching regret. They fell back from the plaza now swarming with shadows, and into the relative safety of their companions. The blackness closed around Loressai as the moon's light disappeared at the height of Ka-Ma-Sharri. The celestial doorway was open. Once again, Loressai was hopelessly trapped inside the relentless prison of her mind.

4

Priestess makes thy hand to stay
the promise of the warrior's way.
He who seeks to take her heart
is forced with love to sorely part.
His is just the way of thieves
practicing their craft.
Their way is merely wandering,
without their souls intact.

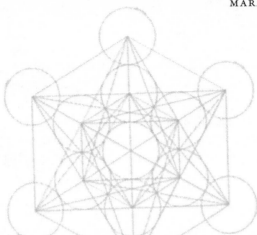

It was the quietest time in Poseidia, when night revelers drifted to sleep, and day dwellers awoke in silent greeting of the sun. Reeling from their jilting confrontation with the shadowmancers, the companions of the hunter conclave gathered at a deserted nodeyard.

They maintained equality among their group, though the most advanced among them, Fa'nariel and Atheerian, acted as leaders. The other companions respected them even more after they nearly became willing sacrifices to the strange servants of darkness.

Cloaked by ribbons of blue mist, they slipped through fog like phantoms. The fabric of their clothing seemed to mesh with the air. Atheerian stood at the base of the towering obelisk. The act of reaching to touch the surface was a whisper of a movement. The others lifted crystals to their lips in support. Their humming buzzed into a resonance. The obelisk sputtered to life, shimmering with waves of sound that harmonized with the still morning.

Atheerian's eyes flew open. Their multi-colored irises reflected the light of the cosmos, then disappeared with a series of blinks. "I got it. I know what this sacré moré is. Let's go," he said.

Fa'nariel stopped as they prepared to leave. "I have to return to the palace before I'm missed," she said. Atheerian faced her. The others waited for them. "Don't give me that look." She glanced around at the conclave. "I have gathered more information in the king's bed than any of you have in cycles."

Atheerian wrapped his hand around her wrist. "I will let you know what happens when I achieve symbiosis with this download."

One by one, they slipped deeper into Dreamtime and dissolved into the morning fog. Fa'nariel maintained her connection with

Atheerian.

"We shouldn't have left them there," she said.

"We had no choice. Where would we put a bunch of dead shadowmancers? The guardians will find them. It's out of our hands."

Severity vibrated between them.

"We can't do everything, Fa'nariel. At some point the other conclaves will have to unify. They all like to pretend everything is still like it used to be. It's not." He breathed steadily. They put their foreheads together and raised their eyes to meet. "Go in the vortex," they said together.

Watching him leave made her sink into a mire of sadness. She flipped her hover disc toward the ground with a click. Soon she was silently gliding toward the center of the citadel.

Fractured sunrays spilled through prismatic windows, casting light into a mirror of marble floors. Breaking the morning's lazy stillness, faint pattering echoed among foliage lining the temple's open-air corridor. Robed figures marched in silent formation. They passed through elegant archways and fragrant, hanging bouquets. A group of temple clergy guarded a set of double doors.

The sentinels straightened as the procession appeared, preparing to challenge their entry, but relaxed as they recognized the leader. He was a priest with long, sandy-colored hair tied back in a ponytail. His face had the wizened lines of an old one, and yet his blue eyes were fierce. A twelve-pointed star medallion fashioned in amethyst fell to the indentation of his throat.

They dared not object as he reached to push open the frosted glass door, its smooth contours etched with the same star symbol. His entourage waited outside.

Inside stood a statuesque woman, her alabaster skin like a beam of moonlight that would vanish in the harsh light of day. She wore a white robe embellished with gold and embroidered with the star burst symbol of the highest priesthood, known as the Alta. Her eyes focused out the window on a view of Poseidia from its highest point, but her thoughts were turned inward. She fidgeted with a staff of cylindrical quartz, its clear, fragile body wrapped in sinuous, silver snakes. At its top rested a perfect ball of rose quartz.

"High Priestess," the man spoke gently.

She turned to face him. Her eyes were clouded. "Ah, Ilorian Thoth," she said, addressing the High Keeper of the Archives Nexes. "Is there still no news from the king's betrothed?" Her voice sounded distant.

"The dreamseers sensed her arrival. However, the temple escorts sent to greet her were attacked last night. They were massacred by something savage, some kind of beast. But it is said the Queen Impending was not with them when it happened."

The priestess fixed her eyes out the window again. "I believe she is alive."

He regarded the High Priestess soberly. "I have something else to report... about the king."

She waved him on, preparing herself for whatever he might say.

"The king has prepared to request ancient war technologies from the archives. It seems he wishes to activate the Fire Crystal."

The news did not disturb her placid face, though she closed her eyes for a drawn-out moment. "This is curious information. How do you know this?"

"One of the king's scientists reported it to me. He was terrified we may break his anonymity. Since he is afraid to testify publicly, we don't have enough evidence to take the king to public mediation. I do not blame the scientist for this. Priestess, this has bolstered our suspicions enough to identify a pattern in the king's actions. He is much like his father. I fear he is positioning himself to use Atlantis as a weapon for his own ambitions."

She began pacing. "The royal family is connected to the Grid by blood. If the king has suffered his father's ailments, then it is merely a reflection of the corruption in the Grid. And if he is corrupted, then you know it must be systemic. We cannot even trust the orders of the Temple Sect to be pure anymore." She placed her fingers in a steeple. "We are all doomed if we do not purify the Grid. The rest of the world will be in jeopardy. The other realms will not take it lightly. Especially if we are forced to break the treaty because all the emissaries have been wiped out."

"Understood, High Priestess."

"In the meantime, King Kyliron must be reminded of his role. The young king must know he does not possess unlimited power. Even if the mediators back him, we overrule him in temple matters. It seems I should arrange to educate him, myself." She glided toward the window, placing her hands on the sill.

Silence engulfed the chamber, and the sound of rushing water could be heard in the distance. Golden sunbeams filtered through the windows. The stillness caused them both to pause and reflect on the many peaceful rotation cycles Atlantis had seen during its third age. But it seemed this peace would soon be at an end.

She drew a long, steady breath and looked suddenly resolved. "If the Queen Impending has indeed arrived, she will possess the power to make this right. The emissary of the Watchers must take her place immediately at the king's side. It is obvious she is cunning, and the Fates are on her side." She turned to him. "We are limited in what we can do, I'm afraid. But there is one thing we *can* do to protect Atlantis. We must activate Grid lockdown protocol."

A look of dread suffused Ilorian Thoth's face.

She turned toward him and beckoned. He covered the distance between them and gently grasped her hand. Together they stood gazing out the window at the sunlit glory of the temple grounds.

"We must begin by activating the Lost Temple Children." Thoth's words were nothing more than a whisper.

She nodded. "It has already been done. The geneticists have been reporting to me with stories of their awakening throughout the ten kingdoms. We must find a way to bring them guidance, but I must admit I do not yet understand how they have organized. They call themselves the Conclaves. Others call them the Children of One. This is the generation they are supposed to activate. The upgrade we have placed into the populace is supposed to develop an immunity to the shadow madness."

"I realize this project is a favorite among your order, High Priestess. But I must warn you, if they are not properly trained to use their powers, they could be led astray."

"That should be impossible," she retorted, turning to him pointedly. "In order to create an immunity to the shadows, the geneticists had to breed out a connection to them. That is why their development has taken seven generations."

"We cannot separate from the shadows, High Priestess. They are part of humanity. To ignore them is to ignore our own hands. Our own eyes. Our own hearts."

"I realize you think this way, my dear Thoth. And yes, the shadows have been created by humanity. The genetic upgrade is our only hope in controlling them. The Children of One will find a way to integrate this."

"Hope is the child of wishes and probabilities."

"We have other precautions in place. The dreamclans bring with them the next level of the upgrade. The Lemurian dreamclans will infuse their blood into the upgrade. Their return is imperative to the project."

"Which leads us to their destruction. Priestess, if the shadows from the Grid of Atlantis have been spreading into Dreamtime to destroy the dreamclans, then perhaps something or someone is trying to infiltrate your project. That something may be aware of your genetics."

"Then it will be up to the Lost Temple Children to make this right. It is why they were designed. Atlantis is theirs to inherit." She sighed. "Go now, my friend. Prepare to activate Nexes lockdown protocol. We must do our part. I await a sign from the Watchers. Once the key comes into alignment, and I know it is in the right hands, we will take the Grid offline. No one will be able to access it unless they possess the key."

Brigitte awoke to a gentle tapping on her door. She popped up, gasping as she realized her nakedness, in the same instant recalling she no longer possessed her heart, her purity, and perhaps even her soul. Anything that would have bound her to her future mate had been utterly stolen, and willingly surrendered. She looked around frantically. D'Vinid was gone. A wave of confusion washed over her. What had happened? She remembered those eerie orange eyes and a feeling of effervescent love. She could barely contain the blissful feeling in her heart, though a sinking dread began to surface in his absence.

The tapping persisted.

"In a moment!" she called, hoping beyond reason it would be D'Vinid. She threw on her overcoat and cracked the door to peek through. Allondriss greeted her, calm and poised, her golden hair pulled into a braid, hands folded within the wide sleeves of her coat. Her clothing bore a mark of the Warrior Sect, undoubtedly Pan's symbol. Brigitte ushered the young girl inside and closed the door.

"Hello, Allondriss."

"Good morning, mistress." The fair-skinned servant lingered curiously.

Brigitte sighed, feeling D'Vinid's absence acutely, and crumpled on the bed. "What can I do for you?"

"I have come to see if you require anything for your journey."

Brigitte traced her finger along the stitching of the pattern on her bedding. "Perhaps a way out of all this. Is that something you can do for me, little dreamseer?"

Allondriss looked ahead steadily, biting her lip. "I am not a dreamseer." She lowered her eyes.

"Then what gives you premonitions?"

The question startled the girl momentarily, but Brigitte somehow made her feel comfortable. "A gift of sight, perhaps, but I am not trained as a dreamseer. There is a difference."

"The Watchers can be cruel when they direct the Fates." Brigitte's smile was reassuring. Her attention blazed on Allondriss with eyes far older than her human cycles. "My guess is the Fates have interesting plans for you." Brigitte began to warm up to the girl. "And tell me, young seer. What path would you prefer? A path more predictable and measured?"

The girl kept biting her lower lip. It was unusual for anyone to ask her so many personal questions. She summoned the courage to open up. "Mistress, my choices have never been my own. My mother made sure of that from the moment I was born. She sent me from the Temple Sect in disgrace to be traded as a servant with low-born citizens. If not for the kindness of Pan Aello, my shame would have been unbearable. This is the most I have spoken of her in many rotations."

Brigitte looked at her with a depth she had seldom experienced. Being a servant had always kept her more or less invisible.

Narrowing her eyes, Brigitte perked up, "And why were you cast from your order, Allondriss?" She stretched to a sitting position on the bed, feeling more sensually alive than she had ever been. "What reason did your mother give you? She wouldn't do this without giving you a proper reason, would she?"

Allondriss bowed her head. "She cast me out of my teachings with disgrace because I questioned the order of the temple, mistress." She paused. "I was impetuous. I always questioned why the Temple Sect was set apart from the rest of Atlantis. In the first and second ages, every Atlantean had temple teachings. Now we are born into it like royalty. I have always thought the priesthood should be available to anyone. I had many other ideas, but this was the main one. I was supposed to follow my teaching without question. Ingenuity is said to lead to the dark path. Thus, I was cast from my order, and even forced to leave the sect altogether." She looked nervously at Brigitte, uncertain of how the news would land.

Brigitte sighed. "It could mean one of three things. Either you are some kind of radical who has learned the error of her ways, or the Temple Sect is unreasonably strict. The other more likely reason is the Watchers have arranged one of their curious paths to align things for a moment in the future." She rolled out of the bed. "If your mother is a direct servant of the Watchers, as my people are, then you and I are merely servants, ourselves. Therefore, your mother's action is a literal means of teaching you one simple lesson."

"What is that, mistress?"

"That you, too, are a servant of the Fates. Once you understand this, you will have merged with your life purpose. And here we are," she smiled, her lip twisted in irony. "You, a temple outcast, and me, a dreamclan woman in Atlantis. Both of us servants. Neither of us living the life we would choose." Brigitte chuckled, making a move for her scattered clothing.

"And what life would you choose?" asked Allondriss shyly.

Now it was Brigitte's turn to be at a loss for words. She had always accepted her fate. Another knock sounded at the door, saving her from having to answer. Allondriss hesitated, studying Brigitte intently.

Brigitte smiled. "I hope my words are helpful."

Allondriss nodded quickly. "Yes, my lady. They are."

"Now, I suppose you can answer the door," Brigitte cocked her head compassionately, a smile brightening her beautiful face. "Not because you're a servant, but because you're standing right next to it."

Allondriss paused before opening the door, allowing Brigitte the chance to straighten herself.

Pan Aello's grinning face greeted them. Another servant accompanied him with a tray of food.

"Might I share a word with you as you eat your breakfast, my lady?" he asked, his voice pitched to a delicate volume.

Brigitte nodded. Pan waited for the servant to place the food and head toward the door. Allondriss stole another look at Brigitte and followed the other servant into the garden, which had somehow grown more lush and bountiful overnight. Pan shut the door as they left. "Let us be honest with one another. Last night there was a murder in our fair streets. Your brother said there was danger, and he was right. But it was not just any murder, but a mass slaughter."

Brigitte gasped. "Who?"

"It was the temple contingent sent to fetch the Queen Impending who had arrived in Poseidia. But this *dreamclan* queen is nowhere to be found. I am not a stupid man, my lady, and the Watchers are never without purpose. They trusted me, and so can you."

She sighed. "If I were to tell you I am this queen of yours, what would you do then with the information?"

"I would be your servant and true friend for entrusting me with such a secret. But I already know this to be true. You are King Kyliron's betrothed."

"Then I will hold you to your promise of friendship." She offered her hand.

He took it up gallantly, and bowed, touching it to his forehead. "Your Majesty. I am honored to receive you in my estates. The Watchers were right to send you to me. I can help you."

"And I thank you for your generosity. But I am not yet queen. My journey has been barred. Something does not want me to take the position. Not that I was meant to take the position in the first place. I was taught the ways of queens, although I always thought Kyliron's brother would be king, and I would be a lady of the court with the job of having royal children." Her thoughts drifted to D'Vinid.

What had she done? Her eyes landed on the rose. Its petals remained crisp and fresh, although she had neglected to place it in water.

"We all thought Prince Bavendrick would be king, my lady."

They stood in silence for a time as she examined the small feast of fresh fruit on her tray. She had always held tight to her slipping idealism, battling her tutor Indrius's harsh teachings. It was always preferable to spend her life in denial, embracing instead the bliss of nature, rather than the intricacies of Atlantean socio-political, economic, and historical facts. But all of this had been destroyed in a single evening of terror when dark shadows descended on her people to ruthlessly consume them. "Who killed the temple contingent?" she asked, shivering.

"It is not known."

"I am so sorry." She sank down on the bed, her eyes fixed darkly on the floor. "They were after me."

"You must have protection. I can see this now. I will see to it you are granted whatever warriors you desire from now on. This is all because of the madness. We grow farther away from who we truly are every time someone separates from the Grid in favor of freewill."

Brigitte glanced up.

He continued. "If we connect to the Grid for a few moments every day and night as we are supposed to, we contribute to the mental power which illuminates every aspect of this city. People are starting to believe they have the right to refuse illumination rituals. But this, of course, makes the rest of us work harder. Having a small amount of discipline every day to connect to the nodes keeps us connected to the collective.

"The rulership of Atlantis has fallen into the hands of people who have proven to disregard the Watchers and the laws set to guide us in this age. King Koraxx repeatedly used his birthright to disobey these laws of nature. He has started a trend of disregard toward the ways of our ancestors. And now the madness has swept across the land. It's because people have disconnected from the Grid! I can promise you this. We have gone terribly wrong, my lady. I fear your task will not be easy. The Watchers are not as highly regarded as they once were."

Brigitte scowled. "Watchers hold the keys to time and space. Their actions can't always be understood, but they are for the best, because they see outside the scope of what humans can perceive. They hold the best interest of the planet eternally. Everything that happens is guided by them, regardless of whether it is believed by humans or not."

"I think you will find many Atlanteans have replaced their faith in the Watchers with the worship of free-will," answered Pan.

Brigitte smiled as she answered. "Watchers are subject to the laws of nature just as humans are. If they guide us along a path benefiting us, it is because they see a future that is best for us. To choose to have faith in the Fates is to choose an easier life, guided by faith. By choosing free-will, Atlanteans have demanded to be the masters of their own fates, and so have taken control. If they refuse to take responsibility for their mistakes, then they might curse the Watchers for their self-induced suffering. The Watchers merely promote oneness with the laws of nature.

"Atlanteans worship free-will as if it were a deity. The laws of nature are unerring, and no matter how much we become masters of the Fates, we are still subject to these laws." She brushed a lock of hair from her face, chuckling at his thoughtful expression. "Forsake the Watchers if you must. Control your own fates, if you wish, and blame your mistakes on them. But I would beg you, do not underestimate them. They are as old and as young as time itself, and they see things we can barely hope to understand. They do not encroach on our free-will because they cannot intervene. All they wish is to preserve humanity. And they do so with the neutrality of the laws of nature."

Pan nodded, amused at her brilliance. "Your words are wise beyond your rotations," he bowed. "And welcome in my presence. What I will say to you, my dear, is the line of Atlas is not so bright and glorious amid their distaste of the Fates. There are many things amiss in our governance. I do hope you find the power to help us. I am in your service, my lady. You have but to call on me, and I shall respond."

"Thank you, Pan Aello." She hesitated. "I promise to remember your friendship. It has been arranged by the Watchers, and so it shall be sealed."

Warriors arrived at Pan's estate. The group was silent, led by a tall man with a broad chest. His face was painted black and white, and peered out from beneath the shroud of a shadowed hood. His eyes knew the face of death as if they were created by it. He examined the courtyard with passive menace. Three warriors accompanied him, hovering silently, looking as if they were perched on the edge of rapid motion.

The warrior leader's name was Stixxus. They were from the Bull League known as the furies, who harnessed the power of pure rage in their fighting style. The group approached Pan and his guests as they prepared to depart on their foreboding journey.

Brigitte and her brother stood at the entrance to Pan's gardens. Lukias watched his sister carefully, trying to seem casual, knowing he had allowed her to step down a path that would cause her suffering. He watched her fidget with the rose she still carried and wondered why it remained crisp as if it were still growing from a bush.

Brigitte watched the warriors with blazing intent, her mind set only on the future. She examined the hardened expression radiating from Stixxus's black and white painted face. His dark eyes watched them with curiosity buried beneath disciplined complacence. Pan met the warriors' advance with his arms open in welcome. Stixxus's response emerged in deep, rasping tones barely audible above its nearly whispered resonance. Once negotiations were completed, the warriors stepped aside.

Pan faced his guests with a look of triumph on his impish face. Allondriss stood at his side, her hands buried in her sleeves. Her blue eyes devoured the scene.

"As you can see, I've done as I said I would. Let us not forget one another, then." Pan wrapped his fingers with a clap, drawing in a pronounced breath through flared nostrils. A flowing gesture summoned Allondriss to his side. "I would like to send Allondriss with you. She knows all the paths of Poseidia. Allow me to offer her as your personal guide during your time here among us."

Lukias lifted his hand. "Thank you for your gift, but I beg you to reconsider. I would not be comfortable compromising her safety."

Pan's eyes questioned Brigitte.

She smiled as best she could amid her rising anxiety. "Lukias," she interjected. "I would be pleased to accept her company."

Pan clapped again. Delight lit his features. "Keep her with you from now on, in fact. I would like for her to be your servant."

"Thank you, Pan Aello. I would be honored to accept your gift. I have begun to like this girl." She smiled at Allondriss. "And I expect your warriors to keep her safe, as well." Her eyes shifted to Stixxus, who nodded with silent menace.

"My family and I are your devoted friends." He grabbed her hand up with both hands and kissed it. "It is an *honor* for me to pass on my favorite servant who I have treated like a daughter. She is meant for better things than what I can give."

"It is I who is honored." She kept her eyes pointedly on him, and then smiled at Allondriss.

Pan cupped Allondriss's cheeks between his palms. "See, my sweet child? One day you were destined for something even more than you imagined. I am honored to have been *your* deliverer, as well."

Allondriss knew she was being given in service to the Queen Impending. Still, she wondered if his motivation was politically inclined. She knew it would be to his benefit to have the loyalty of a queen's personal servant. He was right. She was loyal to him.

She couldn't help but admire his political agility. His wealth and position made him practically untouchable. He could enjoy any style of theatrics he could dream up without fear of reprimand, because his station was not about anything Atlanteans considered serious. The famous fireball games, no matter how popular, were considered merely a pastime.

Despite this, everyone wanted to be a part of what he offered, so it was up to him who he allowed into his sphere. And most often he championed misfits like Allondriss or D'Vinid, and now Brigitte.

If anyone decided to hate him for his mind boggling-antics, He didn't care. He was quite simply a clown savant with a golden heart and a tendency to manipulate politics for his own entertainment. And it was a game he somehow always won, because he had no real ego-driven ambitions. Or so it seemed.

His friendship made Brigitte's heart glad.

"I have but one favor to ask in exchange for all I have done here," he added.

She cocked her head curiously. "Anything."

"I ask for you to keep my assistance a secret. It's better for you. Trust me on this."

"Very well." She shifted her attention to Stixxus, noticing how he calculated his task with predatory precision. She could feel an unspoken bond forming between them. The warrior took a step closer, standing behind her as if an order was decreed by the

Watchers themselves, and he could hear the call in the depths of his steadfast soul.

She quickly scanned the area one last time, hoping beyond hope that D'Vinid would arrive to say goodbye. Her heart screamed in agony, wanting to stop everything, needing to know he had not forgotten, even though the idea seemed preposterous. She knew what they had done would not be spoken of again.

"Are you ready, Brigitte?" Lukias spoke softly. His glare suggested he wondered why Pan was doting on her so completely. He was clever enough to figure out she had informed the mediator of her secret identity. But soon she would be queen. Soon enough her own choices had to be made with unerring confidence, and this was where she would begin.

She forced her eyes not to search for D'Vinid anymore. With a final goodbye, she allowed Pan to guide her step as she boarded the hover-carriage that waited to take her to meet her betrothed at last.

From high in the branches of a nearby tree, D'Vinid watched them depart. His heart ached more than it ever had. He knew she needed to see him. He felt elated at the memory of her touch, though he barely remembered any specifics from the night. All he knew was he had awakened in the night with her in his arms, and the feeling could barely be contained. He had held her closer. She had moaned softly and moved to match every crevice of his body.

He had been the downfall of many beautiful women, who now wallowed in despair over the carelessness of his seduction and abandonment. Their hearts threatened to unite and strike out in revenge, forming a barrier between him and this woman named Brigitte who made him feel so utterly alive. This was the very woman for whom he had searched in all the others. He now knew what it meant to feel the perfect connection.

But she was a Watcher. He knew it all had to be some kind of trick. And she would not be his. Not ever. She belonged to her mate impending. Of course, he could pursue her. A lover being mated to another man had never held him back before. Chasing a lover he could not have was somewhat of a specialty. It was a skill he was not proud of, and more so, something he would not allow

the Watchers to force him into.

He knew she would be hurt when he did not show up to bid her farewell. He wanted desperately for her to know the depth of his love. But he could not do that to her. He knew it would be better for her heart to harden as she was brought to face her mate, whoever he was. D'Vinid just sat and watched until the carriage disappeared past the confines of Pan Aello's estate.

"I want D'Vinid brought to me immediately!" A loud baritone voice seemed as though it would tear a hole in the sky. A deathly silence descended on the garden. Even the birds stopped their chorus. "I must know if it was he who started this movement. Curse these Children of One. How dare he move against me! I will crush him with my bare hands!"

"Your Majesty, you must calm yourself." The voice of the king's maydrian spoke as if telling a bedtime story. "A king's power does not outweigh his self-control." The priest tried to soothe Kyliron's anger. His even temperament often served to balance the king's moods.

"Jamarish Ka, I will ask you when I wish your opinion." The king's voice strained to escape his clenching jaw. "I want everyone out!" A commotion arose in the royal courtyard as a flock of kallistas rushed to escape the king's fury.

"Your Majesty, you have a visitor in the antechamber. You should attend to this at once," said Jamarish Ka steadily.

Kyliron glared at his personal advisor. "In this moment, what makes you think it wise to tell me what to do?"

"Your Majesty, the High Priestess of the Temple Sect has requested a private audience. You must pull yourself together. She has the right to see you when she calls on you."

A silence followed.

The High Priestess backed away from the doorway where she had overheard the scene and took her place casually next to a window in the antechamber. Flimsy drapes billowed in the breeze, filling the chamber with movement. She glanced out the window, and when she looked back again, a woman was standing behind the drapes as if she had materialized out of thin air.

Presumably, she was one of Kyliron's kallistas. Her curves were

73

evident through a sheer gown. Gold dust was painted on her nails, an essential of courtly fashion. Tattooed snakes intertwined up her legs, extensions of her sandal laces. Her hair had a reddish tint and fell in many braids over an ample chest.

She regarded the High Priestess with calculating, feline eyes. "Your Grace," she bowed. "I am Fa'nariel. One of the king's kallistas." She looked back quickly to see if he was coming and lowered her voice. "I know what happened to the temple clergy who were sent to find the Queen Impending." She handed the priestess a crystal. "This is a summoner. Use it to find me."

Heavy footfalls approached. Fa'nariel took one last look at the High Priestess before her body faded into Dreamtime. The priestess watched the girl disappear and buried her surprise as best she could. This was an advanced level of training among the Temple Sect. She wanted to think the girl was from the dreamclans, but she seemed purely Atlantean. Shock sent a tingling wave of excitement through her body as she realized this girl was one of the Lost Temple Children. She had no time to ponder its significance before a shadow fell over the threshold, and the king strode into the room.

King Kyliron had a perfectly chiseled form. Charisma radiated from a bold smile framed by a square jawline. His copper skin shone with oil. Jet-black hair was cropped close to his head. Most women looked to him as an object of perfection, and it was obvious he saw himself in the same light.

The priestess bowed, keeping her eyes soft. It was necessary for all to act with the proper respect afforded a king, regardless of any ill feelings.

Kyliron was dressed in his bed pants with an open robe exposing his chiseled chest. His movements were lazy. Without a word, he brushed past the priestess, and perched in the window where she stood. "High Priestess." He examined her with cool detachment. Sexuality poured off him in unnoticed waves. "To what do I owe the honor of a visit in my private suites?"

"Your Majesty." She allowed her salutation to linger for a moment. She knew he responded favorably when treated with respect. "I wanted to forgo the complication of a formal visit. I hope you and I can gain a certain trust. If we learn to compromise and agree outside of formal argument, we can get things done quickly and easily."

Kyliron studied her, calculating. The Temple Sect, in order of precedence, was considered equal to his own hereditary position. They controlled the Crystal Grid. And he could not gain access to any knowledge without their approval. This woman was in charge of the entire sect, just as he was in charge of all mediators. Her words were within reason.

"You are just as wise as you should be, High Priestess of Atlantis." He studied her carefully.

"All beings should strive toward wisdom, Your Majesty, especially kings." Her eyes flashed as she issued an unspoken challenge.

He leaned back in the window seat and folded his arms. A wicked smile crept onto his lips. "Yet it remains to be seen whether you or I will be the more persuasive of the other."

She paused, examining his cool composure. "Let us discuss the arrival of your betrothed."

Kyliron shifted his posture to suggest his care toward the matter. She was masterful at reading body language. His hands began to fidget. His dark eyes flinched. "This has weighed on my mind all day, High Priestess. I expected to be in a joining ceremony last night, but instead I linger in my bedchamber in despair, worried for her well-being."

"Perhaps instead of 'lingering in despair' you might take greater measures to find her," she suggested, trying not to sound snide.

He looked into her eyes from beneath a lowered brow. "I thought the Temple Sect was in charge of greeting dreamclan dignitaries. Do you have a suggestion? I have already launched an investigation into the deaths of the temple entourage."

She remained impassive at his accusatory tone. "Perhaps an announcement over VC waves would be appropriate, so the people know she is at-large."

He looked away angrily. "I cannot authorize that."

"Your Majesty, ultimately it is not your decision. The Temple Sect controls the viewer-crystals." The VC network was traditionally used to transmit messages to the populace. It was believed that keeping secrets from the populace was a breeding ground for malicious rumors.

"I understand, High Priestess. But the mediator controls the content. Since the VC mediator has fallen to the madness, the duty falls on me. I am now in charge of all VC transmissions."

She kept her face straight while studying his determination. "Your Majesty, there is a successor to that mediator line. From what I understand, the duty falls to the heir."

"She is unfit to assume her position," he spat. "She is too young. I have taken her into *my* court under *my* command."

"I see." Her angelic presence radiated a calm that washed over the room. Technically he was well within his right to do so. But he was not exercising the rules VC mediators were trained to follow.

"Priestess," Kyliron approached her slowly. "I wonder how well you knew my father."

"I knew King Koraxx quite well."

"Then, know this," he leaned closer, a smile brightening his perfectly symmetrical face. His breath brushed her cheek. "My father was a great king because he found a way to get past your temple rules. I am his son. Don't forget that." He ran his finger up her arm. His eyes flashed. For a moment she thought they shifted like an elemental's.

"I can see this, Your Majesty." She lowered her head, muttering. "But I can see your mother in your eyes, as well. We shall see which aspect of your bloodline prevails."

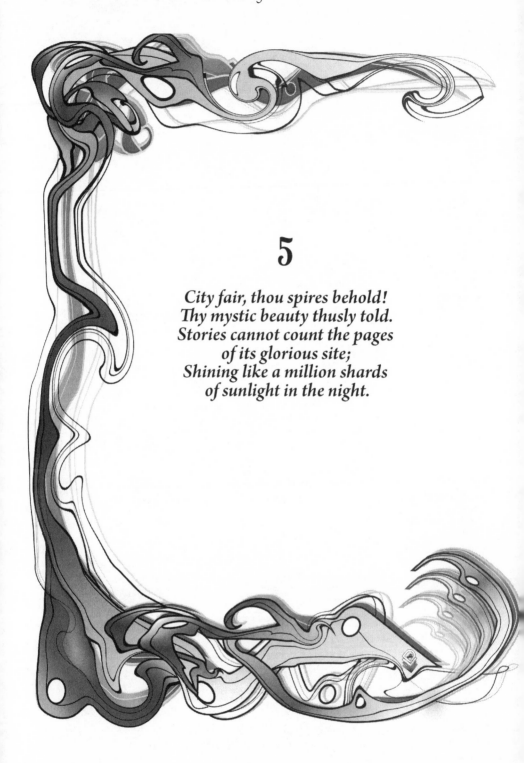

5

City fair, thou spires behold!
Thy mystic beauty thusly told.
Stories cannot count the pages
of its glorious site;
Shining like a million shards
of sunlight in the night.

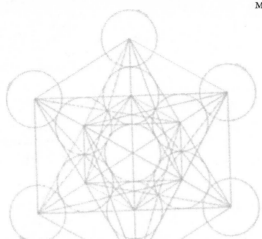

Pan's estate in all its opulent majesty could not raise D'Vinid's spirits. The Ka-Ma-Sharri festival had moved into its third and final day. The guests lay around the garden in various states of undress, their eyes wide with the effects of elixirs. D'Vinid always thought the aftermath of revelries to be the least attractive state humans could be in.

He wandered to the bungalow where his dabrina was still set up. He laughed to himself. Despite Pan's attempt at sending his sons to fetch him, he had still failed at keeping him from getting distracted. He took up the dabrina in his lap and began strumming the chiming chords. The song echoed across the cove, summoning courtiers to witness the show. The sound of a dabrina captured the souls of its listeners. Layers of harmonies wove up and down the scale in fluid melodic textures unlike any other instrument. He began to hum along. His voice wove into the buzzing frequency like a celestial current.

Once he was done expressing his melancholy through music, the courtiers showed their love to him. They came bearing gifts and offers of attention. He just wanted to keep playing. Pan Aello crossed the bridge, triumphantly waving a piece of paper that looked like an official mediator document. D'Vinid made a point to make it clear he was being disturbed. Pan waved the gathered guests away proclaiming he had business with his favorite musician.

"D'Vinid, my boy! It's always exciting to have you around," Pan chimed laughingly as he shook the document. "I just received some news from the palace courier. I'm afraid you won't like it. But let me assure you, I can turn this to our advantage."

"I don't want to know." D'Vinid flipped his hand dismissively as he frowned at the dabrina, hearing off-pitch notes in the perfectly tuned strings.

Not realizing D'Vinid was serious, Pan continued. "Apparently, it has reached the attention of King Kyliron you are a regular musician at my court. So, he is sending a general warning that he has ordered you to cease playing your music until you appear in formal argument before him."

D'Vinid stopped strumming. His shoulders fell. Pan had said the key word to ruin his day. Kyliron. He did not attempt to mask his anger. "Kyliron said *what*?!"

"Now, now, now," Pan comforted, taking a seat on one of the chairs, his fingers unrolling the parchment. "There has been an argument which has reached royal mediation this past week. You seem to somehow be involved with it. The Followers of the Axiom of One have been causing quite a stir. They have been saying on the streets that the madness is a punishment to Atlantis for our greed and selfishness, and we have gone down the path of our own destruction. Kyliron has made a decree their beliefs are counteractive to our peaceful ways."

D'Vinid smirked. "Well, they're probably right."

"A-ha!" Pan pointed his finger. "The king has decreed they must be ordered silent until such time as he decides their dissent is not what is causing this downfall they speak of. It seems *you* are accused of being a leader among a faction called the Children of One."

"All of this is written on this parchment?" D'Vinid laughed dryly. "This is insane!" He buried his face in his hands. Kyliron had made up yet another story about him. He had never even met anyone in the conclaves. "How am I supposed to make a living if I can't play music?"

"Well, since I am your patron, I shall continue my patronage of you until the argument has been resolved. It is my duty, after all."

"Kyliron has been out to get me for so long now. I don't think he knows how not to hate me." He pressed his fingers to his temples.

Pan laughed and reached out to squeeze D'Vinid's shoulders in a side hug, a dismal attempt at paternal comfort. "Why should you stop singing? It goes against our highest law of free-will. I, of course, do not agree with our wise young king."

D'Vinid looked up suspiciously at Pan.

Pan smiled. "You must understand, your involvement in this is a political wish-come-true for opponents of Kyliron… like me. And you forget, I am the king's relative by blood. I do have a say in things, my boy."

D'Vinid shook his head dismally.

"You have great influence among your fans, D'Vinid. Your voice going public about this forced silence would bring many important people into the argument. What is considered a trivial matter by Kyliron and his supporters could be his undoing. You know how Atlanteans detest the suppression of the arts!"

"You don't understand. Kyliron was my friend. Like a brother. I don't want to have any part in this. I wish him no ill will. I just don't want him to know where I am."

"Yet he has selfishly undermined your career at all stops. You have an opportunity to fight back. Why would you not take it?"

"I can't lower myself to his level." D'Vinid paused in introspection. "But I can't spend my whole life running from him, either. All I want to do is play music."

"And Kyliron has now managed to cut that off, as well. How much more convincing do you need to fight? Where is the limit?"

D'Vinid scowled, wishing he could scream at the top of his lungs.

"Unless you want to stop singing, I think you have no choice." Pan squeezed his shoulders again, bobbing D'Vinid's head back and forth. "Here. I wanted to bring this to you." He produced a single dabrina tuning peg. A golden chain was threaded through the loop, transforming it to a pendant. "This was given to me many cycles ago by a lovely visitor. We had a bit of an understanding between us. If we could have known each other longer, we would have been closer. But we had a lovely evening of conversation, and she gave me this as a gift. She was a master dabrina player. Much like you."

D'Vinid felt somehow compelled by the story. He studied the peg as he wrapped the gold chain in his fingers. His eyebrows knitted as he held it up. One of the pegs on his instrument had always been missing. Its jeweled brilliance stood in stark contrast to the faded pegs. To his astonishment it was an exact match. He checked again. Even the symbol of its creator was etched in the same place as the other pegs. "Who was this visitor, again?"

Pan smiled. He knew his gift would get D'Vinid's attention. "She was a bit of a refugee. My family was asked to protect her until she could leave the city. Apparently, she had somehow offended King Koraxx. This is all I know."

"But what was her name?"

"I believe it was Indrius."

D'Vinid choked. He was inclined to reject the gift, and yet he couldn't. His dabrina was the only thing he possessed of his mother's. The Watchers had finally acquired his attention.

People on the Grand Esplanade barely exchanged words. They all seemed trapped in a daze. A mysterious fear had washed over the people. In the distance in every direction, a wall of black clouds closed around the city. Every district featured a VC courtyard. Here citizens gathered to watch the viewer-crystals for any news. So far, no one appeared to offer an explanation for the strange elemental activity.

It was a humid morning. Heavy heat blanketed the entourage, who were covered with tiny beads of sweat. They turned onto the Grand Esplanade and hovered toward the great brass wall marking the first ring of the citadel, which loomed in the distance.

Beholding in awe Poseidia's open-air patios, Brigitte peeked out of the fabric of the carriage and turned her face upward. Dwellings were built one on top of the other, terraced at an angle, reaching toward the sky in tribute to the stars. Their bases framed the streets. Crystal and stone architecture shone in the light of late morning. Creeping vines and draping flowers wrapped the city's curving minarets into the planet's pulsing life force. The intricate masonry was made mostly of white, black, and red stone, quarried from the native lands. Columns supported arched bridges reaching across the streets, connecting higher levels of passage. Brigitte was consumed by the city's intricacy.

She slowly plucked the thorns from the rose's green stem, tossing them from the curtains as if to leave a trail for D'Vinid to follow. Lukias and Allondriss were her comfort. The warriors enclosed the carriage in a tight formation. On the road mound they moved past crowds of sluggish, perfumed citizens.

Atlanteans were generally dressed in multicolored fitted garments with colorful sashes and sandals. Women wore fitted dresses with fabric draped over their arms. Men wore short vests or light tunics and took to tying wide sashes around their waists over baggy pants that fell mid-calf. She knew the sashes were embroidered with symbols that marked achievements in the lives of men. The older they were, the more designs covered the edges.

Most of their skins glistened with an oily sheen. Many donned intricate jeweled necklaces, arm cuffs, and headbands. Most carried a double-waist satchel, held by leather straps crossed at the back to balance the weight of goods or hover discs in their retracted state.

The road was shaded by tree branches and elegant hanging vines. Sparkling banners mingled with the leaves and balconies above. Ocean breezes kept the city's host of fluttering colors in constant motion. Pollen floated through the air, pervading the sky with white, puffy dots in every direction.

Exotic, colorful birds sang in the trees. Some of the people leashed dogs or lambs, ranging in all hues from bright white to black. Cats of all shapes and sizes could be seen everywhere, lounging in high places or creeping low to the ground. Horses were a popular pack animal, used for transportation when a hovercraft was not present. The islands were known as a natural habitat for elephants in Atlantis's earlier ages, so the occasional beast could be seen along the road, decorated with fringed blankets. Brigitte felt increasingly intoxicated from the floral fragrances.

Sandwiched between busy esplanades, the entry channel, flanked by the Grand Esplanade, was the main passageway through the Outlands of the citadel. Bridged by shining overpasses and aqueducts, it was populated with ships whose tall mainsails could easily pass beneath the massive structures. Flocks of birds floated in rippling waters, mere specks illustrating the canal's width.

Their hovering carriage was restricted to road mounds, which had their own path along the esplanade, so they had to wait for traffic. It was bustling with activity: artists displaying their work, people cooking food, artisans shouting introductions of their crafts and goods.

"The Grand Esplanade is where people display their talents,

gather to exchange goods and services, and network between guilds," Brigitte recited, sharpening her memory of Indrius's endless lectures. Lukias surveyed the unfolding scene with a hint of mania in his expression. His world was seen through the eyes of a dreamseer, which saw past the veil of consciousness, beyond the solidity of perception. He watched the world around him as if it were overlaid with the colors from his vivid dream states.

Brigitte's dreams were like most, vague and fleeting, so the workings of the dreamseers stretched past what she could imagine. They lived tortured lives, as they were chosen by the Watchers to impart knowledge of the past, present, and future. They carried information that could not be wielded by average human beings. Brigitte did not envy his life. Their father was always better at hiding the mania all dreamseers were predisposed to develop. Lukias was still young, and his position as hereditary high seer had not yet been initiated.

Roadways twisted off the esplanade, passing dwellings and small shops. Branching pathways offered a look at complex gardens and spiral staircases bridging the gap between the street and walkways. Brigitte could barely suppress her curiosity. She wished to explore every corner of Poseidia's maze.

The carriage glided forward. She projected her thoughts into a future she dared not imagine. The mind of her betrothed was ever nearer, and it filled her with a sick dread, despite her wonderment of the city. She debated whether to slip away and disappear forever into the crevices of the streets, wandering like a small insect in a vast alien world.

Brigitte reached for a snack from a golden tray, which lay atop a table between them, giggling at the thought of Pan Aello and his excitement at being their host. The snack was a soft velvety nut, wrapped in salted meat strips and buried inside dark orange fruit. The seeds of the fruit crunched delicately while she chewed. It was impressive enough to venture another. Lukias noted her enjoyment and copied.

"This is one thing I have anticipated," he delighted, "Atlantean cuisine."

"This place is like a dream." Brigitte shook her head in awe. "More incredible than a dream."

"Dreams are just as real," Lukias smiled.

"Perhaps for you, brother." She punched him lightly on the arm.

Lukias chuckled as he pushed her fist away. But then his face grew serious. "The closer we get to the inside of the city, the more I can feel the Dreamvale, sister."

"Yes," said Brigitte. "I can feel it, too."

"We are getting closer to the Temple District," said Allondriss. "The Temple Sect lives in the Dreamvale, like the dreamclans. If a non-initiate attempted to enter the Temple District, they would merely find a temple with statues. They would not enter the Dreamvale, and therefore not be able to see what is truly there."

Brigitte's eyes fixed. "And the Great Crystal is there."

"Yes," Allondriss nodded. "The Great Crystal is an interdimensional being of light, residing at the power vortex of this sacred mountain. It exists at the heart of the citadel, and stores power for the entire Grid across the ten Atlantean kingdoms. As we get closer, we feel its effects stronger."

When they reached the beginning of the citadel, the entry channel circled into a lagoon filled with circular marinas. The two Grand Esplanades joined on the far end of the lagoon and formed into a round plaza, as the channel emptied on either side into the first water ring. From this plaza, massive bridges reached across the channel entries and over the first water ring of the citadel. Framed by magnificent colonnades, the bridge of the Grand Esplanade's wide expanse would easily accommodate one hundred people walking shoulder-to-shoulder. A great brass wall encircled the first land ring beyond, shining in the light of Ra.

The warriors escorted the carriage up the arch of the road mound and across the stone bridge. Looking back at their path as they moved along the first land ring, Brigitte noted how the city was built on a gradual incline.

While the neighborhoods of the rings were terraced with steps and built level into the hillside, the Grand Esplanade was almost like an optical illusion in its precision. Brigitte looked out the curtains at their path as they neared the bridge over the second water ring. The top of its arch offered a view of the ocean past the expanse of the Outlands.

Inside another hover-carriage, one of its passengers leaned out the window to examine the carriage they passed. Billowing drapes made of red silk fluttered in the breeze. One of the passengers held them aside to get a good look at the warrior contingent. The fabric of the dress she wore laid on her body like a layer of skin. Her jet-black hair was tied up in an intricate headdress dangling with chains of beads and shells.

Corenya Shanel leaned back in her seat again and caught the breeze up in a fan of lace to cool herself down. She gazed at her company, a younger woman of exceptional beauty, though dressed in simple, common street wear. She stared out the window, uninterested. She had brown skin like all Atlanteans, with reddish-brown hair falling in loose waves past her shoulders. Her eyes were framed with thick lashes. Defined eyebrows and high cheekbones set her beauty apart with timeless elegance. The carriage maintained its pace toward the inner ring of the citadel.

"I wonder what sort of passengers might require a warrior escort." Corenya's voice was strained with laziness. "They are sexy, aren't they, my little Vinesia? I suppose you can have any man you desire now that you are a common builder. The Mediator Sect has such rules."

Vinesia bellowed a heavy sigh. "Why did you come and fetch me, Aunt?"

"I wanted to see my niece. Do I need a reason? Besides, there are previews today at the cartel docks. I thought maybe we could go do some shopping."

"Corenya! Just… Tell me what this is about."

They reached their destination. The carriage pulled into an alcove set aside for hover carriages. Vinesia was driven to exhaustion already trying to comprehend her aunt's incessant chattering. She spoke of nothing that mattered, the affairs of other people, what someone wore to Pan's Ka-Ma-Sharri revelry, what kind of elixir she had with breakfast.

"I heard your friend D'Vinid was supposed to be playing last night."

It was the first thing she said that piqued Vinesia's interest.

"But he never showed up. Typical. He was probably with some lucky woman. Hey, you're free to pursue him now! Why don't you?"

"Corenya! I may as well fuck Kyliron, too. How about all of Bavendrick's family while I'm at? I can be like everyone else in this crazy city, obsessed with sex and status and elixirs."

Corenya wrinkled her nose. "D'Vinid isn't Bavendrick's family."

Despite her intolerable personality, Corenya was the only member of Vinesia's family she allowed to visit. Their proximity in age made them more like sisters.

Corenya reached out a delicate hand. She watched Vinesia as she stared out the window in surrender. The girl she used to be was now buried beneath heartbreak. "So, how are you handling the news of Prince Bavendrick's new betrothal?"

Vinesia folded her arms. "So, that's what this is about? I'm fine."

"Are you sure you're fine? He is the reason you left our family."

"Corenya, I left *him* because of our family. Don't ever forget that." She moved to get out of the carriage. "If I need time to heal, I'm entitled to that."

"Vinesia, wait. Look, don't walk away."

"What do you want from me, Aunt Corenya?"

"I just want you to be happy again. You are a lady of the Mediator Sect. You don't belong here among the Builder Sect." Their silence revealed the racket from the street.

"You will never understand." Vinesia stepped out and waited for Corenya to join her.

"You can have anything you want, and yet you choose nothing. You were betrothed to the heir of the high throne of Atlantis, Vinesia. You would have been queen. You are important, an emissary of the dreamclans."

"Half dreamclan."

"My sister told me Bavendrick was sent away to be joined on the Ka-Ma-Sharri. I wanted you to know."

Vinesia stopped, bowing her head in tortured silence.

"Your mother. She wanted me to tell you something."

Vinesia stared at the ground. The neighborhood noise interrupted again.

"The dreamclans are being attacked. Those emissaries who possess the blood to renew the treaty are disappearing. Just like Bavendrick's first betrothed. Your mother is worried about you, here alone, unprotected. She wants to send help."

Vinesia creased her eyebrows, a movement she had become all

too used to. "That's nonsense. The emissaries are needed for the treaty. How will the Crystal Grid be used if the treaty isn't renewed?"

"How am I supposed to know?" she giggled.

Vinesia shrugged. "I can take care of myself." She turned around and scanned the area. She knew the cartel docks well. It was the site of a legendary conclave headquarters. She didn't know who organized it, but that came as no shock. Vinesia was fairly new to the awakening, and the conclaves were excessively exclusive. She squinted into Dreamtime and wasn't surprised to see floating masses of blue mist that formed into patterns. She could feel the message left by the patterns, as well as their intensity. "Danger."

"Corenya," Vinesia stopped. "Let's not go shopping. Let's go to a bath house instead. Come on, you love the bath house. Let's go to one of the nicer ones up here in the Mediator Heights."

"And miss the preview? I could never do that. We get first pick on all the goods today." Her hips thrust to the side with every step as she moved toward the docks. The beads of her headdress dangled as she fanned herself. Her silent footman followed, carrying empty satchels. He was a well-formed male animata servant she called Breeze. Vinesia always hated the use of animata. Most people called them Things. Vinesia had discovered they had a sweetness that perhaps made them more pure than humans, definitely more tolerable.

"But..." She didn't know how to explain the danger sign to her aunt without revealing secrets. The warning about her safety started to rattle her intuition. Her thoughts swam with reasons why there could be danger. She had no choice but to enter the dance of the elementa. Drawing on the dreamclan teachings passed down by her mother, she dropped into a centering pose. Dreamlight swarmed from telluric cracks into her fingertips. With her eyes open to dreamsight, she followed her aunt into the bustling marketplace built into a labyrinth of floating shops.

Wearing dark goggles and a black scarf around his face made D'Vinid seem less approachable, and it was times like these when he needed anonymity. Ultimately, he assumed the Watchers knew he would do the opposite of what they tried to force on him, to trick fate off course. But the defiance of their guidance only united him with Brigitte. It was a two-sided trick, and he had fallen into it.

He fiddled with the tuning peg Pan Aello had given him, feeling torn about putting it back on. His dabrina only had eleven pegs. The twelfth had always been missing. It was the top peg, and the most prominent part of the instrument. He had never desired to replace it, because its absence represented the absence of his mother. His playing style on eleven strings was of his own devising, and it created chord patterns and melodic intervals interesting enough that many other musicians adapted it. He let the peg fall back against his chest with a thump. He shuffled along the Grand Esplanade leading up the entry waterway. At the Grand Lagoon marking the entrance to the citadel was the marina he called home.

Dafni's Enigma was an older vessel, an oceangoing ship of great renown in her day. When Queen Dafni died, the ship was decommissioned, and D'Vinid's father, having gained freedom from his service to the royal family, prepared to leave on his own quest. D'Vinid was in the throes of his fight with Kyliron and wanted to accompany him. But his father wanted to take the journey on his own, and asked D'Vinid to stay and help the first mate, Hanonin, with the ship.

D'Vinid watched the horizon every day, knowing Atlantis did not take long to traverse. But Chaldeis, Captain of *Dafni's Enigma,* never returned. Given its age, the ship could not make a profit against other, more advanced passenger ships, and so Hanonin used its antique craftsmanship and notoriety to their advantage.

He negotiated a permanent slip in the Harbor District of the Grand Lagoon and made *Dafni's Enigma* into a world-famous elixir den and social hub. The marina had a lot of foot traffic, since it was at the entrance of the citadel. D'Vinid built up his career as a performer on the stage of the *Dafni's* main hall. He played not only for the courts, but also for the people, and this was the main ingredient of his rise to fame as the Prophet Singer.

The water was like glass. He watched it for a while, waiting for emerging fish or diving birds to disturb its perfection. Sounds of laughter drifted into earshot, and he knew it to be coming from his home. He padded through the docks, some of them built into multiple levels over their allotted slips. *Dafni's Enigma* was the crown jewel of the marina.

An intricate structure of stairs crisscrossed up three stories of open-air decks built over the ship. Each level provided a view of the waterway and private seating for small groups. From the deck of the ship, one could see up into the spiral pattern created by the deliberate spacing of the patios and stairs. A group of young people caroused on one of the levels. Their laughter filled the air with abandoned propriety.

The ship's interior held a dark romance. The windows were changed from nautical portals to large crystal windows. In any given direction, one could behold a view of the city rings, or the rising buildings of the Outlands along the entry channel. Its main hull had been gutted and redesigned. At the stern, the elixir bar was carved to look like the trunk of a tree. Stairways reached into the upper decks of the ship, and a balcony circled the room, all of which were part of the carving. At the bow, stylized branches framed a stage.

The entire vessel was built in homage to Queen Dafni, who was said to have been turned into a tree by the Watchers. D'Vinid always felt honored to be connected with the queen. He had never met a woman like her. People often asked him if he believed the queen had suffered such a fate. He would never admit his answer. But he had always thought it to be the most insane rumor he'd ever heard.

"Ah, D'Vinid! Just when I thought I'd never see you again," Hanonin's voice sailed out from the bar. D'Vinid shot him a sharp look and closed the distance between them. About a dozen guests in the main parlor sat quietly conversing. All eyes landed on him for a moment, then looked away again.

"One day, Hanonin, I promise you I will walk out that gangway and never return." In truth, he never wanted to leave his home. And since they had the same home, they had always tolerated each other, despite their deep-seated disdain.

Hanonin produced a royal parchment from behind the bar.

D'Vinid shuffled his foot on the ground and clenched his teeth, trying to fidget away the frustration.

"I see you know what this is."

D'Vinid nodded and sat at the bar, his eyes downcast.

"Look, D'Vinid. I'm a fan of the day you finally get out of my hair and stop bringing me into your many troubles." He rolled up the parchment. "But as far as I'm concerned, I haven't received any royal decree." He lifted two empty hands with a pronounced look of innocence. "If you wish to play your shows, I will allow it to happen until they tell us in person to stop."

D'Vinid smiled.

A woman sat at the smallest table overlooking the channel. Her booted feet rested on another seat, crossed at the ankles. A delicate glass filled with amber liquid lightly balanced between a gloved thumb and index finger. Her look was that of a seafarer. Practical yet stylish, her fashion could easily denote a commanding officer.

Her chameleon eyes had been fixed on him since he entered the ship. Loose dark curls spilled out from under the blue scarf tied on her head. A smile crept onto her lips as his eyes landed on her. She flipped her head to summon him with many layers of telepathic awareness. He had no choice but to obey.

"Let's see," she declared seductively as he ambled into earshot. "How long has it been since I saw you last?" her laugh was infectious. "I do lose track of time."

He found himself staring at Ofira Pazit and wondering what yet another ghost of past lovers had in store for him. D'Vinid had known Ofira most of his life. They had both traveled the world over many times, often crossing paths in ports across the ten kingdoms.

D'Vinid smiled as he placed his dabrina carefully against the wall. He eyed her with a rascal spark, while positioning himself to sit where she had rested her feet. He carefully raised her boots to place them in his lap. She leaned back, admiring his every move, while shifting the weight of her feet to balance on his legs.

"You get better looking all the time, D'Vinid." She swirled the elixir in her glass and took a dainty sip, just enough to evaporate down her tongue. He found his desire ignited by the sensuality of her lips.

"I could say the same for you, my dear Ofira." He wrapped his finger with one of her curls. "The Dreamvale suits you well. I may have even seen your ship arriving yesterday." He thought of the ship of clouds he spied on the horizon when all this mess started. "What brings you to Poseidia this time? I'm always curious about your adventures and agendas."

"These days I seem to always be doing errands for the Watchers." She looked at him severely. "Do you realize the dreamclans have been attacked? Dreamships are in terribly high demand. So that makes me quite busy." She spoke abruptly, chopping her words.

"Sounds like a real dilemma."

She leaned closer and lowered her voice to a conspiratorial volume. "I feel there are some things I should show you."

She produced a crystal vial from the pocket of her overcoat. It was filled with fine white powder that sparkled when it caught the light at a certain angle. "This is my work when the Watchers aren't calling me off to save dreamclan emissaries, which I'm fine with because it keeps my karma clean." She handed it to him. "Keep it. My ship's hold is filled with cases."

"This is sha'mana," he marveled.

"The treasure of the Watchers. The purest of the pure."

He recoiled from it. "I can't take this. Kyliron is on a blood hunt for me. If they find it on me, I am done forever."

"Just consume it now," she laughed.

"Why would I do that?"

"Because the treasure of the Watchers is meant for all of us. We are the denizens of this planet. It is our birthright to receive her gifts. Just as Atlantis is our gift." She brushed his ear with her lips. "Yet someone is taking our gifts from us, and for some reason we are letting them."

D'Vinid pulled away, trying to fight the passion she ignited.

She leaned back in her seat again. "Have you gone through the blue-dream awakening yet?"

"All I know about this blue dream is that Koraxx outlawed it, and Kyliron is implementing punishments for its use." He was growing increasingly uncomfortable.

"You really aren't aware of the movement? The Children of One? I can't imagine you wouldn't be."

"I know *of* them, of course. I know they call themselves the conclaves, and I know they operate in secret. I know they call their initiation the blue-dream awakening."

She shook her head. Amusement shone in the multi-colored facets of her eyes. "For someone so well-connected, D'Vinid, you are behind on what you *should* know."

"I can't get involved. Particularly right now. I would only be a danger to them. The less I know, the better."

She grabbed him by the arm. "All the more reason to *be* involved. The conclaves can hide you. The king would never find you again. Or maybe you should just join up with my ship if you're determined to hide. I'm barely involved. I just help the conclaves. Besides, even if he wanted to, the king could never catch a dreamship."

"And work for the Watchers? No, thanks," he snorted.

"It's not so bad as you might think. I do their bidding, which has always suited me well, and in turn they grant me more power than I could ever use in my lifetime. I choose to share it with those who need it."

"Aren't you the humanitarian!" He laughed. "And where do you get this sha'mana? This belongs to the Watchers. You're stealing from your own bosses, who can see everything."

She slapped him on the forehead. "Wake up, D'Vinid. They *give* it to me. I have *earned* this gift from my *bosses*. Believe it or not, some of them want us to have it. Belial wants us to have it. I earn it more than the Temple Sect does. I choose to allow the conclaves to use it, because that is what is right.

"The Children of One are born with powers. They are a genetic upgrade. It's confusing for them because they are not supposed to be this way. Only the Temple Sect is supposed to have these powers. Once they begin taking sha'mana, they can access the telluric intelligence of the planetary consciousness and begin to understand themselves. Otherwise, only the Temple Sect has the means of training those born with the gene. This lovely dust opens a channel for them, so the planet herself can teach them." She handed the vial back to him. "I encourage you to begin taking it."

He sighed.

She dropped her feet to the ground and examined him closer. She had the wily shiftiness of a free-marketeer, and yet her heart was pure.

He thought of the decree associating him with these mysterious conclaves. D'Vinid didn't know much, but he knew they were more than their predecessors who followed the Axiom of One. The Children of One were an entirely different animal. He always felt that he should have existed in Atlantis's golden day. The Axiom of One was the only principle followed by the people back then.

His imagination sparked.

"D'Vinid, you were one of the greatest heroes during the foundation of the conclaves." Ofira ogled him and shook her head. "You practically invented being a hover-trickster just by who you were during the renegade revelries."

It seemed like another lifetime to him. Since he had been punished by Koraxx for participating in the renegade days, he had abandoned that world so completely that he barely remembered. He shook his head as if trying to wake himself.

"You mean the conclaves started back then?" He scratched his head.

"Like I said, I travel in Dreamtime so often, I really don't know how long it's been. But I remember those days like they were yesterday. You are a legend to them."

A thought occurred to him. "Do you suppose that's why Kyliron wants me to answer for the conclaves as one of their leaders?"

Ofira rolled her eyes and snapped her fingers in a spiral. The movement of her fingers made another crystal vial appear out of thin air. It was filled with a blue elixir. "All the more reason to see what you helped create," she said with a wink. Everything she did was seductive, down to the way she spoke in a whisper made just for him. She held the vial between her thumb and two fingers. "This is the blue-dream awakening. It will make you see the signs which lead you to the conclaves."

"You distribute this, too?" He didn't pretend to hide his apprehension and made a careful survey of the parlor to see if anyone was watching. No one seemed to be paying attention. "This is contraband. You put yourself in danger being around me, Ofira."

She waved the blue liquid enticingly. "It only affects those who have the gene. You can disappear, D'Vinid. Dreamship! Remember?" she teased, thrusting a thumb out to the water ring. He looked toward where she gestured. Nothing was there except a black mass of swarming sea birds above open water. He knew she had a different perspective of the world than most. She was above Atlantis's laws in many ways. Being a servant of the Watchers had its perks. He thought about what it would feel like to be completely free of Koraxx's laws and Kyliron's wrath forever.

He slowly reached out to take the blue elixir. She snatched it back just before his fingers closed around it. "Before you take this,

I must warn you. It comes with a price."

He threw his hands up. "A price? First you entice, now you bargain? Make up your mind, my dear."

"It has a cumulative effect. If you have the gene, once you go through the awakening, you will never be able to return to ignorance. The blue-dream elixir has a base of sha'mana. It will prepare your body to receive the activations that will come with consuming the treasure of the Watchers. It will send you into the vortex. You may want to think about it." Her smile betrayed the pleasure she got from giving her warning.

He narrowed his eyes and looked at her. "Why does everything always have to be a riddle with you?"

"Because we are dealing with Dreamtime." He knew her position as captain of a dreamship made her formidable. Since she had given herself to the Watchers, D'Vinid could never love her. But unlike other lovers he'd had, she never needed him, and this was why he soundly trusted her.

He nodded, closing his eyes. "You're right. I need to think about it." He tried to hold his breath steady. Fear gripped his throat. "I don't know enough about this. What's the vortex? What is this gene you speak of?"

"Remember when hover-tricksters first started operating hover-discs off-mound? We could feel the telluric lines. We could charge the torsion-crystals with our auric field. We didn't need the road mounds to operate. *That* is the gene. We've discovered that thousands of people have been born with it. It's an evolution. We can access the Archives Nexes, D'Vinid. We don't need to go through the Temple Sect anymore. We can activate our mindlight and become one with the Grid. As for the vortex," she smiled again deliciously, "you will just have to wait and see."

At the snap of Stixxus's fingers, the fury warriors watched a series of simple gestures. Nodding one at a time, they fell wordlessly into another formation. One of them disappeared ahead.

When they crossed onto the first land ring of a citadel, Brigitte felt as though she had stepped into the future. A cylindrical craft silently glided overhead, stopping at elevated platforms to load and unload passengers. She turned to look out over the Outlands.

The view of the sweeping urban mass was stunning. They hurried across the ring up to the next bridge, which brought them to the great copper wall of the central land ring.

On the second ring, the architecture was not as close together as in the Outlands or the Ring of Commerce. Long courtyards, gardens, and flat walkways of colonnades led off into winding roadways and canal offshoots.

"This is the Ring of Learning. It is where Atlanteans go to find their life path," Allondriss explained. "This ring represents the wheel of life. Here there are libraries, educational houses, and reflection gardens. The Warrior Arenas are here, as well. There is also a race track where athletes, horses, and other beasts compete in games of speed."

"I have heard many stories of the fireball arenas," Brigitte said. She wondered what it would be like to be hosted by Pan during one of these famous games.

Allondriss nodded. "It is awe-inspiring."

"I look forward to seeing it," Brigitte remarked. "It's interesting how the Warrior Sect works. I understand if anyone as a child exhibits violent tendencies that cannot be harnessed, they are sent to train in the Warrior Sect. Some of them become great heroes of the fireball games."

"Yes. It's a bit of a contradiction, mistress," Allondriss answered. "Atlanteans detest the spirit of war, and yet we idolize the warrior games. When there is a fireball game, you can hear the crowd in the arena out to sea. There are thousands of people who go see the teams perform. But it's also a very wise way to harness our warrior spirit, so I cannot criticize. People with violent tendencies turn it into something constructive, and therefore they are not cast out."

Brigitte sucked on another delicacy, nodding her head. "Pan must enjoy his position," she said whimsically.

"Yes, mistress. He is very popular and wealthy because of the attention the games receive. He is their mediator by lineage. His ancestor, Prince Aello, was the inventor of fireball. The Aello lineage is of the royal line of Atlas."

Looking back over the widening panorama as they crossed the second land ring, Brigitte admired the rolling hills extending into the agricultural land beyond. Its lush plains were perfectly divided into curving contours, and butted up against the foothills of the mountainous region beyond. Thick layers of humidity blanketed the mystical terrain.

She turned a hesitant eye toward the approaching land ring. Surrounded by a great wall of silver, it was known as the Mediator Heights. Apprehension grew in her heart as they crossed the bridge. With every inch forward they grew closer to her fate, and farther from D'Vinid.

Allondriss continued her guidance. "This is a ring of hereditary palaces. Mediators are born into their positions. They are all like kings and queens unto themselves."

Lukias lifted his head like a dog catching an interesting scent. "Wait," he whispered harshly, closing his eyes.

Allondriss directed the hover-carriage to stop in an alcove off the road mound. The warriors pulled into formation around the carriage.

"I began sensing a presence in Dreamtime last night," said Lukias ponderously. "It was at Pan's estate. I have followed its trail today. Here it diverges from the esplanade."

"Let's follow," Brigitte's voice raised.

Lukias hesitated, fear reflecting in his eyes. He looked back toward the road mound. "We should get to the palace so you can find safety."

"Lukias!" She found her temper flaring. "What makes you think I will be safe there? I have to face this danger, regardless."

A smile crept onto his face. "I should know better than to try telling you what to do," he almost laughed. "Very well," he agreed, sensing the waves of probability through Dreamtime. Curiosity overruled his sense of caution. "Head down that way." He pointed to the right, where the esplanade began its loop around the Ring of Mediation whose affluent complexes rose toward the sky.

They followed the road mound until Lukias directed Allondriss to stop again. He looked over a series of terraced gardens to the road systems beyond. The mounds did not lead to where he knew they needed to go.

"We have to continue on foot if we must obey these laws," he shrugged, feeling limited.

Allondriss saw his line of thought and directed the carriage to a parking alcove. Brigitte immediately sprung to action, determined to continue on their tangent.

With a sigh, Lukias followed. Allondriss accompanied them. Lukias's dreamsight had captured her curiosity, as well. One of the warriors stayed in view of the carriage, while the others followed them at a distance.

Their path led through the gardens to a courtyard, deserted but for two temple clergy, a woman wearing a purple robe and a man in a yellow robe. At its center rose a ten-foot crystal obelisk, which the clergy were examining. Two warriors stood to block the entrance. Both were tall with fierce, penetrating eyes. They were clothed in long leather coats emblazoned with a dragon emblem.

"This is one of the nodeyards," Brigitte remarked, knowing there were hundreds of these crystal-nodes around the city. These resonant capacitors created the nodesong, which called the people daily to illumination rituals. The nodes served to collect the psychic energy of the people and power the Grid.

The sentries prepared to intercept them.

"What is your purpose here, dragon warrior?" Lukias asked.

"This node has been damaged." The dragon answered, posturing defensively. "What is *your* purpose here?"

"We are here for illumination rituals." Lukias immediately regretted his feeble lie.

The warrior glared at him. The miscalculation of lying to a dragon warrior became immediately clear. The warrior league studied the arts of telepathic combat, and thus could detect lies with ease. "This nodeyard is closed."

"Wait!" The purple-robed priestess stepped out from behind the node. Her ice-blue eyes studied them carefully. Her psychic presence bridged their distance and fixed on Lukias, who threw a decisive glance at Brigitte and met the woman's telepathic incursion with more force than she could throw at him.

"Let them pass," she ordered the sentries. Brigitte and Allondriss followed him into the courtyard. The furies spread around the perimeter, ready to strike if necessary. The dragons watched carefully.

"You have been led here, dreamseer. Why?" The temple woman scanned them in dreamsight. Purple-robed temple clergy were the dreamseers of Atlantis. She was the first one Lukias had the chance to meet.

"I have sensed the murders that happened here last night,"

Lukias blurted the truth. It was obvious they were following the same psychic trail. He could not hope to deceive a fellow dream-seer.

"It is a high level of training to detect such a trail after it has dissipated overnight." She scanned him deeper. "I know you're not Atlantean Temple Sect. I could venture a guess." She looked back at her companion.

The yellow-robed priest stepped closer. His was the order of Grid-tuners. "I would say dreamclans," he referred to the trident clan sigil on Brigitte and Lukias's bracelets.

"And you could be who we've been looking for," the priestess bowed her head to Brigitte. "I would be honored, emissary of the Watchers, to be the first to welcome you to Atlantis."

Brigitte stared transfixed into the crystal-node, melding with it telepathically. A terrible sense of loneliness reached out from its telluric consciousness. "This node is cut off from the Grid," Brigitte said.

"Yes. We cannot be sure how this happened." The priestess was now more interested in Brigitte. "We are downloading whatever has been imprinted in this node. However, it has been tampered with in ways only temple clergy know, though it was not done by our orders." She produced a crystal, presumably a downloader of some sort, meant to absorb the information.

Brigitte maintained her connection with the node. Her attention phased in and out of what was being said. Ghostly faces watched her from within. They seemed as though they were trapped as two-dimensional images in the obelisk's shining façade. She looked closer, confused. Their faces were covered in blood and gashes. Their terror shimmered in waves as they reached out desperately for help.

"…Brigitte," Lukias's voice broke the spell.

Fear gripped her throat. "What?" she answered, breathlessly.

"I was introducing you." A closer look registered the terror in her eyes, and he stepped into her line of sight.

"I was looking into the node." She shook her head. "They are trapped in there. What happened to these people?" She directed her question to the priestess, who watched them with curiosity.

"You can see them?" The priestess lifted her eyebrow. "I don't recommend you connect with them anymore. Their deaths were violent. Only those trained to speak with the dead should make contact."

But Brigitte was already sucked back in. *She saw a vision of the same dark-haired woman she had seen the night before. The Neter. Only her face was changed, twisted into rage and hatred as she tracked a group of temple clergy like a beast in the wilds. With a fierce howl, she jumped onto one of the priests, raking his eyes with her fingernails. Her teeth sank into the vein on his neck, and blood spurted in all directions. The other clergy watched in stunned horror. She chased every one of them down, hunting them until no more were left alive.*

Brigitte felt a grip on her shoulder. She let out a startled cry and jumped in recoil. But the kind concern of her brother was all that greeted her. Soon after, she realized her mistake, and threw her arms around him, sobbing.

Allondriss placed her hand on Brigitte's back. She felt a jolt from the servant's touch, and suddenly her emotions disappeared. She looked back at Allondriss, surprised. "What did you do?"

"I disconnected you from the crystal. Your thoughts became one with those shadows who are trapped in there," Allondriss answered quietly.

The other two clergy looked at Allondriss curiously. "Which order do you belong to?" the purple-robed priestess asked.

"I am not of the Temple Sect," Allondriss shied away.

Brigitte's gaze drifted back to the apparition of a bloodied priestess who had become trapped in the surface of the crystal, captured in the imprint of her terrifying death. A rush of fear seized her. She ripped her eyes away.

Lukias stood frozen, his eyes fixed on the node now. This brought Brigitte comfort, knowing he would get the answers.

Allondriss made a point to ignore the crystal-node. Despite being a temple outcast, Brigitte suspected that Pan may have taught her things no one in the temples would ever know. She copied Allondriss in ignoring the node and set to the task of buying Lukias the time to discover pieces of the puzzle. The priest and priestess made ready to interrupt him.

Brigitte barred their path. "My brother will discover what you have been searching for," she eyed them with command.

"But you must understand, this is delicate business," the yellow-robed priest protested, distressed.

"We understand you are trained to work with the Grid." Brigitte's voice softened but kept its force. "My brother is high seer of our dreamclan. We are your allies, sent as emissaries from the Watchers. We all follow the neutral laws of nature, do we not? So, what would you have to hide from an ally who is here to help you? Is this not why you invited us into the nodeyard, anyway?"

The priest stiffened. "We have laws here, my lady. There is a reason why we cannot reveal our protocol."

"Yes, your protocol seems very specific. As I said, I know you have your ways. You, then, should understand we have ours. You need not reveal your protocol to us. We have come to join with your city, and we have only found it to be tainted," she gestured to the node. "I have been chased. My people have been destroyed. And I have come to a place once rumored as the center of the world, now plagued by madness and violence. I have little interest in your protocol, because obviously it is not working, nor do I suspect your protocol will give me the answers I need." She felt her temper flaring.

The priest squirmed, suddenly uncomfortable in his skin.

Brigitte looked away. She knew his discomfort was her fault, and she did not like to hurt people accidentally with the powers that flared with her emotions.

Allondriss covered her mouth to stifle astonished laughter. Lukias continued his survey of the crystal.

The priestess gestured to the dragon warriors, who immediately jumped to attention. "In the name of the king, I must request that you vacate this nodeyard immediately," she demanded.

"Excellent." Brigitte clapped her hands together like Pan Aello. "Then take me to him. It is our right as dreamclan to request immediate audience with the king and the High Council."

The dragon warriors sent out a psychic blast. Brigitte felt insatiably compelled to leave the nodeyard. Allondriss began to leave. Lukias stood his ground, untouched by their collective psychic command. The fury warriors entered while the dragons focused on her. Brigitte turned her attention to them and broke out of the spell caused by the psychic blast. Stixxus approached Brigitte. She held up her hand toward him and faced the aggressors, who recoiled at her ability to resist their suggestion.

Lukias pulled out of his trance. "Interesting," he puzzled.

The crystal-node began to resonate. Its gentle humming penetrated the nodeyard. It captured the attention of the clergy.

"Impossible," the yellow-robed Grid-tuner gulped. "This node is detached from the resonators! And the nodesong has not been activated!" They backed away as if it would soon explode.

Brigitte looked around while the others stared at the crystal obelisk. She opened her eyes to dreamsight.

A ragtag group of figures wearing revelry disguises had surrounded them. They could not be seen easily, as they were hidden in a pocket of Dreamtime. She tugged at her brother's sleeve. The figures all held small crystals to their lips and were pointing them at the node while humming softly. Their humming magnified through the crystals and seemed to be the cause of the rogue resonance. Among them, she noticed a man dressed in the clothes of a nobleman with his hair and beard cut in patterns. He saluted, noticing Brigitte's attention.

The dragon warriors sent a shock-wave attack outward in all directions. In tandem, the entire group faded deeper into Dreamtime, into a translucent blue mist. A man's voice echoed in Brigitte's head. "*You must reach out to the conclaves, dreamclan emissaries. There is an invisible war happening, and you will not find your answers among the Temple Sect. We are your allies. We are the Children of One.*"

Brigitte and Lukias melded psychically. Lukias reminded her of their final days on the ship that brought them from their home. "*Remember the blue elixir the captain gave us?*"

Brigitte nodded and answered with her mind. "*She called it the blue-dream awakening. She said it would help us see these conclaves.*" After what seemed like a short silence, Brigitte nodded to Lukias and turned to the clergy. "We can help you with your investigation."

"Are you in league with those people?" The priestess was almost speechless.

"This is the first I have seen them," said Lukias. "I wonder why you wouldn't know who they are. Are they not Atlantean?"

"They are Atlanteans, yes, but they possess temple skills. They are not of the Temple Sect, yet they dreamwalk masterfully. We must inform the Alta immediately." The priestess was babbling in distress. Brigitte felt her respect for them slipping away.

"I don't think they are the problem," said Brigitte. "I think you need to find the one who killed the temple contingent. Those poor murdered clergy whose spirits are trapped in the obelisk must be set free."

"Sister," Lukias put his hand on her arm. "These apparitions are not spirits as you suggest. They are emotional constructs trapped in the Grid. They were created when each of those clergy died. They are made of fear. Nothing more. It would be wise to pay them no mind." He turned to the priest and priestess. "My sister is right about one thing, we need to find the creature that killed them. I suggest you leave the dragon warriors to seal off the nodeyard and come with us. We have our furies to protect us." He reached out a beckoning hand to the priestess.

The priestess's eyes grew wide. She shook her head, almost an involuntary twitch. "We must report to our temple Alta. This would be a renegade investigation without their approval."

"Then we will go ourselves," said Brigitte.

Lukias moved to place his hands on the priestess's shoulders and made the mental link, injecting his thoughts directly into her mindlight.

The priestess began to tremble. "We will accompany you, my Lord High Seer," her voice quaked.

"Then we must waste no more time." Lukias waited for everyone to fall into step. He shifted his vision to the frequency of Dreamtime where the trail left by the attacker was still visible and, together, they continued their journey.

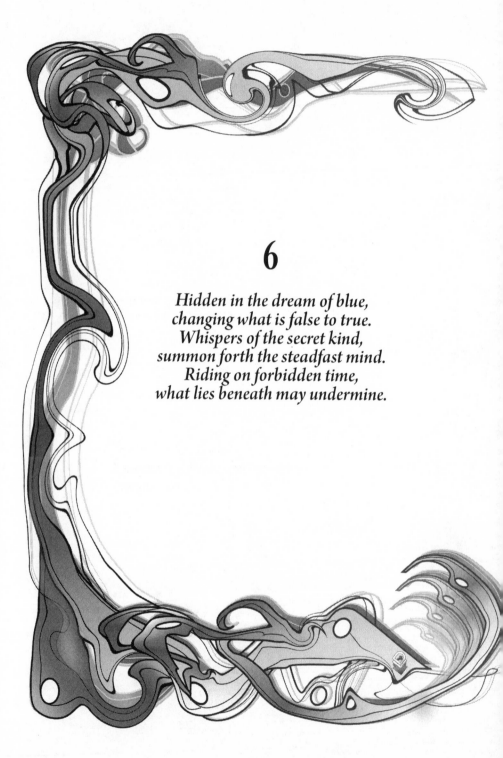

6

Hidden in the dream of blue,
changing what is false to true.
Whispers of the secret kind,
summon forth the steadfast mind.
Riding on forbidden time,
what lies beneath may undermine.

An orange sun climbed to its height on the third day of Ka-Ma-Sharri. The city languished from the previous night's celebrations as two silver streaks approached Poseidia at blinding speed. They skimmed the surface of the ocean, skipping like flat stones hurled by a giant from the wild lands beyond the sea. A closer look revealed two ancient flowcraft from the Golden Age of Atlantis. Not many possessed the influence to acquire these powerful vehicles, which gave Atlanteans the ability to navigate every element.

The flowcraft neared the entry waterway and sped up to spring themselves into the air off one of the ocean swells. On each craft, a lone rider leaned forward with palms resting on crystal spheres held aloft by metal pedestals. A red cape billowed from behind one of the riders as the craft took flight and shot like an arrow straight for the heart of Poseidia. In the air, they diverged, and one banked to the right, circling around the palace to calculate its point of entry. The other banked left. Despite their tremendous speed, their turns began to gracefully slow their descent until both encountered one another in a tight spiral and came to a hovering stop in front of the palace's main entry.

The drivers exchanged salutes. The red-caped rider pulled the gloves from his hands finger by finger and nodded at his companion, a Nubian woman, dark brown of skin. Her hair was woven into numerous tiny braids. Both wore goggles.

He peered up at the gigantic entrance looming ahead. Two silver colonnades with bases of alternating orichalcum and gold marked the entrance to a silver brick path framed by ornamental trees and bushes. Vines climbed tree trunks, displaying throngs of flowers in every imaginable color. The pathway branched off into garden walkways, and trees grew in a tunnel of green foliage.

The man directed his flowcraft down the silver path, ignoring the calls of servants who begged him not to. His dark companion followed. The path opened into a floral courtyard. A series of silver stairs led into an arching set of double doors framed by two towering colonnades. Palace guardians approached them as the flowcraft sank slowly to the ground.

"Don't bother trying to move it," the red-caped rider proclaimed arrogantly. "I am the only one who can activate it." He lifted the goggles and placed them on top of his disheveled head, pushing his hair back into an unkempt array. Sure of step, he bound forward on an urgent mission, bursting past the guardians into the palace. His dark-skinned companion remained ever at his side, casting a menacing presence.

The room beyond boasted a magnificent domed ceiling of rainbow-colored glass. Sunlight poured through windows, creating fragments of dark colors lighting the room in a prismatic mosaic.

The floor, inlaid with abundant Atlantean metals arranged in geometric precision, formed pictures and patterns inside triangles and octagons. A platform rose well above the tallest head in the place. It was made of solid orichalcum, looking like an ocean tumbled by imaginary winds. Oceanids, horses, and sea creatures made up the crests of the waves, as if they were one. Sea nymphs and nereids could be seen playing flute-like instruments. Some were laughing, and two were splashing at one another in joyful frolic.

Steps curled up either side of the platform in the form of sea folk holding up their hands in solemn offering. On the very top rested an empty chair of gold, held aloft by two beautiful women emerging from golden waves, their hair flowing into the tumult. Two dolphins formed the arms of the chair on either side. The room stood silent, but for the echoing footfalls of the invaders. They stood beneath the fractal rainbow shards of filtered sun and regrouped as two guardians approached them.

"I have no time for this. Deal with them, please," he moaned to his friend, whose savage beauty sprung to life as she faced the guardians, now trying to block their advance. Her voice reverberated through the domed room to announce their intent to the guardians.

Never skipping a beat, his booted feet strode down the glass corridor leading off the royal audience chamber. The red cape flared behind, billowing with the force of his movement. With the guardians deterred from their path, his companion caught up and followed him to the inner sanctum of the palace.

They pushed past servants who tried to step in the way, sometimes twirling and ducking to avoid their touch. He burst into a large, oblong room where glass walls offered a view overlooking a garden paradise below. Sunlight spilled through geometrically cut windows. At its farthest extent, the room featured an elevated stage with a luxurious throne seemingly suspended over the garden.

This was a private audience chamber. Today, the king's maydrian took appointments for arguments to be heard by the king. The entry of the newcomers startled everyone in the room. Palace guardians leapt forward, then caught themselves mid-stride and stopped when they recognized the intruder.

Jamarish Ka rose from the throne. He was the temple delegate of the High Council, and yet had managed to become the king's maydrian, as well. It had been King Koraxx's parting wish for the priest to advise his successor. Most of the Alta opposed his dual role, and yet the High Priestess did not. Wearing a blue, pleated robe, the edges of which flared at the wind of his movement, he spread his arms in welcome. A gold circlet rested on his bald head. His skin was flawlessly white, an indication of pure temple lineage.

He bowed at the entrance of the royal prince of Og, the most powerful and opulent kingdom in Eastern Atlantis. "Prince Azai! What, may I ask, is the reason for your visit?" Jamarish Ka's blue eyes looked tired and sunken.

Azai's companion was a Nubian named Rayliis from the oldest empire of the planet. It was said she was of royal lineage, and she and Prince Azai were childhood friends who often dashed around the ten kingdoms looking for adventures. He claimed she was his personal bodyguard, and most believed it. She went to work ushering the petitioners from the room, silently suggesting this was urgent business for the maydrian's ears only.

Azai stared at Jamarish Ka and waited until the last petitioner left the room. His chocolate-colored eyes scanned around, seeming warm and friendly, yet when he spoke, his voice was strained.

"I come on behalf of my father to inform His Majesty, King Kyliron, our beloved cousin, that his brother's ship arrived at its rendezvous point last night," he shrugged. "Regretfully, Prince Bavendrick was not on board. My father demands Bavendrick be hunted down and brought to justice for insulting my sister, Princess Nazira, by deserting her on her joining day." Prince Azai's words were calculated. There was a coldness in his delivery, but his speech lacked the passion that would have been delivered by the King of Og himself. It was quite obvious he was merely the messenger.

His hair stuck every which way from the goggles resting on his head like a headband. He flipped the red cape over his shoulders and folded his arms, waiting for a response.

Jamarish Ka flinched and closed his eyes. "I assure you Prince Bavendrick will be found. This is unfortunate news. King Kyliron will not be pleased."

"Not be pleased by what?" Kyliron's voice resounded from a back entrance. He stalked into the room, his eyes fixed on those assembled. His presence filled the space to the point of feeling crowded. He was adorned with the jewels he often wore. His coppery skin was complemented by an iridescent robe, which was left open to expose his shaven chest.

Kyliron's manner was indifferent as he slumped into the throne where Jamarish Ka had been. A spark appeared in his dark eyes as he examined his reckless cousin with calm intelligence. "Prince Azai, it's good to see you again so soon. And how fares my brother, soon to be your brother?"

"Missing, cousin." Azai fixed his eyes on Kyliron to illustrate the complexity of the situation.

Kyliron folded his hands together and buried his lips behind his fists in disturbed silence.

"He left with the ship, Your Majesty," Jamarish Ka assured.

Azai took a step forward. His voice was calm, though his words radiated threat. "Everyone knows Bavendrick resisted this betrothal from the start."

After a considerable silence, Kyliron's eyes flared and turned red by the gathering of angry tears.

"My father insists he has fled in cowardice," said Azai flatly. "And he demands justice."

Kyliron began to tremble. "My brother is not a coward! Nor is he dishonorable as you dare to accuse him. He had accepted his duty, and he resolved to carry it through. He told me himself. He would *not* lie to me." His voice shook. "There is one explanation alone. He fell off the ship in the middle of the sea with no one to notice. Did you have the ship searched? I made sure he left. He became Og's responsibility then! I will be sure your father is held accountable for this." Tears escaped the king's red-rimmed eyes, which he immediately wiped away.

Azai paused, unsure what to say. His cousin's words seemed just as unreasonable as his father's.

Kyliron pounded his fists on the arms of the throne. "Your father planned this, didn't he? This is his revenge for the death of your brother, isn't it? This betrothal was not enough of an apology for you? I have broken the sacred Telluric Treaty and angered the Watchers for your father! And now this?"

Azai flinched, visibly disturbed. "Cousin, don't be foolish, my father believes Bavendrick ran away. He does not think the prince is dead. You are the only one who has suggested that." He made a sign to the Watchers, and muttered under his breath. "You do not insult the Watchers, cousin. You are the insult."

"What was that you just said?" Kyliron narrowed his eyes.

"Let's not squabble, Your Majesty, Your Highness," Jamarish Ka interjected.

"This is not a squabble!" shouted Kyliron, his voice turned to ice. "My brother is dead! Can't you see? I sent him away and he was not safe!" He glared at Azai. "You tell your father I will hear no more of it. Your brother is dead, and now so is mine. I'd say it makes us even. Any more words about it could tempt me toward retaliation."

Azai bowed and gave his cousin a searching look. Knowing better than to say anything else, he headed for the entrance. "I will show myself out, Your Majesty."

"No, no, cousin," Kyliron reached out feebly. His demeanor flipped dramatically. "I have nothing against you. Please, be my guest in the palace. I have always felt comfort in your company."

"You must forgive me, Your Majesty." Azai studied the high king even more carefully. He continued, his voice dripping with sarcasm. "But I must refuse your generous offer. My family prepared a joining feast for Ka-Ma-Sharri. I must return to help my sister face her shame and grieve the loss of her betrothed." Prince Azai was the most diplomatic choice for his father to send. Of all the royal family of Og, Azai was the most tolerable. He bowed once more, gathered Rayliis with a glance, and walked quickly out of the chamber, shooting one last look of pity and concern at his royal cousin.

After many moments in uncomfortable silence, Kyliron looked at Jamarish Ka through bleary eyes. "And what of *my* betrothed? Has there been any news?"

"This is why I summoned you, Your Majesty. I was contacted by the Grid-tuner I sent to the node where the temple entourage was attacked." Jamarish Ka spoke steadily, studying the king's fragile mood. "I believe the Queen Impending has been discovered. Are you ready to meet her?"

Kyliron shook his head, and blinked the tears out of his eyes, which streaked down his handsome features. He used his sleeve to wipe them away. "No. I am not prepared to meet her. Jamarish, I have begun to fear myself. I wished for my brother *and* my betrothed to perish. What have I done?"

"Nothing here is of your doing, Your Majesty."

"You think not?" His eyes lit on fire. "I *wished* for both of them to die. Look at what happened! What am I becoming?"

"These were merely coincidences." Jamarish Ka reached out a hand to touch the king's shoulder. Kyliron pulled away, crossing his arms.

The king's maydrian continued. "You don't know if your brother is dead, Your Majesty. And you can most certainly still save your betrothed."

The king's voice shook as he spoke. "He was taken by the elements. Just like our mother. Mark my words, Jamarish Ka. He was taken by the ocean."

"But, Your Majesty…"

"Just *leave* me! If I have to listen to your voice any longer, my head will explode!"

Prince Azai made a quick exit with Rayliis in stride. He stared straight ahead, brooding as they retraced their steps back to the courtyard where they had left their vehicles.

Azai muttered toward Rayliis. "Of course, I didn't mention that this wouldn't have happened if he had allowed us to transport Bavendrick *our* way. I don't understand what he has against vimana." He angrily shook his head. "He has brought this on himself. And my father is no better."

Rayliis answered quietly. "Your family does hold on to the ancient technologies. They are jealous and selfish. The high king, I am sure, wishes to possess his own flying fortress. It is always futile to argue with pride."

"Right, as always. So now the great mystery begins. Where is Prince Bavendrick? Perhaps my father is defying the Watchers by attempting to steer his betrothal to my sister. Though the joining would strengthen Eastern and Western Atlantis, my sister is not of the dreamclans. Bavendrick was correct to resist this betrothal. We are all supposed to join with dreamclan mates. It is our duty."

A small group of citizens had gathered to gawk at the two flowcraft. Both were etched with ancient Keylontic codes, the magic symbols that balanced them with nature.

Each flowcraft had one seat. Its back curved to head height. A bubble of glass usually shielded the rider from all elements, yet both had been retracted to a rounded windshield for their trip from Og, since they had only skimmed the ocean rather than submerge. Azai preferred to feel the occasional splash of water when he traveled that way at top speed.

Sensing their approach, both vehicles sprang into action, scaring the wits out of those who had gathered to study the ancient relics. Azai's pace quickened as he donned his gloves and goggles. His last steps built momentum to spring himself into the seat. He acknowledged Rayliis with a salute and leaned forward in the craft to direct it back down the silver path. They scaled over the great orichalcum wall of the inner circle of the city and downward toward the water. Hovering slowly over the inner water ring, Azai and Rayliis directed their crafts to keep pace.

"Back to Og, Your Highness?"

He smiled and shook his head slowly. "My father suspected our royal cousin would be unreasonable, so he ordered me to track down Bavendrick myself once I delivered the news. He knows this is a better task for me than comforting my intolerable sister. I can't say I blame my cousin Bavendrick for running. He was always the most sensible among us."

Rayliis nodded knowingly as he continued.

"I think we should begin with the woman he claims to be in love with. What was her name again? The one who was cast from the courts in shame?"

"Vinesia Shanel, Your Highness."

He beamed a half-cocked smile at his friend and bodyguard. She knew him well enough to anticipate his every move. Without another word, he leaned forward in his seat. The flowcraft picked up speed along the water ring and took flight, capturing the attention of pedestrians as they passed. Once airborne, they banked in sync and headed toward the Outlands.

From the highest deck of *Dafni's Enigma*, D'Vinid stared at the horizon. He held the blue-dream elixir between his fingers.

His eyes drifted to the tuning peg on his chest and slid to his instrument. He tucked the elixir vial into a pocket and picked up the dabrina. After aligning it, the peg fit perfectly into the one empty notch. He twisted it, and it clicked as it turned. A jolt shocked his finger. He pulled away and realized how replacing the peg had created a crack in the wood.

He cursed, tracing his finger along the crack. But it did not have the random pattern of a crack. The wood crumbled away like a clay shell at the touch of his finger, and revealed a small, secret compartment. Puzzled, and driven by curiosity, he pried at the edge of the compartment with his fingernail. It popped off, and he cursed again under his breath.

Beneath the plate was a symbol. But not a symbol he liked seeing. He tried desperately to replace the plate, but it was too late. It would not go back on unless he could replace the sealant that had somehow crumbled at the tuning peg's replacement. He let the dabrina fall into his lap and stared over the edge of the deck.

"You must have faith when you jump from high places," Ofira's voice came from behind as she joined him. "You must trust that you will grow wings and the wind will catch you." She ran her finger down the skin of his arm.

His attraction for her ignited. She pulled a hover-disc from a satchel at her side. "I need to go on an errand. Would you like to accompany me?"

"I have no hover-disc." For the first time in many rotations, he regretted it. He casually covered the symbol on the dabrina with his hand.

With a sneaky smile, she pulled another disc from her satchel. "I never leave home without an extra."

"You lie."

"You're right. I brought that for you. I knew you didn't have one. Unless, of course, you've dropped your stubborn protest. But I knew you hadn't."

He studied the disc suspiciously. Of course, he had not made the bond with it, so he couldn't necessarily leap off the top deck like he wanted to. He longed to feel the wind in his hair again, to search for telluric currents with his senses. "You offer me so much, Ofira. What's the reason?"

"Would you believe me if I say it's a task I've been assigned by the Watchers?"

He shivered. "So, they sent you." He shook his head. "What do they want with me? They should know I am not interested in being their minion."

"Do you think that's what I am? A minion?" She raised an eyebrow. "Being favored by the Watchers is a tremendous honor, D'Vinid. Only you would resist something like that." She laughed to herself. "What if I were to say you were already chosen by something far less savory than the Watchers, and you are simply being used to entrap this unsavory entity?"

He thought about her words very carefully.

"Okay, I'm kidding. I *want* you to come with me," she admitted. "I've decided I want you in my life."

He squirmed, wanting to run, though he admired the curve of her hips, the oval perfection of her face, and thick curls of her dark, auburn hair. He wondered if her lie was not a lie at all. In his mind, the unsavory entity she spoke of was Kyliron. He could not help but feel trapped between Kyliron and the Watchers, although he would choose the Watchers if given no other way out. He focused on the hover-disc and placed his hand over the imprinter panel, connecting with the torsion-crystal at its center.

Ofira followed him down the stairs to his cabin, which had been his quarters all his life. He carefully stashed the dabrina, covering

115

the symbol with a blanket. It mocked him until anger clutched his throat. Even his music was being tainted by the royal family. Quickly, he tore his eyes away and triggered the door shut in an effort to entomb his rising dread.

He closed his eyes and tried to imagine anything but the personal seal of King Koraxx etched into his beloved dabrina and hidden from him all of his life until now. He shivered to imagine what it could mean, though he couldn't even begin to come up with any reasons why it would be hidden there.

"Are you coming back tonight?" Hanonin shouted after them as they left the ship.

"I will do what I want, when I want. How many times do I have to say this?" he shot back, looking at Ofira the whole time with a half-cocked smile.

Hanonin shook his head and went back to work, grumbling about D'Vinid earning his keep, but knowing better than to interrupt his female conquests.

The moment they were off the ship, Ofira activated her disc and threw it into the air. It clicked open with a snap, fanning its mesh of copper wires into a spiral around its spherical central crystal. It glowed as it spun and vibrated quickly up the frequencies of sound until it was beyond human hearing. She winked, and in one graceful move, hopped on the footpads and bounced off the dock.

"You know that's still illegal here," he teased.

Her answer was to simply speed up and circle around, creating an impression in the water where she passed. D'Vinid knew how extremely difficult this was. Hovering over water was one of the more advanced trickster techniques. Some of the guests on *Dafni's Enigma* applauded her skill. He held the disc she had given him, making the bond was easy enough. But he had to use it for a while to seal it. He stretched his mindlight into the central torsion crystal, feeling the pulse of its life force. When he knew the bond was complete, he flipped his disc toward the dock and the footpads clicked open.

The disc bounced under his weight. It took a few moments to steady himself, but his old skills started to come back as he slowly drifted in several directions. Careful to avoid her more advanced techniques, he reached his energy into the torsion-crystal. When he was finally able to match its vibration, he felt his awareness spring through the web of copper wires into the telluric currents of Sophaiya.

At the end of the docks, he dismounted and walked toward the road mound.

Ofira hovered up to him. "What are you doing?"

"What I'm supposed to do," he grumbled, not wanting to attract undue attention.

"I have a better idea. Follow me if you can." She sped off down a side street, grinning while completely ignoring the road mounds. Against his better judgment, D'Vinid decided to follow.

They banked off walls, up steps, and onto the rooftops of Poseidia, skipping off buildings, across chasms and balconies, feeling through their discs and into the surfaces beneath. They quickly fell into a deep meditative state which kept them keenly aware of the pulsing of their auric fields into the torsion-crystals and created magnetic waves which propelled them wherever they wished to go.

They slid down the face of a crystal minaret, bounced onto the esplanade of the outer land ring, and joined the road mound running alongside the second water ring. They reached the great bridge on the Grand Esplanade then crossed with traffic all the way to the third land ring, where the mediator estates rose in terraced affluence.

Ofira glanced back at him and hovered to the edge of the great silver wall overlooking the water ring. Looking quickly over her shoulder, she catapulted over the edge. D'Vinid watched in awe as she landed just above the water. He tried not to think about it too much, and instead sucked in a deep breath and followed. He plummeted several stories, breathing steadily, sending his mindlight into the crystal, waiting in vague dread to feel the water below.

The instant he made contact, he slammed his auric field in a spiral into the crystal and accelerated it to its limits. His field merged with the hover-disc and leapt outward below him, pushing against the bonds of the water, rocketing him forward like a meteor. Steam rolled off his disc as he caught up with Ofira, who nodded at his resurrected skill, and together they skimmed the surface at breakneck speed.

Ofira suddenly leaned right, toward the hull of a ship. She ricocheted off the side, arching into a backflip as she spun the disc's field into a harsh resonance pattern, and landed squarely on a dock reaching into the water ring. D'Vinid copied her move, but with far less grace. She dismounted, laughing while applauding his flailing attempt to re-enter the world of hover-tricksters. He kicked the hover-disc away and leaned forward with his hands on his knees, breathing heavily.

The hover carriage came to a stop. Lukias tossed a hurried glance at his sister. Brigitte noticed a pier stretching over the water toward the Ring of Learning, its entrance marked by a sunken nodeyard plaza. Her eyes were open to Dreamtime, though she could not see as deeply as her brother.

Blue tendrils of mist weaved in and out of patterns and pointed off in different directions as they traveled. They did not seem random, like other wisps of color in Dreamtime, but perhaps signs left by someone to convey a message. As her brother directed Allondriss on where to go, Brigitte wondered if these were what guided him.

The priest and priestess occasionally shot concerned looks at one another. Stixxus and his team of fury warriors escorted them in formation. They came to rest in one of the many alcoves where unmanned carriages clustered, bearing flags and décor.

Allondriss parted the curtains. "This is the Commercian Cartel District," she said to Brigitte quietly.

Lukias was in one of his trances and said nothing.

Stixxus and Allondriss remained with Brigitte while the other furies stayed in step with Lukias and the temple clergy. A stone archway marked the entrance to the cartel docks. Without a word, Lukias headed for a nodeyard plaza at the edge of the water ring. The yellow-robed priest took out his gauge and began measuring the node.

Unlike the first one they encountered, this one was attached to the rest of the Grid. Brigitte could feel her essence stretching into the crystalline network covering all of Atlantis. But the nodes only offered a small glimpse of its vastness.

A tingle ran up her spine, and she noticed a face watching her, a hologram trapped in the crystal's surface, the same face that watched her from the first node. Chills covered her body. The woman's bloody hand reached for her. Her mouth was open in terror, fixed in an eternal scream of pain.

Brigitte began to feel the pain. She wanted to run, but instead her feet carried her closer. The entity tried to reach out but remained trapped in the crystal. She approached the node as if caught in a magic spell which usurped all control of her body. Her hand lifted to touch its surface. The entity's two-dimensional hand escaped the crystal, and Brigitte felt a jolt as their fingers touched. An icy-cold stab crept up her arm and into her heart like poison. A scream was trapped in her throat. She was paralyzed with fear.

"Brigitte!" Her brother's voice shocked her into awareness. The entity's hand recoiled back into the node. Lukias stepped between her and the crystal. "You must stay away from the nodes. This creature has attached itself to your fear. Banish your fear and it will have no hold on you."

"What *is* it?" she sobbed, feeling the poison spread through her body.

"When those temple clergy were murdered, a part of them remained. They are an imprint of that one moment of terror. I think isolating that node from the Grid kept them trapped there. Otherwise they would be in the Grid. But this one managed to attach to you. I think you may have set it loose in the Grid. Unless you allow it to attach to you, it will find someone else." Brigitte pondered her brother's words. He was suggesting that she voluntarily take on the shadow madness.

The dreamseer priestess stepped closer, examining Brigitte with concern.

"You say you have no idea how that node was isolated?" Lukias directed his attention to the priestess.

She lowered her voice while tossing a wary glance at the yellow-robed priest. "That's the claim of the Grid-tuners, at least. It is they who work with the nodes."

Brigitte knew there were eyes on her. She peeled away from her brother. A slow, casual turn revealed their audience. Hidden in shallow Dreamtime, they surrounded the nodeyard and watched intently. It was the same group they had seen before. In unison, they lifted crystals to their lips and began humming. She could feel the resonance on a higher frequency. It pulled at her soul. She could not resist.

All sensation began to drain away. She lifted her hands to make sure they were still attached to her body. At that moment, their spell was complete. Brigitte's body crumpled to the ground, and her dreambody was yanked away by the resonance they created. As an apparition, she drifted closer to the man she had noticed earlier. Sounds and colors swirled into Dreamtime.

The man bowed to Brigitte. *"Emissary of the Dreamvale. It is we who disconnected the node from the Grid. The Temple Sect does not know how this was accomplished. They cannot be trusted."*

"How did you force me into dreambody?" Brigitte looked around in confusion.

"We have many skills. They are granted to us by the spirit of the planet. We summoned you into dreambody because you are accompanied by Temple Sect clergy. We had no choice but to approach you without their knowing. We are in need of your assistance. We would ask you to help us capture the creature that murdered the Temple Sect victims. We encountered her once last night, but she has escaped. The shadowmancers are trying to find her, too."

Brigitte scowled, not liking the sound of that.

"My lady, Atlantis is suffering from an invasion, and no one seems to want to do anything about it. Most of our people would rather remain in denial."

"My brother is on the same trail. He will find her."

"What will you do once you find her? You will have to face the shadowmancers. They would kill you if they find you. Believe me, your fury warriors are no match for them. Your brother can find her, but she is hunting you. You can lead her into a trap we have set for her.

"If the Temple Sect takes her, we will never know the answers we seek. Right now they think the attack of this entity in the node is why you have passed out. We must keep it this way, and you must lead her to us. If you stay in the blue dream, the creature will not be able to see you."

Brigitte examined the ribbons of blue essence around them. As she gazed at him, she quickly re-evaluated her situation.

High sun approached. Citizens slowly gathered for illumination rituals at the entrance to the nodeyard, but the furies blocked their path.

"We must let them enter," the Grid-tuner priest said to Lukias and the dreamseer priestess. "We need devoted citizens to attend illumination rituals. The power of Atlantis depends on their mind-light donations."

Still cradling his sister, Lukias looked up at the priest in shock. "You would endanger all of these people? The entity that attacked my sister is still in there."

"It looks as though it has entered her. She must be brought to a temple healing center." The priest's voice pitched into urgency. "You don't understand. Citizens have been neglecting their duties to attend the rituals. We have not reached our mindlight quota for many rotations. We must let them in. The resonance will start soon."

Without another word, Lukias picked Brigitte up and walked to the carriage. Allondriss followed. Stixxus fell in step. Lukias carefully arranged her body in the back seat. He opened his mind to Allondriss as he nimbly crouched at his sister's side. "*Allondriss, you must make sure the fury warriors keep those priests away from us. I will enter into dreambody and summon my sister.*"

"*I can help you,*" Allondriss responded with easy telepathy. She opened the curtain and spoke in hushed tones with the warrior outside.

Lukias reached out his hand. "*Stay with me, then. Be my ground.*"

She took his hand and sat on Brigitte's other side. They locked expressions as he slowed his breath to a rhythmic cadence. Absorbed in her ocean-blue eyes, his fingers pressed against the softness of the skin on her palm. They both took Brigitte's hands. Thousands of subtle sparks passed between them. After a few moments, he closed his eyes, just as the nodes began to sing. Waves of sound rippled over Atlantis, and Lukias flew out of his body. Brigitte was waiting for him.

The resonance of the nodesong cascaded down the slopes of the citadel. D'Vinid closed his eyes.

Ofira tapped him on the arm. "If you were to actually take the elixir, you would be able to see the blue-dream markers," she laughed. "This is a conclave sanctuary." She wiggled her index finger, looking him squarely in the eyes as her finger lured him closer. She cocked her head playfully, revealing the definition of her jawline. "This situation would be a far different experience if you awakened your mindlight to the blue dream."

His head twitched. For a moment he forgot what was happening, as her beauty further awakened his desire. "How can I know what to decide if I can't even imagine what it is you're talking about? Look. At least let me see the contrast."

Her smile brightened. "Perhaps you are wiser than you seem." She gently tapped his cheek with her index finger and turned laughingly to stroll down the dock with her hands behind her back. She allowed the heels of her boots to drag along the boards as she walked, enjoying the hollow sound echoing off the water below. At this point, it felt as though he would follow her anywhere if she continued her flirting. It was becoming a welcome distraction, which was managing to lift his spirits.

The dock reached the wall of the canal and branched off in two directions. Each led to the famous cartel docks, the richest, most exotic market in Poseidia.

She turned to glare at him. "Now, let me do all the talking. If I say something you know to be untrue," she shrugged, "just go with it."

He covered his dashing grin with the scarf he kept around his neck at all times for just such an occasion. Seduction flared in her eyes as she slowly turned and led him onward.

Ofira pointed to the wall at the dock's end. "You don't see the sign, because you didn't take the elixir. But if you had, you would see that is not really a wall." She continued, taking one of the other routes toward the cartel docks. These docks were a special place of commerce. Commercians were the commercial networkers of the ten kingdoms, and so their markets were places of business where they could match goods and services with those who had the means to channel them through the kingdom.

Ambassadors frequented commercian docks to find out the news of all trade trends through the kingdoms. Mediators would find leisure among its international visitors. There was no telling what exotic surprises would present themselves amid those who came to register with commercial cartels. As such, the docks were kept in pristine condition, and served as a marketplace as well as mooring for the most important visiting vessels. For the last day of Ka-Ma-Sharri, the docks were adorned beyond their usual gran-

123

deur.

"Aren't we going into the magical wall?" he asked with a laugh.

"We have other business in the market hub first, my love." She directed their whimsical journey down the dock to the right. To the left lay a quay belonging to the Telleria family, who controlled the cartel.

The quay gave the effect of being suspended above water. In actuality, it rested on giant pedestals anchored at the bottom of the canal. From the building, docks jutted into the water ring, providing moorings for ships to unload supplies onto hover-sleds. Ramps stretched from the unloading zone straight to the doors in the side of the main building.

The pier above them separated the work area from the public area. Anyone who walked along the esplanades could divert their path along the pier to overlook either side. D'Vinid knew there was a popular nodeyard at the entrance to the pier.

Ofira and D'Vinid ambled onto the main ramp of the marketplace. Ofira did not seem to be trying to get anywhere in particular. She casually enjoyed each moment. They perched next to a temporary shop.

The people filling the floating market had come to see what surprise bargains had arrived in the cartel docks for the holiday. Traders and marketeers who traveled the world had no doubt signed up with the cartel to display the goods they transported, filling the temporary shops provided by the cartel. Merchants who bought from the previews would be here to buy goods to supply their local stores. The other attendees would be from wealthy families who wanted to have the first choice of everything.

The smell of spices and perfumes filled the air. Where they stood, cages of exotic animals hung from the ceiling of a cubicle that had been reserved by an animal merchant for the preview. D'Vinid poked at a monkey, who stared at him with eyes that asked to be set free.

Ofira winced. "Don't get attached. These creatures don't always find good homes."

Ofira's family had a shipping business that was highly connected with cartels in all ten kingdoms. But along the line she had acquired a crew who could command the elements, and the ship she inherited was able to travel into the Dreamvale.

Her business then expanded far beyond that of her commercian lineage. She had once told him she left her family behind when the Watchers took her into their favor. They could never understand how her new existence brought her to a land somewhere between waking and lucid living. This had significantly changed her priorities.

She began to count backwards slowly from ten. A wry smile spread across the fullness of her lips. The moment her counting hit one, a gravel voice bellowed across the din of revelers. "Ah! Ofira Pazit!" An old seafarer stood across the market hub, waving eagerly. He had a barrel chest and a big nose with a handlebar mustache. Beads dangled at the end of his braided beard.

In the confusion of those arriving for the preview, few took notice of the scene he caused pushing across the docks to unite in a hug. When he reached her, she expertly evaded his advance, leaving him standing awkwardly next to an array of colorful fabrics rolled vertically at the entry of a merchant's temporary shop.

"Oh, little captain!" He slapped toward her with a limp hand. "You aren't still mad at me, are you?" He uncomfortably scratched an itch on his head.

"Not at all," she seemed more interested in a piece of fabric. "I just don't trust you. There is a difference." She raised an eyebrow at him.

"Fair enough." He swung his giant hand to slap her on the shoulder.

She dodged it adeptly.

He let out a belly laugh and pulled his hand away. "At least let me make you a peace offering," he suggested.

"How about you let me know what you're doing in Poseidia," she blurted, finally making eye contact.

"Very well. I have sailed from Og with a shipment of animata servants. We are preparing for a showing very soon, in fact. This batch is strong on pleasure animata."

"And what is your involvement with the attacks on dreamclans?" she changed direction.

"No, no, no!" His look shifted into animated concern. "I have nothing to do with that! I would never hurt the dreamclans. I don't think it's the smartest idea to anger the Watchers." He leaned in conspiratorially. "And as you know, one has to be clever to be a free-marketeer."

"So, what do you know about it, then?" She shifted impatiently, cocking her head to the side. She examined him intensely. He retracted from the heaviness of her glare.

"Look, little captain. I don't make it my business to follow the doings of the other realms of the planet. I deal strictly in the Meridian Realm. The rest of it is beyond my comprehension. Dreamtime. Watchers, Telluric Realm, Subterra, Oceanus, Celestius. Bah! To Incendius with it all. I'm a human, not a traveler of Dreamtime!"

"But you know what is going on in the free-market guild. Come now. You do want favor with the winds, don't you?"

"Fine. I know you will find out eventually. I will tell you what's going on in the guild, just to make things easier for you. There are new animata being produced in Og. I cannot name names! But some of the free-market ships have been taking madness victims to these compounds. Some believe they are turning said victims into animata."

"How would they do that?" A look of horror formed on her face.

"You know how this is possible. When animata are created, they are simply bodies made of human tissue. Imagine how few resources they would have to expend if they already had human bodies and didn't need to make them from scratch. Once the madness consumes them, their soul is gone, leaving just an empty shell. All these dealers have to do is extract the parasite, send the soul on its way and recycle their body for a more useful purpose. It's better than allowing them to suffer and die mad. At least, that's what they think."

"This is making me sick." Ofira looked pale.

"I don't trade in these new animata, but I do have a warrior with me on this trip."

"An animata warrior?"

"That's right. It seems to be in style these days, dealing in war technologies. The spirit of war is spreading all over the Atlantean kingdoms. I can guarantee you, the free-market guilds know this, and they are figuring out how to profit from it."

"You disgust me."

"Hey, little captain! I already told you, I don't deal with all this. I just *know* about it. Consider this information a gift for our continued good faith."

126

"If you don't deal with it, then why do you have an animata warrior?"

He shrugged almost shyly. "If you must know, I saved it. My crew found it wandering on the beach on an island we were visiting. It had somehow escaped from where it was spawned."

"And you just stole it?"

"I found it fair and square! It needed a new life, and so I brought it along." He scratched his head again. "I figured the Watchers guided it to me."

"How do you know it's a warrior?" she demanded suspiciously.

"How do you know when an animata is created for pleasure? How do you know when an animata is created for manual labor? You just know. What more can I do for you, my lady of the Watchers?"

"How would they know how to extract the parasites from madness victims?" She squinted, not sure she wanted to know the answer.

"It's not known. But I have heard whispers of alliances. A dark priesthood of some sort."

She paused, contemplating the information. "You know nothing about the dreamclan attacks?"

"Well, my guess is as good as yours. But I think I may have given you a good starting point." He winked and licked his lips at her.

She shuddered. "I want the animata warrior."

It was his turn to look at her incredulously. "I suppose you have something to trade for it, then?"

"I thought you found it. Now you're selling it?"

"A man's gotta make a living somehow."

She shook her head and pulled a vial of white dust from her pocket.

He nodded, not having to be told what it was. "Of course. The price is right. The deal shall be yours. Make sure and watch the showing. I will make sure everyone knows your warrior is pre-bought."

She wrinkled her forehead. "I would prefer the warrior be left out of the showing."

He smiled treacherously. "I know you've been out of the cartels for a while, little captain, but technically, you can't make those demands until payment has been made."

Her expression shifted. "Very well. Take this as an offering in *good faith*." She handed him the vial of sha'mana. "I will come back shortly with your payment. My associate here, Jorious Oceanflyer, will accompany you as collateral in the meantime." She winked toward D'Vinid.

"Of course, my lady! I would expect at least five more of these vials. The warrior has a crystal imprinter installed in its brain, so you can link with it. I expected to fetch an excellent price for it in the open market."

She flipped her hand dismissively toward the marketeer. "I will bring you three."

"No less than four. And something else. Something personal. Perhaps information."

Ignoring him, she turned to D'Vinid. She grabbed his hand and pressed something into his palm. "I activated this locator-crystal. Make sure and imprint it so I can find you." The next moment, she abandoned him standing next to the free-marketeer in awkward silence. He stared at the crystal to imprint it, then tucked it into a pocket.

"Ooooh, I'm in love with that woman!" The tiny beaded braids dangled from his chin as he spoke. He clapped D'Vinid on the back, who tried not to fall over from the unexpected force. "One day she will love me," he gazed after her.

D'Vinid wondered if he was joking at first. Close observation revealed he was serious. He couldn't blame the unfortunate fellow. She was spellbinding in many ways, a magic trick of exceeding delight.

"What was it she said your name was, lad?"

D'Vinid had already forgotten the name she had assigned him. "J... Jorious... Flavious.... Ocean. Rider."

"Well, keep up then, lad. My showing starts soon." Without introducing himself, the free-marketeer cut through the action on the docks. D'Vinid followed at his own pace. He was already tired of keeping up with Ofira, and he hadn't signed up to be her collateral. He quickly invented a reason why Jorious Flavious didn't need to hurry. Perhaps he could say he was a prince.

He thought of how Queen Dafni used to call him Prince of the Sea. It made him sad. He had always loved the queen. She was kind to him, perhaps the only one who had shown him that kind of love. It was said the Watchers had taken her because she was too beautiful for the eyes of men. He never believed the story, although it was plausible. She had been the first woman to whom he had ever been attracted. It was an uncomfortable memory.

The docks formed a labyrinth of floating shops. He could see nothing but aimless greed everywhere. He tried to keep an eye on the mercenary. It was apparent enough he was headed to the center of the market, where all the showings were held.

A commotion broke out on the dock, blocking his path. While trying to see what was happening, he lost his footing, and was pushed into a corner by the unforgiving rabble of shoppers. Another body broke his fall, and both found themselves tangled in a mess of shoulder satchels on display at the threshold of a shop.

A woman's voice cried out in startled concern. He tried to pry himself out of the predicament, while reaching out to save her from falling. He looked into the eyes of the woman he was trapped with, and the bottom fell out of his stomach. Loressai Torbin gawked back at him, her eyes wide with disbelief. Movement caught their attention. It seemed as though smoke billowed in the air above the market center, but a closer look revealed a fog was rolling in.

Her astonished look quickly shifted to intense fear. Out of breath, she buried her face in his chest. "Hide me, D'Vinid. They're coming to get me."

He looked up quickly, and although he didn't see anyone in the crowd, he took her word for it and pulled some bags over her. He sat there mesmerized by the gathering smoke above the marketplace.

"Are they gone?" she asked after a few moments.

"Who?" He began to peel bags away, trying to ignore the way she was moving next to his body. She slid up his chest like a snake and wrapped her legs around him. A savage look pulsed from her eyes, hypnotizing him with a passion so seductive it ignited his inner fire almost immediately.

She writhed in his lap as she ran her lips up his neck and into a kiss. He wanted desperately to throw her off, yet he couldn't. All he could do was kiss her back. The smoke gathering in the market thickened, and in moments fog covered the marina and blocked out the sun.

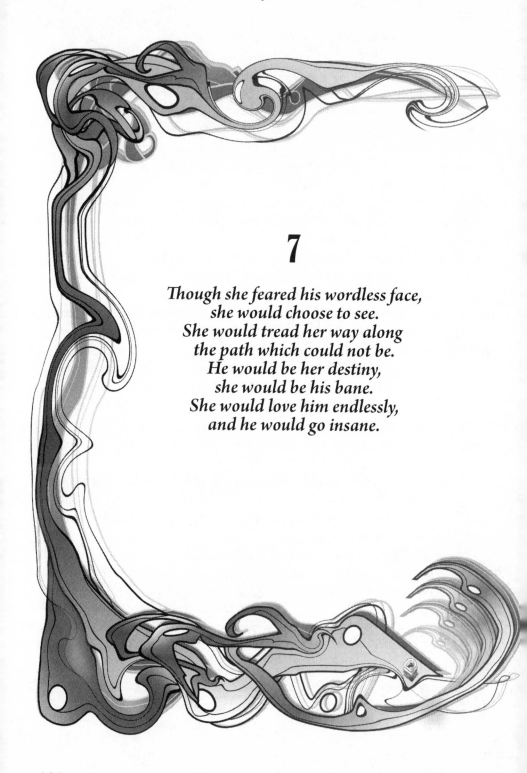

7

Though she feared his wordless face,
she would choose to see.
She would tread her way along
the path which could not be.
He would be her destiny,
she would be his bane.
She would love him endlessly,
and he would go insane.

Sunlight blazed into the garden courtyard of King Kyliron. The centerpiece was a deep blue pool of sacred waters pumped straight from the center of the mountain. It was embellished with aquatic terraces connected by warm waterfalls.

His collection of kallistas lounged in the waters. Each lady was stunning and eclectic, of varied shapes and coloring. Kyliron sat in his favorite seat overlooking it all. His murky eyes brooded as he twirled the jeweled trident of his office.

His eyebrow lifted when he saw Fa'nariel enter the pool, one of his favorites. He beckoned to her. She was dressed in next to nothing, exactly the way he required his collection of feminine beauty. She watched him with a steady gaze as she approached. Water dripped down her skin. He pulled her into his lap, skimming her curves with the point of his trident.

"Where were you last night? I sought you out for the Ka-Ma-Sharri."

"I didn't think you would miss me, Your Majesty. I had to go to my family. My brother has been sick again."

He smiled, pulling aside what little she wore with his trident. "You'd better be careful or I might grow jealous of this brother you always disappear to care for. Of course, you will have to make up for it." He gazed on her with the hunger of a man never satiated.

Jamarish Ka approached him with caution.

"What do you want?" grumbled the king dully. His eyes remained fixed on his prize.

"I received word from the investigation team I sent into the citadel. They have found your betrothed."

Kyliron shrugged, running his lips on her golden skin. "Where is she?"

131

"I would like to encourage you to go out among the people and meet your Queen Impending." Jamarish Ka had a hypnotizing effect when he spoke. The priest reached his arm up to brush the sweat from his bald head. His blue eyes captured Kyliron's gaze.

The king sighed deeply. "Let her find her own way. If she does, I will join with her. It is in the hands of the Watchers now." He continued his exploration of Fa'nariel's body.

Jamarish Ka gently touched Kyliron's arm. "Why do you resist her arrival, Your Majesty?" His voice was soft and calming.

"Haven't you noticed?" Kyliron spoke in a pleading voice. "I have gotten worse since she has arrived in the city. I have dreamt of her since I was a child. She accompanies my greatest nightmares. I fear her more than anything in this world, Jamarish Ka. She is my undoing." The color of his eyes shifted, as if they had suddenly turned to liquid.

"But you really must go to her now. It is your duty."

Kyliron shook his head fiercely. He pushed Fa'nariel off his lap. She caught her footing and tried to avoid the hypnotic gaze of the priest.

"You *will* go to her now," Jamarish Ka repeated, this time with more force.

"I have made you aware of my decision. Your words will have no further effect here." Kyliron's voice began to waver.

The priest waved his hand across the king's eyes and began chanting in a guttural tone.

Kyliron's expression went blank.

By now, Fa'nariel made it across the courtyard. She turned to watch, taking note of the change in the king's manner.

"You *will* go meet your Queen Impending."

The king nodded vacantly and stood up.

The priest snapped toward the kallistas and raised his voice for them to hear. "Help your king dress in his finest street wear. He will go out in public now to meet his new queen."

It seemed as though night had engulfed the city, though just moments earlier it had been a sunny afternoon before the fog covered the market in a matter of moments.

"You two! What are you doing to my shop?" A man's angry

voice broke the mood.

D'Vinid pulled out of the spell which had entranced him. Just as angry as the shopkeeper, he pushed Loressai from his lap. She landed awkwardly, her limbs entangled in bags. The trader began pulling the bags away. She remained still, watching D'Vinid struggle from his entanglement.

Once free, he rolled to his feet and eyed her carefully, half-tempted to run away into the crowd. But guilt robbed him of his escape. There was something terribly off about her, and it made him nervous. Against his will, he reached out a hand to help her up. Back on her feet, she watched him with hungry eyes. D'Vinid tried to help the trader organize the mess they had made, but it only complicated matters.

"Jorious!" The free-marketeer's voice cut through the chaos. "By the Watchers, what are you doing?" The barrel-chested man marched through the fog up to D'Vinid. "I am running out of time! I thought you were behind me! I was walking along talking to no one and making a fool of myself. Then this fog came and I thought you were lost." He closed D'Vinid's arm in a tight grip and yanked him along. "What are you doing shopping?" he called, as if to a deaf person.

D'Vinid felt an ironic sense of relief. Looking back, however, his heart sank as he realized Loressai was following them, her eyes fixed in that same hungry reptilian gleam.

They neared the central hub of the docks, which was kept empty to serve as a floating stage so whoever was officially showing their merchandise could be seen from every direction. The dock leading to the central platform was covered by an awning sided by drapes. The free-marketeer was using it as a staging point for his animata merchandise.

D'Vinid allowed himself to be dragged past the sentries, straight into a group of silent animata. They stared ahead with blank expressions, merely human bodies with no spark of consciousness.

He felt a sense of relief as he noticed Loressai being blocked by the sentries. Undaunted, she merely took a few steps to the side, and waited for them to let their guard down. D'Vinid shivered, gripped by dread and a strong desire to jump into the water.

The free-marketeer pointed out the animata warrior Ofira was set on acquiring. Its eyes were fixed on nothing. A permanent furrow knitted its brow. It stood at least two heads taller than D'Vinid, who was already tall. Its empty presence radiated an imposing calmness. Its hands looked like they could break a person in half.

D'Vinid remembered his cover as this Jorious Ocean-Fellow and contemplated the character he was drafted into playing. He forced his expression to assume a look of expertise as he examined the man-creature. "You say this warrior has an imprinter-crystal in its brain?" He wondered at the practice of making models of humans that could be so entirely controlled.

In a way it felt like slavery, although these creatures were supposedly merely bio-organic vessels with no souls. He shivered, thinking about the claim that madness victims were being transformed into these slaves. It was a terrifying thought that could only lead to moral disaster.

The free-marketeer captain patted his hand on the warrior's head. "Once you make the imprint, this creature will always take your psychic commands, no matter the distance."

D'Vinid kept half of his attention on Loressai, who was stalking along the perimeter of the docks, materializing in and out of view among the fog. "How do you know it has an imprinter, anyway?" He stepped back in case his blunt suggestion should incur some kind of wrath. "I heard you tell Ofira how you found it wandering."

The free-marketeer cast a long, assessing look at D'Vinid. "How do you know Captain Ofira?"

This was D'Vinid's chance to deliver his acting role. He feigned aloofness while staring at the warrior. "Let's just say, she has been campaigning for my friendship. But I don't know why she's associating with the likes of you." He raised an eyebrow and curled his lip, pretending to examine the warrior closer.

"The likes of me?! I am Jonda Dex! One of the best free-market traders you will ever meet. We are made for each other, Ofira Pazit and I." His jowls trembled as he made a growling sound.

"Is that right?" D'Vinid drew back. "Oh, yes, I can see that. A lovely match, indeed." He only slightly masked his sarcasm. "Now, if you don't mind, I will wait right here until the captain returns." He stole a casual glimpse at the locator-crystal while Jonda Dex fumed at him, hoping to be relieved of his "job" soon.

Across from the viewing stage floated a dock adorned with stacked seating for spectators to view the previews. It was between showings, and the curators of the docks had announced they would pause until the fog cleared. Vinesia accepted a pastry from Breeze. Corenya wrinkled her nose, an expression that often revealed her dissatisfaction, which was quite frequent. As she nibbled on the delicate morsel, Vinesia watched the commotion of the upcoming animata showing.

"I hear these animata are sexual. Maybe I'll get one. Breeze already has his hands full with all the things I need done." Corenya smiled with a devious twist of her lip.

Vinesia thought she recognized someone pacing back and forth on the docks. She looked closer and froze. It was Loressai. She watched the woman's feral behavior with some trepidation. When Loressai arrived in the palace for the first time, it was the beginning of the end for all of them. Vinesia realized she had been harboring blame and resentment all this time. She opened her eyes to dreamsight. Corenya's chattering became background noise. What she saw made her shiver.

Floating above the marketplace, it was evident the fog covered only the cartel docks. Brigitte and Lukias hovered in dreambody. Energy swirled above the city, a visible wind caught up in an elemental torrent. The dreamclan brother and sister watched the fog form into a web over the market. The ethereal sound of chanting drifted through the air, suggesting the fog was trapped by magic. On the outskirts of the fog stood a ring of people dressed in black, the source of the chanting. People with the madness stumbled toward the docks.

Brigitte and Lukias knew they had little time to recover their vulnerable bodies lying dormant in the hover-carriage with Allondriss. Stixxus and the furies would defend them, but for how long?

They directed their dreambodies into the soup of fog and followed the apex of the web over the central market, where three entities hovered in the air. Their bodies were made up of the darkest pitch. Their appendages seeped into the fog as if to wield the elements. Their faces were hollow voids. Pinpoints of red glowed where their eyes would be.v

One had engulfed a woman, the one Brigitte recognized as the target of their new conclave allies. One stayed at the crux of the fog, weaving it like a web, and the other, to Brigitte's overwhelming dismay, hovered over D'Vinid.

"Brigitte! We must enter the blue-dream frequency now!" Lukias projected.

But it was too late. The creature hovering over D'Vinid had already noticed her. It hurled itself toward them with a terrible screech. Brigitte froze in fear. Thoughts of the storm that hunted her people laid siege to her mind.

Lukias moved in front of her. The outline of his rugged face took shape in the essence of his spirit form. He urged her to lift her heart and release the fear. It pushed her into action. Together they shifted their dreambodies into the secret blue level of Dreamtime, which now seemed to be ideally crafted for hiding from these creatures. The entity flew past them, suddenly blinded to their presence. It floated around the market with the anger of a beast having lost its prey.

Once they entered the blue-dream frequency, she could see some of the group who called themselves the Children of One spread through the marketplace. They walked invisible to most, cloaked in the blue mist. She swooped down to the one who appeared to be their leader, the one who had spoken to her before.

Atheerian Telleria had already witnessed what the shadowmancers were willing to do the night before when they almost killed him in their ritual sacré moré. He looked at her pleadingly. *"You can lure these creatures to the nodeyard. We will take care of the rest. Once they enter the perimeter, they will be unable to harm you."* He signaled to his team, and they all fell back.

Brigitte gestured to her brother who still did not approve of using her as bait.

"I have to save him." Her ethereal eyes referred to D'Vinid.

Lukias sighed in reluctant acceptance. *"Let's do this fast and get back to our bodies. I will spot you."*

A man stepped out onto the viewing stage and called out for the attention of those assembled. The Children of One stared at him. Atheerian was gripped in a surge of panic. The man was the same one who had killed himself at the height of the eclipse. His face was empty of tattoos where there had been before. He was dressed

137

in the clothing of a merchant.

Atheerian thought for a moment that he was mistaken. But a closer examination revealed the scar on the neck of the fallen shadowmancer. He began shouting, and his voice was unmistakable. "The Children of One are upon us!" His words added to the confusion of citizens already alarmed by the fog.

Citizens at the market were frozen in fear, making ready to head for the exits. The docks would be an awkward place to be stuck. The zealot's eyes were wide and serious. "They walk among us like ghosts! They have stolen the power of the Watchers! It is forbidden for those outside the temples to possess such powers! They must be stopped! They will be the downfall of Atlantis! You wait and see! They have declared themselves akin to Watchers and they will be punished for their arrogance!"

D'Vinid felt the locator-crystal pulse to life. He took it between his fingers, projecting his thoughts to reveal his location to Ofira. Guardians came to usher away the man on the stage. He continued his rant, raising his voice higher. "It is they who have caused this madness! They have stolen from us! When one of them takes from the Grid, another of us falls to the madness!" His shouting trailed off as he was dragged away by guards.

D'Vinid felt a shiver up and down his spine. A voice whispered in his thoughts: *"D'Vinid, why are you marked?"* He turned around quickly. But no one stood nearby. No one seemed to even pay attention to him, except, of course, Loressai.

A rush of triumph washed over him as Ofira Pazit materialized from the fog. Riding her hover-disc, she skimmed the water to the central platform and bounced onto her feet. She stomped on the disc with her foot. It clicked closed as it flipped into her hand. "D'Vinid, now would be a good time for the blue-dream awakening," she said breathlessly, tucking the disc into the sack at her hip.

He recognized the urgency in her eyes. The words were more than a suggestion. His fingers fumbled for the vial of blue liquid as she approached Jonda Dex.

"I'm waiting for this fog to lift before my showing!" His booming voice was edged with anxiety.

Ofira reached for a small sack she carried inside the hover-disc bag. "Here is your payment. Three vials of sha'mana. I will take my warrior now, if you please."

He looked into the sack and cracked a smile. As she stepped toward the animata, he blocked her path. "One more thing," he grinned, revealing a golden tooth. "I would ask for a kiss to seal the deal."

Ofira balled up her fists. "Jonda Dex. I would not kiss you even if the Watchers threatened to take my ship. You disgust me. Get out of my way."

He reached his giant hand around her waist. "You are so lovely when you're angry."

She twisted nimbly past his reach and made contact with the warrior. She focused into its eyes to bond with the imprinter-crystal in its brain. The warrior animated and stepped between them.

"D'Vinid," she barked. "You'd better hurry."

"D'Vinid!" Jonda declared. "The Prophet Singer? You lied to me!"

"The liar has been fooled, and he's upset about it," she snorted to D'Vinid.

"Now I'm hurt, little captain," he pouted. "I told you the truth earlier about the animata! Don't you think you owe me something?"

"I owe you a kick in the head." Ofira looked past him nervously. "But I will tell you the truth. We are all in grave danger right now. We need to get out of here." She tossed the hover-disc to the dock and hopped on.

D'Vinid swallowed the blue elixir. A strange, liquid sensation began to rearrange his molecules. He looked at his hands. They were still hands, though they felt like they had lost their cohesion. His focus shifted, and he could see into an unusual pocket of Dreamtime.

His movement seemed to manipulate a subtle, blue-translucent mist. He waved his hand around, watching the paths his hands created in the dense misty layer of blue essence. As he scanned the area, he noticed a blue apparition hovering beside him. Startled, he jumped. "You!" he gasped.

Brigitte's ghostly appendages reached out to encompass him. Her almond eyes took shape in her misty form, watching him urgently. *You must leave here now.* She touched his head, and he could see what she wanted him to see. The profound love that had ignited in his heart quickly turned to terror, as another being

139

materialized over them both. Its pitch-blackness blended into the fog. Its eerie red eyes watched him. A blast of cold seeped into his bones.

Another creature just like it hovered over Loressai, its shadowy appendages reaching into her body. Guilt seized his heart. He felt as though this was his fault. A rush of adrenalin boosted his movements. "I have to try and help her!" He looked pleadingly at the apparition of Brigitte. "Whatever you are, if you are a Watcher, have pity on Loressai. Don't let them take her!"

Ofira grabbed him by the arm. "We need to get out of here. Now."

He wavered, and his breath trembled as he watched the black figure reach further into Loressai's body, animating her like she was its puppet. Her lips fluttered into a wicked grin.

"*You can save her if you run, D'Vinid.*" Brigitte's voice appeared in his head. "*Don't look back.*"

Without a word, he sprung his hover-disc open with a flick of the wrist, tossed it, and hopped on in one fluid motion. He was relieved to discover he was slowly regaining his trickster skills.

Watching from the viewing platform, Vinesia leapt to her feet. "Stay here, Aunt. You will be safe now." She hurried off into the crowd in pursuit of the action.

Together, D'Vinid and Ofira bounced through the docks, trying to avoid the many people who had become obscured in the fog. The hair on D'Vinid's neck stood on end. He knew the creature was in pursuit. He widened his stance, leaning over to pick up speed. The fog had to end somewhere.

"What about your warrior?" D'Vinid called out to Ofira as she sprung off the side of a crate to avoid hitting some frightened shoppers.

"Don't worry about that. I am bonded with it. It will come to me when I command."

They cleared the cartel docks, but the fog remained.

Loressai emerged from the docks, sprinting at unnatural speed. The blackness was attached to her as if it had become part of her body. D'Vinid wanted to continue but he remained engrossed as Loressai stopped and turned her attention to the apparition of Brigitte, who very purposefully shifted her body from the blue-dream into the shallows of Dreamtime.

Like an animal, she began sniffing the air. The shadow creature consumed her. The puppet master dug its dark claws deeper into her body. The other shadow entity followed D'Vinid. It did not have the same hold on him. Yet the more guilt he felt at seeing Loressai, the more he could feel its icy touch.

"What are you doing, D'Vinid?" Ofira called back, while making a wide loop on her disc. D'Vinid's heart clenched as he realized where Loressai was heading. In a parking alcove, surrounded by four fury warriors, rested the same carriage in which Brigitte and her brother had departed from Pan's estate.

Brigitte realized her ploy to lead the creatures to the nodeyard had failed. They were too smart. They understood she was separated from her physical body, which meant somewhere she was lying completely vulnerable. She had no choice but to re-enter her body.

She opened her eyes to the concerned look of Allondriss. Lukias's eyes fluttered open a heartbeat later.

"We have to lead her there on foot," Lukias whispered harshly. "Are you ready?" He turned his eyes to Allondriss. "You'd better wait here. It will follow us, and if I'm right, you will be safe once we leave."

Outside the carriage, Loressai jumped onto the back of a fury warrior, sinking her teeth into his neck.

Brigitte and Lukias dove from the carriage and made a break for the nodeyard.

Seeing this, D'Vinid sped back on the hover-disc, ignoring Ofira's warning to keep going.

Brigitte and Lukias ran with surprising agility.

Loressai disengaged the fury, leaving him twitching and bleeding.

The other three furies pounced on her.

"Stixxus!" Brigitte called back. "With us!"

The fury leader left the other two to fight and ran to catch up with his charges. When they reached the nodeyard, they turned back to see Loressai in hot pursuit, somehow disengaged from her attackers.

Just before she reached the nodeyard, D'Vinid hovered between them and dismounted from the disc.

He reached a hand out to Loressai. "Don't hurt these people!" he demanded. "Whatever you want from me, you can have it."

Loressai stopped outside the perimeter of the nodeyard.

Brigitte and the others cringed, hoping they would take a few steps into the waiting blue web created by the conclave.

"Very well. We will take you, then." The entity above him closed in on D'Vinid, reaching into him like the one who had taken Loressai.

D'Vinid reached out his arms and surrendered. "Leave this place!" he called back to Brigitte. The black tentacles wrapped around him, sinking into his dreambody. He began trembling. Tears rolled down his cheeks. "I am sorry, Loressai," he moaned in pain. "I am sorry for what I did to you and Kyliron. I have always regretted what I did." He sank to a knee, trying to fight the pain.

The rage in Loressai's eyes faded for a moment. A tear rolled down her cheek. "D'Vinid," she gasped.

"You are a fool!" the shadow screeched as it dug into his body. *"There's no giving yourself to us. You are already taken. You gave yourself to us cycles ago when you surrendered to your guilt."* Laughter ripped through the nodeyard as the creature burrowed deeper into D'Vinid's flesh. *"I will take you, and then your friends will die."*

Seeing this, Vinesia lifted her arms, weaving a ball of crackling electricity. She sent it hurling at D'Vinid. His body seized from the jolt. The shock wave from the blast sucked the air out of the node-yard, causing the demonic creature to shrink.

Ofira tackled D'Vinid into the nodeyard, hurling herself at full speed on the disc, and throwing herself bodily through the air. They landed close to the crystal-node.

Loressai took a few steps toward them, placing her at last in the waiting trap. The Children of One were ready for her. The node began to resonate. The sound maintained its oscillation between dissonance and harmony. Everyone in earshot recoiled.

D'Vinid's eyes flashed orange, and the entity retracted from his body, retreating into the fog. Its shrieking, pain-filled screech sailed through the air.

Loressai collapsed on the ground. A sunbeam broke through the clouds, rapidly dissolving the fog.

Brigitte uncovered her ears and rushed to D'Vinid's side. They melted into a hug. She noticed recognition in D'Vinid's eyes and looked up at Vinesia, who rushed into the circle.

Lukias reached his hand out to Ofira and yanked her to her feet.

"Didn't think I would see you two again so soon," Ofira smiled at the dreamseer, and then to Brigitte.

D'Vinid pointed back and forth between them. "You brought them here?"

"Dreamclans. Dreamshiiiip," Ofira sang.

Looking around, they realized the Children of One had taken their solid forms. Brigitte marveled at their skill. Projecting her consciousness into dreambody was very different than lifting the molecules of her physical form into Dreamtime. They moved toward Loressai's unconscious body.

"We will take her," one of the men spoke as another scooped her up. Their leader had a powerful presence. His hair and beard were cut in jagged patterns, framing his chiseled face. Gratitude shown in his expression. He approached Vinesia. "Was that you who sent that elemental blast?"

She nodded.

"What method are you using?"

She glanced at D'Vinid. "It is the Dance of the Elementa. It's a dreamclan method."

Brigitte and Lukias locked eyes with the newcomer. She was impossibly beautiful though simply dressed. She did radiate a spark of telluric consciousness.

"I learned it from someone named Vektra."

D'Vinid wondered why Vinesia was lying. He knew it was her dreamclan mother that taught her the Grid dance. He could tell in her expression that she wanted him to keep his mouth shut.

Brigitte reached out to clasp the leader's hand. "What is your name?"

"I am called Atheerian Telleria. We are in your debt, emissary."

"Where are you taking her?" D'Vinid demanded.

The sound of a horn blurted through the area. The conclave faded back into Dreamtime, taking Loressai with them. Atheerian raised his hood with one last look at Brigitte. As if he had stepped across a threshold, his body faded into invisibility.

"All hail, King Kyliron!" a blaring voice followed.

D'Vinid froze in dismay. He looked at Brigitte, breathless. "Come with me." His expression was deflated. He began inching away.

"I can't." Brigitte's triumph collapsed.

Ofira wrapped her arm around his shoulders and guided him in the other direction. He wrapped his other arm around Vinesia and they all slipped into the multiplying crowd.

Brigitte watched as he left, feeling helpless. She debated whether to follow. But, how could she? Her moment had arrived. She watched D'Vinid. He threw her one last pained expression before he quickly made his exit.

Her attention shifted as they passed a man watching from the crowd. It was the same man that had shouted from the viewing stage in the market earlier. He stood out from the others like a drop of black ink in a pool of color. A frozen smile wrinkled his face.

Lukias grabbed her arm, nodding toward the arriving royal entourage. The man in black turned to follow D'Vinid. His body faded into Dreamtime. Her heart was ripped in half as she turned to face King Kyliron, the man to whom she had always been betrothed.

A tunnel stretched impossibly in both directions, making it seem as though one could walk forever. The underground passage was made of smoothly-hewn granite. The way was lit by luminescent moss growing from the walls. The High Priestess of the Temple Sect walked alone, adorned with the flowing white and gold robe of the Alta. The ball of rose quartz atop her crystal staff had ignited to light the way. The air was as still as death.

Eventually the walls gave way to a yawning cavern. On the far end, a smooth wall of water fell into an aqua-colored lake. Dancing lights played off the tumbling waterfall, casting its shimmering chaos on the walls of the cave. These were fresh waters flowing from the heart of the mountain. An underground channel connected the lake to the ocean. It was said to be a sacred place where oceanid royalty held court with the most privileged of Atlantean temple nobility.

In the center of the lake was a small island upon which a fire raged in a massive cauldron. Above it was suspended a throne where a woman sat, her golden hair flowing over the edges. Her eyes were closed. The High Priestess tapped her staff on the ground. A singing resonance echoed through the cavern, and its light brightened. The woman on the throne opened her eyes.

"I bring greetings to the Oracle of the Six Realms!" the priestess called out. Her voice ricocheted through the cave.

"High Priestess of Atlantis. I welcome you." The woman's voice cracked as if it had not been used in ages.

"I have come for your wise guidance, Oracle."

"Your questions have been brought to me by the elementals. You have chosen to activate the Nexes lockdown protocol."

"Yes." The priestess had regret in her voice.

"Your caution is indeed necessary. The Blood Triad has descended on this land. The three Nephilim rulers of the Bloodfire Nations have been released from their icy prison with more hatred in their hearts than ever they once possessed. Their dreambodies are twisted into vengeance. They seek to dominate Atlantis.

"But Belial has returned, using his cunning. They do not know of his presence. There is another who works from within to bring back the Triad. Seek out the shadow who hides in the faces of many. He has deceived even you. If they take over the Grid, they will have more power than they must ever be allowed."

The priestess nodded. "So, I am correct in disconnecting the Nexes."

"You possess the key, do you not?"

The priestess lowered her eyes. "It is hidden from me."

"If the key returns to you, then it will serve as a sign that your decision is correct. The Grid of Atlantis must not fall into the hands of those who would misuse it. If the Triad succeeds, the Grid must be destroyed. Remember this, only humanity can choose to rise above this. It is the task of the Moirae Dreamclan Emissary to judge the fate of Atlantis. The Watchers will do what they can to assist you, and so will the elements… You have another question."

The priestess produced the summoner-crystal given to her by the kallista in Kyliron's chambers. "At the beginning of the third age, a genetic project was initiated among the temples. This is the generation they are supposed to take form. I have watched my whole life for signs of their awakening. Today I have met one at last."

The Oracle's eyes rolled back in her head. Moments became swallowed in convulsive thought until she opened her eyes and spoke again. "As you seek to isolate the Archives Nexes, your actions will initiate the shutdown of the Atlantis Project. These Lost Temple Children you created will be the ones destined to disassemble the Grid. But they can also re-assemble it. There are those born with the upgrade who have been altered. Beware of your creations, High Priestess. They can spell the doom of Atlantis.

"They have already been unleashed upon the world. They will bind themselves to the planetary being, Sophaiya, until the Grid is ready to be assembled again. Even if it takes millions of rotations around the solar entity, they will return and destroy what is in the way of unity, so the human project may continue.

"They operate in secret, and yet they are more advanced than even they understand. They are wild, and if you do not nurture your creations, they will accelerate this destruction. They wish to understand the reason for their existence. You must help them understand."

"How do I find them?"

"The key to Nexes will have the power to activate all of them. They cloak themselves in mists of blue. King Koraxx knew of them. He tried to eliminate their practices. Beware of his son, the one who has taken on Koraxx's folly. The other son is destined for greatness. His fate has been activated. He will find his way soon and take his place among your Lost Temple Children.

"The elements are your allies, High Priestess. Take care to recognize the signs they leave. The oceanids are on the rise. They have taken notice of the change in vibration emanating from the powerful Grid of Atlantis. They will destroy the Grid before you if you are not careful. Look to them as you initiate your lockdown of Nexes. You will know the way. All is in your capable hands now."

As a girl growing up, Brigitte would catch glimpses of his face in her dreams, the boy named Prince Kyliron. His eyes burned into her memory. She always thought she loved him. But often he visited her nightmares. She closed her eyes to send a prayer to Belial. The time had arrived when she would once again meet the man who had always inhabited her visions.

She lifted her eyes and tried to swallow the lump in her throat. Brigitte could not bring herself to look at his face at first. Trembling with anguished apprehension, she forced herself to step into his presence. He scanned the group with a predatory spark in his dark, shining eyes. A jeweled crown rested on top of jet-black hair, cropped close to his head in thin strands. His long neck was adorned with an ornate necklace of orichalcum, and a large aqua pendant rested on his throat.

He glimpsed Brigitte with calm intelligence, just as her eyes lifted from the pendant to look at him. Their gazes locked, and Brigitte knew him at once. The boy had grown, his face shaped into the rugged, masculine angles of manhood. All surrounding sounds faded into the background as Brigitte and Kyliron renewed their psychic link. It was as if no time had passed since their first meeting as children.

In a moment of seeming endlessness they became one. Her body refused to move. She felt if she stood there holding her breath, she would wake up from a dream, and be back home in her own bed. The moment continued, nonetheless.

One disturbing thought remained in her mind: D'Vinid. At the memory of his face, her entire body lit up. She cursed the fact that they had been reunited in the moments of Kyliron's arrival. The Watchers had played a mean trick on her heart. In the moment she had prepared for all her life, the face of another man was the motivation guiding her toward her designated mate. The danger was staggering. She wanted to hope she would never see the musician again, but desired to see him above all things. She attempted to bury him deep in her heart instead.

A priest robed in light blue approached the node. He was one of the record-keepers of the Temple Sect. They dealt with the transfer of information and knowledge, and among those duties was the function of VC waves. The priest took out a small crystal, presumably a programmer, and ran it over the crystal-node.

Kyliron waited for the record-keeper to program the crystal-node so it would record this moment to be featured on viewer-crystals around Atlantis. Those citizens who hurried to the scene immediately recognized they were involved in a VC transmission being recorded for all time. The word spread as quickly as the hush that followed.

The priest nodded, and Kyliron began his speech. "I am pleased to see you have made it to Poseidia, Brigitte of the ocean's dreamclan." Kyliron's voice rang through a dreamlike silence. He guided her tenderly to face him. His pose was lofty. His copper beauty shone in the sunlight. To those who were fleeing the cartel docks, it looked as though the king had dispersed the fog. They felt as though the fear had been banished by his arrival.

Brigitte met his gaze, spellbound by his resplendence, reluctant to speak, for fear she had lost her voice in the panic of her heart.

"You are more beautiful than I imagined." He assessed her from head to toe. His movements were like a pantomime, staged not only for her but also for everyone assembled. To those who watched, their meeting was the romance anyone could ever hope to experience. But his eyes said something only she could see.

He gently rearranged her wild auburn locks to spill down her back, watching the way her hair fell. He lifted her hand to his lips. But he closed his eyes. Though his actions were a show of gallantry, he seemed only interested in her outer appearance. She searched for his eyes, trying to mimic the way she had become lost in D'Vinid's. He avoided her gaze, and looked around at the gathering crowd, holding up her hand to show her off.

A gasp emerged from the audience. Kyliron was the image of perfection; an icon, just as the Adonis of legend who remained unreachable for all women. And now, as his betrothed took her place at his side, a flash of envy rippled through the city, and quickly turned to inspiration at the sight of Brigitte's otherworldliness. News traveled quickly. The dreamclans had finally arrived to take their place at the heart of Atlantis in the name of the Watchers. The frail mood of the city shifted.

Brigitte wondered how the king had found them, until she caught sight of the priest and priestess who accompanied them to the cartel docks. They stood with another man, who had the alabaster skin tone of a priest, but did not dress in a traditional Temple Sect robe. Instead, his dress was rich like a mediator's, suggesting wealth and status. He had an imposing presence. A circlet on his bald head suggested he was a member of the High Council.

King Kyliron signaled to him. At his approach, Brigitte scanned him with dreamsight, half-expecting he would have a shadow attached. To her relief, he didn't.

He strode toward them, his arms held wide in welcome. "I am relieved you have been found at last, Brigitte. I am Jamarish Ka, temple delegate of the High Council and the king's maydrian. I bid you welcome to Atlantis," he bowed with a flair. He turned to Lukias and glanced briefly at the furies. "Your companions?"

"Oh, yes," Brigitte nodded her head. "Forgive my rudeness. Allow me to present my elder brother, Lukias." She paused awkwardly. "He is high seer of our dreamclan."

"I see. And what of your father, Denikon?" asked Jamarish Ka.

"It is with great despair that I inform you of his demise." Her eyes slid to Kyliron. "Our clan was attacked by a horde of shadows from Dreamtime. It is only by the grace of the Watchers we have survived and come to these shores alive."

Kyliron's eyes clouded over, and darted to the blue-robed priest, but the priest was already ahead of him. He had cut off the VC transmission in the midst of her statement.

"This is grave news," Jamarish Ka consoled. His eyes studied the king's reaction carefully.

"Obviously, my Queen Impending has been through much." Kyliron's voice was tinged with irritation. He pulled her into his embrace, and lifted her chin delicately, whispering, "So much sadness." He pouted his lower lip, while gently caressing the side of her face. "We must bring you at once to your suites where you will be safe. And you can bring your fury warriors for protection." He was very aware of the gathering crowd.

"I have stored this transmission in my downloader-crystal, Your Majesty." The record-keeper priest nodded to Brigitte. "My Queen," he bowed, a hint of regret in his eyes. "My condolences to you and your brother on the news of your clan."

"Thank you for your kindness," Brigitte bowed back.

"My dear, I trust you have been well tutored in the decorum of your station, but a queen bows to no one but her king," Kyliron chuckled.

Brigitte noticed Allondriss among the gathering onlookers.

"Your Majesty," Brigitte smiled, "if it's all the same to you, I choose to honor those who treat me with kindness. A queen is still human is she not?"

Jamarish Ka nodded. "Should we be on our way? I guarantee you the council will vote for the ceremony to take place this night, in time for the third night of Ka-Ma-Sharri. Our gracious Queen Impending will need as much rest as she can get."

"If you please, we have our own hover-carriage," said Brigitte. "I would like to keep it, if possible."

Jamarish Ka chuckled. "You will have access to the finest hover-craft in all of Atlantis, my lady."

"The lady wishes to keep her carriage," Kyliron snapped. "I will ride with you, my love." He trapped her arm in the crook of his elbow and pulled her along. As they walked, the people naturally parted, forming an aisle to let them pass. Brigitte was careful to meet the eyes of the people and send them respect. As they neared the carriage, she reached out to Allondriss.

"This is my companion and adviser on Atlantean ways. She will be joining us."

The king nodded and helped Allondriss into the carriage like a perfect nobleman. After Brigitte and Lukias entered, Kyliron blocked Jamarish Ka.

"I want to know exactly what happened here," he said, gesturing to the wounded fury warrior, who was now being attended by a priestess. "I wish for you to stay and be sure your investigation continues. Take my hover-carriage when you are finished."

"As you wish, Your Majesty." Jamarish Ka bowed and stepped backward.

One of Kyliron's servants climbed aboard the carriage to take control of its imprinter panel.

"This is an impressive vehicle," Kyliron remarked, as he made himself comfortable beside Brigitte. His eyes landed on Allondriss. "Aren't you a curiosity. Temple Sect?"

"No, Your Majesty," Allondriss looked downward.

"She is my companion." Brigitte's tone suggested she wished the subject changed.

Stixxus and the remaining two furies fell into step on the road, along with the entourage of servants who accompanied the king. The crowd from the market followed. Word spread quickly. As they made their ascent through the remainder of the citadel, their makeshift royal parade became a source of increasing interest. Brigitte's exhausting and dangerous journey quickly transformed into a spectacle, with fanfare more befitting the arrival of the new Queen of Atlantis.

8

Celebrations through the night,
to strike the flame of life to light.
Underneath the shining moon
is Ka-Ma-Sha's unerring boon.
Maiden touched by lover's match,
yet seeing some new plot to hatch.

*E*vening sank over Poseidia's majestic tiers as nodesong echoed across the heights of the citadel. The sky radiated orange and purple hues, reflecting off dark clouds in the distance. The moon was a sliver less than full, having been eclipsed the night before. Its light gradually lifted over an oceanic horizon, as large as the city itself.

Resounding horns echoed across the city's steps, proclaiming the last night of Ka-Ma-Sharri. It was a night of solemnity, when Belial and Kama were separated once again. Atlanteans looked to one another for community. Music and laughter echoed from all directions.

The appearance of Vinesia had filled D'Vinid with nostalgia for what they all once had. Bavendrick and Vinesia were the perfect model of devotion. Everyone wanted what they had. And when the time came for them to seal their love at last, the Fates ruined everything. Many lost faith in the perfection of love after that. No one rejoiced when Kyliron promised Bavendrick to the Princess of Og. Koraxx was considered a tyrant, but Kyliron was becoming an imbecile.

Dimples formed in his cheeks as he pressed his lips together, squeezing Vinesia's hand. "I can't tell you how much I needed your light today, Vinesia," he said. "It is good to see you."

She laid her head on his shoulder with a glance to Ofira. "I don't understand much of what I just saw."

"That makes two of us," he answered with an uneasy laugh.

"Three of us," added Ofira. She stared at Vinesia.

"Not even you, Ofira Pazit?" Vinesia laughed. "You seem to always be at the heart of the matter. And how fares Dragonspine? Sometimes I miss my home island."

"I was just there, in fact. Your mother sent me with a messenger-crystal to give to you."

"I got her message. From my Aunt Corenya." She glared at Ofira.

"It does you well to mingle with the citizenry," D'Vinid changed the subject.

"There are no expectations among the working sect. No families betraying one another for the sake of status." Despite maintaining her resentment, there was a grounded solid quality about her. It was different than her sprightly manner as a lady of the courts, but it radiated a calmness that felt good to be around. She stopped and patted his hand. "My aunt is back there in the market. I should go fetch her. You will see me again, D'Vinid."

"You should take the messenger," Ofira warned.

"Keep it," she answered.

"I saw him," D'Vinid called after her as she walked away. She looked back. "He's still good and perfect."

She turned away with a sad smile.

D'Vinid walked with Ofira in the failing sunlight. Flower petals drifted through the air, floating specks of color dotting his vision. He couldn't shake the memory of how he had felt when Brigitte's carriage disappeared, or the sickness he felt when he turned his back on her because he couldn't face Kyliron.

Brigitte had captured his attention completely, and he was not sure how it could be possible. He told himself the obsession would soon pass. She was simply another beautiful woman he could not reach. He knew it was this very fact which made her so desirable. The less he could have her, the more he wanted her. He just had to wait out the fever.

He listened with Ofira to the gentle sound of crystal-nodes, as the setting sun brightened the horizon into a vivid orange masterpiece. D'Vinid kept his eyes down while weaving through the alluring stares of fashionably beautiful would-be lovers. Not even Ofira's wiles could distract him.

His heart set with the sun. He took a deep breath as they reached *Dafni's Enigma*, where his first love awaited. He went to her immediately, caressed her silky strings. Taking her into his embrace was all he usually needed to feel better. But even she didn't comfort him this evening. She sounded the same at the strum of his fingers, but now Kyliron had managed to extend his ever-pursuing shadow over his beloved dabrina.

His hands shook. He felt miserable. What was he, but a charlatan and a maverick with a lazy, self-indulgent lifestyle? Kyliron was the High King of Atlantis. Surely a king would always be more important than D'Vinid. He never understood why Kyliron was so threatened by him.

He put his head down just to close his eyes for a few moments. He was drowning in regret. As he lay in his cabin, that familiar liquid sensation filled him. His heart pounded like a drum, threatening to deafen him to all other sounds. *"I am for I am thou,"* a voice reverberated through the incessant heartbeat. His vision went black. His heart pounded harder.

Loressai Torbin's voice emerged in an ethereal whisper. *"You can stop this before it happens."*

"Loressai?" He twitched, looking around in the darkness. But another vision faded into view.

Brigitte stood before him, dressed in the finest of Atlantean noblewear. She was alluring beyond all temptation. He reached out to touch her, but she faded away. He burned for her, longed to touch her again.

Suddenly he was in the royal courtyard. Brigitte graced a balcony, overlooking throngs of people.

Kyliron appeared at her side, his eyes red-rimmed and bloodshot. He took her into his arms.

D'Vinid wanted to cry out, but his voice would not cooperate.

In front of the entire kingdom, Kyliron suddenly grabbed her by the hair and yanked her head back. He struck her across the face with the back of his other hand. She crumpled to the ground.

D'Vinid startled back to awareness. Darkness had engulfed the cabin. His dabrina lay beside him. Quickly, he rolled over, and carried his instrument into the main hold of the ship.

Ofira sat on the stage measuring his mood.

"You're still here?" he marveled. "Don't you have a ship to command?"

"Oh, D'Vinid. I will leave soon. Don't you worry about that. I have one more thing to help you with."

"Oh, is this another one of your jobs from the Watchers?" He tried not to sound bitter as he wrestled with the seething anger he carried toward Kyliron. He didn't want to take it out on Ofira.

"You did a good job earlier," she remarked.

"What do you mean?" he grumbled.

"You offered to sacrifice yourself. I didn't think you had it in you. One could say it was heroic. Stupid, but heroic."

He shrugged and looked down at his dabrina. He touched the new tuning peg and traced his finger down the crack leading to the once-hidden symbol now defacing his beloved companion. Having been protected all his life, the symbol stood out, perfect and untouched by the cycles of time. It filled him with dread and shame.

He couldn't imagine why his mother would have hidden the sigil of King Koraxx on her dabrina. There were no stories he could muster from his imagination to offer an explanation. Perhaps it was a magical instrument she had stolen from his treasure trove. Or perhaps they knew one another. This would explain how his father had become captain of the royal flagship.

He thought of his father, the long-lost captain of *Dafni's Enigma*. Captain Chaldeis always kept his eye on the horizon, forever searching for his missing love who had been D'Vinid's mother. When he left, he claimed to be on a dangerous mission to find her on a far-off shore where no mortal could go. For the first time in his life, D'Vinid wondered if his journey was into the Dreamvale. Lukias and Pan had said the same name: Indrius. His father never said her name. "You brought Brigitte and her brother to Poseidia," he said to Ofira. "Where did they come from?"

"I told you already. From the dreamclans."

"I have never understood the dreamclans," he admitted, as his fingers slid up and down the silky dabrina strings.

She laughed. "Dreamclans live in the valley between the Meridian Realm and Dreamtime. The Dreamvale. It is the place between waking and sleep. In fact, everyone goes there on a daily basis."

"Can you take anyone there?"

She frowned. "Into the Dreamvale? Yes. To Brigitte's clan, I don't think so." She visibly shivered. "If you think what we experienced today was terrifying, what I saw there would turn your hair white."

"What happened to all the people you left behind?"

Ofira shook her head. "I don't think they made it. They sacrificed themselves so Brigitte and Lukias could escape."

His fingers ran nimbly up and down the dabrina. There were still eleven sets of strings, though he now had 12 pegs to tune them with. A few easy twists of the pegs, and the instrument sang in perfect harmony. Everyone inside stopped their conversations to pay attention.

He wondered about Loressai as his fingers absently improvised a melody.

"*I am for I am thou.*" The words appeared in his head as if audible. He paused and looked around, thinking perhaps someone had spoken. Ofira watched him carefully. His fingers began again almost without his consent. Words spilled from his lips with a singing voice that could rend the heart of even the most jaded soul.

> "There were once two brothers.
> Both loved a girl.
> Both became her lover,
> one more than the other,
> though the other loved her more.
>
> All have lost their way.
> Nothing more to say.
> Afraid to apologize,
> all would personify
> the spiral to guilt and shame.
>
> There is a debt to be paid,
> a story yet to be told.
> In time the fire will be stayed
> or magnified tenfold."

When King Kyliron and his Queen Impending reached the palace, a crowd swarmed the base of the steps. Brigitte greeted their wonder with a weary smile as she emerged from the carriage. Lukias stole a look at Allondriss, who seemed just as nervous as Brigitte. He reached out his arm to escort her, mimicking the king's gallantry. Kyliron waved to the people while carefully guiding Brigitte to the looming threshold of the royal audience chamber.

As she prepared to take her first steps into the palace, Brigitte recalled echoes of her lonesome childhood by the seashore. The ocean's song had always been her refuge. She strained but couldn't make out the distant surf past miles of city. She felt strangely isolated outside its sound.

She wanted to cry out. Madness crept into her thoughts. An icy chill of apprehension caught her in a mental backpedaling frenzy. But instead of succumbing to its power, she allowed herself to draw on the calm strength of her companions and move forward.

They stood within fractal lights and rainbow patterns spilling through stained glass in the domed ceiling. Brigitte tossed her head back to bathe in the colors.

"Welcome to your new home," Kyliron's smile radiated. She gawked at the intricate oceanic statue that served as a throne. The High Council entered the royal audience hall in single file to meet their Queen Impending. Seven council delegates governed seven Atlantean Sects. Together they made up the highest authority in the land next to the king and queen. Each one fixed their attention on Brigitte.

Six of seven delegates were introduced. Jamarish Ka was the seventh, though he had remained in the city. The names of the others quickly vanished, swept into the current of her panic. She relied on Lukias and Kyliron to do all the talking. Allondriss stayed at Brigitte's side, her face and hands hidden in her embroidered overcoat. Stixxus and the furies stood in the background.

Just when she felt she could handle no more, one of the High Council women – perhaps the warrior delegate, for she had the same emblem as Pan Aello – seemed to take pity, and urged them to allow her a rest.

The only interaction that stuck in her mind was the discussion of their joining ceremony, which would commence at the height of the moon. She tried to imagine how she would muster the strength. Despite their many delays, they were still on time for her to be joined during the exalted festival of Ka-Ma-Sharri, though not during the eclipse. By the time the sun rose, Brigitte would be High Queen of Atlantis. Expediency was necessary, as the Telluric Treaty needed to be sealed before elementals were released from their service to the Grid.

Kyliron left to prepare while the rest of them were led down a series of brightly lit hallways, their polished mosaic surfaces gleaming. Stone hallways gave way to tubes of paned glass looking into magnificent garden scenes, their views obstructed only by thick, growing trees. Brigitte's thoughts whirled, and she didn't know whether to cry for it to stop, or to let herself swim in the glory of it.

Numbly, she allowed herself to be brought to the suites designated as her new home. Her thoughts lingered on Kyliron. His elegant mannerisms and robust physique made her heart flutter anxiously. Brigitte had loathed him and loved him all at once for as long as she could remember.

She could barely keep her eyes open to examine the rooms, which were luxurious beyond what she had ever imagined. The sitting room emptied into a chamber where the bed was obscured behind curtains and raised on a platform. Mirrored walls were lined with lush plants, making the rooms look even more expansive. An archway enticed her outside following delicate flower essences to a balcony overlooking an expanse of gardens.

Carved stairs curved up to a large tub of white marble and black onyx inlaid with gold. A wall of windows overlooked the garden. The tub was filled with steaming, aromatic water. Beyond, another room was enclosed by glass, perhaps a hot steam room, as she had been taught Atlanteans were fond of.

In the main room of the suite, an open archway led to a garden patio. Stairs descended to a polished pathway, where blooming trees and thick foliage quickly swallowed them. The garden seemed maintained exclusively for whoever lived in the suite. It was the perfect gilded habitat. At least her captivity promised unsurpassed luxury. Drunk from the fragrances, she sauntered back to the bed.

The thought of D'Vinid flooded her eyes with tears. She laid the rose on the pillow, and silently wept herself to sleep.

The main hold of *Dafni's Enigma* filled with D'Vinid's fans as word spread through the Outlands that he was making a public appearance. The revelry spilled out into the Harbor District esplanade. He had not really given thought to how much they loved him. Perhaps his own sense of self-loathing made him unable to accept it. He looked on them with new eyes as they focused on his music.

For the first time, he wondered how they would all react to the king's decree. Pan's plan began to make sense. He watched how his music moved their reactions. He had always played with no regard for their emotions, but now his attitude was changed. He scanned their eager faces, and this time, he allowed himself to care.

Dabrina chords folded around D'Vinid's voice. His fingers wove a poetic approximation of underwater arpeggios.

"The realms of possibility have fallen into dream
as echoes of the rational
would fly away to seem.
Its path is chosen nonetheless,
its life is since unknown.
And nothing would suffice to know
its duty to atone.

Far across the distant stars
it cries in memory.
And distant points of cosmic life
have vowed to set it free.
Twice the dream has called to me
and touched my soulless flight.
I cannot figure if its darkened face is truly light.

And fate is just a causal spark,
inventions of the mind.
Its weavers are oppressive still,
though meaning to be kind."

Dabrina music gradually slowed, ending on a sustained chord. Its chilling melody sent a shiver through the ship's occupants. Accepting praise from his fans with a nod, the world seemed to slow as his fingers danced across the dabrina once more.

Music exploded into an airy dance rhythm, laced with a dark, grooving melody. With intense eyes, D'Vinid scanned the main hall of *Dafni's Enigma*. His fingers explored the spidery dabrina, leading those gathered into a rhythmic cadence. Everyone began to dance. The melody fell into a rendition of a favorite song he had written about the joining of King Koraxx and Queen Dafni. The group erupted into cheers. His voice entered, humming the tune. The whole room seemed to hum along.

> "O lady, lady of the night,
> sing to me your heart's delight!
> Run away upon the shores,
> and sing to me my heart's allure.
> O Atlantis, fair and true,
> my gift of love released from you.
> I have felt my lover's thrall,
> and I shall have her, lest I fall.

> "Lady, lady sing to me,
> trust in all the things you see.
> I am the ruler of this land,
> but I pray for your sweet hand.
> Curse the day my mate may come,
> for to you my heart is won.

> Try and stop me, Fates above,
> for I shall choose my own true love.
> And try and overcome my might,
> I stand beside my heart's delight!"

The music escalated, weaving itself into a tale of passionate doom. D'Vinid closed his eyes and drove the song into spinning fury. The room went mad, people danced and hollered in response. After a long, musical interlude, he grabbed everyone's attention with a raised hand, and the bottom dropped out of the song with a clench of his fist.

Dabrina chords cascaded into sharp strumming, reviving the original dance groove. One string at a time joined back into layers of harmony until the entire party danced again.

> "Dream Watchers! O Star Watchers!
> Why have thou forsaken me?
> My kallista loved me clear,
> gave to me two children dear.

Take her from my royal bed!
And take her from my royal home!
But you shall never take me from
the hearts you leave alone.

And upon this line
I leave a curse most foul and black.
And you shall never find a way
to take my curses back..."

The song lingered until each layer of harmony peeled away, leaving D'Vinid strumming two strings in bouncing dissonance. Someone climbed on a chair and raised a glass, grabbing the attention of the whole room. "To King Koraxx's folly!" he shouted.

The room exploded into sound.

Another guest raised his glass. "And to the Queen Impending! May Kyliron be a good boy and treat her right!"

The room responded with uproarious laughter all around.

"To King Kyliron and Queen Brigitte!" shouted another voice.

The color washed out of D'Vinid's face. *Brigitte*. She had recently arrived to meet her betrothed. *Kyliron's betrothed*. He nearly fainted from the realization. He was now hopelessly trapped in a nightmare from which there was no way out.

He wandered to the back deck in a daze, wading briefly through appreciative guests. *Dafni's Enigma* hoisted long, graceful streamers and colorful flags from her masts in replacement of sails. Wind chimes captured ocean breezes, singing their eerie musical scales in chaotic, melodic perfection.

He could feel Brigitte somehow, perhaps through the Grid. He gazed out over the lights of the Harbor District, taking slow, deep breaths.

"You are amazing!" A man's voice interrupted his anguish.

He grunted in response.

"You had the entire room at your command in there."

He turned to passively examine the intruder.

"I've heard much about you, D'Vinid." The kind face of Keymaster Torbin from Subterra greeted him. "I'm told you may be able to tell me the whereabouts of my daughter, Loressai. I understand the two of you may have met yesterday before she disappeared from Pan's estate."

D'Vinid closed his eyes. His stomach churned. Shame wrapped around him. He could not get himself to look into Loressai's father's eyes. "Yes, I saw her."

Torbin urged him on.

He placed his hand over his mouth. "I feel sick." D'Vinid politely excused himself and strode through the entrance. Just in time, he fell to his knees on the dock and vomited into the ocean.

"From the Cantos of Belial it is said of the joining ceremony: 'As two beings choose to join themselves in the oath of procreation, they move their hearts into the beginning, where once Belial and Kama, the Watchers who weave the light of the sun and moon, existed as lovers in union.

"'The discs of gold and silver exist within a place we can all access at the merging of the mindlight and heartlight. A witness of the temple shall clear the path as the oath begins with the turning of the discs until they spin as one. When that occurs, the oath is taken, and the joining complete.'" Allondriss effortlessly projected calm strength while she read from the Sacred Cantos. She had been delighted to discover the heavy golden tome featured on a pedestal in Brigitte's new home. Allondriss had proclaimed her love for the Cantos, and immediately explored its thin pages.

Allondriss's words were buried in the panic of Brigitte's mind as she paced the room, calling the Watchers to take away her growing fear. An armada of servants had arrived earlier to help her bathe and dress for the ceremony.

Her joining gown was a complex silver ensemble that trailed on the floor. With golden, painted lips, she prayed to the ocean breeze, which blew the few curled strands of chestnut hair left untied on her head.

Soft ribbons of silver material were twisted around her arms and legs, highlighting gold-painted fingernails and toenails. The bracelet on her upper arm sat in plain contrast to the rest of the ensemble, a tarnished tribute to her days of freedom on the seaside. Brigitte caressed the dreamclan signet nervously.

"My lady, the time has come," a servant's voice came from the door.

Brigitte reluctantly turned to face Allondriss. "I don't think I'm ready." She managed a weak smile, noticing the concern in Allondriss's ocean-blue eyes.

"I wish I could do something for you, mistress. I don't blame your apprehension." Allondriss's eyes fixed on the floor. "I can only imagine how overwhelming this is for you." Together, the two young women stood in empathy, wanting to hold each other, but refrained for fear of crying. A feeling of kinship buzzed between them. Somehow, it renewed Brigitte's strength.

"Let's just get this over with, Allondriss. The Fates await." She gestured toward the door. "Lead on."

Jamarish Ka stood in the sitting room of her suites. His smooth head was polished to a shining luster. "My lady," he greeted as she approached. His expression shifted to Allondriss for a moment as he bowed solemnly. Brigitte nodded in return. He radiated a softness she felt she should be comforted by, yet something in his eyes made her wary.

"You look stunning." He admired her joining ensemble for a few moments then joined his hands in a prayer position. "It is my honor to greet you on behalf of the High Council and the Temple Sect on this most joyous eve, as you are led to join with your life mate."

He guided them through a polished corridor. As they walked, he glanced back at Allondriss. "And just where did these clansfolk find you?" He paused after a few steps, examining a lock of her blond hair with his fingers. "A temple misfit, obviously."

Allondriss lowered her head. "I was brought by the Watchers."

He raised an eyebrow, slowing his step for a mere moment. "Truly," he responded. "And what of your lineage?"

"It is unknown, my lord," she lied without a problem.

"I look forward to speaking with you more at length." He shrugged her off and turned his attention toward Brigitte again. "We are entering the inner sanctum of the temple. This is one of the entrances from the palace. Your joining ceremony will take place at the heart of Atlantis in the Temple of Light."

They reached a foyer made of tiles formed into multi-colored patterns. An arching entryway looked out on an opulent landscape beyond. Brigitte closed her eyes, absorbing the essence of her surroundings. Allondriss suddenly seemed more nervous than

Brigitte.

Their growing contingent crossed through a yawning doorway into a wonderland of moonlit brooks and lush vegetation. A chorus of light, chiming bells could be heard from all directions. Brigitte knew the use of bells created openings into Dreamtime. It was apparent the Temple District was a gateway into the Dreamvale.

Up ahead, a tall hill held aloft a looming pyramid, rising higher than the smaller pyramids surrounding it. Trees and flowers twisted in a mad conglomerate, dangling from sloping rooftops in cascades of weeping vines.

"That is the Temple of Light in the acropolis," Allondriss pointed to a pyramid at the top of the highest peak. This was the center of all Atlantis, where the telluric lines of the ten kingdoms united to nourish the Great Crystal.

Brigitte wondered at its glowing walls that matched the blue blanket of moonlight illuminating the sweeping hillsides. A dizzy spell slowed her step as they passed into the Dreamvale, though it was the world she was used to. The heaviness of being in Atlantis had begun to settle in her body.

But here her feet glided along the switchback path they climbed.

Golden statues of Watchers supervised their journey. A thin, moonlit waterfall plummeted from the glowing temple of light. The entire district seemed vastly larger than the small space it occupied at the heart of Poseidia. She knew the Dreamvale stretched its limits to accommodate more of itself.

They silently entered the temple acropolis and were greeted by an atmosphere of sacred tribute. There were no trees in the multi-tiered brick courtyard, but a splendid, misty view of the vast city and distant ocean spread out in all directions.

Directly across from the opening emerged a series of golden pedestals displaying statues of oceanids riding dolphins. In the courtyard's center was a depiction of the Sea Watcher Poseidon himself. He held the reins of six winged horses that pulled the golden chariot he rode, while brandishing a trident with the other hand.

He guarded a rounded doorway of highly polished gold. On each side of the opening stood a temple priest, holding the massive doors ajar.

165

Jamarish Ka bowed low to Brigitte. "I take my leave of you now. When I see you again, I shall call you my queen." His eyes darted to Allondriss, and he stepped back to the rear of the entourage.

Twelve reverent women in different-colored temple robes assembled around the Queen Impending. One of the priestesses held a silver robe open for Brigitte. She draped it over Brigitte's shoulders, and clasped it across her chest with a ruby brooch. Pangs of nervousness greeted the temple woman, who cocked her head and sent a wave of love through sea-green eyes.

The temple priestesses sent thoughts of strength to cradle her. Brigitte swooned among their power. The robe trailed behind, as long as she was tall, gliding smoothly on the shining floor of the courtyard. Upon their passage through the doors that closed with great, heaving effort, everyone was sealed inside. The joining entourage captured the attention of those already assembled.

The temple walls were made of rose quartz crystal, with contrasting floors of black tiles. A soft hum filled the air, raising the vibration in the chamber to a higher frequency. In the center, reached by three steps, stood a diamond-shaped platform made of clear quartz. It was encircled by twelve rutilated crystal columns that reached above the tallest head in the room. Each column was crowned by a crystal skull that glowed with soft light.

The life source within them called to her in waves. The world seemed to distort around the skulls. She knew these pillars to be the main conduits of the Great Crystal, from where the entire Grid was powered. The skulls were known as the Crystal Council, a gift from the Star Nations to Atlantis.

On the central platform stood the High Priestess dressed in a pure white robe, holding a staff. She stood between two waist-high pedestals crowned with panels of quartz clusters. These were access portals for the Archives Nexes. The tall staff she held was the hereditary power tool of the High Priestess, and was made from cylindrical, transparent quartz wrapped in sinuous silver bands that coiled into a cradle crowned by a perfect ball of rose quartz.

The High Priestess phased in and out of dreamsight. She looked like a Watcher: statuesque and endowed with majesty. Beams of dreamlight spiraled from the pillars, stitching together through her body and the staff.

The High Priestess's eyes pierced the assembly, landing ever so subtly on Allondriss. Brigitte felt something electric pass between them. Twelve rose-clad temple clergy emerged from behind the platform. Humming a soft song, they formed an aisle for Brigitte to traverse. The priestess's aloof gaze lingered on Allondriss for a few more moments, then shifted to Brigitte.

Kyliron stood on one side of the circular pulpit. He looked like a crowned statue, dressed the same as Brigitte, but all in gold with silver lips and nails. His robe was arranged to cascade down the steps. Serpentine trails of smoke surrounded his body, and he rocked back and forth in a trance.

Brigitte reached the steps, and dizzily stepped to meet the priestess. Her consciousness buzzed within the pillars. She knew to take her place across from Kyliron. Two temple women arranged her cloak down the steps and set a golden incense brazier at her feet.

The smoke consumed her in a thick, musky cloud. One of the priestesses struck two cymbals over the top of her head, creating a high-pitched oscillation. The sound wavered as she moved the cymbals down Brigitte's auric field. It instantly catapulted her into a deep meditation.

She was standing in an empty stadium shrouded in mist. Kyliron's disembodied essence stood across an expanse of grass. Above and between them hovered two mighty discs of silver and gold. They were the discs of inner union, the ethereal symbols of the love affair between the sun and the moon, the lovers whose longing regenerated the world each day.

One disc was slowly spinning, and she realized she had to make the other one spin with her mind. Kyliron watched her. Visions flashed of the two of them intertwined in love-making. The discs spun faster and faster until they were blurred circles. Eventually, they moved together and became as one. Brigitte felt his essence weave into the core of her being, binding them on a molecular level.

She rocked back and forth in blissful completion, as the joining seemed to fill an empty space she didn't even know existed. Every fiber of her body vibrated as an electric current enclosed them in a serpentine continuum.

At the height of the greatest bliss, pain jolted through her like light-ning. With Dreamsight, she saw a black cord wrap around them, just as the discs spun together to form a sphere. The cord originated from the darkness of Kyliron's mind and twisted insidiously into the electric-ity fusing them together. With pure reflex, she lifted her defenses to protect its target, her womb. In that instant, she knew she was already carrying a child.

She was jolted back to the awareness of her body facing Kyliron on the pulpit. He opened his eyes, and the High Priestess stepped forward chanting a verse in ancient Lemurian.

The priestess put forward the ball of rose quartz. Kyliron rested his hand over the sphere. Hesitantly, Brigitte laid hers on top. A cry went up from the assembly.

"All hail the King and Queen of Atlantis!"

To Brigitte's knowledge, even the priestess did not see the attack of the black cord. Her head spun in confusion and desperation. The joining had not been completed. She felt it in the depth of her soul, and she seemed to be the only one who knew.

Looking around the room, it took all her power to remain com-posed. She stepped into place beside Kyliron and placed her hand over his lifted wrist. The rainbow-robed assembly filed out quietly. Together they stood on display, a vision of seemingly perfect mates, destined to carry on the line of Atlas together.

Brigitte suppressed a scream. She yearned for it to be a dream from which she would soon awake. Her brother came into view. He watched with beaming pride. Not even he had seen what had happened. The only ones who could experience the joining cer-emony were the ones who were there. She glanced at Kyliron, but he looked straight ahead. She sank further into despair.

They slowly paraded from the crystal room, and Brigitte re-solved that the Watchers had meant for her alone to carry the burden of an incomplete joining. The only thought consuming her now was of the child in her womb, and the child's father, the musi-cian named D'Vinid.

9

Atlantis never would forget
her peaceful golden years.
But when the land and sky unite,
it would unveil her tears.
Something they could never dream
in night's caress to pass.
And darkness took its hold beneath
the shadow of the mass.

Moonlight danced on the water as it rippled in the breeze. D'Vinid sat on the dock, watching the circular patterns illuminated by the sparkle of the full moon. He had been waiting for his stomach to settle.

"Are you feeling any better?"

D'Vinid closed his eyes, wishing Loressai's father would disappear. He was in no state to inform him of her strange fate. In many ways, he didn't understand fatherhood, though an interesting level of empathy accompanied him regarding a father's love for a daughter, as he felt himself to be the cause of suffering for so many daughters. It was just one more regret weighing on his soul.

"I saw her today, at the cartel docks," he acknowledged. "She was not herself." He couldn't make himself meet Torbin's eyes. "I tried to help her, but there was nothing I could do."

"What was she doing there?"

D'Vinid squirmed. "I wish I could tell you, but I have no idea. I saw her last night at Pan's estate, but she left. And by the Watchers, I ran into her again today." He made a sign to the Watchers just to seem as though he was pious about their guidance. "She was not herself."

"I was there." Ofira's melodious voice came to the rescue. "I saw him try and save her." D'Vinid closed his eyes in relief. "In fact, we were running for our lives, and he went back to help your daughter."

"What happened to her? Where is she now?" Torbin asked again with a steady voice. His patience was growing thin.

D'Vinid struggled to his feet to meet Torbin face-to-face. He knew Torbin's position as keymaster to be highly important in Subterra. Loressai was somewhat like a princess from the inner realm of the planet. He hated to think of her so conquered. D'Vinid finally found it in himself to greet Keymaster Torbin with the respect afforded a ruler.

"I don't know," said D'Vinid. "But I saw who took her. I think they were intending to help her." He hesitated, unsure how to proceed. "They needed to take her. She was acting strange. Violent, in fact."

Torbin nodded sharply. "Can you find these people?"

"I wish I knew, Keymaster. There was a lot going on at the time." He shook his head.

"Keymaster Torbin," Ofira intervened. "There are things you should know about your daughter. D'Vinid has acted nobly on her behalf. I don't think he should be the one to inform you of the details. It would be to the advantage of all if your daughter could be put into your care. I would suggest we send D'Vinid to search out her location while I explain the extent of her troubles." Her eyes urged D'Vinid to use this window as his escape.

"Upon what authority do you speak, young lady?" Torbin asked suspiciously, eying her weathered sea-faring outfit.

"I am Ofira Pazit, Captain of the Dreamship *Vex Voyager*." She bowed with a flourish of her hand. "I have come to Poseidia on a mission from the Watchers."

"You have my attention," Torbin nodded, folding his arms.

"I will begin searching for Loressai," D'Vinid quickly interjected, and backed away as Torbin's attention shifted darkly to Ofira. He flashed the locator-crystal at her, and headed quickly toward the esplanade, floating on a wave of gratitude.

Where the dock ended and the land began, Ofira's animata warrior stood like a statue with its arms folded. When it caught sight of D'Vinid, it animated and moved toward him. Gently it reached into a sack over its shoulder, producing the hover-disc Ofira had given him earlier that day.

"Hey! Thanks, Thing!" D'Vinid was relieved to see the disc again after leaving it behind in his flight from Kyliron at the node-yard. His gratitude for Ofira's cunning redoubled. He flicked the disc toward the ground and found himself wondering if perhaps it wouldn't be so awful to have her ability to know what was about to happen all the time. With an unnecessary salute to the warrior, he sped off toward the Grand Esplanade.

At first, he couldn't be sure where he was headed, until he began noticing the wispy blur of blue-dream markers leading down a side street. He noticed they carried feelings with them, the energetic signatures and emotional imprints of their makers.

His hover skills were finally becoming second nature, as he could split his attention between navigating and contemplation. This ever-present feeling of guilt seemed to have become part of him. He knew he was a better person than he had acted through the cycles of time. He wanted to imagine it wasn't too late to change. That lifted his spirits slightly.

So many looked to him for leadership and companionship, but he often interpreted their admiration for mockery, their smiles for ridicule. The arms of women were his eternal refuge, and yet they lacked any real comfort for him. The attraction and the wanting were what made him have any feeling at all.

But once it shifted, and his lovers decided they wanted to hold onto him and turn the discs of joining, he would run. He had no interest in nursing the attachment many women grew toward him. Their hopes were a delusion, and he could never meet them there.

It was the disavowing of poor Loressai's delusion that made D'Vinid believe he had tossed her to this cruel fate. He felt helpless. It was his fault. He began to wonder if his life's random wanderings had always been influenced by the Watchers. He rarely made appointments, and yet he always seemed to be right where they wanted him.

Perhaps if he stopped resisting, his choices wouldn't always transform into mistakes. It was becoming obvious that if he could reunite Loressai with her father, he could begin to make up for the wrong he did to her and to Kyliron.

And to yourself, a voice appeared in his thoughts. He shivered and sped up.

Following a trail of blue markers, he buzzed through the luminous streets of the Outlands, allowing his mind to relax. He felt a profound connection to the Grid.

In a sudden move, he slipped from the road mound. The torsion-crystal searched for traction and caught on a wispy current. He bounced the disc off a wall and tried an old twisting flip he used to do. As he flew through the air, he stretched out his senses to find another current, and skimmed down a footpath.

A peculiar sensation pricked the back of his mind. He hopped off the hover-disc, trying to place the agitation. His ears perked at the sound of pebbles falling from above. He fell into a ready stance. In the night's shroud, his breathing became shallow. The city was teeming with life. But around him, death seemed to gather on all sides, threatening to corner him.

A passage from the Cantos sprung up, and he repeated it over and over again to occupy himself from the nagging presence. *"Darkness is a measure of thy mind. If thou chooseth to walk the paths of night, then thy world shall shape itself to fit thy journey. For the nature of matter is truly fluid; and thy desire, that which shapes it."* He concentrated into the locator-crystal to make sure Ofira knew where to find him at all times. The night air smelled of mildew. The shadows seemed to stir in every direction.

He slid back against a wall, clutching the retracted hover-disc. He could sense the cold prickle of invisible eyes on him from all angles. "Who's there?" he shouted. Taking a few steps toward the edge of a small canal, he closed his eyes. Trying to shake the fear, he broke out in a sprint toward a nearby bridge. Though there was no physical sign of it, by now he understood; something unseen was stalking him through the misty night.

Lights twinkled in the trees and flowers. Brigitte stood on the landing of her private chambers, gazing out over the moonlit garden. Servants worked to peel off her silver joining gown until only her painted body remained.

One of the servant girls prepared the steam room. She lifted a handle connected to a small, sliding hatch, rerouting hot water flowing through hollow tubes above. This created a strong flow of showers in every corner, as well as a lazy waterfall in the center. Closing the door trapped the steam inside. "When you are ready, Your Majesty." The servant bowed and stepped aside. Brigitte entered the shower to wash off the metallic color, which pooled in silver tributaries and ran down the drain in a glimmering vortex.

With the joining ceremony, the night had only begun. The servants prepared an outfit for her. The custom for a joining celebration required the bride to activate her sexual magnetism, so the clothing was meant to be revealing. Seeing the admiration of other men would arouse the male mate.

The servants went about highlighting Brigitte's features with plant-based dyes, dabbing her body meridians with floral essences, and tying an array of hanging red ribbons to her ensemble. The ribbons would soon be tied to ribbons hanging from Kyliron. It was an age-old tradition that allowed family and friends to acknowledge the new mates in the eyes of the public. Her hair was arranged in a pile on her head, with strands of curls spilling over her shoulders.

"Will Pan be here at the celebration tonight?" Brigitte asked Allondriss. A flutter of eagerness touched her heart.

"I don't think so. His court is celebrating the Ka-Ma-Sha. He does not attend royal courts, I'm afraid. He has too rich of a social life at his own estates." Allondriss was interrupted before she could reveal Pan's real reasoning, how he had publicly vowed to counteract everything Kyliron stood for. He would never be invited to Kyliron's courts. It was the reason he had asked her to keep their friendship a secret.

"Beautiful. Simply breathtaking," a male voice came from behind. The servants sprung to stunned attention at the king's intrusion. He closed the distance between them in a few long strides. Stepping gently into Brigitte's personal space, his fingers brushed the smooth texture of her skin. She did her best not to show her apprehension.

He took in a slow inhale of her perfume. His languid eyes examined the bare contours of her waist. "I am a lucky man," he spoke, shaking his head in disbelief. "My mate, I wish to escort you to our joining revelry, if you feel you are presentable to the public."

She forced herself to submit to his tactile exploration. "I would be honored, my lord."

He was wearing court fashion. A red leather vest cut in intricate stencils was fashioned to fall below the rib cage in front, and long in the back. Red fitted pants were cut low, revealing the lines of his abdomen. He wore a sheer red pleated robe with golden accents, hung open to show his chest. A gold crown accented with rubies rested on his head. Just like hers, his ensemble had an array of hanging ribbons tied to it.

He lifted the back of his wrist to raise her palm in a formal escorting gesture. She marveled at the king's exquisite presence, wishing she could love him as completely and suddenly as she did D'Vinid. He guided her into the gardens. With a look of invitation, he encouraged Allondriss to follow along.

"I have welcomed Allondriss." He waggled his fingers toward the young temple outcast. "She is to be your official companion."

Brigitte nodded, taking comfort in the information.

"I have also welcomed your brother as your personal dreamseer. And your fury is now your bodyguard. My father and I have taken steps to raise the position of the Warrior Sect in our time. Bringing a warrior with you has caused some resistance within the High Council. But I am pleased. It is a good queen who can further the causes of her king."

"Thank you, my lord," she bowed. "I feel safer having him around. After the attack…" His grip on her hand tightened, suggesting she remain quiet.

"As queen, you will be required to appoint a personal maydriss who will advise you on all affairs. You must also appoint an external naydir to keep your public appointments." Brigitte tried not to roll her eyes. With her extensive training, this was basic knowledge.

"For me," he continued, "Jamarish Ka occupies my maydrian position. I will make sure you are presented with candidates so you can have one as good as mine. My naydir is Tashan Balinor. You will have more contact with my maydrian than with him. He represents me in the city."

One of the paths ended at a set of double doors. Kyliron stopped to face her. He held out a golden bracelet with a clear crystal wrapped in a simple mounting. With a sly smile on his face, he waved it over a panel. She watched as the doors swung open to reveal a beautifully carved chamber with five walls and five different sets of double doors.

"This is the royal staging area for court. One leads to your personal court. Access will be granted to you when you are ready. One leads to my court and my suites, to which you will not have ready access. The other leads to our shared court."

"Where does this one lead?" she gestured to the fifth door next to the one they entered through.

He pulled her into his embrace. "I will show you."

He slid the crystal bracelet onto Brigitte's wrist. Her thumb caressed its facets.

"Pass the accessor over the lock," he guided gently. Imitating the Children of One, she lifted the accessor-crystal to her lips, and hummed a note into its surface. Her lips created a vibration that set the crystal buzzing in her hand. She passed it over the side panel. The door lit up, and a jolt of electricity veined through the etchings.

Kyliron sputtered. "What did you just do? I've only seen soul-crystals do that." He stewed on it for a few moments.

Brigitte bowed her head humbly. "My people are in tune with elementals. Crystals are some of the more conscious of telluric beings." She gasped at the sight ahead. Beyond lay a magnificent open courtyard built around a tree that looked remarkably like the shape of a woman. She recognized it instantly as the one from her vision when D'Vinid gave her the rose. She felt an overwhelming sense of welcome radiating from the shivering branches. She began to wonder how D'Vinid had gotten hold of the rose in the first place.

Kyliron knelt beside its thick trunk. "Mother, give me strength," he prayed with clasped hands, looking at the hanging leaves with love in his eyes. Brigitte watched with reverence, taking note of Kyliron's gentleness toward it.

"Mother, meet my new mate," he smiled. "Brigitte, this is the shrine of my mother, Queen Dafni, your predecessor. She would have loved you as she loved all beings."

"Hello, Dafni. Is it true what they say about your mother?" she asked. "That the Watchers transformed her into a tree?"

"It made my father believe in Watcher magic again." Kyliron's voice grew distant. "But it's a poor replacement for my mother. She was more lovely than all the islands of Atlantis."

After a long moment, he turned to leave. For an instant, she felt hypnotized by the tree. She shuddered, feeling a sense of deep sorrow. A powerful elemental presence inhabited this courtyard, and it was not happy to see her leave.

She pulled herself away, and they returned together to the royal staging area.

He beckoned to the door of her private court. "You may explore your domain at your leisure. I am certain you will find it to your liking. And should you not, simply say a word, and it shall be transformed to suit your whim." He leaned in close and spoke softly into her ear. His voice caused a ripple of pleasure through her body. "The queen's court should be a center of culture and beauty," he continued. "It is up to you and your entourage to populate this court. Soon you may choose from the house of courtiers, or welcome any from the mediator households.

"Tonight, there will be many petitioners who will approach you for a position at your court; musicians, dancers, historians, artisans, Temple Sect advisers, trainers, philosophers, poets, mixologists, lovers. Wherever your interests point, my love. I look forward to seeing what you choose." He reached his lips down to her face, brushing ever so slightly across her cheek.

Her apprehension faded. She gazed up at him, longing to always possess such tenderness.

"Come now, our celebration awaits us in our shared court." His moves were smooth as a cat's. With a gentle, caressing touch, he guided them toward their adjoined court. The opening doors revealed a landing with two thrones. Their arrival captured the attention of the colorful courtiers mingling in the moonlit courtyard beyond. A wave of approval gradually erupted, as the first courtiers noticed their unannounced arrival, and passed on the news with their applause.

Kyliron guided Brigitte to a throne and stood at the one beside her. She was careful to maintain delicate movements, though she felt heavy with fatigue. When they sat, Kyliron beckoned for the revelry to continue.

A musical ensemble created a high celestial chorus. Allondriss stayed behind Brigitte's throne, trying to remain elusive, although everyone strained to have a look at the queen's unusual temple companion. Lukias approached, oblivious to the admiration of the court ladies. He had bathed and brushed his hair, and looked more handsome than ever in a clean, hooded robe. Brigitte flashed a dazzling smile at her brother. He kissed her hand with a wink. "I barely recognized you, brother," she laughed.

He smiled back, returning her laughter. "You and me both, sister. The servants insisted that I display myself thus." He bowed to the king and slipped behind the throne to stand beside Allondriss.

Festively dressed courtiers mingled throughout the courtyard, which was decorated to look like Dreamtime. The court styles were far more grandiose than those on the streets. Women's dresses were shining colorful fabric hung in layers, sometimes gathered at the sides, or in thick ruffles. Their bodices and collars were cut in patterns, exposing skin. Headdresses boasted arrays of feathers cascading down the back.

Men wore pleated robes with high collars fastened up the front and parted at the bottom to show the signature short pants made of rich shining fabrics and lace-up shoes. All men wore wide sashes in many different colors.

Brigitte had learned that sashes were a symbol of the life accomplishments of men. Upon emergence as an Atlantean, they received an embroidered symbol on their sash, which was granted to them at their passage into adulthood. Through the years, the symbols accumulated, and the sashes were kept in the family to honor the memory of their ancestor long after their souls had passed through the death gateways.

A table filled with delicacies and delights was set up before them. Servants carried out plates of savory foods, delivering them to rows of wide tables in the courtyard. A seductive servant woman approached, balancing two crystal goblets on a silver tray.

Kyliron took both goblets in hand, his eyes lingering on the woman hungrily before turning his attention to Brigitte. "A tribute to you, my love," he handed her one of the goblets. "This is an aphrodisiac elixir for desire and fertility. You will become intoxicated." He smiled wickedly, placing the rim to his lips. "We often indulge in such elixirs. I should hope you soon become accustomed to it."

She sipped and almost immediately her senses danced to life. The taste was fruity and pleasant, and she found herself compelled to take another deeper drink. Her eyes searched the assembly, looking for familiar faces. The High Council was in attendance, sitting at their own table, speaking in hushed tones. She tried to memorize the many beautiful faces of the courtiers who came to pay them tribute and contend for her attention.

The joining celebration spilled by in a swirl of tastes and sounds, smells and sights. Brigitte and Kyliron were given performances, gifts, and presentations. Dancers held fire in their hands while moving in ways she had never seen. They lit torches at the end of chains to spin in intricate patterns. The Order of the Spiral Dancers made a special presentation Brigitte particularly enjoyed, performing amazing tricks by spinning variously shaped rings around their bodies.

Intoxication saturated the many beautiful courtiers as they mingled in the gardens. Bodies began to move, snakelike as the music gradually fused with deep rhythmic sounds. Their musical journey slowly elevated the celebration to a new level of excitement.

Eventually, Kyliron coaxed her from their landing and led her around the crowd, showing her off like fine jewels acquired in an exotic market. She could barely walk or talk. Anyone who touched her skin became the newest object of her desire, but knowing the elixir's effect on a first timer, Kyliron would jealously snatch her away the moment her eyes lingered on another. Guests began to tie the ribbons hanging from their outfits to recognize the couple's union.

At midnight, the palace gardens came to life. A layer of fog cast long shadows over amber and purple lights. It rendered the scene dreamlike, as if that which was solid would soon fade. The moon illuminated the festive scene. Glowing insects sparkled in the gardens.

Walking barefoot across carpets of green moss, Brigitte beheld the nighttime wonders of the courtyard with abandon. Kyliron remained at her side. The ribbons bound them together so if one were to fall, the other would soon come tumbling after. A small entourage tagged along, laughing and showing Brigitte mysterious, floating bio-luminescent creatures, explaining how they had been created for this very courtyard by scientists.

She could not remember a time when she had enjoyed herself more. They danced close in the twinkling lights as thousands of flower petals were let loose to float over their heads. Effervescent fire exploded in the sky and echoed off Poseidia's heights, raining streams of cascading sparks. Brigitte watched in wonder and tossed her head back in laughter.

As if on cue, the High Priestess, followed by a processional of temple priestesses, entered the courtyard, and all fell into reverence. Brigitte searched the recesses of her foggy mind for the reason, and then all at once, fear attacked her heart. This was the fertility blessing. And Brigitte thought again of D'Vinid.

The courtiers paraded Brigitte and Kyliron to their thrones. Temple women filed around them. Chanting, they placed a series of crystals at their feet and arranged small crystal bottles on the table in front of them. An incense brazier was set burning and waved around their heads. Brigitte prayed to the Watchers.

The High Priestess began muttering a lyrical, ancient Lemurian verse. She waved the crystal staff around them and placed a hand on Kyliron's stomach, then on Brigitte's, who watched the High Priestess nervously. The priestess paused for a moment, stealing the slightest look at Brigitte's stomach. With barely a furrow of the brow, she continued, moving toward the crystal bottles.

Arranging two goblets as receptacles for the fertility potions, she removed multi-faceted lids one by one, and began pouring various colored liquids into each goblet, chanting as she worked. Smoke billowed from the incense, and the crystals lit up at their feet. When the incantation was complete, she handed the goblets to Brigitte and Kyliron, who drank deeply at the nod of her head.

"The queen is fertile!" the priestess announced. "Tonight, we welcome the conception of our heir!"

A cheer erupted from the courtiers. Kyliron stood and offered his hand to Brigitte, who lingered darkly on the High Priestess, wondering if she knew about the child that was already conceived.

The priestess nodded. Her voice appeared in Brigitte's mind. *"You are Moirae. The Watchers know what is best."* It was in this moment Brigitte knew the High Priestess may have been on her side, for whatever reason a side was necessary.

Kyliron snatched Brigitte into his arms and devoured her with a ravenous kiss. The courtiers let out a drunken cheer. The priestess tied the final ribbons to complete the binding of the couple. Without another word, Kyliron carried her from the landing into his personal chambers while ladies of the court commented on how lucky she was.

Gaseous blue energy formed into cords, twisting and turning through alleyways. D'Vinid could see them clearly. They steered him to a part of the city seldom visited. Here, part of Poseidia had crumbled into the sea. Its remains stood forgotten, hanging from the cliffs of the shoreline. Very few people ventured here. No one wanted to imagine Atlantis could ever again experience catastrophe as it had at the end of its previous two ages.

He moved cautiously, unsure if or when his stalker would spring to attack him. The path headed to what looked like an old palace. As he approached, the sounds of rhythmic thumping drifted out of the moonlit rubble. He hopped off the hover-disc and brandished it like a weapon, careful not to lose it again.

As he crested to the hill to get a look at the source of the sound, D'Vinid couldn't believe his eyes. The gathering was in a natural amphitheater looking out over the ocean. The scene reminded him of the renegade revelries many rotations back when he was at the height of his hover-trickster fame.

Everyone moved to syncopated beats he assumed to be amplified through resonance amplifiers. The revelry was pure chaos. Those who weren't dancing on every available surface were somehow creating light from their hands. As they projected the lights toward each other, they created intricate geometrical symbols.

Laughter mingled with the pulsing rhythm. D'Vinid was enthralled. They seemed like celestial beings who had stolen one night on this side of the Dreamvale. Their collective chaos seemed like an incantation. The spell cast with their lights and sounds banished the shadows. D'Vinid had a hard time staying still as he watched.

"*It's too late for your Loressai.*" A voice merged with his thoughts. "*She belongs to us now.*"

D'Vinid jumped, looking around. No one was there. He held his hover-disc at the ready. "So, you have been following me."

"*We have always been with you. Give yourself freely to us, and we will spare your queen. We can make her suffer. You can save her still from this fate.*"

"What would you want with me? I'm a nobody. Surely there's someone else…"

"*It is Atlantis we want.*" He could feel the creature reaching into his thoughts, filling his head with mockery. "*And it is you who brings the king the most anguish. We can help you be rid of him. And you can have her to yourself.*" The guilt tried to consume him, as it usually did. The creature seeped deeper into his head with every wave of self-loathing. It snaked into his blood like poison. His hands trembled violently as he raised them to eye level.

Chanting emerged from the rubble in a hissing chorus: "Moela mesh maaah sacreeey moreeeey." The phrase repeated itself in perfect cadence until D'Vinid could feel his head swim. Shadows converged into physical beings, cloaked in wavering darkness. Even the runes on their faces wavered. Their chanting grew louder as they enclosed him in a tight circle.

He wanted to dash away, run to the safety of the revelry, but his body was too heavy. The chanting continued. The circle shrank. He was trapped in their web. Shadows swarmed in a vortex, wrapping him in a cocoon. The creature that stalked him reached into his body to claim its chosen host. He trembled. Tears poured down his face.

Visions danced in his head: *Cities burning. Crowds bowing in worship. Darkness descending on the land. Wars. Black tar bubbling from inside the planet. Humans dying in terrible rituals of sacrifice.*

A silent scream formed on his lips. The smell of sulfur burned his nose. Smoke drifted through the air. He fell to his knees.

He looked up, suddenly engulfed in a newfound strength. His eyes flashed orange. His mouth formed a devious smile. The creature retracted. The beings encircling him faded away.

"If you're so confident I will succumb to your influence, why ask me to give myself to you freely?" He stood up with clenched fists.

Darkness pressed in around him, and fear tore at his resolve.

"Come with us and we will spare your queen."

The thought of Brigitte as Kyliron's queen irritated him. But thinking of her ignited the love he had felt in her presence. Embracing the feeling made the darkness shrink away. A reckless grin touched his lips. "Something tells me you wouldn't be offering me this bargain if you could actually claim me on your own," D'Vinid chuckled. "In fact, I find myself wondering if this horrible guilt I always feel is you trying to take over my mind. Who are you? What do you want with me?" D'Vinid could feel the creature swirling around him like a hundred spiders crawling on his back.

"We are the Triad." The voice reverberated in his head. *"You will assume a place of glory in the new order. It's more than Kyliron will offer you."*

D'Vinid gathered his energy, feeling the darkness fold inward upon him. "Triad. I see." For a moment he appeared to be considering the offer. "You seem to have no idea who I am. Glory is the last thing I care about." A surge of passion swelled his heart. "In truth, I would prefer to see you banished from this planet." His eyes flashed. Light appeared out of nowhere and bathed the area.

The creature screeched in agony and was hurled into the nebulous night. The chanting circle faded and disappeared. D'Vinid sat for a while in silence, evaluating his options.

As if in answer to his inner turmoil, another shape approached in the darkness. Though obscured under a full-length, hooded robe, D'Vinid easily recognized the feminine fluidity of her movements. Her feet were adorned with sandals, her toenails painted gold. The cords of the sandals wrapped up her calves and merged with snake tattoos. She took a prolonged look at D'Vinid with cat-like eyes.

She was accompanied by another woman with the stature of a warrior and a shaved head. The sight of them filled him with relief.

"You, over there. Did you feel that?" she demanded. Caution stuttered her words. Her face was steady.

"You mean, the darkness that just flew off… into the darkness?" he grimaced. "I'm afraid I may have led it here." His answer was honest, though he was not entirely sure it should be.

"What have you done?!" the shaved-headed woman snapped.

"Well, I didn't know where I was going in the first place! Your blue-dream markers led me here."

"Newbies." She sneered at her companion. "He should be banned from the gatherings."

D'Vinid shrugged innocently. "At least now they're gone. I suspect when I leave, they will follow me."

The woman with the snake tattoos stepped closer to him. Narrowing her eyes, she tilted her head. "What do you mean, they?"

"I don't know who they were." He frowned.

"Did they mention the sacré moré?"

"I don't know. They were chanting something. They seem to think they own me for some reason. There was something about the return of the Triad. What does that mean?"

"Sacré moré means sacred death. It's what they say when they're about to sacrifice someone to help them bring back the Blood Triad."

"Hold on a minute! Blood Triad?"

"What is your name?" she laughed.

"I might ask you the same question," he said as he leaned on one leg, tossing a worried look into the darkness.

"I wouldn't worry about them showing back up. My conclave is patrolling the area. They know better than to cross us." The beauty of her face shone in the moonlight.

The woman with the shaved head crouched at a sound in the ruins nearby and went to inspect it.

The other woman inched closer. Her movements were the definition of eloquence. "My name is Fa'nariel Ma'at," she said. "Now that I see your face, I know who you are. You're new to the awakening aren't you, D'Vinid?"

He propped his leg on the base of a toppled column and returned her attention levelly. She lowered her hood. D'Vinid did his best to appear aloof, though his body still trembled. Under normal circumstances he might have tried to flirt with her. She was his savior, after all.

"I hear you were at the cartel docks earlier." Her voice was almost musical as she spoke. "What you did was very brave." She flipped her head, sizing him up with measuring eyes. "Although you did almost spoil the trap."

He pointed at her sharply. "You were one of those people who took Loressai!" He marveled at the thorough perfection of the Watchers' web. At the same time, his heart ached imagining Loressai's face contorted in its madness.

Fa'nariel seemed to look directly through him. "I am one of them, yes. But I was not there." She paused, studying him. "You possess the innate wisdom of our Source creator. It's up to you to tap into it. All the answers will come. You must simply ask and surrender to the answer."

"I am not really interested in your Axiom of One dogma."

She smiled. "As you wish."

"All I have is one simple question. Where is Loressai?"

The humor of her expression faded. "You will not like what you see if you find her."

He leaned closer. "Her father may have me tortured if I don't find her."

Her eyes were piercing in their intensity. "Perhaps she is safer where she is. Did you give that any thought?"

"Safer than with the Luminari? You may overestimate yourselves."

"Are you certain your heart is true in this matter? Is this simply an attempt to keep yourself from harm? Or do you really care about her well-being?" She sat on the edge of a fallen rock. "The madness takes people all the time. *That* is unfair. The madness does not discriminate. But what if there is a possibility she could be saved in our care? Wouldn't you choose that path for her?"

He opened his mouth to respond but found himself frozen by her line of questioning. He exhaled, folded his arms, and copied her movement, seating himself on a rock to face her.

"Fa'nariel Ma'at," he chanted. "I will remember your name."

She adjusted her position, and one of her legs peeked out of the robe. "What just happened to you may have happened to her. Obviously, you are tainted. If you go to where she is, you could lead them there."

He raised his eyebrow in dismay.

"Look," she continued. "I see you have been awakened to the blue-dream. There is no turning back now. You are part of this whether you like it or not. Your next step is to wait for your soul-crystal. We all have one. It's the key to unlocking the gateways of initiation."

D'Vinid shifted, scratching his head. His thoughts began to darken.

She produced a small quartz crystal in the shape of a wand, with one end rounded and the other terminating in a point. She dangled the crystal enticingly. "Once you figure all that out, use this to contact me and I will help you find her." She handed him the crystal.

D'Vinid sank into confusion. He was drawn to what she said, yet he fought it. He reached for the crystal.

She lowered her voice, as if preparing to impart a great secret. "Everyone has accessors built into their mindlights. We call these inner gateways. The Temple Sect has been hiding this from us for generations. You become the master of your own fate when you go through inner initiation. But first you have to go through symbiosis with your soul-crystal." She recognized his interest. "When you go through initiation, you learn to access all human knowledge stored in the archives of our own DNA. This access is simply stimulating a remembrance of what we already know."

"If you can know anything, then tell me what it is that I'm dealing with here."

"My conclave and I specialize in hunting the shadows that

have been terrorizing Atlantis. We have been on their trail. These creatures are living in the same realm as the shadows, and their servants may be like us: Children of One who seem to think it's a good idea to use the shadows as their tools. They may be worshipping the Triad. They are called shadowmancers." Her expression sobered. "The Blood Triad are mentioned in our history chronicles: the Nephilim kings of the ancient Bloodfire Nations. They were the ones who enslaved the peaceful cities of Lemuria and caused the war of the Watchers. In the end, they were said to be imprisoned in ice by the Fire Crystal of Atlantis."

"I remember the stories. They got their power from ritual sacrifice. The nations of humanity fell under their tyranny." He pressed his head with his hand. "They said they wanted to take over Atlantis."

She opened a portable elixir jar and took a sip, offering it to him. He reached for it. "What is that?"

Her smile was an invitation. "It's for clarity and stamina."

Shrugging, he accepted the jar, hoping it would settle his nerves.

"If they're trying to use you as a host for one of the Blood Triad, you may be more important than you think."

D'Vinid looked around, paranoia prickling his spine. Fa'nariel caught the eye of her companion, who indicated there was still no sign of the creature.

"The conclaves watch as our society crumbles around us. We see the monsters who haunt our Dreamtime. And every day we are developing more immunity to their poison. Most of us just want to exist in peace so we can practice what we learn from the Nexes." She gestured toward the revelry. "Most of them don't want to be involved. All they care about is their free-will. Perhaps you can relate."

D'Vinid grinned. "Maybe I have something in common with them, after all." He waved his hand, feeling energized by the elixir. He jumped up and lifted her hand to kiss her fingers. His senses danced to life, and the crashing cadence of the ocean sailed above the music. He felt drawn to it, like the tide tugged at his body. He winked and tipped his hat, then turned and began picking his way through the shattered estate.

She followed. "You will need friends in the coming days. Trust me on that."

With heavily placed footsteps he wandered through the rubble. "I came to find Loressai, not get involved in your secret society."

The blue haze faded in and out of existence around them. She noticed his awareness of it. "You are in the vortex. That is what brought you here."

"What is the vortex, anyway?"

Her laughter was bright and cheerful. "When you relax into the flow of the One, you are swept into the currents of the vortex. You can control your direction if you learn the proper technique."

They picked their way through rugged ground until the music faded in the distance. The cliff sloped down to a place where land met sea. As the waves crashed rhythmically, he took note of a strangely shaped rock. Moonlight mingled with the blue mist as they drew closer. His hackles rose. Each step brought more certainty. It was not a rock but a human body.

D'Vinid shuddered to think of why the Watchers would guide him to see such a thing. Fa'nariel bent over what looked like a man and touched his head gently. Receiving no response, she placed her fingers on his wrist. She looked at D'Vinid eagerly and nodded. Carefully, she cradled the man in her arms and turned him over. He moaned.

D'Vinid knelt, and as the moon caught the man's features, he cried out, "Watchers! No!" He yanked the body from Fa'nariel and slapped the man's cheeks briskly. "No, no, no, no. Wake up. You have to wake up." D'Vinid rocked the man in his arms. "Help me," he looked on her pleadingly. "We have to get him somewhere safe."

She gestured to her companion, who had silently followed them. She responded by running back along the path.

"Bavendrick," he muttered. "If this was Kyliron's doing…"

The prince's eyes opened. The color in them shifted as though they were made of the ocean itself. D'Vinid marveled at the sight and wondered if he was dreaming. He had never seen eyes turn to liquid before. "D'Vinid," Bavendrick smiled weakly. "Are you a Watcher?" His strange eyes fluttered as he passed out again.

D'Vinid cradled the prince in his arms and sobbed. He looked into the sky and out into the ocean, holding his childhood friend. He squinted. He thought he could make out the shape of a woman on a rock in the middle of the cove. Moonlight glimmered on her wet skin. Her hair was thick like fins. But when he blinked the tears

from his eyes, the vision was gone.

They sat in silence. Every breath Bavendrick took flooded D'Vinid with gratitude. After a while, approaching footsteps drew his attention. The identical smiling faces of the Aello twins greeted him with surprise.

Fa'nariel's companion accompanied them. "These two came in a hover-carriage! They can help us take him somewhere safe."

The twins examined the scene with mouths agape.

D'Vinid could do nothing but sputter into maddened laughter at this new synchronicity. Was this the vortex? He squeezed his eyes closed, feeling the sting of exhaustion. He could feel the touch of the Watchers, and helplessness brought him to a point of trembling desperation. Jensyn put his hand on D'Vinid's shoulder. "The Watchers work in mysterious ways," he said with a cunning smile.

Kayden brought a blanket and wrapped it around Prince Bavendrick.

D'Vinid tried to collect himself, rubbing tears from his eyes. "Obviously, we can't take him to a healing center," D'Vinid sighed. "Your father will know what to do." He pointed a stern finger at both of them.

They nodded in unison.

"Of course," Kayden agreed.

His slightly wider features were barely apparent in the blue light of the moon, but D'Vinid could easily tell who was who.

Kayden continued. "Sometimes it seems our father has more resources than the king." They picked Bavendrick up between them and began climbing the steep beach.

Fa'nariel and her staunch companion followed to the waiting carriage. After Bavendrick was safely tucked inside, she turned to D'Vinid. "We can help. Our healers are highly advanced. We have achieved access to ancient Nexes records, and we don't have the rules that restrict us like the Temple Sect does. Let us care for the prince."

"In whatever secret place Loressai may or may not be that I would have to awaken my gateways to access? No, thank you."

The twins watched with growing interest.

"You will understand eventually. Once you pass through the gateways, you will no longer be vulnerable to the emotions that can be used to control you. You will need our help passing through the city. Aren't you worried about what is trying to find you?"

He squinted. His eyes flashed orange. "I don't think so. For some reason, I don't think there's any room for that Triad thing inside me."

"You should be wary of the shadowmancers. They are very dangerous and very evil. If they are after you…"

"Hey, no need to worry! I've got the Aello twins on my side!" he interrupted. The twins nodded and patted his back.

"The king thinks his brother is dead," Fa'nariel blurted out as they prepared to leave.

He glanced at her and noticed a bracelet that had slipped out of her robe. He grabbed her hand and examined the royal trident etched into its silver surface. He looked up to catch her triumphant gaze.

"I am one of Kyliron's kallistas," she admitted.

A wave of realization nearly knocked him over. He knew she seemed familiar.

"I'm not the only one. The king has a voracious appetite." She watched his reaction.

He stared at her closer. "For how long?"

"I have seen you before, D'Vinid. Many times. I have been a visitor in Kyliron's bed since before you left the palace. Since Loressai came. Since the beginning of Prince Bavendrick's ill-fated series of betrothals. This is the vortex at work. I am part of this, D'Vinid. Make no mistake about that."

He squeezed his eyes shut, pushing away the sickening dizzy spell of coincidence. "Then I trust that you will keep this to yourself."

"You have my word," she nodded. "You will receive your soul-crystal. You will achieve symbiosis. You will open your inner gateways. It is a natural progression. Contact me once this happens and I will offer you answers. I will take you to Loressai when you are ready. The vortex will unite us again, D'Vinid. Take care of yourself." She nodded to the Aellos and slipped away with her companion.

D'Vinid pulled the new hover-disc from his shoulder satchel and tossed it to the ground. Both twins examined it with delight.

"Well," Jensyn smiled, clapping his hands. "A fine hover-disc you've acquired." He bobbled his head from side to side.

D'Vinid shrugged off their leering faces and gestured to the hover-carriage. "Let's move."

As the twins climbed into their sleek vehicle, D'Vinid felt for Bavendrick's heartbeat. The pallor of death spread a blanket over the prince's repose. He did not want to return to Pan's, and yet could not bring himself to leave Bavendrick, not just yet. For now, he would continue his journey within the vortex.

Brigitte barely had time to examine the king's court, but it was as magnificent as any other place she had seen that day and was designed almost entirely with water features. Their walk was exhausting. He had to hold her up as she often melted in his arms, giggling at her loss of control. She could barely contain the bursting feeling in her heart. The ribbons on their arms now linked them, and even when she fell, she was held up by his weight.

He said nothing, merely dutifully remained at her side until they entered his suite. Quickly, he unlinked the ribbons from his outfit, and relinquished their bond. "This is a stupid tradition," he growled, unlatching the ribbons from her outfit. They crumpled to the floor in a red heap. He disappeared, leaving her to look around.

The room's main attraction was a very large pool of shallow blue water, fed constantly by a fountain depicting a shapely sea nymph, whose hair and clothing were made to seem as the fountain's flowing water. Brigitte blinked at the illusion, watching it curiously.

Her fingers traced the edges of dimly lit crystal walls, which were warm to the touch. She squinted at the reflection in the surface of the crystal. She wondered if the elixirs were tricking her perceptions. Leaning in closer revealed it was not a reflection at all, but the face of the apparition who had appeared in the crystal-node. Panic clutched her heart. The woman's bloody face was trapped in an eternal scream. Brigitte stumbled backward.

Kyliron appeared with two crystal goblets. "What's wrong?"

Wide-eyed, she stared at the surface of the crystal wall.

"Are you afraid of your reflection, my darling?" He laughed and handed her one of the goblets. The sight of the red liquid turned her stomach. She could not bear the thought of entering the elixir fog even deeper. She stole another look at the shiny wall. The apparition was gone. She watched his perfectly formed arm as he handed her a goblet. She was afraid to speak. No matter how kind he acted, she could not dispel the fear.

"I have received news that has caused me great sorrow." His pensive voice mingled with the delicate sound of trickling water. "I believe my brother Bavendrick to have been taken by the ocean. I don't know what to do with my feelings about this." He lowered his head, his face full of despair. "It was with great regret that I had to send him away to join with the princess of Og. It was an excellent political choice, but it pained my heart."

"Do you think that choice angered the Watchers? Your line is slated to mate with the dreamclans in this generation."

His murky eyes scrutinized her. "The people wanted me for their king because I have lived my life among them, concentrating on the sects and their happiness. They love me. This is what matters to me."

He had not yet drunk from his glass. She held onto hers, hoping he would turn around, so she could pour it out somewhere. "You joined with *me*. Obviously, the pact did carry some weight with you," she suggested.

"I am king. I have done my duty. My brother would remain prince so he could be spared. He was betrothed to a dreamclan half-breed. But she was an unscrupulous slut. She was chosen by our mother. But my mother was not politically intelligent. My father never wanted this woman in the royal dynasty. I have carried out our father's wishes, because he knew what was best.

"My brother hated me for it. He claimed to love Vinesia still. A monarch has to make difficult decisions sometimes, my love, and people don't always like us for it." He reached out his hand to touch her hair. His caress was soft, his eyes warm. With a strange facial twitch, he raised the glass toward her in tribute. "To you, my royal mate. Your coming is a great honor for me. And to my brother Bavendrick. May his soul find rest from this unjust world."

She mimicked the action, wondering why he almost seemed happy his brother was gone. He drank the liquid in one long gulp. When he was finished, he shattered the crystal on the ground and wiped his face. His eyes dilated, spiraling into a frenzy.

"Drink yours. Go on, drink it like I just did." She was dismayed when he leaned in to watch her closer, urging her with his bleary eyes.

Frightened, she choked it down. Some of it dripped down her cheek. He licked it with his tongue, and grabbed the glass from her, tossing it to shatter on the marble floor. Animata servants appeared from the shadows to clean it. He pulled away as if he had felt a sudden pain. He doubled over, sucking in a shallow, labored breath.

"What is it?" She wanted to touch him but held her hand back. Fear began to clutter her mind.

He lifted his face. His eyes gleamed with cold malice. The energy in the room shifted. "It's you," his voice strained to a deeper pitch. "You're making this happen. It started when *you* arrived."

"Making what happen?"

"You are here to destroy me!" he shouted.

Brigitte backed away in alarm. His words stabbed like a serrated blade. "How can you say that?"

"The Watchers want me to fall!" he gasped. His eyes shifted madly to the window. "They hate me! Like they hated my mother! No matter how much the people loved me, or how much my father loved me, the Watchers hated me! And now they send you to undo me! I hate them, too!"

Brigitte stared in stunned silence, trying to stifle her expression under the weight of the realization that all her childhood fears were coming true on the very eve of her joining. His deep preternatural eyes seared into her like molten steel, and she burned from the pain of his gaze. Could it possibly be the King of Atlantis, her new mate, was falling to the madness? He staggered to the window and buried his face in his hand.

She was dizzy from the elixir's effects.

"You bring me these emotions." His voice was calmer, though just as filled with malice. "You did so when you first looked into my eyes, when your mind came into mine like a Watcher." He began laughing. He propped himself against the wall, hugging his body.

Brigitte did not know what to say. She stared in confusion for a few moments then headed toward the pool, sinking into her own thoughts. She didn't notice him follow. The moment she put her feet into the water, his hands gripped her shoulders. A rush of adrenaline seized her in shock. Resisting the urge to flee blindly,

194

she turned her head to feel his breath upon her cheek. Her breathing shallowed.

"Why have you come to me, Brigitte? Do you feel love for me?" She writhed to free herself, but he gripped tighter. "The less you struggle within my grasp, the less pain you will feel." She could feel him smiling with his lips pressed against her cheek. "I asked you a question. Do you feel love for me? Or did the Watchers train you to destroy me?" He nudged her shoulder back with a sudden tenderness in his touch, guiding her to face him.

"I have always loved you, Kyliron! I love you even now as you tell me I am destroying you. I would seek to help you, and you do nothing but scorch me with false blame!" Tears flowed from her eyes.

He caressed her skin. "You are so wondrously lovely, Brigitte, especially when you are in pain. How could I ever bring myself to destroy that? I would rather watch your beauty gradually fade than see it snuffed out before it has a chance to suffer. I will show the Watchers what I think of their trickery." He delivered the words with an eerie tenderness.

She flinched, unable to control the trembling of her hands.

"Look at you," he continued. "Every feature, a masterpiece. The very essence of temptation. The Watchers are so clever, seeking to lure me from my path with the sweetness of beauty." There was a wickedness to his smile as he continued to pet her face. All the while he avoided her gaze, examining the rest of her like an animata appraisal. "I will use this gift for all it's worth," he spoke into the air as if to an invisible floating entity. He pushed her away and stumbled to the wall. With his full weight against the surface, he sank into a crouch and clutched at his head.

She gazed at him in awe, wanting to fear him, wanting to pity him.

He fell silent, hunched over with his face between his knees. "What have you done to me?" he choked helplessly. "I must free myself of this." He buried his face in his hands, turning his back to her.

She approached. "Please allow me to help you." She reached out to touch his back. He flinched at her touch. "Free you from what, my lord?" she begged him to respond. A sense of futility caused her tears to flow, and they wept together.

She knelt in front of him. "My tears I shed for this land, and for you, Kyliron. My life I give to this land, and to you, my mate. *My King.*" She gently pulled his face up to meet her. He gazed at her beauty. "I am here to help rid you of that which plagues your mind and your heart. I am not your bane. I am your strength. Your lady and queen."

Without warning, he jumped up with all his might, shoving her away. She tried to gain her footing, but his momentum forced her into the water. Fighting the water's resistance, she stood up as quickly as possible. Dripping wet, she poised in a defensive posture.

His eyes burned, red-rimmed with hatred. "You are trying to manipulate me!" His words rang out in a mocking tone. "You can't fool me! Your very presence has been the catalyst for all this to begin! Are you proud of your role, Brigitte? You are my destroyer. You are the destroyer of Atlantis." His voice broke in the rage.

Brigitte edged herself away into the depths of the pool. Water dripped down her face, and she reached up to wipe it away. "The answer is obvious, my lord." She eyed him, reaching blindly to feel for a solid object as she waded backward. "I have been sent to help purge you of whatever this evil is." Her voice shook. "I cannot judge you, nor will I speak of it to anyone outside of this room.

"Whatever is in you was already there before I came. It would be here if I weren't. I am your joined mate now. It is my duty to help you. Perhaps my presence has made it more apparent, but you cannot continue denying it. You must be strong and face whatever it is that makes you suffer." She couldn't help but doubt her words as she spoke.

"I c-could be happy before," he stammered, sobbing. "You make me f-face it and I had the s-strength to s-suppress it b-before you c-came." Like a child reaching out for his mother, he entered the water, crying as he reached for her.

She accepted his embrace with as much invitation as she could pantomime despite the terror in her heart. The aphrodisiac working through her system activated further. His hands began exploring her curves. His fingers worked feverishly to strip away her clothing as he pressed her body against the fountain. Alarmed, she felt her arousal ignite. The effects of the elixirs wove into sensations she could not begin to separate. She had no choice but to surrender to their complex chemistry. Her body lit ablaze with burning desire.

As he fumbled with her clothing, he quickly gave up, and made his way around the fine fabrics with nimble fingers adept at the art of touching women, yet disregarding of tenderness. He tore his own leggings away and entered her in a passionate rage, claiming his mate. As his movement increased, tears streamed down his face. Sobs of agony escaped his throat. He could not contain the pain lodged deep in unseen corners of his mind.

She could feel his anger coursing through her in electric jolts. He sculpted her body against his with powerful arms, pressing the breath out of her. Every thrust filled her with despair, and yet her body exploded with passion. She had never known greater physical pain in her life, but the pleasure of it was equally unbearable. She had no choice. She could not separate from him if she wanted to. The elixirs had completely taken control of every faculty.

Her mind's grasp on awareness disappeared further. She sighed in resignation, closed her eyes, and began breathing steadily. Slowly the sensations turned from pain to pleasure, as she let her mind release. She floated into a cloud of stillness, where an apparition of D'Vinid swept her into a dream, hovering further away from her tortured body.

10

Once more to resonate
among the hills so fair.
Those who suffer blindly
must force themselves to care.
For once the winds begin to blow,
and transfer words that all must know,
aloft upon the highest hill,
the mother must redeem them still.

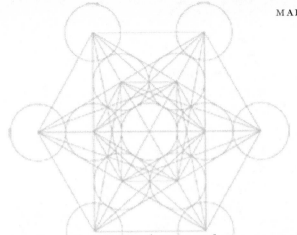

In the queen's garden, meandering paths converged on a node-yard. The obelisk reached toward the stars, a celestial antenna in the eerie light of crystal-illuminators. The air was filled with a chorus of singing insects. Allondriss sat on the ground beside a meditation bench. Her pale face was fixed in a trance at the sky. Lukias approached the scene quietly. She didn't seem to notice.

The node was not much taller than Lukias. It glowed translucent blue under the towering moon. A perfect sphere of clear quartz lined with copper filaments balanced impossibly on the point of the obelisk. It was built into an elaborate fountain made into a mound of amethyst, rose, and clear quartz. Water trickled a smooth flow from the base of the obelisk, its gentle spill constantly purifying the crystals. Canals trailed away from it, fashioned into winding streams traversed by low foot bridges. The bed of the canal was smooth, white marble, and at various junctions along the paths, gushed through smaller fountains.

Lukias sank down on the bench beside Allondriss. Her eyes were focused into dreamsight. Tears rolled down her face, and yet she showed no signs of emotion. He dared not disturb the meditation.

"Lukias." She blinked out of the trance, but her sight remained fixed on the node.

"What do you see in there?" he asked.

"It's not what I see." She nervously scratched the marble. Her eyes darted around, avoiding contact with any one thing. "It's where I go." Finally, she looked toward him. The intensity of her gaze fell short of the space he occupied. Struck speechless by her luminosity, he reached for her hand. But her fingers remained limp in his grip. "This is where I belong." Her attention gravitated back

199

to the node.

"Allondriss." He squeezed her hand harder.

"Ouch!" she cried out. Awareness dawned in her eyes. After a few unsettled moments, she finally bounced back into awareness, and tightened her grip on his hand.

Something sparked between them, an understanding from a dream long forgotten.

"I try and stay away from the nodes." She looked downward in an effort to hide her discomfort. "They suck me into the Grid. Someday I feel like I won't come back. I don't know why I came out here. It was as if the Grid summoned me." She struggled to her feet. He reached to help her up. "I must get back to my bed chamber." Shyly, she looked away. He offered to escort her by wordlessly presenting his elbow.

"The elementals have a message," she remarked, hooking her arm through his. She shook her head, trying to break out of the swirling confusion as he guided her along the moonlit path. "Something about the oceanids. They bring a gift for the arrival of the Moirae to Atlantis. I don't know this word Moirae."

"That is what my sister is called in our dreamclan. She is a Watcher in human form, chosen to judge the Fates of Atlantis. You would never know it, though. She has chosen to focus on the experience of being human. Her powers are not yet awakened."

In her heart she was surprised that Brigitte was a Watcher, and yet she had released her ability to react to emotions long ago. She stared ahead. Silence consumed them as they walked slowly through the garden.

"You say the oceanids have brought my sister a gift? What sort of gift?"

A crease appeared on her forehead. "It is vague. All I can see is someone washed ashore. I get a distinct feeling that Pan is involved." Allondriss stopped to face him, noticing how looking at him made her feel something, which was unusual. Her eyes landed on the crystal at his chest. With a graceful gesture, she reached for it. "The Keylontics are very old in this crystal." She studied it closer. "It's set to someone's blood. You can see it in the shards. Look." She pointed to its surface, and as she turned it to catch light in another way, the rainbow cracks under the surface were revealed.

Lukias took the crystal and rolled it around in his fingers. "You are learned in Keylontics?"

"All temple children are given the chance to advance in Keylontics. We are at least able to read the Fire Letters."

"You must teach me." He was sucked into the beauty of the crystal.

She smiled sweetly. "Of course."

"My sister's tutor gave this to me when we left the shores of our clan. She was Atlantean. She and my sister barely got along, but she treated me like a son. She was as close to a mother as we ever had. Her name was Indrius."

"Why did she give it to you?"

"Indrius said her real son was left in Atlantis, while she was sent to the dreamclans by the Temple Sect. Her last wish was for me to find him. She said this would lead me to him."

"And what would you do when you are led to him?"

"I believe I would give it to him."

"Why didn't you give it to him?" She looked at him knowingly.

He lingered, knowing she shared with him the dangerous secret of Brigitte's unusual rendezvous upon their arrival in the city. "He was not ready to receive it." He shrugged and stared inward. "I believe he may soon be ready. I can feel the crystal's pull. I must leave soon. There are many questions I need answered, but I worry for my sister's safety." He faced her and took both her hands. "I would leave her safety in your hands now, and that of Stixxus. I serve my sister best by gathering information she will need in order to do her job as queen."

She nodded, turning away to conceal the blushing of her cheeks as she felt a pang of regret at his impending absence. At the base of the stairs to her area of the suites, she stopped to steal one last look at him.

He was still watching her, his rugged features framed by the mess of his hair.

"I will stay with her," she promised.

They lingered under the waning moon until, overwhelmed by the feelings he conjured, she turned and quickly ascended the stairs.

Tucked in a quiet social hub on the Ring of Commerce, a rather unremarkable elixir den had a cave-like appeal on the inside. Aside from the bar where the mixologist served his concoctions, every seat was built into its own recess, which could be sealed off by its own door. It was known as a place for private meetings. This night most of the seats were filled with locals laughing and feasting for the Ka-Ma-Sha, reminiscing about their Ka-Ma-Sharri stories.

Fa'nariel Ma'at pulled the door closed in one of the larger private rooms and took a seat at a round table. The members of her conclave occupied the other seats. Atheerian surveyed the group with the depth of his brown eyes. His features were blessed with sharp angles so his hair could grow to any length and frame a handsome face. Four other members of the conclave sat back in their seats, their faces darkened by shadows.

The only newcomer was a man who sprawled in his seat with a casual demeanor. "Ah! You must be the notorious Fa'nariel Ma'at!" He laced his fingers into a formal Atlantean greeting.

She acknowledged him with a bow of the head.

"I am honored to sit with Atheerian Telleria and his special conclave of hunters I've heard so much about." The stranger examined each of them one by one. "Who would think the son and heir of the Telleria Commercian Cartel would be a great leader of the Children of One? But we all have our alter-egos." He devoured Fa'nariel with hungry eyes, suggesting he knew of her other role as kallista. "And to what do I owe this clandestine visit?"

Atheerian, being the chief negotiator on behalf of his family's cartel, was no stranger to politics, as his life path often found him at the courts of mediators and kings. He gestured to Fa'nariel and nodded for her to present their case to the man who called himself The Pathfinder.

Fa'nariel leaned in, lowering her voice into a conspiratorial volume. "We are searching for a Grid Dancer named Vektra. It is said she teaches a variety of dance passed down from the dreamclans."

Atheerian added, "we hear she has single-handedly reprogrammed the Grid in this section of the city."

The Pathfinder smiled and folded his arms. "Why do you seek her?"

"A Grid Dancer as powerful as Vektra should be able to teach other Grid Dancers to reprogram the Grid. Together."

The Pathfinder chuckled. "Oh, I see. You speak of unification. I'm aware you are well-known unificationists. I realize this is a tired argument, but don't you think uniting the conclaves is risky business? Our secrecy, even from one another, affords us privacy from those who would wish us out of existence."

Fa'nariel carefully considered his words, trying to gauge his trustworthiness. She leaned forward for emphasis. "Just like everyone else, I am aware the ways of the conclaves have been banned since the days of Koraxx. I realize Kyliron is carrying on his father's edicts with his ridiculous crusade to silence us. I understand why the conclaves want to hide. But our days of comfort and revelry are over."

Atheerian joined in. "On the night of the Ka-Ma-Sharri, we tracked down a blood ritual here in Poseidia. We haven't seen the shadowmancers often, but their intrusions have become more frequent of late. They worship Watchers who require blood sacrifice to gain strength. I believe they are Children of One, like us. They seem to believe it is our birthright to purge the Grid of those who have fallen to the shadows because they are weak. If left unchecked, they could be the biggest threat Atlantis has ever seen. Can you imagine if the conclaves were to adopt a twisted doctrine of believing we must use our gifts to murder innocent Atlanteans?"

"They were using the eclipse for a ritual." Fa'nariel said. "A blood sacrifice to open a portal and solidify a human host for one of the Blood Triad. We have captured her."

Atheerian leaned back in his chair. "And so, you see, Pathfinder, the stakes have been raised. We need to be ready for unification, if not unified already. We believe Vektra can help us. You should know we are not personally motivated. The unification would not be for glory. It is for the good of all Atlantis. No one, not even the conclaves seem to understand that we are part of nature. We are an evolution. They can try and stop nature, but it will keep growing, regardless. We have it in our power to become a revolution. We can take over the Grid. We have come to believe this to be our responsibility."

"Those are ambitious words." Pathfinder folded his hands in thought. "And I think Vektra will like them." He breathed steadily, cupping his hands before his mouth in measured thought. "You are obviously well-tuned to the Grid to come to this place." He stood up and parted the curtains covering the outside window. The elixir den was surrounded by an elaborate stone deck where a network of stairways joined multiple levels of dwellings overlooking the terraced courtyard. "Vektra's dwelling is nearby. I can fetch her for you." He winked at Fa'nariel. Activity caught their eyes through the window. Two figures ascended the stairs to a higher level of the dwellings and reached one of the doors on the third level. One had a red cape. The other was a woman, lithe, elegant, and black of skin.

"Who do you suppose...?" The Pathfinder squinted. "Looks like Vektra has visitors already."

Fa'nariel and Atheerian exchanged telepathic messages and focused again on Pathfinder. Fa'nariel spoke. "We will investigate." Atheerian nodded to the others and, one by one, they faded into the blue dream.

"Where can I find the singer D'Vinid?" A gravelly voice interrupted Hanonin's thoughts. He turned from his work. The main hold of *Dafni's Enigma* had emptied out considerably since D'Vinid had stopped playing music. A tall, black-clad man stood at the bar. By the looks of his long robe, Hanonin gathered he had come from somewhere in the Learning Sect.

"I hear he was playing music tonight." The man's attitude was arrogant and impatient.

Hanonin looked around, noticing the dabrina abandoned onstage. D'Vinid had left it there before disappearing, presumably courting some young woman. Shaking his head, he pointed at the dabrina. "Alas. That's all I have left of D'Vinid tonight," he grumbled.

The man turned to examine the instrument with aloof interest. "Is this some kind of joke?"

"But of course it is. Life is a joke, and so are you. Are you here to socialize or annoy me with questions?" He gestured to the empty room.

The man began to drum his long fingers on the bar. "I have little respect for these elixir dens, and no love for the Outlands. You must know I detest this errand. But I assure you, when I sleep comfortably in my bed, I will put you and your kind well out of my mind."

"You don't like the elixir dens?" Hanonin leaned in. "And yet here you stand. I am a citizen of Atlantis just like you, whoever you are — and please spare me that knowledge. Whether you like it or not, we are from the same place. Now I don't know where D'Vinid ran off to. If you're quite finished insulting me, I would appreciate it if you left my establishment."

The man strode to the stage, wrapping his spindly fingers around the dabrina's handle. "If he asks," the voice hissed over Hanonin's mumbled curses, "he can retrieve this at the speaker grounds. By decree of the king, he is hereby banned from singing until he appears in formal argument to prove he is not spreading lies against the king's laws on behalf of the Followers of the Axiom of One."

On a quiet street in the Ring of Commerce, Ofira Pazit hovered up to a low-key social hub, tucked away in the central circle of a small neighborhood. Laughter spilled from inside. Shafts of glowing light escaped its windows.

The hub and its intricate patio were built on lower ground. Stairs ascended in all directions to the entry streets and the multiple levels of dwellings surrounding it. One of the city's many canal branches circled the neighborhood, making it a small harbor for private water-crafts. As with all neighborhoods of Poseidia, it was thick with lush greenery and floral fragrances.

The captain dismounted the hover-disc and perched on one of the staircases, casually examining her gloved hands. Her face was hidden in the shadow of her hat. "Are you ready?" she muttered to the imposing warrior who approached, even though she didn't have to speak to it. They were linked, and she could feel it as if it were an extension of herself. A fluid movement rolled her to her feet and up the stairs.

On the third landing, she approached one of the doors and pressed an index finger to her lips. She listened intently and began counting backward from ten. When she reached one, she stepped back and kicked the door with all her might. The door flew open. The dwelling's occupants retreated from the entry except for a tall, black-skinned woman who moved to block the path. She crouched into a fighting stance, holding a small dagger. Many twisted locks of coarse hair framed the savage beauty of her face.

Prince Azai and Rayliis had many resources in the ten king-doms. It took all afternoon, but calling in favors and visiting Og ambassadors around the city had finally led them to the residence of Vinesia Shanel, who had been known as the long time love of the elusive Prince Bavendrick.

Ofira raised her hands. "You don't need that weapon. I'm not here to fight. I'm just here to collect Vinesia." She sauntered into the room.

"How did you know we were here?" Rayliis inquired, maintain-ing her stance.

"I am a servant of the Watchers. And they are not particularly pleased with your actions at the moment. This woman is in their favor. I must ask you to release her to me immediately."

Inside the inner chamber, Prince Azai pulled Vinesia toward a balcony. His face was covered by a revelry disguise. A red cape flipped in the breeze wafting in from the patio. He drew a knife and held it to her throat.

Ofira laughed chirpily. "Oh, come now, Your Highness, none of us needs this show. We both know you won't be killing her," she teased. "We all know you need her alive. Drop the act. It's almost insulting. Set her free and let us negotiate like proper Atlanteans." She examined Azai, the younger Prince of Og. He was reedy of stature. His clothing was functional for travel, yet easily distin-guishable for its courtly fashion. His ruffled hair was held from his forehead by goggles used as a headband. His dark-skinned partner backed toward the balcony, blocking Ofira's advance.

Held in his grasp, Vinesia stared at her with pleading eyes.

"Who sent you here? How did you know we were here?" Azai demanded, pressing the knife closer to her throat. Vinesia panted.

Ofira casually ran her hand over the surface of the entry table. "I told you. I am a servant of the Watchers. By their decree, this woman is favored. So, I wouldn't think about hurting her. Need I remind you the Watchers are the guardians of the threshold between life and death? You would discover the truth of this the moment you hurt her."

The prince continued to stare at Ofira. His eyes held no regard for her warning as he backed toward the balcony, dragging Vinesia along with him.

Ofira mentally summoned her warrior.

Prince Azai noticed the imposing shadow darkening the threshold. "Look, I just want to know where to find my cousin Bavendrick." He pushed Vinesia toward them and tucked the blade back in its sheath.

"What do you mean?" Vinesia demanded, her voice raised to a higher pitch. "Bavendrick is supposed to be in Og." She rubbed her throat. Finally free from his grasp, she recognized the prince.

"He was not on the ship sent from Poseidia. Look, I need my cousin to come and join with my sister. My brother died at your betrothal ceremony. That makes me heir to the throne of Og. If Bavendrick comes he can have the throne."

"But that doesn't answer my question." Vinesia leaned toward his face with her eyes narrow. "Where is he?"

Azai turned around with a frustrated swing of his fist toward air. "I was hoping you would tell me."

The temperature in the room dropped. Their breath turned to vapor. Shadows darkened the corners. Rayliis drew two blades from her belt and stood back-to-back with Azai. The shadows grew faces, moaning with treacherous intent. They reached out from all directions.

Dark vortexes materialized next to Vinesia into the form of cloaked men. Their faces were covered in black runes, their arms and legs wrapped with death shrouds. Their icy touch spread across her skin like poison. She could feel herself losing consciousness as they muttered a guttural incantation.

The animata warrior tried to grab one of them. His hands passed right through. Ofira watched with wide eyes. Before she could react, an explosion of light sent the shadows screeching into the night. They were surrounded by Children of One, brandishing blades of light. One of them stepped up with a mighty heave of his sword and sliced through the body of a shadowmancer, who disappeared in a whirl of shadows. The Children of One disappeared in kind.

Azai saluted with a flick of his fingers and slid over the balcony. While free-falling, he clicked open a hover-disc. The torsion-crystal spun into its high-pitched whirl as it searched for a telluric current that did not exist three stories up. Rayliis copied his move, and together they fell from the balcony, expertly using narrow surfaces to bounce to the ground and speed away.

Ofira leaned out to watch them leave, her mouth downturned, impressed with their skill.

Vinesia collected herself. She had an air of equanimity even in the face of danger. With graceful movements that covered the shaking of her hands, she went to work picking up the items knocked to the ground in her struggle. She carefully avoided the animata warrior. "Ofira Pazit. I never thought I'd be happy to see you."

Ofira was lost in thought. "Were those…"

"Shadowmancers. Like at the docks earlier. I guess they figured out I'm a dreamclan emissary. I guess you can tell my mother she's right. I am in danger."

"Well, as you seem to know, your mother did send me to find you."

"She's suddenly begun to care, then?"

"She's your mother. All mothers love their daughters. It's the daughters most of the time who choose not to believe it. You will be safer with me for a while."

Vinesia looked at Ofira, deadpan. She shifted her stare at the warrior and wrinkled her brow. The shock was beginning to wear off. She let out a trembling breath. "Let's be forthright. Why did she send you?"

"I am a caretaker of the dreamclans. Your mother is a very important part of the Watchers' workings. You must not forget your birthright, my dear."

"On the contrary, I know it all too well." Vinesia sat down, fixed ahead with a vacant stare. "What do I do? I want to run. But where do I go? I can't go out into the night. I can't stay here."

"You have me and Ritt now. Oh, I named him Ritt." She gestured to the warrior.

Vinesia stared ahead. "I rue the day I was born into nobility with dreamclan blood. My parents thought it would be amusing to negotiate my life away to the royal family after Bavendrick's first betrothal ended. They thought because we had true love, we would make adorable mates." She ground her throat. "And when Kyliron ruined me at court, they didn't stand up for me. They just bent to his wishes to preserve the family standing. You can't use love as a tool and expect everything to be ok when things fall apart. I took the fall for them. The least they can do is let me grieve."

"My dear, your father is the mediator of all sha'mana mining in the ten kingdoms. He could wave his hand, and everyone would conveniently forget. His sister is the mediator delegate on the High Council. Your family's standing is well entrenched."

"Then why couldn't they stand up for me? Why did they let me take the fall?"

Ofira shrugged. "Because time is the great eraser of memories. You are still young. In a few decades, who will remember?"

Vinesia buried her face in her hands. "That's not good enough." Her voice wavered.

"Don't be too sure of the future, my dear." She reached out a hand to pat Vinesia's back. "The new you is still the old you, Vektra." Ofira winked and plopped sideways into a chair, kicking her feet on the table beside it.

Vinesia snapped upright. "How do you know that name?"

"Your mother taught you the Dance of the Elementa. It is a specialty of her people. Your people. The Dreamclan of Hermes are known for their ability to align the Grid. The work you've done reprogramming the Grid in this sector is no secret among those who are awakened. Vektra is a hero."

"What does my mother want?"

"How should I know? I'm sure you can find out in this messenger-crystal." Ofira produced it from her shoulder satchel.

Vinesia stared at the crystal.

"You know how to use these, I take it?"

Vinesia wrinkled her face as she took it. "This is encoded. I need to go to a nodeyard and unlock it with the Grid."

"There will be one where we are heading."

Vinesia nodded, conceding the argument. She gathered some outfits from the cabinets and stuffed them haphazardly into a satchel. "And where, may I ask, might our heading be?"

Ofira smiled. "To an old friend's place. Someone who will be able to keep you safe."

Prince Azai and Rayliis watched from the darkness as the two women hovered away. The animata warrior trotted easily behind.

The night seemed still, despite voices spilling from the neighborhood elixir den.

Azai lowered the embroidered scarf from his face and nudged Rayliis, tossing his head toward their departure. "I do think she is still our best lead in finding Bavendrick," he calculated, stroking his chin. A smile formed on his lips. "I see why my cousin Bavendrick has stayed in love with her. We are stubborn with our freewill, the line of Atlas. A very big mess has been made, and I don't think it was Kyliron who caused it. I think he is a victim who is merely trained to perpetuate it."

"She is important for other reasons, my prince. Need I remind you that her father is the mediator of sha'mana processing in Dragonspine?" Rayliis prepared her hover-disc. "You should think about that the next time you decide to hold a knife to her throat." She raised her eyebrows severely.

He nodded with a deep sigh. "Of course, I was only bluffing. I don't know who that other woman was, but she has made this task significantly more difficult." He mounted his hover-disc and winked back at her. "But you know how I love a challenge."

Rayliis stared at him as he hovered away, and quickly joined in pursuit of Vinesia and her mysterious liberator.

Two figures materialized out of Dreamtime as Prince Azai began his hunt. Atheerian glanced at Fa'nariel.

"Was that Vektra?" he squinted. "She's the one who told us about her in the first place. She was talking about herself?"

"You know who that is?"

"Vinesia Shanel, formerly betrothed to Prince Bavendrick," Atheerian spoke in a distant voice.

Fa'nariel continued. "She was a famous Grid dancer in her day. Her mother was a dreamclan emissary. That makes her a first-generation hybrid. It would make sense Vektra would be her hidden identity." She flipped her head back in revelation. "Why did the shadowmancers follow her here? They may be trying to destroy the treaty. But why? What would they have to gain unless they're trying to destroy Atlantis?"

"Maybe they're trying to change them into shadowmancers." Atheerian suggested.

Fa'nariel pondered his theory. "That bears some thought."

He added. "That woman with her was at the cartel docks today with D'Vinid. The vortex has made itself clear."

"Who do you suppose those other two are, following them?"

Atheerian shook his head. "I didn't get a good look at them. But I think it might be wise to lead them astray. I don't like them."

Fa'nariel smiled. "Neither do I." She lowered her goggles. "Let's have some fun, shall we?"

They simultaneously vanished into the blue dream and began hunting the hunters.

Under the cover of darkness, a hover-carriage passed through an elaborate gateway, embellished with tridents and other nautical symbols. A single rider hovered alongside. The twins sat at the controls, caught in a bickering clash of wills. "You were the one who told father we rearranged the seats at the feast. Why could you not have the sense to keep your mouth shut?"

The other twin opened and closed his fingers to mimic his brother's incessant yammering.

"I'm not arguing with you anymore. You're wrong. Just like you're always wrong. And I don't even see why I argue with you in the first place. It's just a waste of breath, because not only are you wrong, but you don't believe you're wrong! That makes you good for just about nothing."

They directed the hover-carriage to a roundabout and climbed to the ground. One of them belched as he stretched his arms back.

"You two are never subtle, are you?" D'Vinid reined in the Aello twins as he dismounted the hover-disc. "Nor are you aware of your surroundings. I have never understood why your father places so much faith in you in the first place."

"We're his sons!" Jensyn put his fists on his hips, incensed. "He *has* to trust us."

Kayden nodded in agreement. It was the first thing they had agreed on since their long hover from the ocean to the Aello estate.

They were approached by a pair of servants.

"Ah!" Jensyn threw his arms wide. "I'm glad you came to greet us! Please see to it our guest in the carriage is brought to the water bungalows. Put him in the third one, and make sure the doors are

locked. He had too many of the wrong elixirs at the revelry." He winked at D'Vinid to point out his clever subterfuge.

The servants assessed the situation, and one went in search of a smaller hover-sled from the Aello gatehouse.

"Come on!" Kayden beckoned to D'Vinid. "Let's go see our father."

D'Vinid lingered on Bavendrick. "I don't think I will be leaving our friend's side. Have your father come see us."

The twins formed identical frowns.

"We could just not tell our father," Kayden suggested.

"And what would that accomplish?" asked his brother.

"Well," Kayden pondered. "If we just take care of our 'guest' ourselves, it will keep the secret even more secret. We can't have people knowing where he is. If father doesn't know, then even fewer people know."

Jensyn hit Kayden over the head. "Don't be ridiculous! Our father knows everything! That would only get us in more trouble! That's the dumbest idea you've had all day."

D'Vinid released a heavy sigh of impatience. By now the servants had loaded Bavendrick onto the sled. The prince moaned while he was being moved.

The twins gave in and followed the processional to the water bungalows. When Bavendrick was safely tucked into bed, D'Vinid flipped his head toward them. "Don't you have any healers to summon?" he suggested.

"Oh, yes, of course!" Jensyn stuck his head out the door to the departing servants. "Fetch some sentinels to watch over this bungalow, and a healer. Oh, and food to eat."

"And something to drink!" Kayden added.

Jensyn slammed the door.

D'Vinid sat down in the seat next to the bed. "Let's play an honesty game while we wait. How were you able to find me on Ka-Ma-Sharri?"

"We didn't have a locator-crystal, if that's what you're asking," Jensyn answered, as he went to work checking for dust on the surfaces of furniture around the bungalow.

"Then, how?" D'Vinid flipped his wrist to encourage an answer.

They both looked around conspiratorially and pulled crystals from their inner pockets. "Children of One have soul-crystals we use to tap into the Grid," Jensyn explained. "There are so many ways you can use them. We happen to be really good at locating because we can triangulate someone's location using the Grid."

D'Vinid produced the crystal wand Fa'nariel had given him from an inner pocket. "Can you help me access this? There's an energy signature in it I need to locate."

The twins' eyes lit up. Jensyn snatched it from his hand and rolled it around between his fingers.

They focused on each other. "Should we take him to the estate nodeyard?" Kayden suggested.

"I think it's the best idea," Jensyn agreed.

D'Vinid snatched it back.

A healer woman arrived at the door, interrupting the moment, much to D'Vinid's relief. Of course, Pan employed only the best onsite healers. This one was another temple outcast like Allondriss. Immediate recognition widened her eyes as she carefully assessed the prince's recovery protocol.

Kayden leaned in close to her ear, massaging her shoulders. "Of course, no one is to be told of this. I do hope you understand."

She nodded, holding Bavendrick's hand, gently probing his auric field with a crystal. She eased and looked up. "He has suffered from elemental invasion. But he will recover with proper rest and care."

"We will be going to fetch our father now," said Jensyn. "Stay with him until we return, yes?"

She nodded again.

The twins and D'Vinid took one last look at Bavendrick and stepped into the moonlit gardens of Pan's estate.

"The nodeyard first, then?" said D'Vinid in a tone suggesting that "yes" would be the only acceptable answer.

Using enthusiastic gestures, the twins directed their path to the estate's nodeyard. The node glowed from within, as if it had absorbed the lunar blue flooding the sky.

Crystals of all shapes and sizes were configured in a formation designed to amplify the six-foot-tall capacitor. Jensyn crept through the crystal garden and took a position next to the node. Kayden did the same. Inching closer, D'Vinid held the crystal given him by Fa'nariel. Assuming it had been with Loressai at some point, he concentrated on her.

As the clouds covering the moon parted and the sky brightened, the Aello twins touched their soul-crystals to the surface of the node.

As they began to concentrate, a rush of images flooded D'Vinid's head. He quickly pulled away, stunned by the vastness of the Grid. He could immediately tell it would take practice to get used to the images. The twins convulsed as they pressed their crystals to the node. D'Vinid decided to try a different approach. He focused on projecting his thoughts to the twins to harness their alleged ability to locate through triangulation.

They both jolted, and an image of Loressai appeared. Suddenly, it sizzled with static and noise, and was replaced by the menacing shadow face of the demonic creature who had possessed her. D'Vinid cried out. Dropping the crystal, he tried desperately to block out the terrifying image.

"What was that?" Kayden's voice was awash with anxiety.

"That, I'm afraid, is our adversary," D'Vinid confessed.

"Then we must not ever get its attention again," said Kayden.

"But we have the upper hand," Jensyn countered. "If we don't do our duty and find a way to banish this creature, we will be no better than anyone we despise in Atlantis."

"You can't be serious. Us?" Kayden grunted. "How do you figure we have the upper hand?"

D'Vinid rolled his eyes. "Here we go again, you two bickering away."

The twins flanked him, Kayden on the left and Jensyn on the right, appealing to him as the judge of their new argument.

"Why is it our responsibility to do something about this?" Kayden pleaded. "Just because we saw it doesn't mean it's up to us to face it! We don't even have the skills!"

"But that doesn't change the fact we saw it! That means the Watchers have given us a mission." Jensyn had a look of longing on his face.

"What if it's a trap? What if it's trying to lure us so it can suck us into its lair?"

"Then we will have given our lives for a noble cause." Jensyn looked meaningfully into the sky.

"Enough! Both of you need to just... shut up!" D'Vinid stormed off into the garden. They stared at one another, their clash simmer-

215

ing. The sound of approaching voices echoed through the garden. The twins remained silent and ducked into a shadow to get a good look at who would appear out of the darkness.

A beam of golden light shone into the courtyard of Queen Dafni. The tree branches stretched into the stars. Brigitte bathed in the gathering light, allowing it to purify her body. Two roses grew from the ground, marking the entrance to a cavernous opening. The darkness led to a view of stars inside the planet. "As above, so below. As within, so without." The words were a floating whisper on the wind. Brigitte wanted to leap into the opening and escape, but somehow she remained held in the light, unable to move.

"I must find answers, sister." The voice of her brother drifted through the dream. "I will be gone when you awake."

"No! Lukias, I need you."

"I am with you always. Never fear. I will return."

Brigitte opened her eyes. Overwhelming discomfort overtook her body as she realized she was pinned beneath Kyliron as they slept. A subtle snore labored his breathing. She carefully pushed him away, but he pulled her into a tighter lock. She struggled harder until she was free of his grasp. Gently she crawled to the other side of the rounded bed, and curled into a fetal position, relieved to be free from his suffocating weight.

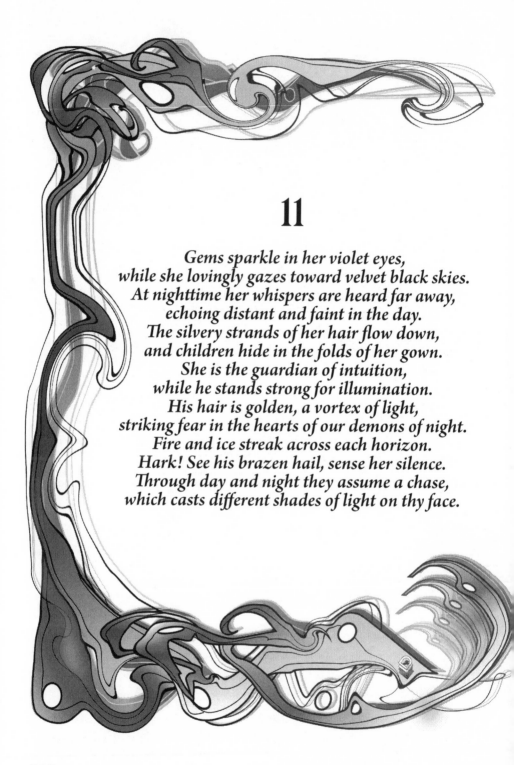

11

Gems sparkle in her violet eyes,
while she lovingly gazes toward velvet black skies.
At nighttime her whispers are heard far away,
echoing distant and faint in the day.
The silvery strands of her hair flow down,
and children hide in the folds of her gown.
She is the guardian of intuition,
while he stands strong for illumination.
His hair is golden, a vortex of light,
striking fear in the hearts of our demons of night.
Fire and ice streak across each horizon.
Hark! See his brazen hail, sense her silence.
Through day and night they assume a chase,
which casts different shades of light on thy face.

The twins huddled in the shadows of a low-hanging tree and watched as Pan entered the courtyard escorting two women. Their voices were hushed, though accented with hints of urgency.

D'Vinid snuck back, having heard the same approach, and watched from afar. He immediately recognized the two women as Ofira Pazit and Vinesia Shanel. D'Vinid had always sympathized with Vinesia's downfall. Since it was Kyliron who ruined her reputation, he always wondered about the truth of the matter.

But then it dawned on him with a shiver. It was Pan who stood up for her in the courts. Pan didn't know about Bavendrick's presence, and yet, here was Vinesia. Or did he know? Or was this Ofira's doing? He produced the crystal she had given him and wondered if it had some kind of spying ability. Was the vortex that specific?

"My dear Vinesia, you are looking more vibrant and beautiful than I've ever seen you." Pan's high timbre bounced vibrantly through the courtyard. "I have been wishing I could see you more often. Please consider attending my revelries from time to time."

"Thank you, Pan Aello." Vinesia's smile was genuine. She was dressed in simple Builder Sect clothing which failed to flatter her figure. Her dark skin was flawless, showing the upbringing of a proper Atlantean noblewoman, although she didn't carry herself with the refined grace of her station any longer. Once, there had been a chance she would be queen. And now, she had chosen simplicity.

Pan liked to make sure she never forgot it. He accepted it was most likely the reason she avoided his hospitality. D'Vinid had never known anyone who had more fortitude of spirit than she.

219

And for that, he admired her profoundly. "I have recently made a new friend," Pan chirped as they entered the nodeyard. "She is from the dreamclans. Her name is Brigitte. And tonight she has become Queen of Atlantis."

Vinesia shuddered.

"Soon she will need to appoint a maydriss in her court. I was thinking about recommending you, since you have all the courtly training of a queen."

Vinesia stopped, stunned by the audacity of his suggestion. "Pan, why do you insist on teasing me?"

"My dear, I would never tease you where it hurts. But I would offer you a chance at revenge. Pay it no mind. It was just one of my outlandish ideas." He waved it away. "Why don't you take care of your business with the crystal-node, and then Ofira and I shall escort you to your guest room."

Vinesia thanked him, then stepped to the node and sank into a meditative state, feeling the edges of the messenger-crystal between her fingers.

Pan stepped aside with Ofira and began talking quietly as not to disturb Vinesia's meditation. Their conversation brought them closer to where D'Vinid was hiding. Though they spoke in hushed voices, D'Vinid could easily overhear them.

"It's been a while since we've had one of our talks," said Pan to Ofira.

"I see you've acquired some excellent pieces for your gameboard." She matched his volume. Together they ambled in silence with their hands clasped behind their backs.

"Were you able to coerce D'Vinid with your insatiable magnetism?" he poked playfully.

"I have my reasons for wanting him around. They're not all your reasons, Pan."

"I understand. The two of you would make a lovely pair."

"Don't even imagine you know my reasons. Tonight I waited at *Dafni's Enigma* after he played that show. And just as you said, they came to get him. Since they didn't find him, they took his dabrina instead. I'm afraid the king will have his hands on it before too long."

The twins shared a glance, shrugged, and decided to reveal themselves to their father. And they did so with great panache.

Their ungraceful ambush managed to inflict a sense of unwanted panic on Ofira and Pan, yet they both managed to keep their composure.

"The puppet master with twin fools for sons," Ofira mumbled.

"Ofira Pazit," Jensyn scowled. "You owe me a favor. I won that bet, and you disappeared like you always do, because you lost."

"You're still holding on to that, Kayden?"

"I'm Jensyn. He's Kayden."

"Fine, whatever, whoever. You're both so far from my mind, I nearly forgot how the Fates granted you one instance of being correct."

"Now children, you must not quarrel. Our guest is communing with the Grid," Pan interrupted.

"We have brought other guests, father," Kayden leaned in to whisper in his ear. But Jensyn pushed him away. "I wanted to tell him! You didn't want to tell him at all!"

Pan laughed. "Jensyn, you tell me the name of one guest, and Kayden you tell me the other until you are finished with the news."

Jensyn leaned in to deliver his news in a whispered secret. Pan's eyes widened. He looked back at Vinesia and stroked his goatee in thought. "Prince Bavendrick?" He looked at Kayden. "And how did you come about this prize?"

"It was D'Vinid who found him," Kayden announced proudly. They began looking around in the garden, but the singer was nowhere to be seen.

"You mean D'Vinid is in this garden?" Pan peered at Ofira. "Do you think he overheard what we said?"

"Last thing we saw of D'Vinid, he was leaving the garden. We should try Bavendrick," said Jensyn.

"What about Bavendrick?" Vinesia interrupted them, having finished her meditation. She wiped tears from her eyes.

Pan scanned the twins, wordlessly ordering them to remain silent. "Word in the courts is that Bavendrick claims he is still betrothed to you. When Kyliron offered him to the Princess of Og, Bavendrick insisted he already had a chosen mate. You. And yet, he left on a ship bound for Og."

"Oh, please." She folded her arms indignantly. "Only a fool holds onto romantic memories of first love."

"Then what you say is you don't love Bavendrick anymore?" Pan asked.

"Of course, I love him. But I am realistic. He is a fool to hold onto me. I have moved on."

Pan gestured to the twins. "My sons will lead us to where you will be staying." He nodded, hoping they would bring them to Bavendrick without making it known.

They both nodded back, a bit too obvious in signaling their understanding. Pan shook his head and cracked a smile, his upper lip twitching.

"I take it you've accessed your mother's message?" Ofira asked to draw attention from the comic display.

"I have. What do you know of the attacks on dreamclans? My mother says our entire clan has gone missing. She wants me to visit her in person."

"I have been investigating these attacks. But I'm afraid I have few leads. It seems as though the shadows that cause the madness have been harnessed by something else. If you wish to accept your mother's summons, I would be honored to grant you passage on the *Vex Voyager*. As you know, Dragonspine is a few hours away by ocean. I can cover it in one hour if the ship takes flight."

"Thank you, Captain. May I think on it?"

"Whatever you wish."

They arrived at the over-water bungalows and began crossing the walkway. Sentinels stood watch at the third bungalow.

"Am I in so much danger as to have my own guardians?" Vinesia asked.

The door swung open at Pan's order. Past the threshold, the bungalow opened into a rounded bed chamber. But the bed was not empty. "They are not for you, my dear. But for him."

Vinesia rushed to the bed. "Bavendrick!" she cried. "What happened to him? Is he hurt?" She brushed a lock of hair from his face, examining him feverishly. The fear in her eyes betrayed her love for him.

"I see now how you've moved on," Pan chided. "I will leave you two alone for a while." He walked back outside where Ofira and the twins awaited. "Now, where is D'Vinid?" Pan searched the night.

"He was here with us." Kayden scratched his head.

"Don't worry," said Ofira. "D'Vinid has a locator I gave him. I just have to access it."

"Then do so." Pan seemed impatient. He turned to the twins and shook his finger at them. "The next time you run into D'Vinid, you make sure he stays with you. Do you understand?"

They nodded furiously.

"He should be in here." Ofira pushed at the door of the neighboring bungalow. It swung open. But the room stood empty except for a locator-crystal resting by itself on the bed. She looked at Pan gravely. "I imagine he did overhear us."

"Something tells me you're right." Pan cast an accusing glance at his sons but couldn't bring himself to say anything.

"I bet you didn't see that one coming." Ofira leaned against the wall with a sideways smile.

Pan's look was bordering on ferocity. "Being human has its limitations, my dear." With one more look of disdain toward the twins, he turned and stormed toward the main house.

"You've done it again!" Ofira laughed dismissively at Jensyn and Kayden.

"What did we do? It was you who said things D'Vinid shouldn't overhear. That's one of my father's main rules: Never say anything out loud you don't want overheard. We can find him again whenever we want, anyway." Kayden nudged the railing of the bridge with his toe.

"Well, show me to my quarters, then," she ordered. "I will fix this in the morning when I have rested. It's been a very long, busy day."

"Not until you grant me my debt." Jensyn folded his arms. Kayden did the same, showing support for his brother.

She sighed heavily. "What is it you want from me?"

"I want you to answer a question honestly."

She tilted her head and gestured for him to say it quickly.

"What do you know of embodied Watchers? And is our father one of them?"

Ofira sputtered into laughter. "Which question would you like me to answer?"

Kayden hit his twin on the arm. "You are so stupid," he complained.

Ofira decided to be generous. "Pick one."

"Can I decide later?" Jensyn fidgeted nervously.

"Show me to my room."

They both gestured to the neighboring bungalow with identical devilish grins.

She stepped through the entry and turned around. "There *are* Watchers walking among us. And rest assured you've met one or two in your lifetime."

With that, she shut the door and prepared to slip into the comfort of the bed. She picked up the locator-crystal and squeezed it in her hand. She hadn't told Pan, but she knew D'Vinid was right where he was supposed to be. "You will come back, D'Vinid. You cannot escape the Fates once they have been cast." She smiled to herself and dropped into a dreamless sleep.

D'Vinid walked slowly to *Dafni's Enigma*, feeling entirely horrible. There was a nagging at the back of his mind. Sometimes the feeling was worse than other times, but mostly it lingered like a gray haze.

Entering the main hold of the ship, he crossed straight to the stage where he had left his dabrina, hoping Ofira's words were untrue. But it was indeed gone. He couldn't even begin to comprehend why she wouldn't prevent it from being taken. Then again, she worked for the Watchers, and this was exactly why he despised them.

The moment he entered, Hanonin's cynical voice called his name. "I guess they found out about your little show. You might have been able to stop him if you had been here. Tall fellow from the Speaker Sect. Rude. Arrogant. You know, the punchy type. Not the kind throwin' the punches, if you know what I mean. Be thankful this is the worst thing that happened."

"Hanonin, you let him take my dabrina!" D'Vinid's voice shook.

"I was over here! I'm old. I can't go chasing tall men down the street. I'm no hero. You should know that."

"They can't just take my dabrina!"

"He did say you can get it from the Speaker Sect when you appear in formal argument. He didn't steal it. He just confiscated it. Would you stop singing if he didn't take it? I doubt it."

"But I'm not spreading lies about Kyliron, and I'm definitely not involved with these crazy Children of One. Kyliron doesn't even know what he's talking about." He paused, not wanting to quarrel with Hanonin.

"Then you have nothing to worry about. Just go to argument and say you're innocent. The crystals can tell if you're lying."

"I will never be innocent in Kyliron's eyes. Never mind." He stormed out the door, adding under his breath, "You don't know Kyliron like I know Kyliron."

As he walked, he wrestled with half-plans, all of which ended with terrible consequences. The thought of Kyliron's hands on his beloved instrument filled his blood with fire. The dabrina was his only family. It was his connection to a mother he knew only in dreams and imaginings.

This is ridiculous, he thought. *I'm getting my dabrina back.*

A cold wind rushed through the esplanade corridor.

He felt suddenly drunk. The air turned to gel, impeding his movements, brushing across his skin like velvet. His mind flashed a momentary universe of information. The bliss of it was unsurpassed.

A voice rang through his head like thunder. *"You have nothing to fear, for I have chosen you. We are armed with the Cunning, hidden by the folding of space. The more they pursue you, the more they will fail. I am for I am thou."* D'Vinid stumbled along the path, holding his head. Everything faded into a slow-motion dancing tapestry.

Shadows swarmed as if the streets themselves were alive. He tried to steady himself and focus on something solid. They called out to him. He pushed them away with all his might, collapsing in the corner of an alcove to shield himself from the unwelcome awareness. Lightning flashed in the sky and a sudden peace descended upon him.

" ....*Darkness is a measure of thy mind*," he thought. *"If thou chooseth to walk the paths of night, then thy world shall shape itself to fit thy journey. For the nature of matter is truly fluid; and thy desire, that which shapes it…"*

Brigitte watched the sparkling undulation of crystal blue waters as ripples formed from her caress. A bird landed, spilling water over its ruffled feathers. The sight offered something of interest in her gloomy fog.

She lay at the edge of Kyliron's garden pool, watching the servants set up breakfast for them. It was supposed to be a celebration of their first morning as joined mates. But as of yet, Kyliron did not emerge. She stripped naked and descended into the pool of his proclaimed magical healing waters. The temperature was neither hot nor cold. It wrapped around her skin with luxurious texture. Her reflection in the water's surface looked back at her.

She barely recognized it.

She tried to summon a memory of where she had been before. She thought of Lukias, her one rock. He was nowhere to be seen. A flash of panic sucked the breath from her lungs. She leaned closer to examine the strange reflection in the water. She was entranced. The woman was beautiful, with honey hair crowned in sunlight. She wanted to reach out and touch her hand, but the water enveloped her fingers, and slowly shimmered into shards of color and light. Her heart pounded in her chest as if it were begging to be released.

She thought again of Lukias, and the thought of him helped her remember who she was. She was Brigitte, joined mate of King Kyliron. Seventh High Queen of Atlantis's third dynasty. Daughter of Denikon, High Seer of the ocean's dreamclan. And sister... of Lukias. Her brother kept her anchored to that past. She remembered he was the newly-ascended high seer of their clan. That meant their father was gone. She furrowed her brow. But how?

She sank and dipped her head into the aquatic underworld. The perfect temperature encircled her into weightlessness, an elemental womb preparing to birth her anew. Her hair flowed with luxurious grace.

Indrius was gone, too. Brigitte remembered the many details of her teachings more than anyone from the dream of before. Indrius had been so luminous and filled with knowledge. But her heart was always distant, pointing like an ever-aiming arrow across the sea. She radiated a point of light across Brigitte's mind.

Then her pondering switched to D'Vinid, and her mind drifted to the light igniting inside her womb. Her heart clenched and she popped out of the water, emerging into the uncomfortable world outside the containment of the healing waters. She gasped for air, coughing and sputtering. As the liquid film over her eyes cleared, she grasped at the edge of the crafted shore and caught her breath.

But how did she come to be here in the first place? The first thing she remembered clearly was overlooking Poseidia from the *Vex Voyager*, the face of Captain Ofira Pazit staring at her. Her next memory was appearing in the mound crossing with Lukias. The rest of her journey was quickly fading like the images of a dream. But from the moment they reached Atlantis, she remembered everything, as if she had been birthed again into the life of someone else.

She reached for the golden gown that had crumpled to the ground and wrapped it around her. She wandered back to the courtyard where servants lingered, waiting to deliver the feast to a low table built into a flower-framed grotto.

"Oh, look! There she is! My wayward queen." Kyliron awaited her in the courtyard, fresh, shaved, dressed, and luminous. Brigitte's heart sank at his bronze beauty.

A chuckle escaped his lips at the sight of her. "I'm glad to see you are enjoying my healing pool. You're late for our joining breakfast, but I will overlook it, my love." He watched her darkly as she approached the dining area. She didn't bother to answer his hypocritical comment. She had been taught they would be equals upon their joining, so she did not bow at the sight of him.

A newfound strength consumed her actions. She brushed past him and pushed into the dining recess to carefully arrange herself amid pillows and cushions. Hints of her curves could be seen through her transparent gown. The dining area was framed by a flimsy canopy, punctuated with golden strands. While waiting for him, she had become fascinated with the shimmering fabric as it blew in the wind. Beauty everywhere captured her attention. Nothing seemed real anymore.

He examined her with a gleam of hunger. "You are radiant, my queen, even still today. This pleases me." He snaked toward her, crawling through the pillows.

"There is more to life than beauty, my king," she answered, her voice flat, poising herself in a warning for him to keep his distance.

He laughed. "On the higher realms of existence, all souls are beautiful to behold. Those of us who have beauty on this plane are closer to our creator." He sat back in the cushions, choosing instead to invade her with his eyes. She squirmed under his scrutiny.

"You know you are mine now, Brigitte. If I choose to touch you, you must obey. It is your duty now as my queen." He crossed his arms. "But I shall give you your space. You may be confined to your suites and your courtyards all you wish. I have given you your own palace. I will stay in my palace until I choose to come to you. And I may come at my leisure."

The food arrived. Delicate aromas from cooked fruits and meats were caught up in the swirling air. She watched him sit up to observe the incoming dishes, nodding as they were placed on the table adorned with flowers. He leaned back to watch her reaction.

Brigitte remembered the previous night clearly, until the moment she had slipped from her body. The horrible things he said attached to her thoughts. She could not be sure what he had done to her. In the morning she could barely move, but the healing waters had soothed the pain. She decided to allow the meal to distract her, and instead focused with feigned delight at the elaborate feast of sensual foods.

Jamarish Ka entered the courtyard, strolling through the scurry of servants.

Kyliron glared at his royal maydrian.

"You must excuse me, Your Majesty," said the priest. "I was coming to see if the feast pleases you."

Kyliron smiled at Brigitte. "Only if it pleases my queen."

She nodded, her face lit with delight from the morsel melting on her tongue.

Jamarish Ka continued in his soothing voice. "I was hoping to update you on your schedule for the upcoming sun cycles. A king's work is never done." Jamarish Ka bowed, awaiting the king's leave.

Kyliron raised a glass of intoxicating elixir to his lips. "I think my queen can hear my schedule report. It will give her an opportunity to know what I do."

Jamarish Ka nodded. "Indeed, Your Majesty. She is the queen, after all." He read off a list of appointments. Kyliron rolled his eyes at each of them. He virtually ignored the list while taking bites of food.

Brigitte, on the other hand, made it clear she was listening.

"And now to the matter at hand. You are to hear the arguments between the Temple Sect and the Followers of the Axiom of One on the next cycle of the sun. You asked for a report on the goings-on of D'Vinid, the singer, who is accused of spreading their lies, and causing a stir among the people."

A surge of adrenalin sent Brigitte's heart reeling.

Kyliron's face turned to stone. His hand froze where it was, holding a piece of food. It began to shake.

"D'Vinid has not yet been located, though last night, he played a concert at *Dafni's Enigma.*"

Kyliron's face reddened. In an eruption of rage, he flung the food to the table. "He did this to defy me!"

Brigitte tried to seem impartial. But it felt as though her heart pounded louder than they spoke. She could feel herself begin to wither from inside.

"If I find D'Vinid is against me…" Kyliron looked at her like he didn't know she'd been there. "What are you looking at?"

"Nothing, my lord." She cast her eyes down. "I am just confused about the subject you speak of."

He snorted.

Jamarish Ka interjected. "My queen, the Followers of the Axiom of One have spoken against the laws of the land. They have begun to preach on the street of a foreboding future, warning we are going the way of hubris, and that it will lead to our demise. Of course, the king is not pleased with this, though he is determined to give them a fair argument. He will decide whether their words are correct, but until then they are ordered silent, as they are causing unrest.

"D'Vinid is a well-known singer, and childhood friend of the king's, and it has come to our attention he is in line with these zealots, and perhaps even a leader among them. His Majesty has ordered the singer silent until he appears in argument to confirm he does not speak against the king." He turned his attention to Kyliron, whose eyes were fixed on the table in fuming intensity. "As far as we know, *Dafni's Enigma* was one of the first places we sent notice to suspend his performances. It can only mean an act of defiance has been made against Your Majesty's decree by not only D'Vinid, but perhaps the ship's owner."

Kyliron's face stretched into lines of contempt. "Then they are part of this movement against me. Seize my mother's ship immediately. Close down the elixir den until further notice."

"Very well. There is good news. The Speaker Sect has confiscated D'Vinid's dabrina. Perhaps now he will show up to present himself."

Kyliron stared ahead, despondent. Brigitte remained as calm and steady as she could, knowing her meeting with D'Vinid had layers of meaning carefully orchestrated by the Watchers.

"Have the dabrina brought to me in my chambers," he grumbled.

"As you wish, Your Majesty."

Kyliron's eyes glassed over. Something dark began to take hold of him. Brigitte could see it, the same raging beast that had taken him before her very eyes on the previous night.

"Jamarish Ka, you have disturbed my joining meal long enough. You are excused." Kyliron regained his composure and glared again at Brigitte.

The maydrian added, "The both of you will be presented in the peoples' square later today. Please rest well for this important occasion."

As Jamarish Ka left the garden, Kyliron took a few bites of food and calmed down. He slipped closer along the soft bench they shared. "Your duty is to please your king, and hear tribute befitting the matriarch of this land." He grabbed her wrist and pulled her close. "I would have D'Vinid put to death if he ever spoke to you, my sweet, beautiful queen. You will be the one thing that will remain unsullied by him."

Her face drained of all color. "You're hurting my wrist, Kyliron." She twisted her arm away, rubbing the red skin where he had grasped it.

He leaned against her. His tone softened. "I have forgone the traditional mating sequence to present you to the people. Usually new mates are not presented to the public until this period is over. Does this please you? My people will be so inspired by your beauty, they will have no choice but to love me more."

She nodded, though inside she wanted to scream. They sat quietly. A truce-like peace settled as they watched the morning drift by. She found herself wondering if there was any escape from the palace. Instead, only a theater of deceit materialized out of the churning panic of her thoughts. Her heart sank into despair as he fell fast asleep in her lap.

She began reciting in her mind bits and pieces of the personal credo taught her as Moirae. *"I am a warrior of the subconscious. I am the observer, the messenger, the weaver."*

Her face set in cold anger as she developed the understanding that she was helplessly trapped. As the awareness took hold, flowers and plants slowly wilted around them until the king's garden was completely dead, destroyed by the raw, unharnessed, elemental power of the Moirae.

A single tree grew from a circle of gardens. Its branches formed an umbrella of twinkling lights. Three roses sprung from the ground at its base. Beneath the boughs stood a luminous being, beckoning toward a broad opening in the trunk, which led below to a starlit sky. As the garden slowly wilted, within the opening, Dreamtime swallowed the tree in an eddy of light and sound.

The inky waters of an underground lake stood still as death. A woman sat in a dangling throne over a burning cauldron. Her hair cascaded over the throne, spilling into the water. Her face was old and wrinkled. Her eyes reflected a universe of planets as she held out a rose in her hand. She spoke, but it was the sound of a chorus speaking in unison. "Where one rose grew are truly three. And only one shall stand alone; its path begets the fourth and final, fallen back to home."

A gigantic whale breached the smooth black waters, and with a mighty movement, the tail slapped the surface. A high-pitched song resounded through the cavern. The water swelled, creating a whirlpool, sucking everything into itself. The suction swept through an underwater tunnel, twisting and turning, eventually spilling out into the depths of the ocean.

Dolphins swarmed in formation and met with a line of oceanids armed with spears and tridents. A woman swam in the lead of the oceanid army. Her fins danced in the current. Prince Bavendrick floated at her side, exuding elemental power through the ocean. The ocean swelled into a wall of water and crashed toward the shores of Poseidia.

D'Vinid jolted awake. The dream quickly faded as he became aware of his surroundings.

The sound of many chattering voices blurred into dullness. Light saturated his vision. He sat up, realizing he had somehow passed out in a bed of flowers. He was near a commons area, but he couldn't be sure where. He rubbed his head, focusing on his last memory. His quest to find his missing dabrina quickly returned. But it had been night, and now it was day. His body ached as he tried to move.

231

The nearby commons area was overflowing with citizens. He tried to remember what day it was. He knew it was the day after Ka-Ma-Sha, when citizens usually stayed at home recovering from the three-day festival. He crept out of the flowers, picking leaves from his clothing and brushing off the dirt. He found his hat nearby and beat the dust out. Thankfully, his hover-disc was nearby, as well. Soon, curiosity lured him to the commons. It didn't take long to realize the crowd was gathered eagerly around the viewer-crystal screen.

VCs were assembled from cubes of selenite crystal and fitted within frames built to receive images from the Crystal Grid. The image of a woman faded into view. Everyone knew her as the palace speaker. She had become famous in the land. As her lovely face materialized on the screen, a hush fell over the crowd.

"Greetings, fellow Atlanteans," she said in a melodic voice. "The Queen Impending arrived in the palace yesterday before nightfall from Poseidon's dreamclan to take her place at King Kyliron's side." The speaker's face faded away, and to D'Vinid's chagrin, the VC showed exactly what happened when the new couple met just moments after D'Vinid abandoned her. The crowd sighed at her wild beauty.

The speaker appeared again. "King Kyliron and his new queen were joined under the last moon of Ka-Ma-Sharri. The king is taken by the beauty and wisdom of his new queen and has decided to present her to you by the bidding of the Watchers. But first they ask for us to perform mudras together at the resonance of nodesong." The palace speaker closed her eyes and laced her fingers together at her heart.

D'Vinid felt his stomach turn.

Nodesong began. Everyone in the commons turned to face the crystal-node and shaped their hands in mudras for illumination rituals. D'Vinid did the same. He wanted to walk away, but somehow felt the urge to stay. His mind wandered, and though he participated in the ritual, his hands merely made the movements. He was losing interest in being part of anything anymore.

"Your Majesty, you were right about presenting your queen." Jamarish Ka greeted the advancing royal processional as they pre-

pared to present Brigitte to the people. "More citizens are attending illumination rituals today than in many rotations. You have managed to increase our power stores tenfold."

"Then maybe they can fix my gardens." Kyliron threw a suspicious glance at Brigitte.

She looked away from his blame. The plants could not withstand the distortion caused by her emotions. And if she was not careful to maintain her equanimity, she would destroy much more than that.

In the final moments of afternoon nodesong, double doors glided open. Sunlight poured through, bathing the advancing processional in its glorious radiance. The thunder of the crowd spilled into the entryway. Everything shifted into slow motion. It was time for the people of Atlantis to meet their new queen.

Along the extended platform, the royal entourage joined with the High Council. The High Priestess had taken a place of honor on an elevated podium. Wordless and meditative, her eyes followed Brigitte.

When she met the gaze of the priestess, Brigitte's eyes filled with distress. She knew the priestess had sensed her pregnancy the night before, and wondered if she could have sensed their incomplete joining, as well. The priestess inclined her head slightly, and Brigitte knew the child would be acknowledged as Kyliron's. The foundation to the house of cards had been laid with terrifying potential for disaster. But it was what the Watchers wanted. Brigitte had no choice but to surrender to the currents of fate.

Wrapped in their joining ensembles, Kyliron and Brigitte walked past the High Priestess onto a balcony. Below, a massive plaza extended wide enough to encompass throngs of citizens, who traditionally gathered to hear the words of Atlas's line in person, rather than on VC screens. It had been decorated for the Ka-Ma-Sharri festival. Its splendor remained as if it had truly been created for this spectacle. A deep roar filled the air as they came into view.

The High Priestess raised her staff, uttering a blessing in old Lemurian. Her voice poured across the plaza. The crowd gradually fell silent. She caught the staff up in a sunbeam, and its refraction through the crystal ball cast shards of rainbow lights over the king and queen. A gasp rippled through the gathering.

The words of the Moirae's credo taught by Indrius appeared in Brigitte's mind, as if programmed to activate at the right time. Their meaning finally became clear as she stood before the people of Atlantis. *"I am trained within the dream world, a warrior of the subconscious. My awareness lies beyond that which is clouded by personal identity. I am created to bring reflection to the masses. I am that which lies between what they see and what they feel. I am the connection of inspiration. I am the observer, the messenger, the weaver, the judge. For this task I am humble and I am prepared."*

In a daze, D'Vinid wandered away from the commons area, allowing his feet to carry him where they would. He felt perhaps he was at the lowest point of his life. He was so weary that surrendering to the Triad was beginning to sound like a relief. His heart ached for Brigitte, for his dabrina. Kyliron now possessed everything he loved. A flashing light glimmered up ahead. Aimlessly, he gravitated toward it.

The road emptied into a courtyard. An old woman sat on a stairway, striking a rock on the stone of the steps. Every now and again the impact made a spark. A closer look revealed she was using the rock to try and destroy a piece of quartz crystal. He sat down next to her.

She had the look and feel of the madness, muttering unintelligibly. She didn't bother to look at him. Everyone who passed quickened their pace to avoid her. D'Vinid sat there for a while, trying to organize his priorities. In a sense, he felt a bit like her. He watched, trying to reach for any shred of motivation. Nothing presented itself.

"They say if we destroy all the crystals, we can have our minds back," the woman muttered.

"Excuse me?" D'Vinid tried to catch her distracted eyes.

"Destroy Belial. Destroy the crystals. It must be done. This crystal stole my mind... stole my mind. We are slaves to the Grid. The crystals are evil."

"What did Belial do to deserve to be destroyed?"

Her eyes clouded over. She stopped her work and scratched her head. He could see her fingers were bloodied by her difficult task. "I don't know," she shrugged and continued. Chips of crystal fell to the ground. All at once, cracks formed in its façade, and it shattered. Letting out a cry of joy, she quickly stood up and swept the pieces into a bundle she created with her tattered dress. She scurried off in triumph. D'Vinid followed her to one of the great walls overlooking one of the water rings. Seeing the copper wall, he finally knew where he was on the central Ring of Learning.

"The end is near," she whispered. "All of Atlantis will crumble into the sea." She stood on the wall and emptied the contents of her tunic into the water ring. She spread her arms and leaned back as if her sacrifice would magically restore her mind. After a few moments, she realized she was still the same. Her expression contorted. "Nooooo!" she screamed. "You promised me!" She clutched at her head.

D'Vinid tried to reach out to her.

She pulled away, and finally looked at him with raging hatred. "You!" she pointed. "You must take your place with them! They are waiting for you!" she panted, clawing at her face as if being swarmed by bugs. "The longer you wait, the worse it will be." Her voice changed. "We won't stop here. We will kill until you surrender to ussss," she hissed. And then without another word, she convulsed and threw herself backward into empty space.

D'Vinid cried out, trying to reach for her, but he was too late. Her cries, mixed with laughter, fell with her and ceased with the splashing impact of her plunge into the water ring. He began shouting to passersby, but they ignored him like he had the madness. Given his shabby appearance and intensity of his outburst, he couldn't blame them.

He began to run. Anger built a wall around his heart.

He waded through the crowded esplanade in a daze, dodging the festive feeling around him. The happier they were at the sight of their new queen, the heavier his heart weighed. A dark shadow closed in on him. He thought again of surrendering to it.

Ahead, the crowd parted, and Lukias stood in a space created by his presence, waiting. His dreamseer eyes landed pointedly on the Prophet Singer.

D'Vinid approached the queen's brother, unsure if he would suddenly disappear.

"I have something for you," Lukias announced, and slid the crystal pendant over his head, reaching it toward him. "I believe it is yours."

Absently, D'Vinid accepted it. A jolt passed between their fingers. Visions flooded their minds. Lukias recognized the download of a dozen images all at once. He knew they would now be connected, and perhaps that was the effect of delivering the crystal. He accepted that this was what Indrius wanted.

D'Vinid immediately connected with the crystal. The images made him dizzy. One stood out vividly: the worn face of a silver-haired woman, her eyes beaming with love, her fingers caressing a dabrina.

Lukias's voice cut through the visions. "This came from my sister's tutor. She wanted me to bring it to the one whose blood was imprinted into it. It was her last wish. Her name was Indrius. I believe she was your mother."

D'Vinid's head pounded. He saw the image of a woman standing on the shore as Brigitte and Lukias departed on a dreamship. He inspected the five-sided crystal. Somehow, he knew this was his soul-crystal. Just as Fa'nariel Ma'at had promised, it had found him at last. There were numerous perfect triangles etched in the crystal's surface, invisible until he shifted the angle of the light's reflection. He knew these to be Keylontic record-keepers.

"Let's go," said Lukias as he started walking.

D'Vinid looked up from his confused misery and began walking in step. "Where?"

Lukias raised his eyebrow. "Indrius was my surrogate mother. That means we're kindred. You and I have some catching up to do."

D'Vinid nodded. Belial appeared in his head again.

Lukias noticed the flash of orange in D'Vinid's eyes. He said nothing of it as they walked toward the edge of the plaza. "Why don't you tell me about the events from yesterday, the shadow entities." He felt D'Vinid tense up, so he began again. "No. How about we start with something more personal. Tell me how you became known as the Prophet Singer."

Thunder rumbled in the distance. Lightning flickered, spreading electrical fingers through the mass of dark clouds gathering on the distant horizon. Above them, the sky was still blue, filled with lazy white clouds. As yet, the mighty Grid of Atlantis held the storm at bay.

ADDENDUM

Visions seen upon the morn,
awakening the distant storm.
The past has come upon him
in a way he can't refuse.
Retreating to the future,
for a distant path to lose.
Friendship never lost in light
of all that has been told.
Summoning the courage
to release the pain of old.

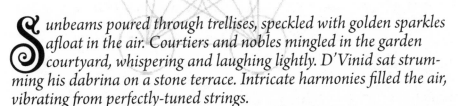

*S*unbeams poured through trellises, speckled with golden sparkles afloat in the air. Courtiers and nobles mingled in the garden courtyard, whispering and laughing lightly. D'Vinid sat strumming his dabrina on a stone terrace. Intricate harmonies filled the air, vibrating from perfectly-tuned strings.

He caught the eye of a beautiful woman peeking at him from behind the lace of her fan. Her eyes summoned him to her innermost secrets. He could feel the craving ignite at the base of his spine. Drawing on the inspiration of her desire, his fingers danced up and down the dabrina, capturing the attention of all. The air had a gilded hue. Thunder rumbled in the distance and a ring of dark clouds encircled the city, held at bay by the mighty Crystal Grid of Atlantis. D'Vinid's words formed a melody, which wove through the harmony of the strings.

> *"What once was one with humankind*
> *now separates the whole.*
> *It hides unseen in folds of time,*
> *its touch is icy cold.*
> *Longing to be known once more,*
> *remaining still unseen.*
> *Its life is hollow*
> *all the more voraciously it feeds.*
>
> *Its longing to be one once more*
> *remains its only crime.*
> *It feeds on what it longs to be*
> *and stimulates the mind.*
> *Though what it is remains unseen,*
> *shadows in the night.*
> *Causing untold damage*
> *in its lonely, anguished plight."v*

When he was finished, Queen Dafni stood from her throne, thanking him for playing music at her private affair. Her beauty shone like diamonds, radiant and pure. Her raven hair fell, a luxurious wave over the high collar of her shining gown.

"D'Vinid. Your words have been spoken of as prophetic." Dafni's voice dripped like honey. The gathered nobility applauded her words. "I have always known you were special, my boy. I think I shall grant you a new nickname: 'The Prophet Singer.' Let it be known throughout the land."

Time stretched into slow motion. D'Vinid was confused as to what Dafni was doing alive. The beautiful queen of Atlantis was long gone, replaced by rumors that the mystical Watchers had turned her into a tree. Lightning flashed in the distance.

D'Vinid's line of sight was obscured by an elongated shadow stretching over the royal courtyard. And then he understood, as he realized the shadow belonged to Lukias. The last thing he remembered, the dreamseer had appeared just after nodesong to deliver a crystal, a gift from D'Vinid's long lost mother.

He blinked again, and he was standing on the road facing Lukias.

"You loved her," said Lukias. "The queen."

"Wait, how did you do that? I felt like I was there."

"Dreamseers have many skills, my friend. All my life I have trained to be high seer of my clan. I can induce waking memories from the depths of your mind, if I please." His eyes fixed in a feverish stare, as if he was looking at the space around D'Vinid.

"Well, I don't please. I would appreciate it if you don't do that again," D'Vinid let out a terse laugh, venturing a friendly pat on the dreamseer's shoulder. "Now, if you don't mind, perhaps we can walk while we talk …" He wrung his hands. "I'm in a bit of a rush."

"Ah, yes, to the Speaker Sect to fetch your stolen dabrina." Lukias gestured for him to lead the way.

D'Vinid clutched his head. "No thought is safe from you, is it?"

Lukias smiled. "You must forgive me. Atlanteans are more guarded with their thoughts than we are in the Dreamvale. I will give you your privacy from now on." He stopped to look at D'Vinid. "My people have no secrets."

D'Vinid tried to keep his unexplainable experience with Brigitte buried, but the look on her brother's face suggested it was not necessary. No matter how hard D'Vinid tried to forget her, she was etched into his heart. He could not explain it.

He couldn't decide what to blame, fate woven by Watchers or the magical *vortex* the conclaves went on about. He couldn't help but wonder if these were just two ways of defining the same thing.

The dreamseer's expression was that of a caring man. D'Vinid felt inclined to trust his intentions as honorable. He cast his eyes to the ground. If anyone was dishonorable, it wasn't this dreamseer who now knew enough to end his life. He only had himself to blame, really. He had slept with the future queen of Atlantis on the eve of her joining – to Kyliron of all people. And her brother knew about it.

A jolt vibrated his chest. Flinching, he pulled the soul-crystal from the folds of his overcoat as if it were on fire. He dangled it from its chain at eye level. Liquid, ethereal whispers caressed his thoughts. His head turned as if on its own. In his view stretched the entrance to a nodeyard. Energy pulsed from the obelisk at its center.

The turnout at Brigitte's presentation as the new Queen of Atlantis had filled the Grid with more power than D'Vinid could remember. He could feel the buzz in the air. Without thinking, he approached and placed his new crystal against one of the shining facets of the node. Lukias perched on a nearby wall, unfazed by the turn of events.

The ghostly form of a woman materialized inside the crystal tower. Worry creased her brows. Her eyes knew the sorrow that wrenched at D'Vinid's heart. *"My son."* Her words were one with his thoughts.

D'Vinid felt the tingle of shock spread across his skin. He studied her face with care, memorizing every line, the depth of her eyes as she gazed on him.

"Are you real?" he gasped.

"I am part of you, my son."

"You are her. My mother. Indrius."

"I am an aspect of her, the part she linked with the soul-crystal. Indrius was taken by the shadow storm that now approaches. You have been marked to join with the storm. They must not have you."

"Why? Why me?"

"You will soon know who you are. There is something you should see."

The cells of his body sped up like effervescence. He felt as though he would melt away and fall upwards. His stomach dropped as he reached out for a solid object to hold onto.

"Relax. Breathe." The voice of Indrius amplified. He tried to relax, and the bubbling of his cells took over.

In a flash, he burst into the sky in his dreambody. He merged with the Grid, traveling at the speed of light straight to the heart of Atlantis. He could see a black rift form above the Temple Sect. It grew bigger as the influx of mindlight flooded to the central torsion field.

Some of it went to the Great Crystal, which looked to him like a corona of light inside a pyramid at the heart of the city. Waves of light emanated from the pyramid and fed the dome-shaped grid. But there was a rip in the fabric of the dome where mindlight poured into the gathering storm. A pain stabbed at his heart, and he jolted back into his body.

"How did I do that?" He stumbled, breathless, looking for his bearings. He felt queasy.

"The Grid has just given you your first inner-initiation. Follow the signs and open your heart to the gateways. Your journey has now begun." Indrius faded.

Lukias watched with casual indifference.

"I saw my mother," he said to the dreamseer.

"I know," Lukias smiled, rising to his feet.

"There was something else. I felt connected to the heart of Atlantis. The Great Crystal. It is being attacked by that storm." He pointed to the flickering horizon. "There is a leak in the Grid. All that mindlight that was just donated. It's not all making it to the Great Crystal." He shook his head, looking inward. "No wonder I haven't wanted to do illumination rituals." He looked up, pleading with Lukias. "People keep telling me I have a part to play in all this. I don't know what to do," he sighed. "What can I do?"

"Who's to know you haven't already done what you need to do?"

"Could it be that easy?" D'Vinid gazed at the sky with hope in his heart.

Lukias gave him a sideways glance and a crooked smile. "Not at all."

"That's not fair! You're a dreamseer. I believe everything you say like it's a prophecy."

"And yet it is you who are the Prophet Singer." Lukias laughed. "To pass through the gates of consciousness, you need to become no one. The path you wish to walk places you on the path of chance. Is chance not still dictated by fate?"

"I said to get out of my mind!" D'Vinid laughed, though he was mostly serious. Lukias had a kindness in his general demeanor, but D'Vinid was starting to see there was a bit of scoundrel in him.

"The only thing you lack is motivation in your heart. Perhaps my sister can help you with that."

D'Vinid eyed him until they both smiled with a newfound understanding between them.

"If I had known who your sister was, I would have run the other direction," D'Vinid confessed. "I'm doomed now if Kyliron..." He creased his forehead. "He hates me. I mean real hatred. I have never understood what could motivate him toward so much hatred. I have always been like a brother to him. He has pushed his family away. Ever since his mother died. She held us all together. Many things went wrong when Dafni left us."

"Perhaps you should evaluate how you treated him in the past and find a way to make amends." Lukias turned toward the black clouds on the horizon. "I know this storm. It came through the Dreamvale, swallowing souls along its path. Its substance is of shadow. We escaped just before it arrived. Now it seems it has come to Poseidia. We thought the Temple Sect would be able to deflect it with the Crystal Grid."

"Well, they've failed," D'Vinid churned, glad for the change of topic, though the new subject was just as uncomfortable. "The Grid is only feeding it through that hole." He pointed toward the center of the city.

The dreamseer ventured a longer look. "I will go to the palace and see to this." He reached his hand out. They clapped wrists in a gesture of farewell. "You and my sister are bound together by the Fates. You will see her again. And you and I ... Your mother was like a mother to me. We are as brothers."

D'Vinid nodded through narrow eyes. "Bring your sister a message. Prince Bavendrick has returned to Poseidia. It seems that he ended up in the ocean, perhaps left for dead. I found him washed ashore and brought him to Pan Aello. If anyone can rise against Kyliron, he can. It is he who is the appropriate heir." D'Vinid gripped Lukias by the shoulder. "I have heard Kyliron thinks his brother is dead. It should be Bavendrick who decides what his brother must know. He deserves the time to figure out if someone tried to end his life."

"Very well. I will tell her."

"Only her."

Lukias nodded with a veiled smile. "Where will you go from here?"

"It seems as though the Grid has initiated me. I have a journey to take, and the Watchers will guide me." He shook his head, sputtering into cynical laughter. "I suppose once you are chosen, there is no way out." With the exchange of another knowing look, Lukias faded into the invisibility of Dreamtime, and the two men parted ways.

When the people of Atlantis first laid eyes on their new queen, a sigh of adoration rippled across the Grid. The royal procession filed from the balcony, pursued by the crowd's dull roar. Kyliron ignored Brigitte. When they reached the palace corridor, he looked to Jamarish Ka. "I have had enough of this royal joining business. I get it, the people love queens." A far-off look haunted the king's eyes as he strode away and flipped his hand. "Have you engaged the warriors to seize my mother's ship in the Harbor District?"

"I have, indeed. The furies and the dragons are sending squads, and the shark warriors are blocking the channel."

"Why would they need to block the channel?"

"In case D'Vinid tries to get away by watercraft."

Kyliron pondered the words until he came to a decision. "Good. Have D'Vinid brought to me when he is found." He strode away and flipped his hand. "See to it my queen begins the building of her court." His searing glance turned her stomach in knots.

She looked at Allondriss as he strode away. A sense of relief blossomed at his absence.

Always imposing, the fury warrior Stixxus stayed close. Brigitte noticed his lips twist into a grimace at mention of the furies working for the king's pointless errand. She liked to believe that with him around, Kyliron could not hurt her. It was a convenient fantasy.

Jamarish Ka escorted them back to her gilded cage. "I wish to congratulate Your Majesty," said the maydrian. "So many citizens turned up to see your presentation that the Grid will be filled with mindlight for the first time since the early days of King Koraxx. I sense you will have popularity with the people. Atlantis owes you great accolades."

Brigitte weighed his words. "You mean, the Grid is never filled?"

"We have not reached our mindlight quota for many rotations. The people have come to believe it is not required for them to attend illumination rituals. It seems that the job of the monarchy has become convincing the people to attend the rituals. It stands to reason you will become the face of this task, so your king may focus on matters of state. You have already proven valuable in that regard."

They reached the entry to her suites.

"Your Majesty, I have arranged a reception this evening to inaugurate the queen's courtyard. You will find within, a team of servants poised to help you make ready."

Brigitte narrowed her eyes. "No rest?"

Jamarish Ka placed his hands in a steeple. "There will be plenty of time for rest, eventually. The king commanded me to present you with retinue candidates. It is imperative that we keep up this mindlight quotient. You need staff to organize your public appearances. Since you do not possess your own maydriss, I will perform the duties of that post until we find you someone the king approves of. Perhaps your new maydriss will be more kind on your schedule requirements than His Majesty."

She muttered. "Let us hope we may relieve you of this extra burden quickly." She tilted her head with growing impatience. "You understand that I have been running against great threats since I left my home? What I want is for you to begin searching for who or what tried to keep me from becoming *your queen*."

Jamarish Ka stared at her blankly. She narrowed her eyes, daring him to answer. He said nothing.

"I wish to rest now." She paused at the door, easing her tone. "I will attend your reception when I am ready. But from what I understand of the law, the queen's retinue is her own choice. I will see the king's candidates, Jamarish Ka, but I should hope that no one plans to step in the way of *my* decision." A silent battle of wills followed in their staring match until Brigitte turned her back. Allondriss followed her into the entrance, and Stixxus blocked the way.

"Quite true, Your Majesty," Jamarish Ka said as she deserted him, leaving only the ominous fury warrior to hear his words. The king's maydrian ran his fingers along his hairless head. Clicking his tongue on the roof of his mouth, he casually fled down the corridor, his red robe flaring at the breeze of his departure.

The Temple Sect lay at the heart of Atlantis. To those who didn't possess the ability to step into the Dreamvale, the palace surrounded a magnificent courtyard with the temple of Poseidon in the middle. But entering the Dreamvale revealed an impossibly large landscape scattered with pyramids. These were the temples to the 12 orders of the sect. At the highest height was the Temple of Light where the Great Crystal lay at the heart of all Atlantis.

Lukias waited in a receiving room. He had requested the presence of the High Priestess. He couldn't be sure of the required decorum. The priests acted as though it was highly irregular to drop into the Temple Sect and request her presence, but his status seemed to reap respect. He stared out a series of lancet windows over the mist of a waterfall. It reminded him of Celestius, the realm of the Watchers where the souls of the dead reunited with their higher selves.

He had been unable to shake visions of the girl Allondriss from his dreamsight. Before he left, she mentioned that the oceanids had a gift for Brigitte. It had been washed ashore, and Pan Aello was involved. He now understood the "gift" as the return of Prince Bavendrick. Perhaps her potential freedom from being queen would be the best boon of all.

The mysterious servant gifted to them by Mediator Pan Aello had become a riddle he couldn't solve. He pulled a twig from his pocket around which was entwined a singular strand of the girl's golden hair. He had found it on his coat after their last encounter. Instead of tossing it aside, he wrapped it around his finger until he realized he must have needed to keep it. Hair was, after all, a good way to check DNA.

He wondered what it had been like for her to grow up in this magical pocket of the world. The pyramids glowed like planets tucked into the terraced hills. The very air tasted like honey and smelled of a million varieties of flower. For a child it would be a wonderland.

He could tell when she arrived, though she made no sound. A whisper of a feeling embraced the room with a sense of serenity. He turned to face the High Priestess of Atlantis.

Servants scurried around the room, preparing garments, body paints and jewels for Brigitte to choose from. Ignoring them, she began to strip her joining ensemble, leaving a trail of silver fabric in her wake.

A slight wind rushed in from the garden, drawing her attention to a gathering storm on the horizon. She recognized the wall of storm. It conjured a memory of the nightmare of her departure from the Dreamvale. A shiver passed up her spine. The wind brushed her painted skin, left bare beneath flowing silver undergarments. She reached for the sheer robe hanging beside the stairs leading to the steaming waters of her elevated tub.

"Allondriss, fetch me the rose on my bed, please."

She contemplated her situation. "I wonder what sort of candidates Pan Aello would have in mind for my retinue," she said as Allondriss returned with the un-wilted flower. "Perhaps you can contact him." She stared at the stormy horizon as she spoke, reaching for the rose and brushing its fragrant petals on her lips. Though she wished she could forget him, the thought of D'Vinid's touch brought her comfort.

It was Pan Aello who had gained her trust by decree of the Watchers. She had resolved to listen to his counsel above all. If Kyliron could dare to assume she had no political acumen, he was mistaken. The teachings of Indrius left her well prepared. And what she lacked in connections, Pan could easily oblige.

She was queen now, against the odds, but perhaps in more danger than she had been yet. Something was destroying the dreamclans. Perhaps it was a prelude to Atlantis. She knew Atlantis's treaty with the dreamclans was a threat to their aggressors. But who and what were they?

Any plan seemed counter-intuitive. Her people were the ambassadors of the elementals and the Watchers. They were crucial to the very existence of Atlantis. The telluric elementals were the reason its technology even worked. To break the treaty could only serve to sever ties with the other realms and, thereby, the mechanism by which to control the Grid. There would have to be another mechanism to take its place, otherwise the Grid would cease to function.

"I will contact Pan immediately, mistress," said Allondriss.

"You must call me Brigitte." The new queen's smile amplified the beauty of her face.

Allondriss nodded. "Very well, Brigitte."

With another look at Allondriss, Brigitte hugged the robe closed, and descended the stairwell into her private garden.

"You seem distressed," Pan spoke to his household healer after intercepting her flight from the bungalows of his estate.

She gave a sharp nod. "Master Pan, I was coming to speak with you. I am not sure how to tell you this..."

"I think words are a good tool to use." He steadied her with his hands on her shoulders, leaning forward to catch her eye. "Have no fear. I am not your enemy." His voice was edged with cynicism.

She nodded again, trying to focus on her breathing. "I think Prince Bavendrick has been taken by the elementals. I thought he had simple elemental invasion, but I have not been able to rid him of it. I believe he is possessed."

"I see. So, he has been inhabited by an elemental?"

"I believe so, master. A powerful one."

Pan cupped his goatee in thought. "Remind me of the popular rumor that his mother was taken by the Watchers?"

The healer priestess's eyes lit up. "She was turned into a tree because she was too beautiful for the eyes of man."

He led her back toward the bungalow dome where they had the prince safely tucked away. At the doorway, he turned to her. "If Queen Dafni was indeed turned into an elemental at the end of her human life, would you think that perhaps she could have been one before?"

The healer nodded. "I will think on this, Master Pan."

Pan reached for a communicator-crystal in his pocket that pulsed with a soft glow. "Ah, excellent. Perfect timing as always, my little Allondriss." He nodded to the healer. "If you will excuse me…"

The gaze of the High Priestess was like a gateway to infinite worlds. Lukias looked away, knowing she could enter his thoughts as easily as he could enter hers.

"I am pleased you came to see me, Lukias Dreamseer." Her voice was a gentle reverberation in the towering, crystal cathedral.

He bowed. "My lady, I have been remiss in coming to see you. The city has given me much to ponder upon my arrival."

"You have come here for a reason," she said.

"There is a matter we must discuss."

She stepped up to the window to stand beside him. They both looked out over the rush of the waterfall. "Beautiful, isn't it?"

He agreed.

"Every tiny particle is a living piece of element. Here you can journey through the penumbra into the other realms of existence. As the Meridian Realm grows denser with matter, it seems that humans forget the subtle realms."

He tried to stay focused on the subject at hand.

She spoke before he could. "You wish to speak of the Crystal Grid, and the shadow madness."

"The rift in the Grid. I take it you know about it?"

She looked at him pointedly. "There is much to know, dreamseer. We will have much to speak of in the coming days. It would be wise for you to show me what happened to your clan. It will help us understand this storm of shadow."

He hesitated. He wanted to confide everything in her, but he couldn't be sure if she was trustworthy. His experience with the Temple Sect clergy in the city had left him with a bad feeling.

"If you wish," she responded to his thoughts again. "You may perform a scan on me to see if my soul is pure. I will open myself to you. Then you can decide if I am someone you wish to trust."

They faced one another, staring into the eyes of the other. Lukias could feel a wealth of information hidden beyond a maze of neurons. But it was the heartlight he sought. She relaxed into his probe.

"You are for Atlantis," he said.

"I am for Sophaiya, the planetary being upon which we exist.

The elementals. The Watchers. Just as you are. The Temple Sect has been overseeing a multi-generational transition. We are required to remain neutral in the face of that which comes to overtake us. We are the hands of the Watchers. The hands of nature."

"Who... What is responsible for this?"

She tilted her head to the side, an apology in her pure gaze. "They are the shadows of Atlantis. This storm was created by the Grid itself. Citizens must be in alignment with nature. Our laws require it, because that is how the Grid works.

"The people have fallen into the traps of identity. The more they separate from the collective, the more they suffer. And when they suffer, the Grid creates an entity, born of their anguish. This is the shadow of the psyche." She pointed to the looming storm front circling the citadel. "Your sister is an emissary, meant to mingle the Lemurian blood of the Dreamvale with the royal line of Atlas. Her journey has always been the same. But since an attempt was made to break the Telluric Treaty, you now have arrived. It is you who are the inquisitor. It is you who, by Atlantean law, must take on the mantle. You have the authority and the right... by the will of the Watchers."

Lukias closed his eyes. A shock of sandy hair jutted from his hood. He reached up to scratch his hand on the stubble of his face, blowing the hair from his eyes with a puff. With a trembling breath, he took her hands. "Very well, High Priestess. Let us begin."

Their connection was immediate as he prepared to bring her back to the beginning of his exodus from the shores of the dreamclan.

The dreamclan village was nestled neatly into the sloping hills of an emerald cove within the Dreamvale.

The central plaza of the village was built around an altar of rings representing the six Realms of Sophaiya. At the center was the eternal flame, a fire that stayed always lit. It was their gateway to the forge of Incendius, where they could communicate with the inner wisdom of the planet.

Around the flames was a ring of rock and moss that glowed at night, representing the caverns of Subterra, the gateways to the deepest wisdom from within.

Next came a circle of water, through which they could see into the realm of Oceanus, the waters of prophecy and all-feeling.

Surrounding the water was a mound of plants, their connection to the Telluric Realm, the whispering whims of the elementals who made up the breath of the Meridian Realm, the physical spectrum of existence on the planetary being of Sophaiya.

And last came a ring of crystals, the Dreamtime gateways to Celestius where the Watchers set the wheels of fate to which all life was beholden.

Here, the dreamclan kept the wisdom of Lemuria, living a simple life within the turning of the seasons. Through the years, the dreamclans had faded from Meridian into the Dreamvale, moving ever closer to Celestius. To many in the world, they were becoming a myth, but Atlantis was still bound to them by treaty.

Lukias watched as the council of elders filed around the central plaza to discuss their flight to Atlantis. They activated the crystals to send out a distress call through the eternal flames into the six realms. Their call vibrated outward in ripples. Sea birds circled above them, a gentle rain fell golden in the sunlight. Elementals sent their whispering pulses across the time-space continuum. The song of oceanids drifted from the cove, awash with the rhythm of the waves.

Indrius looked at Lukias with a face of stone. She showed him a crystal, explaining that it belonged to her son.

The High Priestess broke free from their memory bond with a gasp. "So, this is where Indrius was sent, to train the next Queen of Atlantis. The Watchers are indeed clever." She gazed at him with a new sense of awe. "And where did this crystal lead you? Did you find her son?"

Lukias sighed. "Priestess, I believe there are some things that are best left unsaid. For now."

"No matter," she smiled. "The soul crystal of Indrius's son will lead him to me."

Lukias paused. "Who is Indrius to you? Perhaps you can tell me why you want me to share this knowledge with you."

The priestess looked conflicted. "I can tell you this, Inquisitor. Indrius has a certain genetic code that was monitored by the Temple Sect. Her family is, shall we say, hybrid?"

He furrowed his eyebrows. "What sort of hybrid?"

She sighed. "Perhaps we should continue the memory bond. I can say no more for now. The walls have ears. You will know in time."

The garden path twisted through a verdant wonderland of trees and flowers. The rose remained at Brigitte's lips. Its perfume provided welcome distraction. The path opened into the nodeyard. Water spilled over the impressive collection of crystals surrounding the six-foot obelisk. She could see the water was the source of the creek surrounding the entire garden.

A motion drew her eye to a nearby retainer wall where a black cat sat watching her with jade eyes. She returned the cat's surveillance, hypnotized. The spell between them broke as the cat leapt soundless to the ground, approaching with a creaking meow. It wrapped its elegant body around her legs, pushing her leg with its head and nuzzling into her presented hand. She sat beside the nodeyard on a form-fitting bench. Eager for love, the cat curled up on her lap, purring like thunder. Stroking the cat's soft fur, she drifted into a trance.

"You have done well, child."

Brigitte startled at the sound of the familiar voice. It was as clear as if someone stood beside her. "Indrius?"

"I am here, girl."

"You faced the shadow storm." Brigitte desperately wanted to shake out of the trance. The ghostly image of a woman appeared in the reflection of the crystal node. She had the bloodied face of the priestess who haunted her. But now she spoke, and she had the voice of Indrius.

"I have come back to Atlantis, where I belong." Indrius's voice hissed in her thoughts. Brigitte remembered the harshness of the woman's teachings, the depth of her unhappiness. She was a deeply angry woman who always treated Lukias kindly, and Brigitte with near contempt. Brigitte always knew it was because Indrius hated Atlantis. Brigitte relied on the teachings. It was what gave her the strength to be queen. She remembered how Pan claimed that the palace would destroy any innocence she had left. Indrius had already prepared her.

In many ways, she wished Indrius had come with them. But the tutor chose instead to stay behind with the dreamclan as the shadow storm engulfed them. She would choose that horrible fate over a return to Atlantis. Her skin crawled. Fear began to spread over her body. Her hands trembled. The cat leapt to the ground.

"*And now you are queen of Atlantis.*" the voice of Indrius hissed. "*And we have come to claim you.*"

Brigitte covered her ears and shut her eyes. "You are not Indrius," she whispered. "You are one of those shadows trying to deceive me."

The wind picked up, disturbing the luscious greenery of the garden. She could feel a disembodied presence charging toward her. She opened her eyes and watched the plants part as it passed. The wind gathered in a cyclone around the nodeyard, rustling her hair and prickling her skin. Without thinking, she lifted the rose in front of her face. It began to vibrate.

Its stem sprouted and branched out. It drilled into the ground forming a firm base. Larger and larger it grew until it became a tree. Its petals lifted into the sky. Branches spilled to the ground, wrapping Brigitte in a protective embrace. She opened her mouth in a silent scream, sending a swathe of dreamlight rushing toward the darkness.

The ground split in the wake of her unbridled power. In a blinding flash, a black, smoky essence charged headlong into her attacker, ripping at it with claws and fangs. She tried to catch a closer look at her protector. Her eyes widened as she recognized the jade eyes of the cat. Like the rose, it had grown impossibly into the fearsome form of a shadowy black panther.

A moment later, everything was still. She looked up. The rose lay on the ground. The cat was small again, licking its front paw. The node was pristine. The sky was blue. The air was deathly quiet. But there was a gaping crack in the garden pathway where there had not been one before.

Lukias and the High Priestess watched as Brigitte stood at the bow of the dreamship. They had sailed through Celestius along the skyroads when they escaped the shadow storm. At last they reached the penumbra of Atlantis. An energetic dome surrounded the island empire, generated by the now infamous Crystal Grid.

Ofira Pazit greeted her guests on deck, her expression in a puzzle. "We are unable to enter the skyroads of Atlantis," she said. "The resonance pattern of the Grid has been changed."

Lukias stared at her.

She continued. "We are waiting for the Watchers to intervene."

Lukias could hear the faintest sound in the distance, like the buzzing song of bees. He looked up and a cloud appeared before them, scintillating with dazzling rainbow colors. The lights transformed into the form of a woman floating before them. She reached out a rainbow limb toward Lukias. Wordless, he reached back. When their fingers touched, a bright flash transported them into the sky above the cove of Poseidia.

The priestess broke the bond once more. "You have touched the key." Her expression shifted to a delicate sense of awe. "The key to the Crystal Grid is in your grasp." She closed her eyes. "You have been trusted with the greatest task of all, the knowledge of all humanity. You will know more soon, High Dreamseer. And I daresay, you will know more than I. When next we meet, you will provide me with directions. But first, the key must take its place. I will leave you with this, Inquisitor: these are the days that will determine the Fates of Atlantis. Look to those to whom you are bonded. They will determine the survival of our legacy forever."

Darkness reached up a winding staircase leading into an underground passageway. The only light came from an orb in the hand of a man cloaked in shadow. Its soft amber put up a feeble fight to light the way. The shuffle of his feet echoed against stone. In the distance, trickling water pierced the envelope of silence. The corridor branched off in many directions. He continued along the main path, sure of step as if the maze were his domain. He reached his destination at the hub of four hallways, a large room filled with an assortment of equipment. It had a dome ceiling with a hole at the apex where sunlight cast a single dusty beam into the center of the round room.

With his face obscured by the drape of his hood, he hummed a cheerful tune as he approached a machine crowned with a three-pronged claw. He produced a fist-sized black diamond from a bag at his waist. It rested perfectly in the cradle of the claw. The machine hummed to life and sent an electric jolt into the diamond. The stone trembled in the cradle until a wavering hologram of a man appeared above it. His eyes darted around the room, sagging with torture and impatience.

"Koraxx, my old friend," said the cloaked man in a cheerful voice. He began pulling vials of blood from his pouch and went to work labeling them. "Kyliron has kept me quite busy lately. I just simply haven't had the time for you."

"Pity." Koraxx croaked with an edge of sarcasm.

"In a sense, you really are my only friend. Without you, I'm just this boring vessel with no charm and appeal. All work and no play. I miss the days when my Dafni was around. She made things fun."

"What do you want from me? Can't you just leave me to suffer alone?"

"Oh, but Koraxx, I can't talk to my confidant if I leave you alone. It helps me pass the time in this miserable existence. I'm sure it helps you, too. I had someone go check on your body recently. I had it placed in stasis so one day perhaps one of us may use it again. It was fun pretending to fall to the madness. They were all so shocked when I appointed Kyliron as king. It was amusing. Our younger son is… Just like you."

Koraxx looked away, his shallow eyes devoid of care. "You mean, *your* son is just like *you*. He may carry my bloodline, but he's no son of mine. At least Bavendrick took after Dafni. He will redeem Atlantis still. Mark my words."

The cloaked man twittered into laughter as he shook a vial of blood, staring at the way it clung to the side of the glass. "There is no redemption for my brother's creation. Soon Atlantis will be mine. Poor little humans. You cling to your little lives, desperate to weave your little stories together so you feel like you have some kind of control. In the end, you're just our pawns, stuck in the wake of our rivalries." He continued storing the vials into a lock box with careful fingers. "How are you enjoying your time in the realm of the black diamond?"

Koraxx looked away. "One day you will suffer for what you've done," he muttered.

"That's the funny thing, isn't it? In a free-will zone, karma is the great equalizer. Yes, perhaps one day my actions will bring about consequences for me. I've suffered before at the hands of my brother, when I was imprisoned in the glaciers of the great frozen north. And then he suffered for the way he chose to send me there. Do you realize how much death and destruction he caused just to have revenge on me? Even he was subjected to the great equalizer for that little stunt. But it's been worth it all along, because we each get to win for a while. What better way to spend eternity than locked in a cycle of revenge with my only family. Now it's my turn to win." He paused, waiting for Koraxx to answer. He remained silent. "You never answer me. You can at least nod or agree. All you have to do is say, 'uh huh' sometimes. It makes me feel like I'm not talking to myself."

"You *are* talking to yourself. Why would you even want me to answer?"

"Well, I'm always interested in your opinion. I do consider you my friend."

"Your friend?" Koraxx laughed.

"Theeeere's a laugh. Doesn't that make you feel like you're part of this conversation, now?"

"Very well. You always speak of the Star Nations, and how once this planet was a crossroads. If they closed it off to travelers and turned it into a free-will zone, then isn't it illegal to take away the free-will of its denizens?"

"The thing is, my dear Koraxx, humans are just a step up from animals or elementals. If you misdirect them just a little bit, they will separate from their own free-will every single time. All I'm doing is tricking them into choosing it for themselves. It worked with you, didn't it?"

Koraxx crossed his arms. "Why don't you just kill me?"

"Why would I do that? I like you too much, my friend. Now, relax and let's enjoy our conversation. I am about to become quite busy, so I don't know when I will be able to summon you again. I do so enjoy our time together." The cloaked man sank into a seat and kicked up his heels. "Let me tell you all about the new queen of Atlantis. Her name is Brigitte. I think you might remember her from when she was a child."

"She escaped your dreamclan genocide, then? Or did you let her come so you could renew the Telluric Treaty so the Grid stays functional?"

"To tell you the truth, I couldn't care less if she showed up or not. I like to improvise. I thought you knew that. The dreamclans managed to get her to the palace before the treaty expired. The currents of Fate made it happen. I suppose it had to be done or else I would have to deal with the elementals being released from their bond to the Grid. But the strangest thing occurred during the joining. The elementals allowed her to renew the treaty, even though they prevented the joining from being sealed. I have yet to decide what that means. Is she really Queen of Atlantis if she is not joined with the blood of Atlas? If the treaty was renewed because of her, then technically, she is queen. What do you think? As the former high king, I thought perhaps you might offer some insight into it."

Koraxx had personally made the pact that had betrothed her to Kyliron. But there was one thing he knew that his tormentor did not. He knew she was a Moirae. But not just any Moirae. "This is where your time pretending to be human clouds your Watcher eyes. You may think you are clever, but those of your kind who oppose you can see better than you can. They have anticipated your moves well in advance."

"It's no matter. I will find out their plan in due time. I may be blinded by human eyes. But Watchers are blinded by their laws. Even with this handicap, I intend to outwit them still. They don't stand a chance against me. I have been a denizen of this planet for ages."

"You have admitted to me before that there is one who *can* outwit you."

"Oh, Koraxx, you *have* been listening! I'm just delighted to hear it. Yes. My brother. But the Watchers have made one sad mistake. They have banished him from Sophaiya for the sins he committed to trap me. Their natural laws will be their mistake. Without Belial, they don't stand a chance."

Koraxx smiled ever so slightly. "If Belial is indeed never returning to this planet, then perhaps you *will* win."

D'Vinid watched lightning flicker in the stormy distance. The clouds looked as though they would reach up and swallow the sun as it traveled toward evening. He couldn't keep his thoughts straight. The many choices he faced made him inclined to sit and wait for the Watchers to send him a sign.

He sat on the canal wall, gazing at the swirling chaos of the sunlit ripples in the water ring. He followed the expanding circles and marveled at the way the rings of the citadel mirrored this natural phenomenon. A song began to form in his head. As the words escaped his lips, he could feel the unearthly tingle coming from the soul-crystal he now wore at his chest. It rippled through the water of his own body, and he buzzed with the understanding that he was one with all things.

"Entitled wrath, forgotten propriety.
Vengeance unleashed, fanatic anxiety.
Sovereign blackened, stone on the mountain
reaches his grasp to poison the fountain.
Brother against brother, elements awaken.
Fire unleashed, the heartlight forsaken."

As the words ended, his eyes landed across the water ring where an unusual amount of ships congregated at the entrance to the rings. He realized the ships were gathered in the Grand Lagoon at the Harbor District where *Dafni's Enigma* floated in its berth. Squinting to see clearer, he saw that a crowd was gathered on land, spilling into the marina. He stilled his mind and listened, discerning the distant sounds of shouting.

A vague horror arose in his heart as he realized the gathered ships were the stout predator vessels of the Shark Warrior League, the guardians of the maritime channels of Atlantis. With rising anxiety, he began pacing, wondering what Kyliron was up to this time. And when he couldn't take it anymore, he produced the hover-disc from his waist bag and tossed it to the ground with a whirring click. In a single bound, he leapt onto the footpads with expert agility, bounced over the wall and began skimming the surface of the water toward the Harbor District.

He began to realize his mistake as he skipped nearer to the arriving shark vessels. It was just as illegal to hover over the water as it was off the road mounds. Just as quickly as he approached, a group of shark warriors began closing, expertly outmaneuvering him in their one-man watercraft. They were outfitted in maritime jerkins bearing the crest of the league. D'Vinid had to maintain his momentum or sink into the water. He contemplated evasive maneuvers.

"You will surrender to our custody!" a woman's voice shouted.
He nodded and waved toward the marina.

"The marina is off limits!" she shouted again. They continued to urge him toward one of the small shark vessels. He focused the might of his concentration into the torsion-crystal of the disc, adding momentum to its spinning fury. He circled back and bounced off the wake of a shark watercraft, hurling himself into the air with a twisting maneuver. Applause erupted from those who could see his impressive stunt. The shark warriors circled. He couldn't afford to get in trouble again for hovering illegally.

The soul-crystal began to vibrate. Instinctively, he extended his heartlight to wrap around it. The connection snapped into place. A blue mist rose from the water. His eyes washed with the glow of orange. A devious smile crept onto his lips, and D'Vinid vanished from sight.

To be continued in Part Two:

SHADOWS OF ATLANTIS: SYMBIOSIS

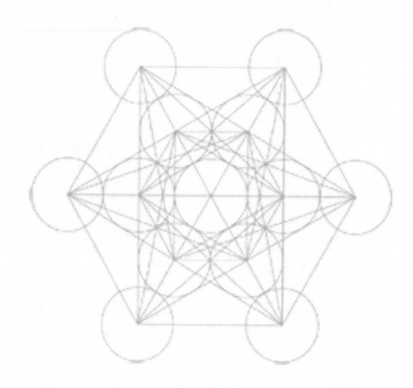

A Letter from Mara Powers

When I discovered Atlantis, I was 16, and hungry for answers. I wanted to find a way out of the "Plato's Cave" of life in America. I remember the feeling I had when I read about Atlantis, as if a spark went off in my brain that ignited an unquenchable fire in my soul. It made sense that nature could utterly decimate any amount of human advancement, leaving behind nothing but a myth. It launched me on a 30-year inquiry that led me on a quest through endless research while wandering the earth like Kane in Kung Fu. My journeys led me over land, air, and sea all in search of Atlantis whether I knew it or not. Even if Atlantis was the furthest thing from my mind, it would somehow find me.

It was at Burning Man where I had "the awakening." I was in search of the ultimate pirate Utopia and felt as though I had been spinning my tires in fun and revelry, much like how you found D'Vinid at the beginning of the book. I couldn't participate in the world unless I had something to contribute. But what? All I had was my Atlantis research. And music. And writing. I didn't want to host the pointless party anymore, so I stepped away from my life as an event producer in Los Angeles and turned my quest inward.

I deconstructed myself, even cut my hair off, and moved to New York in the dead of winter. I spent a lot of years trying to cope with my need to wander, while forcing myself into the role of author, rooted, and patient. These things are against my nature. I always say, that to become a better person, you must first challenge your nature, and learn to do something you are not good at.

Being an author is a solitary path. Any author will attest to the phobia that develops after being locked in the expansive world of one's own imagination. When the time comes to share with the world, it can be pretty scary. It got to where I grew into being an author, and the more that happened, the more I sank into the role. To top that all off, when you go the route of the indie author, finishing the book is only the beginning of the journey, and the invisible route up the giant mountain is harder to find. But I am stubborn, and I don't give up. Whether it be for better or worse, I have been committed to bringing this story into the world.

The small legion of people who have been my refuge and champions have made it possible not only for me to develop confidence in my chosen profession, but also for this project to find its way into your hands. They have believed in me unerringly, and so it is to these champions I owe my greatest thanks.

It is my opinion that artists need patronage. I never compromised my work by balancing it with a job. I gave myself to the flow of chance, and it caught me. I became a penniless wanderer, walking on a path of unfolding miracles, and leaving a trail of good luck and synchronicity in my wake. In the meantime, I maintained a relentless devotion to the work of researching lost civilizations. Deciding what to do with it has been an interesting journey. I wanted to utilize my knowledge but decided not to write about it from a scholarly perspective, instead I chose fiction. Here's why.

There are two ways to approach the study of Atlantis, one is through secular subjects which are often considered "alternative." The other is through the dazzling world of the esoteric. I find the latter reads like a science fiction novel. In choosing fiction, I could use these fantastic stories, and I didn't need to back them up with hard facts. I just had to read and be inspired. To that end, I could also weave in my wider research on metaphysics, sociology and philosophy, as well as storycraft, a sprinkling of Jungian Psychology, and Joseph Campbell's heroes journey.

I understand this story is thick. And to be honest, if you've only read it once, you may have missed a lot of the little gems I've planted. I invite you to read it again and look for treasure. Perhaps start with reading the glossary.

I have sprinkled aspects from many of the great works I've absorbed. Those of you who have delved into the antediluvian mythos may recognize Plato, Edgar Cayce, the Theosophists, the Bible, Hinduism, Greek, Egyptian, Sumerian and Norse Mythology, David Hatcher Childress, Manly P. Hall, Charles Berlitz, Graham Hancock, Diana Cooper, Charles Hapgood, The Urantia Book, Erich Von Däniken, Shirley Andrews, Ignatius Donnelley, Michael Tsarion, Rand Flem-Ath, Colin Wilson, Spirit Science, Ancient Aliens, Frank Joseph, Lewis Spence,

Andrew Collins, Christos Djonis, Marion Zimmer Bradley, Zecharia Sitchen, Col. Churchward, plus various YouTube documentaries, which you can find posted on **"The Shadow of Atlantis"** facebook group going back a number of years.

Do I believe in these stories? The answer is irrelevant. Because even Plato's account of the discussion between Socrates and Solon about Atlantis is said to be an allegory about the downfall of Utopia by its own progress. The wave that sank Atlantis into the ocean is perhaps a metaphor for the destruction of humanity by the poison of our own psyche. These are the shadows of Atlantis.

In popular culture, most believe that Atlantis is an underwater city populated by fish people. This is why I added Oceanus. I just wanted to have fun with that concept. In fact, the first appearance of the underwater kingdom in pop culture seems to be in a 1936 serial called Crash Corrigan. From there the science fiction idea evolved all the way to modern day Aquaman. But all one has to do is Google it, and you will see that Atlantis is actually a myth about an ancient civilization that was destroyed by a massive wave… perhaps the flood endured by Noah and his arc of animals. Checking out the similarities between ancient pyramids around the world begins to unravel a mystery of an ancient time on earth when humans had the ability to transport and carve granite with perfect precision. It begs the theory of a global culture that perhaps had access to spectacular technology.

Looking back through history as we know it, Atlantis was common knowledge. It has made its resurgence in literature and film numerous times, always sparking a common intertest in the subject. When the Americas were discovered, it was believed they were Atlantis. Their first appearance on a map had them named so, according to some tidbit I read somewhere. The 1930's channeler Edgar Cayce said the United States is living out the karma of Atlantis. When you think about an advanced society destroyed and reduced to myth because of the hubris of man, then it does invoke an eerie parallel. So, I have written this series as a warning to my country, as much as for entertainment.

Atlantis remains firmly embedded in our collective psyche. When I meet random people, eight times out of ten they say they have always been fascinated with the concept. I am honoring an ancient tradition by resurrecting the mysterious civilization in fiction.

There are many aspects of my life experience woven into these pages. Struggles with addiction, abusers and sexual assault serve as a lesson for those who may have the same problems. The madness is based on the time I spent living in downtown Los Angeles near skid row watching the homeless epidemic happen around me. It is also a vehicle to demonstrate my theories about evil being an actual disease based on separation from unity consciousness. Hover Tricksters are my ode to the time I lived in Venice Beach where the skateboarders have achieved a level of fame. The conclaves are based on my time in the rave world and the festival circuit. The royal courts are based on the Renaissance reenactment world, otherwise known as SCA.

I have been working on a memoir called "Dreaming up Atlantis." The title is based on a dream I had when I was just hitting puberty. I still remember it because it was the spawning ground of this story. It launched me on another quest for knowledge that has become a thread in the book. The question is: "Why does evil exist?" I like to think I have discovered the answer and perhaps added clues in these pages. It makes up the basis of my philosophy.

And now for my greatest thanks of all. I want to thank YOU for reading all these words that have been so much a part of me for so long. Stay tuned for upcoming installments so you can follow the chronicles of your favorite characters. And if you feel inclined to help spread the word, please share on social media and leave a review on Amazon or Goodreads. It helps the cause of any indie author. Reviews, shares and ratings are key!

Go in the Vortex,
Mara Powers

CHARACTER INDEX

Aeronious, Captain: \er-Ō-nē-əs\ Captain of a neighboring vessel to Dafni's Enigma in the Outlands Harbor District.

Allondriss: \ə-LÄN-driss\ Temple Sect outcast. Raised by Pan Aello in his court as a servant.

Atheerian Telleria: \ə-THEER-ee-in tə-LER-ē-ə\ Oldest son of the Telleria family. Envoy between the Poseidian commercian cartel and the courts. Co-leader of the same conclave Fa'nariel leads.

Azai, Prince: \ə-ZĪ\ Prince of Og. Younger of two princes, older brother of Nazira. Heir to the throne of Og after the untimely death of his older brother Prince Baznar.

Bavendrick, Prince: \bə-VĚN-drĭk\ Older brother of King Kyliron. Son of Koraxx and Dafni. Former heir of Atlantis. High Prince of Atlantis. Betrothed to Princess Nazira of Og.

Belial: \BĒ-lē-ĪL\ Watcher who steals knowledge from the stars and brings it to humanity. Atlantean hero who is said to have brought the Archives Nexes to Atlantis originally from Lemuria.

Brigitte: \brĭ-ZHĒT\ Daughter of the Oceanus Dreamclan's High Seer. Tutored by Indrius. Sister of Lukias.

Chaldeis: \chal-DĀ-ĭss\ Father of D'Vinid. Captain of Koraxx's royal flagship, *Dafni's Enigma,* during the sixth reign of the third dynasty of Atlantis.

Corenya Shanel: \cōr-EN-yə sha-NEL\ Youngest sister of the sha'mana mediator on Dragonspine, and the mediator delegate of the High Council. Aunt of Vinesia.

Dafni, Queen: \DAF-nē\ Sixth Queen of Atlantis in the third dynasty. Mother of King Kyliron and Prince Bavendrick. Mated to

King Koraxx. Died young. Claimed to have been turned into a tree by the Watchers.

Detrew Eljai: \DAY-troo ĔL-zhī\ Brother of Jezeli, ambassador and old friend of Ofira and Pan. Pan's candidate for Brigitte's Naydir.

D'Vinid: \də-VIN-ĭd\ The Prophet Singer. Son of Captain Chaldeis. Childhood friend of Kyliron and Bavendrick. Employed by Pan Aello as a singer at his court. Resides at *Dafni's Enigma*, where he has become famous as a musician among the people of Poseidia.

Fa'nariel Ma'at: \fə-NÄR-ē-əl mə-ŎT\ Female leader among the conclaves. Kallista in the court of King Kyliron.

Hanonin: \hə-NÄN-ĭn\ First mate of Captain Chaldeis on the royal flag ship, *Dafni's Enigma*. Inherited the ship and the care of D'Vinid when Chaldeis left and turned it into a social hub where D'Vinid could play his music.

High Priestess: Head of the Temple Sect. Highest initiate of the temple of light, overseer of all twelve orders of temple clergy.

Illorian Thoth: \ə-LŌR-ē-ĭn THŌTH\ Current temple Alta of the Archives Nexes.

Indrius: \ĬN-drē-əs\ Atlantean transplant and tutor of Brigitte in the dreamclan of Oceanus. Surrogate mother to Lukias and Brigitte.

Jamarish Ka, Maydrian: \ZHÄ-mə-RĒSH KÄ\ Temple delegate of the High Council. Maydrian to King Kyliron.

Jensyn Aello: \JĔN-sĭn ā-ĔL-ō\ Twin son of Pan Aello.

Jezeli: \JĔZ-ə-LĪ\ Elemental navigator of the *Vex Voyager* under the command of Ofira Pazit.

Jonda Dex: \JŎN-də DĔKS\ Free-marketeer from Og.

Kama: \KÄ-mə\ Soulmate of Belial. Watcher who acts as a light for humans in the darkness of consciousness.

Kayden Aello: \KĀY-dĭn ā-ĔL-ō\ Twin son of Pan Aello. Set apart by having slightly wider features than his brother Jensyn.

Koraxx, King: \KŌR-ăks\ Father of Bavendrick and Kyliron. Sixth High King of the third Atlantean dynasty. His reign was considered "Koraxx's Folly," as he created many rules and broke many traditions, principal among these traditions is the breaking of his original betrothal to join with his kallista, Dafni.

Kyliron, King: \KĪ-lə-rŏn\ Seventh High King of Atlantis in the third dynasty. Bavendrick's younger brother. Son of Koraxx and Dafni.

Loressai Torbin: \lōr-əs-Ī TŌR-bĭn\ Daughter of Torbin, keymaster of Subterra's first layer. Previous lover of Kyliron and D'Vinid.

Lukias: \lū-KĪ-əs\ Brother of Queen Brigitte. Hereditary High Seer of the ocean's dreamclan that was destroyed before he and Brigitte entered Atlantis.

Nazira, Princess: \nə-ZĒR-ə\ Youngest child and only princess of Og. Sister to Prince Azai. Cousin to Kyliron and Bavendrick. Betrothed to join with Bavendrick after her oldest brother was killed. Such a political union would unite East and West Atlantis.

Ofira Pazit: \ō-FĒR-ə Pə-ZĒT\ Captain of the *Vex Voyager*, Dreamship of the Watchers. Originally from Yisra. Daughter of a powerful commercial family. Longtime friend and casual lover of D'Vinid.

Pan Aello: \PĂN ā-ĔL-ō\ Mediator of the fireball games of the Warrior Sect.

Pathfinder, the: Mysterious man within the conclaves who people go to for information.

Rayliis: \rā-lĭ-ĒS\ Known as Prince Azai's bodyguard and best friend. Rumored to be a princess of the Nubian Empire.

Stixxus: \STIK-səs\ Fury Warrior, personal protector of Queen Brigitte.

Tashan Balinor, Naydir: \tə-SHON BAL-ĭ-nōr\ Naydir to King Kyliron. From a prestigious mediator lineage.

Telleria: \tə-LER-ē-ə\ Powerful commercian family who owns and runs the cartel docks in Poseidia.

Torbin: \TOR-bin\ Keymaster to Subterra's first layer beneath Atlas. Father of Loressai Torbin, member of the order of Nexes among the Luminari.

Vektra: \VEK-trə\ Grid dancer. The pseudonym Vinesia uses to keep herself anonymous among the conclaves.

Vinesia Shanel: \vin-ĒZ-ē-ə sha-NEL\ Daughter of the sha'mana mediator line and a dreamclan mother from the telluric clan of Hermes. Second in a line of three betrothals to Prince Bavendrick. Kyliron accused her of scheming to take the throne, and had her replaced with the princess of Og, thus breaking the Telluric Treaty. Considered Bavendrick's one and only true love.

GLOSSARY OF ATLANTEAN TERMS

A

Accessor-Crystal: Crystals programmed as keys so people can gain access to doors or devices such as hover craft. They are worn as bracelets or rings.

Agartha: A network of cities within the hollow sphere of Sophaiya, referred to as the Realm of Subterra. They lie deep in massive hollow caverns and are lit by phosphorescent moss that grows abundantly. Beneath Atlantis are six layers of Subterra leading to Agartha. These layers are home to a class of Atlantean priestly scholars called the Luminari, who are the gatekeepers between Atlantis and Agartha. The cities of Agartha are home to a race of Subterran humans ascended to a higher frequency and are the protectors of the passage to the Halls of Amen'ti.

Age of Fire and Blood: Referred to as the time when the three Bloodfire Nations, Sauros, Hyperborea, and Thule waged war on Lemuria. It was the first war on Sophaiya. Sorcerers influenced by the Blood Gods conquered the innocent masses, forcing them into slavery and human sacrifice. Nature was set off balance by the widespread use of magic. Volcanoes and earthquakes changed the face of the planet. The poles shifted and set the planet into an ice age. Atlantis rose at the latter half of the age, at the start of what is now known as the Ice Age.

Alta: Highest ranking priests of the Temple Sect. They wear white robes to set them apart from lower tiers of the clergy. The twelve orders of the temple are ruled by the Alta. They are the keepers of temple rules and higher decision making.

Ambassador Sect: One of the seven sects of Atlantean government. Atlanteans who travel abroad are registered in this sect, and visitors to Atlantean cities are expected to register in this sect during their stay.

Animata: Human-like beings without a soul created for menial and hard labor in Atlantis. The practice evolved in the Second Age of Atlantis, when scientists developed methods to remove the animal appendages from manator. Their science expanded into the creation of biological bodies that could be animated and powered solely by the Crystal Grid.

Anunaki: The original team of scientists who came to Sophaiya to oversee the seeding of life forms on the planet. They were the first Watchers, and took the form of bi-pedal, feathered reptilians. It was their work that created the human experiment. Belial and his brother Sataku were among this team, but they split ways when Belial wanted to liberate the human experiment and allow them to develop on their own, while his brother wanted to be their overlord.

Aphrodisiacs: Elixirs made from herbs to create sexual arousal.

Aphrodite: Watcher of love and sensuality.

Apollo: Watcher of wisdom and prophecy.

Archives Nexes: A bio-crystalline record of all human existence hard wired to the Crystal Grid. The Archives is the mechanism by which the Great Crystal functions. Without it, the Grid would function, and yet humans would not possess the ability to control it. It is highly protected by the Temple Sect and cannot be accessed unless citizens petition in the Temple Sect for whatever knowledge they wish to attain. The Conclaves have, however begun to figure out how to access the Archives through the Grid on their own.

Atlas: Son of Poseidon who became the original high king of Atlantis. All royal lineage is descended from him. The royal line is thus referred to as the line of Atlas.

Atlas, Kingdom of: The island kingdom known as the seat of government in the ten kingdoms of Atlantis. Poseidia, the ruling city where the high king and queen live, is the main city on the island. The rest of the kingdom is known for its abundant agriculture.

Auric Field: The aura, or layer of energy made of subtle bodies that surround every human body. There are as many layers of the aura as there are layers of dreamtime (dimensions). This means every human has an auric body in each of the twelve layers, though they are not generally aware of this unless they practice awareness through activation of the mindlight.

Automatons: The proper term for what Atlanteans call animata that have been created for menial and hard labor.

Avatar: A human who has been chosen to embody the soul essence of a non-physical being such as a Watcher or an elemental. The Watcher piggybacks on the consciousness of the human, thus sharing one body. This is a means for the Watcher to experience physicality without being stuck in an incarnation.

Axiom of One: Said to be the highest of all truths, the Axiom has been passed down since the dawn of time. The Followers of the Axiom in Atlantis are said to practice the ancient ways of Lemuria. It is a simple principle that all life is interconnected.

Azoria: One of the ten kingdoms of Atlantis. A collection of mountainous islands in Eastern Atlantis. Known for its hospitality, the beautiful islands have many small bays with pristine villages of seafarers and fishermen. Because of their location, there are many trade routes that pass through the main cities of Azoria. There is a bawdy quality to the people, who have wild, rowdy revelries, and dress in revealing clothes with tattoos and piercings. Because they place a high value on free-will, they are known as a free trader refuge. Azorian authorities turn a blind eye on pop up settlements of outlaws within their many uninhabited islands.

B

Belial: A trickster Watcher known as the guardian of knowledge and free-will. He was in the first migration from Maldek who came to Sophaiya to develop the human species. Along with his brother

Sataku, he developed the human genome as it exists still to this day, however, he split from his brother, because he didn't believe in using humans as slaves, and so started a movement to preserve their free will. He was a hero of the Lemurian age and brought the Archives Nexes through Subterra to Atlantis. Originally mated to Kama, the two of them vowed to remain separated until they could fix the damage done to Sophaiya by their people. In modern times, Belial has come to mean "To waste one's worth," or "failure to have value." His defection caused his people to redefine his name and accuse him of bringing pain and suffering to Sophaiya by bringing them truth and knowledge.

Belial's Promised Land: Referring to the state of mind connected to Source consciousness past the limitations of physical understanding. (See Halls of Amen'ti.)

Bloodfire Nations: The collective name of the fire alliance during the Age of Fire and Blood, who waged the first war on Sophaiya. They were eventually punished by the elements, who froze them in ice, beginning the ice age. The three kingdoms were Hyperborea, Thule and Sauros. They were ruled over by sorcerer kings with fear and slavery. The war with the Bloodfire Nations is what eventually caused the demise of Lemuria, and thus the rise of Atlantis.

Blood Triad: Ancient Nephilim (beings born from the mating of Watchers and humans) who practiced dark sorcery to gain power and dominion over humans. They ruled with fear and gained power through blood sacrifice. At the height of their power, they ruled over the Bloodfire Nations during the dark Age of Fire and Blood. The most powerful among them were the Triad, who ruled over Hyperborea, Thule and Sauros. They were defeated by the Atlantean fire crystal, which summoned elementals to freeze their nations under layers of glaciers. There they remained in stasis until they were freed in the third age. They exist as disembodied spirits that are otherwise known as demons.

Blue Dream Awakening: Referring to the activation of a new genetic sequence that has been designed to awaken during the generation of this chronicle.

Blue Dream Elixir: A forbidden elixir made from sha'mana and the psychedelic blue lily of Khemet. Used by the conclaves of the Children of One to awaken their genetic sequence. This process is called the blue dream awakening. It is said to activate the ability to see into blue Dreamtime, which is the first step toward activating the gateways of initiation. Only those born with the upgraded genetics can be affected by the elixir.

Blue Dream Marker: When one sees into the blue dream, they are able to see the markers left by those who are adept at creating them. These are ribbons of blue energy made of emotional imprints, meant to lead awakened ones to various conclave meetings and revelries.

Blue Dreamtime: A frequency of Dreamtime vibrating in the blue spectrum. Said to be only seen by those who possess the proper genetic sequence, and who have gone through the awakening. Used by the conclaves of the Children of One to leave signs that could only be seen by those who have been awakened by the elixir. Those who have activated more gateways of initiation can dreamwalk in this frequency, and not be detected by anyone, even by dreamwalkers who have not gone through the awakening. It is said to be a gift from Belial, and perhaps the telluric world, but no one knows for certain.

Builder Sect: (See Sects) Class of citizens in Atlantis who have taken a trade or profession. One does not have to be born into the sect, thus it is referred to as non-hereditary. Anyone in a profession that serves the function of the civilization is known as a builder, from carpenters to entertainers to farmers to kallistas. It is the largest sect of the seven.

C

Cantos: The sacred cantos of Belial are the definitive cultural guide to Atlantean citizens. They are poetic verses describing the reason why Atlantis was created, and what role its citizens need to play. They do not define rules or spiritual disciplines, only values and social morays.

Cartels: (See Commercian) Groups within a trade guild who have formed an alliance to strengthen their hold on their area of discipline.

Cartel Docks: Docks within the urban areas of every Atlantean kingdom where traveling traders and merchants register to set up temporary shops and show their import items to locals.

Celestius Realm: Referring to the realm of the skyroads in the atmosphere of Sophaiya. The kingdoms within Celestius are known as the crystal cities and can be accessed through Dreamtime. The liaisons between Atlantis and Celestius are called Illuminati. Celestius is the first realm anyone enters when they wish to enter the incarnation cycle of Sophaiya, and it is where souls return when they leave their incarnations. It is often mistaken for heaven.

Chakras: Energy centers in the human body of which there are 12. Each chakra is associated with a gland in the human body, as well as one of the 12 auric bodies in each of the layers of Dreamtime. They regulate the flow of spiritual energy between the human endocrine system, the auric field, and connection with the consciousness of the planet.

Children of One: (See Axiom of One, Conclaves, Lost Temple Children) Formal term for the conclaves who sprang up toward the last decade of Atlantis's third age. Called so because they received their initial information from the Axiom of One, an ancient remnant of Lemurian beliefs. They maintain the study of the principles of universal oneness and seek to awaken their innate powers through communion with the Archives Nexes.

Commercians: The trade of networking commerce. Commercians negotiate trade through the kingdoms and represent merchants and trade guild interests. Akin to modern day agents or managers. They also broker the trade of influence tallies, which is the currency of Atlantis. (See Influence tallies).

Commons Areas: Farmers throughout the land give a portion of their crop to the commons, which is distributed in designated areas for any citizen to receive for free. The rest of the food is sold for influence tally or trade in numerous marketplaces or shipped to other islands by marketeers. There are a limited amount of commons areas, thus many citizens trade with local dealers to avoid travel to the commons.

Communication Methods: During the first two ages, long-range communication was conducted telepathically through the Grid. In the third age, psychic awareness has diminished. All long-range communication is conducted through tool crystals. Crystal-transmitters, locators, summoners, and messengers are used for their various purposes. Viewer-crystals known as VC's are used to transmit information to masses through images and amplified sound. The conclaves have begun to unlock the ability to transmit psychically through the Grid, however. In the third age, this has begun to change the face of long-range communication.

Conclaves: (See Children of One, Lost Temple Children) Referring to the secret regional groups of Atlanteans known as Children of One. They are an underground movement who has learned how to access the Archives Nexes through the Crystal Grid. In accessing ancient, forbidden knowledge, they have awakened innate powers. They first emerged during the renegade revelries when hover-tricksters began to operate off-mound. When King Koraxx implemented the hover mound laws, they began to gather in secret and practice their hover tricks. This eventually led to them discovering their genetic abilities, the blue dream awakening, soul-crystal symbiosis, and accessing gateways of inner initiation. Since their practices have been outlawed, conclaves operate in secret, even from one another, though they interact regularly by leaving blue dream markers that lead to their strongholds.

Council of Seven: (See High Council)

Council of Ten Kings: Royal council of regional kings. Atlantis was originally split up into ten kingdoms. Each kingdom was governed by descendants of Atlas's original twelve children. Over

275

the decades these kingdoms dwindled, and in the time of the third age, have been separated into islands after various natural disasters. Poseidia in the kingdom of Atlas remains the ruling city of all Atlantis because it is where the Great Crystal is located. It is thus where the high king and queen reside, who are the figureheads of the ten kingdoms. They are the leaders of the Council of Ten Kings. The monarchs of the ten kingdoms have a vote in more complicated matters that affect all of the region and have full authority over their own kingdom. They are mostly an alliance, though they operate under a set of regional rules that apply to all.

Crux: A point in time and space when fate lines converge to create a moment that could shape the future for good or ill.

Crystal Cities: Majestic ethereal cities along the skyroads of Celestius. They exist in the higher layers of Dreamtime and cannot be detected by the physical eye. It is said the crystal cities are ports of call for intergalactic travelers, and it is from these cities that a soul can decide to enter into the cycle of reincarnation within the Meridian Realm of this planet. Once incarnation cycle is complete, all souls leave their physical bodies and return to the crystal cities and start again. The cities also act as anchor points for the planetary grid of light that encircles Sophaiya.

Crystal Council: Telluric beings representing the cosmic alliance who inhabit twelve crystal skulls. These skulls are situated in the temple of light at the heart of Atlantis where the Great Crystal emanates. They are the regulators and the protectors of the Crystal Grid.

Crystal Grid: A telepathic energy network connecting the people empathically. Anything that happens within the Grid is felt through the network. It also serves to power the cities by creating lights at night, activates the road mounds, and all machinery, running water, and all other automated systems. Essentially it creates an invisible dome that controls the weather over the ten kingdoms, and all currents within Atlantis. It is run by the Great Crystal, a powerful source of free energy. It is powered by crystal obelisk nodes placed at specific vortex points. The Grid works in chorus with natural telluric lines on the planet's surface, and human telepathic emanations. Temple centers are built around the crystal nodes, (also called resonant capacitors) where citizens assemble to participate in illumination rituals. The rituals consist of mudra meditations. The nodes gather the peoples' telepathic projection, send it to a central capacitor node, which then balances and powers the Grid, or "illuminates" the city. The call to illumination rituals is marked by the grid resonance or nodesong; when the grid guardians activate the mechanism that causes the nodes to sing through the city. The Grid is centered on the Great Crystal in the heart of Poseidia and branches out across the ten kingdoms of Atlantis.

Crystal Magi: Those who practice magic with crystals.

Crystals: There are many different types of crystals in use in the Third Age of Atlantis. Most crystals used by the public are tools, programmed to operate symbiotically with the Crystal Grid, and perform various functions such as summoners, record keepers and accessors. The Grid is run by obelisk towers known as resonant capacitors, also nicknamed nodes. Other large crystals in use are viewer-crystals or VC's; akin to modern day televisions. Also, the Temple Sect uses larger crystals for healing, including crystal-chambers that repair the human body through resonance. Hover technology is made possible by torsion-crystals that are charged by operating on road mounds, though hover-tricksters began using them off-mound. This was the beginning of the Children of One movement (See Mound Laws). They have also begun to use soul-crystals, named so because their telluric souls are not bonded to the Grid. When bonded with, soul-crystals grant the user expanded abilities. The use of soul-crystals is currently outlawed in Atlantis. Only the Temple Sect is allowed to use them to harness their telluric soul into the Grid and transform them into tools.

Cunning, the: Referring to a path of discipline spoken of in the Sacred Cantos of Belial. The Cunning of Belial is used by the Conclaves. It is a path of trickery and shapeshifting, meant to keep the soul in alignment with the shifting patterns of nature and the Telluric Realm.

Cycles: Atlantean units of time. Days are measured in sun cycles. Months are measured in moon cycles. Years are called rotations. The cycles are recorded by Time Keepers from the Temple Sect. Every commons area in the cities features a calendar that is changed each day and each hour with the spinning of multiple dials. It is much like the Mayan calendar.

𝕯

Dabrina: Atlantean stringed instrument characterized by spidery limbs that can be adjusted for tuning. It produces an ethereal chorus effect with natural harmonies on twelve sets of strings, said to be connected to the twelve layers of Dreamtime, as well as the twelve levels of human connection to Source.

Dance of the Elementa: (See Grid Dancers) The dreamclan term for Grid dancing. A specialized dance allowing the dancer to communicate with and channel elementals into their movements.

Destructions of Atlantis: There were three ages of Atlantis marked by three major destructions. The first age was ended by a massive fracture in the crust of the Atlantean continent. It happened after the Great Crystal was used to end the great war between Lemuria and the Bloodfire Nations. When turned to a conduit of destruction, the Great Crystal was termed The Fire Crystal, and caused inconceivable levels of destruction through time and space. The Watchers intervened and took the Grid offline while the area underwent massive upheaval. The ice age began at this time. Atlantis was given another chance and the second age achieved great heights and is still remembered as the Golden Age. The second destruction was caused by an experiment gone awry by Aryan scientists, (See Ten Kingdoms) which caused a rip in Dreamtime. This was the arrival of shadows, but most are not aware of this fact. The Atlantic sea floor became destabilized by the experiment, and Atlantis was fractured into islands. The third age began with a new royal dynasty, and a cloistered Temple Sect that guarded the knowledge of Nexes very closely. The great scientific achievements of the previous age have been lost to memory, and this has begun the steady devolution of Atlantean consciousness.

Districts: Neighborhoods within Atlantean cities. Each district has its own set of officials: mediators who oversee law and order within larger regions, speakers who administrate the affairs of the district, and commercians who collect influence tallies from local merchants.

DNA: Nucleic acid containing genetic instructions of all living organisms.

Downloader-Crystal: Crystals programmed to collect energy imprints or information from the nodes of the Grid. They are used by the Temple Sect to collect data. But the Children of One have learned to download information from the Archives Nexes. Some can also use the nodes to unlock information stored in a downloader.

Dragon League: Discipline of the Warrior Sect mastering psychic warfare.

Dragon's Breath: The act of inhaling the smoke of red filaments from the flower of a tree that grows wild in the islands of Atlantis. It has calming qualities on the mind. It is used to dull symptoms of the madness, but its prolonged use has addictive qualities, as well as other unsavory side effects.

Dragons: Referring to dinosaurs that once ruled the planet. They went through mass extinctions in the past, mostly caused by humans. In the time of the third age, there are still dragons in the wilds, though some are kept as pets. They are still hunted by humans and considered a threat that must be eliminated.

Dragonspine: A mountainous basalt island situated between Og and Atlas. This is where sha'mana is processed and shipped to fulfill its various uses throughout the kingdoms. The main authority is the Shanel mediator line that lives in their family estate, a palace at the center of their main port citadel called Urnok. Since sha'mana is so valuable, the sea lanes around Dragonspine are heavily patrolled and regulated. The port is not open to random travelers. Because it is a closed port, it relies on supplies from outside kingdoms. All ten kingdoms send tribute to Dragonspine as an offering for processed sha'mana. As a result, the Shanel mediator line is one of the most influentially wealthy families in Atlantis.

Dreamclans: Tribes who live at the edge of Dreamtime in nature, keeping the ways of ancient Lemuria. They are connected and named for the six Realms of Sophaiya, practice the discipline of ascension into Dreamtime, and maintain a bond with the Watchers. Nephilim blood runs in their lineage, and thus they maintain separation from the humans of the Meridian Realm, so they are not tempted to establish dominance over the human project. They have a special relationship with the kingdoms of Atlantis because they helped Belial bring Nexes from the motherland (Lemuria). It was written in Atlantean law that the royal line has to pair with Dreamclans every six generations so that they can renew their connection with nature, and not be corrupted by the pitfalls of civilization. In modern lore they are akin with the Sidhe of Ireland.

Dreambody: The projected image of any human when they travel in dreamtime. As humans become immersed in the density of physical existence, they lose consciousness of their dreambody, though when they are asleep and dreaming, this is the form they exist in. Those trained in the dreamseer arts are able to transfer their consciousness to their dreambody and walk around displaced from their physical body.

Dreamlight: Light existing in Dreamtime that can be manipulated with human thought. Once a dreamseer becomes aware of how to do this, they can affect entire areas if they become adept at the skill.

Dreamseer: A spiritual adept who studies the intricacies of Dreamtime, and connection to their dreambody. Dreamseers travel in their dreams and communicate with the Watchers. In the Temple Sect their order wears the indigo robes. In the dreamclans they are the central leader of the clan.

Dreamship: They appear as any other ship, but the entire vessel can phase through the layers of Dreamtime. This requires a very high level of magic. Most dreamships travel into the Dreamvale, but more advanced ships can travel the skyroads in Celestius. The crew must gain favor with the Watchers and the elements in order to gain passage into the higher realms.

Dreamsight: The ability to shift one's vision to perceive the invisible world existing alongside the Meridian Realm.

Dreamtime: Subtle layers of reality existing beyond the Meridian Realm. This is how non-physicality is understood among humans in the incarnation cycle. In actuality, the layers of Dreamtime refer to having a connection to the other bodies of the human auric field which are anchored in the other 11 dimensions. Everyone travels there in their sleep, and dreamseers connect to it consciously.

Dreamvale: Threshold between Dreamtime and Meridian. The place where one goes in a visionary state, or right before falling asleep, or while lucid dreaming. Vale is derived from the word valley; of and pertaining to an ethereal valley that is the entrance to Dreamtime. This is the home of the Dreamclans.

Dreamwalker: Someone with the ability to project their full consciousness into their dreambody and walk through Dreamtime while being aware of the Meridian Realm. Their physical body remains dormant in meditation while their dreambody projects anywhere they wish to go, invisible to the naked eye unless the perceiver opens up to Dreamsight. Akin to astral projection. A highly advanced Dreamwalker can raise their physical body's vibration and move through lower Dreamtime, making their body invisible to the naked eye.

Dryad: Tree elemental.

ℰ

Earthforge: Term used to describe the molten center of Sophaiya wherein lies the realm of Incendius.

Elementa: Dreamclan term for a practitioner versed in the ability to channel elementals through their dance movements.

Elementalists: A discipline in the Temple Sect adept at communication with the Telluric (elemental) Realm. They study every aspect of the elemental kingdom and spend their lives in communication with it. Some are able to gain favor and ask the elements to do their bidding. Elementalists in the Temple Sect wear green robes. They run the aspect of the Grid that controls the weather, and the shipping lanes. There are also rogue elementalists who have sprung up within the Children of One.

Elixir Den: A cultural mainstay in Atlantis. Where there are revelries, elixir dens are also set up. However, social houses feature permanent locations for these dens. Mixologists become almost famous with their mixtures of vibrational, telluric and plant elixirs that are known to affect any mood or ailment a human can have. One has merely to communicate their mood to a mixologist, and they should be able to fish through their mixes for the correct dose of what is needed.

Eternal Flames: Sacred fires within the 12 temples of the Temple Sect that are always tended. It is said they have been burning since the beginning of Atlantis. They are ancient doorways to the wisdom of Incendius, which is the realm at the center of the planet.

F

Fale Fruit: Fruit grown in the kingdom of Benini known to create a state of euphoria. Considered a delicacy in other parts of Atlantis but is difficult to procure in the other kingdoms.

Fates, the: Atlanteans consider the Fates a personification of time elementals. Akin to telluric currents, they are seen as conscious, and able to be communicated with.

Fendesia: An herb known for its aphrodisiac and ecstatic properties.

Fireball: A game of physical prowess made famous by the Warrior

Sect. Giant arenas are built for fireball players. The object of
the game is to pass a ball between the players while leaping and
tumbling through an obstacle course as the ball gradually heats
up and eventually catches fire. They build up points by tossing the
fireball through goals, which is blocked by the opposing team.

Fire Crystal: In extreme circumstances the Great Crystal can
be turned into a weapon to harness the rays of the sun. It can
be focused at any point in the world. When the fire code was
activated at the end of the First Age of Atlantis, the crystal turned
red, thus giving its name. It shoots a laser into the planetary grid,
which then ricochets to any point on the planet. It was used in
the First Age of Atlantis to put an end to the war between the
three Bloodfire Nations and Lemuria. It caused so much damage
that it unleashed the volcanic activity in the Atlantic Ocean and
destabilized the region. Since then the fire codes have been hidden
in the Archives Nexes and forbidden.

Fire Letters: Light symbol codes used in Keylontics. The letters
are used to transfer images through the Crystal Grid, program tool
crystals, and download information into human blood cells.

Flowcraft: Ancient, all-terrain vehicles from the Golden Age of
Atlantis. Programmed with Keylontics to harmonize the craft with
tellurics, magnetics and the power of the Crystal Grid. These small,
one-to-two-man vehicles can operate on air, land and above or
beneath the sea.

Flower of Life: A geometric symbol representing the
mathematical order of the intrinsic universe, and the separation of
Source into multiple shards of consciousness.

Followers of the Axiom of One: A group of spiritualists who
study the principles of all life being descended from one Source
creator consciousness. They are what's left of the original spiritual
principle of Atlantis brought from Lemuria, and have over the
years lost their popularity, and segregated into an underground
movement. In the third age, the Followers of the Axiom have had
a resurgence. The youth of Atlantis have adopted their ways in a

rebellion against the Temple Sect. The Children of One are the result of this remembrance of the ancient ways.

Free-Marketeer: A marketeer who operates outside the ten kingdoms. Since they deal with other lands, they often stray outside Atlantean regulations. Most of the time they become akin to modern day pirates.

G

Gateways of Initiation: (See Inner Initiation) A term in the conclaves referring to the activation of the 12 inner gateways connecting humans to their Source code. The gateways correspond to the 12 chakras, the 12 dreambodies, and the 12 layers of Dreamtime. Once activated fully, it is said humans are able to achieve their highest attainment.

Generator-Crystal: A crystal that can work with the Grid to generate power. All Atlantean housing has its own generator that is connected to the local resonant-capacitor.

Glow Orbs: Orbs of various colored glass filled with a chemical similar to what lights up fireflies. Used for light on the streets, in houses or private gardens.

Golden Age of Atlantis: (See Destructions of Atlantis) The Second Age of Atlantis is known as their golden age. This was when Atlantis was at its height, operating with the highest knowledge and connection with Sophaiya and the star nations.

Great Central Sun: Galactic core of the multiverse. All universes orbit around the Great Central Sun, just as planetary bodies orbit around suns. Said to be the eye of Source.

Great Crystal: (See Crystal Grid) The free energy source of all power within the ten kingdoms. Housed in the temple of light at the heart of Poseidia, and regulated by the Temple Sect. Its chamber is kept pure, and no one may enter unless they have achieved the proper frequency through years of meditation.

Great Solidification: A time in history which demarked when humans became separated from Dreamtime. Before then, beings on Sophaiya were ethereal, and could shapeshift into any form. When Sophaiya became open for universal citizens to inhabit, the influx of beings caused a great pain on the ethereal residents of the planet. In order to make room for all spiritual frequencies, Sophaiya shifted her density, and everyone inhabiting the planet was solidified into physical bodies. This was the birth of the Meridian Realm; the moment when the physical became separated from Dreamtime.

Grid, the: (See Crystal Grid)

Grid Dancers: (See Dance of the Elementa) Individuals adept at channeling energy through their bodies and shaping it through movement. Akin to sorcery. Temple Sect Grid dancers, adepts of the yellow robed Grid-tuners, officiate over illumination rituals by directing the mindlight donations of citizens into the resonant capacitors. Grid dancers have begun to pop up within the conclaves of the Children of One. This has allowed them to covertly shift the flow of energy through the Grid.

Grid-Tuners: Temple priests whose life work involves the tuning of the Crystal Grid. In the Temple Sect, their order is denoted by yellow robes.

Guardians: In the Temple Sect, Grid Guardians are priestly adepts within the order of Grid-tuners who oversee the resonance of the capacitors. Guardians in the Warrior Sect have the job of making sure the laws are upheld in every district of the cities. They were given policing powers by King Koraxx during the sixth reign of the Third Age of Atlantis. This was the first time in the third age that warriors were lifted from their mercenary leagues and commanded by the king.

Guilds: Associations of individuals in trades within the ten kingdoms. Once a citizen emerges from the Learning Sect, she or he becomes a member in good standing of a guild. Guild members can connect with others in their trade, network with commercians, who look to the guilds for business connections, be represented by speakers who specialize in their trade, and report to the mediator if they have issues that need to be solved. Other citizens approach guilds to find tradesmen or craftsmen in a specific field. Raising one's standing with the guild brings more prestigious jobs.

H

Halls of Amen'ti: A vortex situated at the center of Sophaiya where physical souls are initiated into higher cosmic learning. It is said to be the brain center of Sophaiya herself. It lies past a network of cities in Subterra known as Agartha. There are 12 Subterran layers through which to pass to find the Halls. They represent the concept that all anyone needs to know lies at the core of our own cells, just as they make their home at the core of Sophaiya.

Harbor District: Area filled with marinas for permanent and temporary docking.

Hereditary Sect: A sect that only breeds within itself. Mediators and the Temple Sect are the only ones with these arranged births. The other sects are entered through training or registration, and considered non-hereditary sects.

Hermes: Watcher of travel, communication and higher learning.

High Council: Also called Council of Seven. Primarily a local ruling council appointed by elite members of their sect. There is a Council of Seven in every kingdom, but the one in Poseidia is called the High Council. It is formed by seven delegates representing the seven sects. Each council member politically represents every citizen who is registered in their sect. Some sects are more numerous, so that delegate has more power on the council. They are overseen by the high king and queen, while they also have the ability to unanimously overrule any royal decree.

High Priestess: Overseer of the entire Temple Sect.

Hover-Carriage: Carriages run by hover technology. They

operate by a central torsion-crystal which is charged by the road mounds and controlled psychically by the operator through imprinter-panels. Typically only used by elite classes as transportation along the road mounds. Larger carriages are used to tow hover sleds for the use of cargo transport.

Hover-Disc: One of the main modes of personal transportation in Atlantis. The central disc is built around a torsion-crystal. When activated, two wings fan out from the center, and become footholds. Users bond with them by accessing a small imprinter-panel. The more it is used, the more the operator bonds chemically with the disc. Upon activation, the disc is tossed to the ground where it hovers a few inches above the surface. The user stands upright on the footholds and thoughts projected through the crystal direct the journey.

Hover Trickster: Referring to a fad created by the youth of Atlantis to operate their discs off the road mounds and do radical stunts. Hover tricksters were banned by King Koraxx, and many young people when caught after the laws were passed, were forced to part with their hover-discs. Since torsion-crystals are programmed to be charged by the road mounds, it is seen as miraculous that tricksters even exist. Conclaves of the Children of One see the original tricksters as the first to have shown signs of the special genetics they possess.

Human Experiment (Project): Referring to the experiment to create a master race of beings on Sophaiya who are meant to be the perfect vessel for the soul in physical form for this universe. Humans were seeded with DNA from many Star Nations and are meant to exist at their optimal design. The experiment was interrupted by the Age of Fire and Blood. However, the Star Nations have not interfered due to the laws of free-will in the universe, though they have placed the Watchers on the planet to oversee the project.

Hyperborea: One of the three Bloodfire Nations ruled by sorcerer kings during the Age of Fire and Blood. Along with Thule and Sauros, they waged war with Lemuria, and caused great havoc on the planet. The elements rose up against their black magic, and a sudden polar shift froze their cities under layers of ice. The legend is Hyperborea still exists perfectly intact beneath glaciers in the North.

Icelands: The general term for the glaciers of the north and south. An ice age is upon the planet during the third age, therefore at least 1/3 of the planet is covered in icecaps. The icelands are said to be inhabited by terrifying monsters, among which is the ice giants, known as descendants of the Nephilim.

Illuminati: Caste of scholars who act as the liaisons between humans and the crystal cities located along the skyroads of the Celestius Realm.

Illumination Rituals: A mandatory practice across Atlantis three times a day. The Crystal Grid generates power to the cities and villas and is fed by telepathic energy projected into resonant capacitors called nodes. The nodes are ten-foot-tall solid crystal obelisks placed through the city in evenly spaced vortex points. The Temple Sect activates their resonance each day at sunrise, high noon and sunset. The citizens are called to illumination rituals by the nodesong. Slang for the rituals is mudras. (See Mudras).

Illuminator-Crystal: Crystals programmed to emanate light when activated. Akin to flashlights.

Imprinter Panel: Crystal panels built into every automated device in Atlantis. Operators must place their hand over the panel and wait for the crystals to create a lock on their bio-rhythms. Once the lock is made, the operator can telepathically operate the device.

Incendius: One of the six Realms of Sophaiya. The fire domain where fire beings dwell. This surrounds and protects the heart of the planet known as the Halls of Amen-ti. Often mistaken for Hell.

Influence Tallies: Currency in the ten kingdoms of Atlantis. Commerce is measured by the trading of influence. When an exchange is made, the tallies are recorded in recorder-crystals usually worn strapped to a palm. At the end of the day, the tallies are downloaded to commercians within the merchant guild, who are able to trade points between merchants and patrons who wish to collect influence.

Inner Initiation: A term among the conclaves referring to the activation of gateways that must be unlocked within the human psyche. Once they are awakened with the blue dream elixir, the Children of One must then undergo the 12 gateways of inner initiation by accessing their personal gate codes from the Crystal Grid with their soul-crystal.

J

Joining Ceremony: Atlantean marriage. The ritual is performed in the temple centers by priests. It involves shifting the frequency of the sacred courtyard into Dreamtime, where the silver and gold discs of union hover above the couple. The clergy causes the discs to spin, and the couple telepathically wills the discs to merge. Once the discs form into one circle, the couple is bonded in Dreamtime, and their genetics are paired for mating.

K

Ka-Ma-Sha: Last day of the Ka-Ma-Sharri festival. Symbolic of the parting of Belial and Kama after their short reunion. There is a traditional feast on this day, in which all Atlanteans join in celebration of their union with friends and family.

Ka-Ma-Sharri: Three-day festival celebrating the union of Belial and Kama. Kama being represented by the moon, and Belial by the sun, the festival is centered around any eclipse of the sun or moon. There are numerous Ka-Ma-Sharri's throughout the year. It is said to be the most exalted time to perform joining ceremonies.

Kallista: Meaning "most beautiful." The term used for those in Atlantis whose beauty holds them in a place of mystique and awe. Those of this beauty who are not born to noble bloodlines can be trained as kallistas, whose job it is to seduce and cater to the nobility in the sensual arts. They are adept in the tantras.

Kama: The soulmate of Belial who has chosen to incarnate in human form and act as the guardian of the Archives Nexes until humans are ready to ascend to their highest attainment. It is said that if humans begin to abuse the power given to them in Atlantis, Kama will return and have the ability to take over the Grid.

Keylontics: Language of symbol codes, light, sound, pulsation and vibration of energy. Based on the intrinsic interior geometric-electric structures that create the foundations for all form and structure within the dimensional systems. Keylontics is represented by living codes of matter and all biologies built on them that serve as the structure upon which all manifestations are built.

Keymaster: (See Agartha, Subterra) There are 12 layers of Subterra, (six leading to the cities of Agartha, and six leading past that to the Halls of Amen'ti). The six layers beneath Atlantis are governed by Atlantean keymasters. The layers past that are governed by the laws of Agartha. Keymasters are much like modern day mayors. Each layer extends deeper into the crust of Sophaiya and must be passed by accessing the keymaster and their subordinates. The citizens of Subterra are surface dwellers, and yet they make their homes below the surface because they are dedicated to moving closer to the Halls of Amen'ti. Those spiritual seekers who dedicate their lives to accessing Amen'ti through Subterra are called Luminari.

Khemet: The kingdom of Egypt, as it is called during the ages of Atlantis. Located in the Valley of Khem, it is part of the network of kingdoms that make their home along the great River Stix. The kingdoms are collectively called the Osirian Nations.

L

Layers of Dreamtime: Referring to the 12 dimensions accessible from Sophaiya. All humans have the ability to ascend through the layers to reconnect with Source. All have a connection to the layers through their chakras, auric fields (dreambodies), and inner gateways.

Layers of Subterra: Referring to the levels below the surface of the planet. Each layer is closer to the earth forge, the molten core of Sophaiya, which is where one finds the Halls of Amen'ti past Agartha. This is another method of connecting with Source besides ascending through the Layers of Dreamtime.

League-Master/Mistress: In the Warrior Sect, one who is appointed leader of each of the nine warrior leagues.

Learning Sect: Sect of Atlantean citizens who are registered as learning a trade, skill or knowledge among the learners. Unless a citizen is born into a hereditary sect, which means they must study what they are born to do, they can choose a skill to learn. As children, they are sent to learning houses, where they live among the Learning Sect so they can choose their training. Once they choose, they move to the school of their choice provided they pass the entrance requirements.

Lemuria: The motherland of Atlantis. Atlantis was one of the eight main colonies of Lemuria. The motherland was destroyed by global cataclysms spawned by the improper use of magic, which set the elements into a state of imbalance. The first nation on Sophaiya, Lemuria was once peaceful, ruled by spiritual principles until it was set into combat by the three nations of Hyperborea, Thule and Sauros. Before they were destroyed, they sent their archives to Atlantis to carry on the secrets of the human project.

Locator-Crystal: Tool crystals used to locate a specific person by searching for their imprint in the Grid. The person it is being set to locate must program their psychic imprint into the crystal by concentrating. Once imprinted, the locator can be used by anyone to find that person until it is reprogrammed. Summoner-crystals can be used as locators as well. Summoners can be used in conjunction with locators if the person holding the summoner is linked to a locator held by another person.

Lost Temple Children: (See Children of One, Conclaves) A project initiated secretly by the Temple Sect at the start of the Third Age of Atlantis. It is a genetic sequence meant to evolve over a series of seven generations. Their original purpose was to build an immunity to the shadows that were trapped in the Meridian Realm after the second destruction of Atlantis. The Temple Sect have called them Project Indigo.

Lower Dreamtime: The layer of Dreamtime closest to the physical world where emotional and mental images created by humans exist as ethereal life forms. Those with advanced Dreamseer abilities can see into this realm, as well as shift the vibration of their physical bodies to walk in this world.

Luminari: Caste of scholars who live in Subterra and study the principles of the 12 levels of connection to Source. They are initiates to the 12 levels of Subterra, and liaisons between the inner and upper world.

M

Madness (the): Term used to define the psychic illness that plagues the citizens of Atlantis in the third and final age. Characterized by the gradual degradation of sanity stimulated by shadows, who attach themselves to humans in Dreamtime, stimulate mental anguish, and feed off negative emotions. It is seen as a madness because the human host slips deeper and deeper into their anguish until they cannot distinguish reality from their suffering.

Magi: A caste of mystics who study the use of magic. In the final age of Atlantis, they are the only non-hereditary spiritual class that can wield magical powers. Those who study magic outside the Temple Sect are considered scholars. In the Temple Sect, their order is denoted by red robes.

Maldek: The fifth planet of the solar system that used to exist between Mars and Jupiter. It was destroyed in the first major destruction of Atlantis, which also incinerated the surface of Mars. It is now a field of asteroids and debris orbiting the fifth orbit of the Ra System.

Manator: Half-man half-animal. Left over from before the Great Solidification. The story of their origin went back to the garden of Pangaea, when all the continents were one mass, and life on Sophaiya existed in Dreamtime. Humans then had the ability to shapeshift at will. When the Solidification happened, anyone who chose to keep their animal forms remained part human and part animal. In the Second Age of Atlantis, the Followers of One declared an edict that manator were abominations and began programs to strip people of their animal sides. In the third age, manator are rare, and almost mythical, as they have found refuge in lower Dreamtime.

Marketeer: A specialist in the markets who works with currency alone. Among those who work in commerce: traders work with trade alone, merchants work with a specific item or items whether through trade or currency, commercians provide and regulate the markets. Free-marketeers work outside the ten kingdoms of Atlantis while marketeers work within its strict laws.

Mars: Planet whose orbit lies just past Sophaiya. Called the fourth planet. Mars was once home to a thriving civilization, but its surface was destroyed, and all civilization moved beneath the surface. Though some refugees fled to Sophaiya and took up residence in Atlantis mainly in the kingdom of Aryan.

Maydrian: Title given to the personal adviser of the king. Maydrians have the responsibility of organizing all the personal affairs of the monarch. This position is appointed by the king and approved by the High Council.

Maydriss: Same as Maydrian, except the queen's personal advisor. Maydrisses also handle the queen's pregnancies, wardrobe, and all personal matters.

Mediator Assembly: When important matters affecting the kingdom need to be weighed, the Mediator Assembly is called. This is when every available mediator assembles in the mediation arena. Assemblies are rare, and can be called by a group of mediators, the High Council, the Temple Sect, a vote from citizens, or the monarch.

Mediator Sect: (Mediator) Hereditary politicians in Atlantis. Bred like royalty, the mediator lines are carefully controlled to produce heirs whose birthright and training are specifically tailored to lead fairly. Each mediator line oversees a specific area of government within the civilization. Every sect is governed by a familial line. Their duties range from mediating disputes to making policy decisions. When a dispute is brought to a mediator, he or she acts as judge.

Meridian Realm: One of the six Realms of Sophaiya where humans dwell. It is known today as the third dimension and is characterized by physical matter.

Mindlight: Atlantean term for the pineal gland. A gland at the center of the head associated with the third eye. In its evolved state, the mindlight is shaped like a quartz cluster, and could be used to create magic, project psychic waves and perceive Dreamtime.

Mixologist: Atlantean profession employing the use of herbs, tellurics, and tonics to create elixirs, which they use for medicine and recreation. There is an elixir for everything. When a mixologist is consulted, it is somewhat like going to therapy or a psychic. They are able to see into the souls of each consumer and tell what kind of emotional adjustment is needed.

Moirae: Dreamclan term for a special being born to influence the Fates of man. In essence, an incarnated Watcher. Title granted to Brigitte during her youth by the Dreamclan council.

Mound Laws: During the reign of King Koraxx, hover tricksters began operating their hover-discs off of the road mounds. This was thought to be impossible because discs are charged by the road mounds. But somehow tricksters had the ability to get past this. The conclaves now see it as the first appearance of the gene that has awakened in humanity. Koraxx restricted hover-disc usage to the mound, citing the reason that tricksters are reckless, and compromised the safety of citizens. But a deeper reason became apparent when his guardian forces began hunting down renegade revelries, where the youth practiced their tricks away from the public. Those who were caught were banned from hovering. This was the beginning of the conclaves who took their practices into strict secrecy.

Mudras: Hand gestures used during meditation to maximize the flow of energy through the hands. Illumination rituals are called mudras as a slang term that refers to the hand gestures they use to channel their mindlight into the crystal nodes and generate power through the cities.

Multiverse: Many universes orbiting around a black central sun, said to be the Eye of Source, watching its creations.

N

Navigators: Adepts of the green-robed elemental order of the Temple Sect. All shipping lanes are regulated in the ten kingdoms. Navigators are trained in the art of communicating with the elements and are able to read the currents and wind patterns, as well as connect with the telluric lines within the ocean. All ships must have a temple navigator. When they register a voyage, they must attain a navigator from whatever port their journey begins. Once the voyage is finished, the navigator must go to the temple center at the destination. A new navigator is usually obtained at the start of another voyage.

Naydir: External advisor to the court of a king or queen. Acts as liaison between the monarch and the public. Appointed by the monarch with final approval by the High Council.

Nephilim (Telluric Nephilim): An ancient race of beings on the planet said to be a cross between a Watcher and a human. The union is often made when a Watcher takes the form of a human for the mating. These beings are said to possess godly powers. The most powerful kind is said to be telluric, meaning they are a cross between a Watcher and an elemental. Since Nephilim had such immense power, they became worshipped and feared. The Star Nations declared Nephilim abominations, and were had thus banished them from the human project. Watchers are now forbidden to interfere with the genetics of humanity.

Nereids: Mermaid creatures living in the depths of the ocean. They are part fish and human, unlike their Oceanid cousins, and considered manator to Atlanteans. They are very shy, and rarely show themselves to land dwellers, but they live harmoniously among the Oceanus Realm.

Neter: A human body carrying the soul of a Watcher. Whereas a Moirae enters from birth, the Neter requires a human to achieve a state of emptiness so their body is surrendered to be inhabited by the Watcher. This can be done by force, which takes the longest, or can be done in chorus with the human choosing to surrender their body to the Watcher.

Nexes: (See Archives Nexes)

Nodes: Slang for resonant capacitors. Called nodes because the crystal obelisks serve as vortex points for the Grid. Citizenry focus their minds into the nodes during illumination rituals to send power to the Great Crystal.

Nodesong: Referring to the resonance created by the nodes to call citizens to illumination rituals. This is a pleasing frequency that oscillates through the cities. Usually programmed to vibrate at 432hz.

Nodeyard: Courtyards built around crystal nodes where citizens gather to perform illumination rituals during the resonance of nodesong.

Nubia: The great continent lying to the Southeast of the Atlantean Islands (modern day Africa). It is filled with lush grasslands and rivers. The people inhabiting Nubia are black of skin and said to be the most ancient race on the planet with a history greater than Lemuria. The land is populated by a confederation of tribes in various states of alliance. There are a number of outposts and cities on the continent, all of them wealthy with vast resources. Sha'mana is mined in abundance there, which allows for global influence among the Lemurian Empires.

Nymphs: Spirits who dwell in the dreamtime and work to protect the Telluric Realm. They are associated with various elements and locations around Sophaiya and possess the power to animate nature.

Obelisk: Crystal tower or pillar with four sides, topped by a pyramidal point. The shape of crystal nodes.

Oceanids: A race of beings who live in the ocean. They are part human and part elemental, and so have evolved to live underwater. They can also come out of the water and walk around, but this is very rare. They have fins for hair, legs with scales, and webbed toes, but mostly resemble humans. They are the masters of the ocean and have their own underwater kingdoms.

Oceanus Realm: One of the six Realms of Sophaiya referring to under the ocean.

Og, Kingdom of: One of the three largest Atlantean kingdoms, and the most powerful of Eastern Atlantis. A vacation destination known for its sensory delights and revelries. Its ruling city Tirnan is one of the most opulent, wealthy cities in the world.

Oracle of the Six Realms: (See Realms of Sophaiya) A position within the Temple Sect. Initiates of the elemental discipline are bred with elemental blood, and those who exhibit the most aptitude at prophecy and connection with the elements are trained to be the oracle. When the previous oracle passes on into the spirit world, the new one takes her place on the elemental throne. It is her duty to travel through the six realms in Dreamtime using meditation. This position acts as an ambassador to the realms.

Order of Nexes: An elite order of high born influential citizens who study the use and principles of the Archives Nexes. They are initiated and trained through various levels of the order, and their intentions always lie in the betterment of Atlantis.

Order of the Serpent: (See Order of Nexes) Another name for the order who studies Nexes. Originally named for the serpentine form Belial and his brother took when they arrived on Sophaiya in the original Anunaki arrival.

Order of the Spiral Dancers: Dancers trained in the use of rings with which they do various tricks while they dance. It is a prominent Atlantean art form, and the order is often commissioned to entertain courts and revelries.

Orders of the Temple Sect: The twelve disciplines within the Temple Sect. Each is connected to a chakra and a layer of Dreamtime. See Temple Sect for listing of the orders and colors.

Osirian Nations: One of the eight Lemurian empires. A loose collection of over 200 cities along the River Stix in the Valley of Khem. They maintain trade along the river and have solid ties to Nubia and Atlantis through river routes. These nations are the forerunners to what later became nations such as Crete, Malta, Thera, Phoenicia, Sumer and Egypt.

Outlands: The outer city of Poseidia surrounding the ringed citadel.

Oversource: (See Source)

P

Panther League: One of the nine warrior leagues specializing in the use of stealth and hunting techniques.

Parnassus: The name of the elemental spirit of the mountain Poseidia is built on.

Penumbra: A shadow layer of lower Dreamtime said to be used by adepts to travel into the other realms of Sophaiya from Meridian. It is also said to be where the shadows are trapped in a holographic reality.

Pineal: (See Mindlight)

Poseidia, City of: The ruling city of Atlantis. Home to the Great Crystal as well at the palace of the high king and queen. Located at the heart of the ten kingdoms on the main island of Atlas.

Predator Vessels: Fast, stout ships belonging to the Shark Warrior League used to patrol the sea lanes and waterways of Atlantis.

Prophet Singer: Nickname for D'Vinid during his lifetime. Referring to his ability to create songs off-the-cuff that often tend to predict the future.

Pythian Games: An annual festival celebrating the heroics of Koraxx in his days as prince. The games were set up to honor his prowess as a hunter. It was at the games when he met Dafni for the first time.

R

Ra: The name of the being who is the sun of this solar system.

Realms of Sophaiya: The six realms of Sophaiya that support life in various forms. Telluric Realm is the home to elementals and minerals. Oceanus is home to sea creatures. Meridian is where humans and animals live in physical form. Subterra is beneath the surface of the planet. Celestius, the skyroads, home to the great Crystal cities in the sky. Indendius is the fire realm at the core of the planet that protects the Halls of Amen'ti.

Record-Keepers: Tool-crystals programmed with information through Keylontics. Akin to Atlantean books.

Renegade Revelries: During the time of King Koraxx, hover tricksters started gathering in deserted areas so they could practice their tricks away from the public. These revelries received widespread fame, and many citizens began to seek them out. But when Koraxx found out about them, he banned them, and punished the hover-tricksters by taking away their discs, thus banning them from hovering altogether. Renegade revelries still happen among the conclaves, but they are done with extreme caution.

Resonant Capacitors: (See Crystal Nodes) Large obelisks named for the resonance they emit to call citizens to illumination rituals. Nicknamed crystal nodes, they are used to conduct psychic energy that is then filtered to the Great Crystal and transformed into electricity to power the city.

Retinue: Officers of the royal court closest to the king or queen.

Revelries: Parties or celebrations in Atlantis. Atlanteans are notoriously prone to revelry in all aspects of life, deriving from their belief that the human experience was meant to indulge in sensual pleasures.

Ring of Commerce: Outer land ring of the citadel of Poseidia where the working class resides.

Ring of Learning: Second land ring of the citadel of Poseidia. Here is where all learners go to attend learning houses and learn trades. It is also where most Atlanteans go for leisure. There are numerous plazas for festivals, a grand fireball arena, as well as a racetrack spanning the entire ring.

Ring of Mediation: Third land ring of the citadel of Poseidia. Known as the mediator heights, many affluent estates span the terraces. This is also where citizens go to report to their mediators, who hold court within their grand estates.

River Stix: Giant river feeding from the glacial lake of Tethys (modern day Eastern Mediterranean.) It extends east of modern day Crete, Malta, and Sicily, onward north of Algiers and into the Atlantic past the Pillars of Hercules. It is home to a vast river economy conducted by the many cities of the Osirian Nations. Ships come and go to and from Atlantis. Their first port in Atlantis is Tartessos of Bascli. From there, ships either head to Atlas, Og or Capraria.

Road Mounds: Raised mounds built along telluric lines acting as roads for Atlantean hover-crafts. The mounds give off a magnetic frequency, which work with torsion-crystals within hover-craft to create magnetic propulsion.

Rotations: Meaning years in the Atlantean measurement of time. Referring a full rotation of the planet around the sun.

Rutilation: Minerals embedded inside crystals creating a striped appearance in the crystal.

§

Sacred Cantos: (See Cantos)

Sacrė Morė: The sacred death rituals performed by the shadowmancers. It is said that the Blood Gods gain power from a soul's passage into death, especially one that is in fear. The creation of a shadow from the fear of the sacrificed brings power to the Blood God to which the sacrifice is being dedicated.

Sauros: One of the fire nations of legend from the Age of Fire and Ice. It is said their kings were Nephilim who ruled with elemental sorcery, enslaving humans as their subjects. They gained power through the fear of their people and demanded blood sacrifice. They hated the free colonies of Lemuria, and waged war on the motherland. They were destroyed when Belial secretly brought the Great Crystal to Atlantis and directed his avatar to activate the Fire Crystal. This attack brought total annihilation to Sauros and its brother nations, freezing them in ice. The legend says their nations are still frozen, awaiting the day they will awaken and seek revenge.

Sea Nymphs: A race of elemental beings living in the ocean. They are mostly non-physical and appear as beings that are one with the water.

Sects: Atlantean citizens are separated into seven sects based on their birthright or their career. Listed in order of precedence: Temple Sect, Mediator Sect, Speaker Sect, Builder Sect, Ambassador Sect, Learner Sect, Warrior Sect.

Shadowmancers: Those born with the activated gene of the Temple Sect who have converted to serve the Blood Gods with the promise of ultimate power. They believe themselves to be the chosen ones of the Watchers.

Shadows (the): Parasitic beings existing as holograms in the Grid of Atlantis. They were born of the rift that was created at the destruction of the second age. They are essentially emotional constructs created by intense human emotions. They do not belong in the physical plane and have survived by feeding off the emotional essence of humans, the essence from which they were spawned. Those who become host to shadows eventually fall to the Madness.

Sha'mana: Minerals from the Telluric Realm. Known by some as gold dust. It is the most magical element on the planet, and one of the most coveted minerals among the Star Nations. There are many uses, though mostly ingesting it repairs the cells of the body, and connects the user with the original human design, as well as the consciousness of Sophaiya. There are many sha'mana mining facilities that are heavily protected. The main production facility lies on the Isle of Dragonspine between Atlas and Og. Most of it goes only to the Temple Sect and the most influential of mediators. The conclaves have managed to find a way to smuggle and use it in their blue dream elixir to activate their genetic upgrade.

Skyroads: Ethereal currents of energy in Celestius connecting the crystal cities together.

Social Hub: Places to meet new people and gather with friends. Akin to modern day bars, they feature an elixir den, as well as performance halls and areas to sit and relax.

Solidification: (See Great Solidification)

Sophaiya: A planetary consciousness in the system of Ra. The most valued planet in the Ra system because she is said to be an actual goddess who descended into the form of a planetary being. The planet is an inter-dimensional crossroads, where many intergalactic beings converge. There are six realms that make up the domains that support life on Sophaiya: Telluric, Subterra, Meridian, Celestius, Incendius and Oceanus. She was later called Earth.

Source: Closest way to describe the word Atlanteans use to refer to God. The Source of all creation.

Soul-Crystal: Crystals that have not been stripped of their telluric consciousness. The use of soul-crystals is banned in Atlantis, as their energy is not harnessed to the Grid, and it is said they pose a danger to the harmony of Atlantis. The conclaves have begun to secretly harvest raw, un-programmed crystals in order to bond with them. They have begun to unlock many secrets in the Archives with the help of these powerful telluric beings.

Speaker District: Area on the Ring of Learning where students rise through the speaker training. It is also where citizens must go to seek the services of the guild, or to attend arguments.

Speaker Sect: (Speakers) A learned sect of Atlantean citizens. Speakers are trained to speak for the laws of Atlantis. Much like modern day lawyers. Upon emergence from training, speakers choose a focus to speak for. When any citizen needs to be represented, they enlist the service of a speaker to argue for them.

Star Nations: Referring collectively to every planet around the universe with advanced life forms. In the Third Age of Atlantis, the Star Nations have been barred to enter all realms of Sophaiya except for the crystal cities of Celestius. From here they are allowed to project their soul into the incarnation cycles of the other realms. In ages past, the Star Nations were directly involved in human evolution, but the Third Age of Atlantis is now a closed experiment, and the human project is considered endangered.

Subterra: One of the six Realms of Sophaiya. Holding the largest sect of scholars who live on 12 underground levels leading to the Halls of Amen'ti at the core of Sophaiya. These levels are called layers. There are six layers leading to Agartha, and six layers past that to Amen'ti. Subterran scholars, known as Luminari, study the records of the human project. These records were brought from Lemuria by Belial and make up the original intent of Atlantis.

Summoner-Crystal: Tool crystals imprinted to one person's psychic frequency. When given to another, the crystal can be activated, and the imprinter receives a telepathic signal through the Grid. They are usually paired with locator-crystals that receive the signal, and the one being summoned can then reveal their location to the one using the summoner.

Syrinx: An herb from a nation called Arcadia in the Valley of Khem meant to be one of the most potent aphrodisiacs in the world. Anyone ingesting it is said to go slightly mad with desire.

T

Tantras: Ancient arts of sexual arousal. Term refers to the teachers and the teachings of the same art.

Telleria Quay: A famous freight warehouse along the Ring of Mediation in Poseidia run by the Telleria commercian cartel. It is connected to the cartel docks where only the most prestigious of merchants are admitted to display their goods. The quay is where the goods are stored before being shipped to the various shopping districts around the citadel.

Telluric Lines: Magnetic currents covering Sophaiya in a grid-like pattern. Atlanteans have methods of measuring the Telluric Realm, so they can connect the Crystal Grid to telluric lines across the planet for power, transportation and communication. Telluric refers to the mineral and elemental Realm of Sophaiya, which has its own principles and rules. Road mounds are built along these lines, so hover-discs can access magnetic propulsion.

Telluric Nephilim: (See Nephilim) The most powerful breed of human/Watcher is said to be telluric, meaning they are a cross between a Watcher and an elemental. They would have godlike powers while also being able to harness and control elementals.

Telluric Realm: One of the six Realms of Sophaiya. Home to elementals and minerals, beings who are incarnations of the life force of Sophaiya. Telluric currents make up the energy that runs through the planet, much like how blood runs through human bodies. The currents are used by Atlanteans in their road mounds, which makes advanced transportation possible.

Temple Center: Centers around the cities set up with nodeyards for citizens to meditate at illumination rituals. They also house healing centers where anyone can receive medical treatment for their ailments. Temple clergy are on hand to council the people at all times.

Temple of Light: Center of the city of Poseidia where the Great Crystal and Archives Nexes are connected to the Grid. All illumination power leads to the temple of light, and is regulated by the temple Alta.

Temple Sect: Hereditary sect of Atlantean citizens. Bred with genetic manipulation and trained as temple clergy with a specific directive to remain neutral so they can tune and conduct the Crystal Grid without bias or corruption. There are 12 orders represented by 12 colored robes. Listed in Order and by color of the order: Magi (red), Alchemists (orange), Grid Tuners (yellow), Elementalists (green), Timekeepers (light blue), Record Keepers (indigo), Dreamseers (purple), Healers (iridescence), Alta first order (blue/green), Alta second order (pearl), Alta third order (pink/orange). Alta fourth order (gold).

Ten Kingdoms of Atlantis: In the beginning of Atlantis the land mass was divided between ten brothers, who became the first kings. After the ages passed, and the land masses broke into islands, the kingdoms became more like provinces, but are still called kingdoms in honor of the previous ages. The kingdoms are: Atlas (the capitol), Og (considered the capitol of the Eastern kingdoms,) The Western kingdoms are: Antillia, Aryan, Benini, and Taino. The Eastern kingdoms are: Azoria, Capraria, Tartessos and Yisra. In the third age, The Kingdom of Albion is the unofficial 11th kingdom of Atlantis. Though governed by their own kings, the High King and the High Council rule them. Once a year, and in emergencies, the ten kings are called to council in Poseidia of Atlas to make kingdom-wide decisions. (See Council of Ten Kings.) In the third age, there are two main alliances, east and west. Eastern islands are allied with Og while west follows Atlas. It is a source of contention between the two main power centers.

Thoth: Known as one of the first high priests during the First Age of Atlantis. It is said he achieved immortality and became a Watcher. He presided over the Temple Sect for 2000 years before he ascended into Dreamtime. Since his departure, a new Thoth from his genetic line always steps into the leadership role as High Alta of the Archives Nexes.

Tool-Crystal: Crystals stripped of their telluric souls. They have been harnessed to the Grid and programmed for specific uses.

Torsion-Crystal: Tool-crystals that harness power from the Grid and spiral it into the device to which they are anchored. Examples are the central torsion crystal that takes mindlight and sends it to the Great Crystal. It is one of the main components of hover-craft technology. All crafts are built around a central torsion-crystal. When activated on the road mounds, they interact with telluric currents to charge, and provide friction. Conclaves first began to realize their innate powers when hover-tricksters realized they could project their energy through torsion-crystals, and harness telluric currents off the road mounds.

Triad: (See Blood Gods)

Triangulate: A principle in magic or energetics. Referring to the act of a third person adding a third point to the magic of two people. The act of triangulation magnifies the magic of two.

Tuaca Solaria: An Atlantean greeting, accompanied by hand gestures.

U

Uiger: One of the eight Lemurian empires. Their civilization lies in the mountains in the area known today as Tibet and stretches into what is today known as the Gobi Desert. At the time of the third age, the Gobi is a vast fertile plane.

Unification: A movement among the conclaves. Those who follow it are called unificationists. They believe that the conclaves should unite and work together. Most conclaves are content to be isolated from one another and maintain a low profile, so they can continue to live their lives in comfort.

V

Vale: (See Dreamvale) Shortened form of the word valley.

Valley of Khem: (See River Stix, Osirian Nations) A vast, fertile river valley in what is today known as the Mediterranean Sea. Along the banks of the River Stix lies hundreds of cities termed loosely as the Osirian Nations. It is one of the most bustling and thriving regions in the world.

Vailix Needle: Cylindrical crafts used as public transportation in Atlantis. With torsion-crystals powered by the Crystal Grid through magnetic propulsion, they propel along thin wires stretching along the main thoroughfares of the cities and stop at elevated platforms for loading and unloading.

VC Waves: Invisible frequencies transmitted through the Crystal Grid to project images and sound into viewer-crystals. Like modern day television waves.

Viewer Crystal (VC): Large flat sheets of selenite crystal set up in all commons areas and connected to the Crystal Grid. They are meant to receive images transmitted through VC waves to send live messages from the government to the citizens.

Violet flame: An ethereal flame (see dreamlight) that can be summoned psychically to cleanse the energy affecting the physical in Dreamtime.

Vortex (the): A term among the conclaves/Children of One referring to the state of being aligned in a state of one-ness. Being in the vortex is indicated by chains of events lining up in perfect synchronicity, and always in the highest good of the one who is aligned. It is known as navigating the vortex.

W

Warriors' Code: A strict code of honor put in place to keep the warriors in check. They are taught the code like a religion from the moment they begin their training. Since the warrior leagues are mostly mercenary, they are only allowed to act within the code, so they cannot be activated for devious reasons.

Warrior Sect: Sect of Atlantean citizens who study the art of warfare. Usually those in any sect who display violent tendencies are sent to be trained in this sect. Since war is frowned upon in the third age, they are shunned in principle, but also revered for their physical prowess. They traditionally act as mercenaries in the third age and can only be employed for a purpose. This is known as activating a warrior force. They are bound by a strict moral code. It is in place to ensure their power is never abused. There are nine warrior leagues. Listed here: Bull League, known as Fury Warriors, studying brute force; Panther League, studying agile movements and covert operations; Monkey Warriors, studying rooftop sentinel tactics; Dragon League, studying telepathic warfare; Ram League, studying terrain tactics; Shark League, studying ocean tactics; Falcon League, studying airborne tactics; Wolf League, studying tracking and hunting; and the mysterious Spider League, previously known as Dream Warriors.

Watchers: Atlantean gods. Beings who exist in Celestius and Dreamtime whose job it is to watch over the Fates of humanity. Although they cannot interfere, they can guide the Fates and send subtle signs through elements, while orchestrating coincidences, and messages in Dreamtime. They are present to make sure the human project does not break the laws of nature and harm Sophaiya.

Water-Craft: Small, one-man sailing vessels used as transportation through the vast canal system of Poseidia. They usually use wind propulsion, though torsion-crystals can be activated for minor propulsion if the winds do not cooperate.

Wolf Warriors: A league of the Warrior Sect. Wolves are used as guardians who specialize in tracking and hunting.

Y

Yazminnia: An intoxication elixir made from an herb growing only in the mountains of Og. Induces an ecstatic dream state.

Yerba Tree: A type of tree growing in Poseidia. It is not native to the area, and yet the climate is perfect to make it grow in abundance. It was brought from Lemuria many thousands of years before the final age of Atlantis thus many yerba trees have thousands of years of growth. Their roots grow in arches above the ground, and their branches become strong and sturdy enough to build houses at the base of multiple levels.

Yisra: One of the ten Atlantean kingdoms. Matriarchal in precedence. Known as a colony of Maldek, it also hosts embassies from all the Lemurian Empires. Its position close to the Nubian Empire makes it an excellent diplomatic entity to the Nubian tribes. It is also known as a center of advanced wisdom and learning.

Z

Zephyre: Watcher of the winds.

Made in the USA
San Bernardino, CA
19 December 2018